Darkened Demig‹

MW00620778

a science fiction / fantasy novel by

Dr. Shawn Phillips

YBCoyote Press

It is his story, a tale told by the first and last modern-day demigod

He was created to defend his nation but warped by his followers into causing the destruction of human society, and then imprisoned for those actions. Relive a jaded past that transforms into an impossible quest to save the last remnants of humankind from the suppression of Marsian rule. But nothing is at it appears, and saving humankind may require even more than he is willing to give.

YBCoyote Press, Publisher
5654 Bienveneda Terrace
Palmdale, CA 93551
www.YBCoyotePress.com

ISBN: 978-0-9826446-2-1
eBook ISBN: 978-0-9826446-7-6

First Edition
1. Fiction   2. Science Fiction   3. Fantasy   4. Mythology   5. Demigod

Amazing cover artwork & stellar front design by Jon Gibbons (https://www.artstation.com/jongibbons)
Back cover layout and graphics editing by Colby G. Phillips

ACKNOWLEDGEMENTS

To the incredible people of the AFRL Rocket Lab, who for the last 65 years have been the unwavering research and development foundation for our nation's rocket propulsion capability. Very few appreciate, let alone acknowledge, the criticality of long-term research and development until it's too late. Thank you for always being there.

This book is dedicated to Pete Huisveld. You sidestep the deserved credit for what you've done for our nation, and are respected by so many for your lifetime commitment to the Air Force; mentoring any that ask, and helping many in need. You embrace differences, and never accept the status quo.

This book could not have been completed without the help of my friends and colleagues. Thanks to Phil Kessel for ideas on the God Device, Pete Huisveld on perfecting the storyline, and Chuck Cross for pulling together the front and back pages. Thanks to Brian Moore and Deb Fuller for reviewing my novel. Thanks to Sergeant Dillen for allowing the use of his persona as part of the storyline, even if for a gruesome purpose.

PRISONER

Chapter 1

My eyes fight back as I open them and assess my bleak surroundings. A yawn easily widens my mouth, though my jaw cracks from lack of use. The soft-glow lights remind me that my underground prison, the shackles, and psychological assessments aren't a mere nightmare. And today they send another human to try and trick me into revealing more about my past. How will I handle this one? Maybe I'll crush him with a rock. No, I'm tired, so I'll take it slowly until my energy returns. I'll show him and his leaders that I'm not some mindless being.

Masking the immense effort it takes, I slowly reach out a gnarled hand from the shadows and wet my index finger in the small puddle of water that lies before my favorite granite chair. The same puddle that has appeared in the ground's depression every day I've been awake for over a dozen years. The wrought shackle clamped around my wrist rattles its chain all the way back to the loop behind me. The diminutive bookworm with horn-rimmed glasses and sharp features—ah yes, I will call him Bookworm—to my right covers his ears to try and dampen the noise as the echoes reverberate off the cavern walls, with black dust lazily drifting to the ground. They are not normal chains; each link twice Bookworm's weight, an advanced alloy eight times denser than Tungsten. Of course, that's not what makes them so special. It's what they are able to hold, or more specifically, whom they are able to hold, that makes them unique.

I fall back to gathering my thoughts as my crooked finger methodically pushes the fluid in a circular motion. My shirtless torso ripples from the underlying muscles. I admire the trailing water as it follows my finger. "You know." I nearly shock myself upon hearing my voice for the first time in months. It has always been deeply resonant and edgy, but the reflectiveness is something new. I start again after clearing my throat. "You know, it wasn't long ago that a simple motion of this finger could topple mountains and force the most powerful leaders on Earth to prostrate on the ground, begging for mercy. Not just figuratively, but also literally. I had that kind of power. I was willingly given that power, and…it was unwillingly taken away."

I don't need to look at the bookworm to know he is furiously writing, noting not only the words I speak but also my movements and behavior so that THEY can study them later. "They" being those who are too afraid to crawl down the hole and visit my chamber. No, enter my prison. A prison that even in my heyday would have been nearly impossible to break free from. A post-apocalyptic, vertical-shaft coal mine whose roof is ten thousand feet of rock. It had been poorly re-mined after our country fell. And that mistake is why I'm here. Too much force and the walls will collapse or the earth will shift. I'd be buried alive. And the elevator shaft itself? I couldn't fit in it if I tried. The only way to get out is the same way they got me in here. A buried memory I don't wish to surface.

A sigh accidently escapes my mouth, but must have sounded more like a growl judging by the bookworm's reaction. I hear his pen hit the ground, but I still don't look at him. My finger does another circle in the water before I set my strong jaw and speak again. "People are a lot like this water. In a group, they always begin standing strongly together, but after you make your way through the first few lines, they gather behind you, follow, and continue to follow until they die out, only to be replaced by the next wave. Ascension to demigod status requires followers, requires me and my kind feed off that continuous replacement, and it's what still keeps me alive despite the slanderous campaign your bosses have been running against me for over a decade."

I pause, not for the brown-haired bookworm to respond but to try and shake my sorrow.

"Faith. That's the word. The strongest word in any human dictionary. Do you know why? Because no other word, nor group of words, can ever erase it. Sure, you may be able to force people to stop proselytizing their faith, but it only slips beneath the surface. Hidden, but never gone. Just waiting to spring forth again. And when it does, the oppressors should beware."

I laugh out loud at the unintentional irony held within my words. Or is it intentional? The second strongest word in the human dictionary is hope. The hope of revenge layers my thoughts. It keeps them from dying out, and keeps me from fading away into oblivion...for now.

I'm surprised to hear his throat clear, as if he is preparing to talk. None of them had ever spoken when they came down to take notes. They would only write as I rambled on about things that weren't important or valuable to their leaders. Eventually they would tire and leave, or accidently get too close and be consumed. That was my fault, and most times it was unintentional. Like a moth to the flame, it feels the heat but the need for light pushes it forward. They all wanted to believe; each human that came down to my prison had a need to touch the untouchable, and that was their undoing.

His throat clears again, but no words follow. Curiosity grips me. What does this bookworm want? What is he doing? No matter. I can wait him out. Time is on my side. Time. My smile is ironic. It looks like today is my philosophical day on the power of single words. Faith, Hope, Time. What will be next?

I have an idea. Time to play with the human.

"Faith will be with most until they die, but hope is what allows one to survive the most abysmal of situations. Take me, for example. My unjustified slavery has lasted for over a decade. However, I have hope that one day I will be freed. I hang my chains of bondage onto that hope because I hunger for what I had before. Hunger. We all hunger for what we had before or for what we most desire. If we knew no better, then we would not hunger. If I had grown up a slave in this cavern and had not lived in our world, I would assume it was how I should live. My chains, this chair, and the insistent invasion by lesser beings would be my norm, my comfort, my belief of reality. However, I know what it's like to be free, to have power. I hunger to have that again, and also...to eat. Where is my food? I asked for crab cakes and some French fries." I sniff the air, trying to draw in any scents that had come down the elevator shaft with the bookworm.

"No food today," Bookworm stammers with a rather effeminate voice.

Rage, always right under my skin these days, boils to the surface. I shoot out from around the outcropping that had prevented the bookworm from seeing me, and I'm within feet of him before he can track me with his fear-ridden eyes. Those blue eyes wash over with a wave of fear and an understanding that it may be the end.

The unbreakable collars around my neck, arms, and legs ring out like a broken church organ as the chains snap to their maximum length—and hold. The ground shakes, and charcoal coats our now-still canvas.

Pain.

I feel the most pain from the sudden stop in my outstretched neck, but my anger won't be choked down. My bloodshot eyes complement the thick veins protruding through the muscles of my upper body. I tower over the frail man in size and stature. The bulldozer coming to wipe out the ant.

Foamed saliva splatters the bookworm as I bellow, "What do you mean no food? That was the agreement!"

I huff and puff, mostly from holding up the tens of thousands of pounds of chains, waiting for a response. The chains could hold a docked ship during a hurricane, but they barely hold me. The bookworm shakes and looks like he wants to become invisible, but much to my surprise he doesn't run away like the others. He works hard to regain his composure, as I fight to hold onto my anger.

"I have been studying you for some time, and I am quite aware that you never give us what is agreed upon for the food that you crave," replies Bookworm. "You instead go off on semi-philosophical rants that reveal nothing about you or your kind. There will be no food tonight, and no substance of any kind until you decide to reveal something for which we hunger. The computer data I looked over said you cannot starve nor die from thirst, so I think time is on your side. However, I have faith that you will decide to talk about what was agreed upon soon enough."

Crave, hunger, time, faith? He's smugly transforming my word strategy into his own sword. Parrying my blows while also waving the point at me.

4

I take a couple steps back to allow a few of the chains to rest on the floor. "You wouldn't be so brash if I were unchained, Bookworm. I would crush you like a rock."

Bookworm takes off his shiny glasses—his hands subtly shaking—and cleans them on his shirt. I'm proud of the volume of saliva that covers him.

"Mr. President. Truth be told, almost anyone could pummel me or even kill me if they wanted, so it does not matter if you are chained. Now, I have a job to do and will try my best to complete it, even if it kills me." Bookworm turns around and continues to speak as he leaves my cavern and heads to the mine's shaft. "And so you know, sir. Just because you can easily crush rocks does not mean the rest of us can. The saying is, 'crush you like a grape.' Probably more apropos, as my blood could be compared to the grape's juice as it squeezed out between your fingers."

Footsteps, fading footsteps.

I glare after him, hoping the intensity will burn through his back. However, after the elevator speeds up the shaft and out of view, I let out a laugh. From that one laugh, it begins, and I laugh louder than I have laughed in decades. The cavern rings out with my joy. Dust begins to extrude from the walls and swirl in patterns from my exuded breath, rapidly growing in volume before I decide it best to stop. It wouldn't be a good idea to be buried alive because of elation.

I like this Bookworm, and I'm pleased that they finally sent down someone with a little character. He will die soon enough, but at least it will be a fun game of cat and moose. Moose? I think that's right.

The calmness that envelopes my body only reminds me of the colossal weight of the chains I'm holding up, which will soon overcome me. I step back toward my granite chair and carefully sit down, as I don't want to crack it. They had told me it would be my last chair if I destroyed it, and I do like the feel of the smooth, cold rock on my skin. It relaxes me. I close my eyes and wait for a new nightmare to remind me of the horrible things I have done and that have been done to me.

****

The peace I experience after Bookworm left doesn't last very long. In fact, anger creeps back to full strength after two more days have passed. When the elevator shaft finally begins to vibrate, I hope he will come a little too close so I can squeeze his neck until his head pops off. Yes, I had done that before to someone—to many, in fact—and yes, the head would actually pop off and roll along the ground if I flicked it with my thumb at exactly the right moment. It's messy, but nothing demoralizes an attacking ground force like seeing such an unusual beheading of one of their own.

The clang of metal as the elevator stops shakes me from my daydream. I'm sitting in my granite chair, hidden from his view—waiting for the guest to say something. The familiar clearing of a throat confirms what my nostrils have already captured. They let Bookworm come back. I had wondered the last two days if they'd released him from his contract or if they'd decided their new approach of bringing in a different type of recorder might work.

"You're not a shrink, are you, Bookworm?" I growl. My anger shows even though I meant for it to be hidden. I didn't want him to have the upper hand.

"What? I thought that was rather obvious," he replies without looking up. He isn't being disrespectful but rather is preoccupied with finding his pen, searching through his belongings.

"Your pen is in your left breast pocket. Also, you said something about a computer the other day. We have those again?" My intent is to let Bookworm know that I'm listening to every word he says and that I will catch any slip-ups. I want him to know that he's dealing with an intellectually superior being.

Bookworm doesn't hesitate as he answers. "Yes, some are up and running. Not many, but some."

He then walks over and sits down on the writing rock. "So, you can see me through the shadows, but I can't see you."

I let the statement, which is actually a question, play in my mind while trying to figure out what is really behind it. When I solve it, I decide it's best to ignore.

"What took you so long to come back? Did it take two days to regather your courage?" My words spread like a slow-moving venom. Starting like an innocent question, but then ending with lethality.

However, Bookworm barely takes notice.

"What? Oh, I was researching another project of mine. Sorry about that. I didn't know I had committed to coming right back." Bookworm's eyebrows then scrunch up as he asks, "How are you able to tell the passage of time down here? Last time you said you had been down here for a decade, and now you mentioned how long I was absent."

Blind, stupid fools! Creating without understanding is just as bad as not creating at all. Why should I help them when they'll only use it to enslave their new creations?

"Sorry if I've offended you; I am just trying to learn," Bookworm said, surely hearing my rapid inhales.

"Learn? What are you trying to learn? About how I got my power? Ask people! That history hasn't had time to be overtaken by the fog of humankind's failures, yet."

This time my scoff is meant to be heard.

"I was hoping for a little more than the usual. I wanted to know when you first noticed the change to a demigod, and what it felt like. I would like your perspective on this." Bookworm stops writing and peers into the shadows, as if he can see me.

I slouch back in my chair. My perspective? Why would my perspective matter? It implies that my subjective inputs are valuable and a key to unlocking the power. Hmm. Maybe they're getting smarter, but I'm not yet convinced.

"I wear my emotions. You've seen it. Just take what has been written and add anger to it. That should complete 99 percent of what your bosses want."

7

"Hmm. That would be after you had gained your power. I want to know about the beginning…starting from the formation of The Americas."

"It didn't start there, Bookworm." I close my eyes and let the images take over. They swirl around like a casino slot machine, not as vivid as I remember, but still there.

"Was it shortly before then?" Bookworm's effeminate voice sounds eager.

I decide that I do crave the crab cakes I requested days before, and the only way to get them is to placate the diminutive man. Besides, what harm will I cause by describing the beginning, or the whole thing for that matter?

"Of course it was. You don't think that this power was a direct result of the formation of The United Americas? That was paperwork and politics. Power like mine is not created by bureaucrats possessing more pen and paper than brains."

I keep searching for the image I want in my mind until I find it. I shape it, cast the line, and reel it to my lips. "We here highly resolve that these dead shall not have died in vain; that this nation shall have a new birth of freedom; and that government of the people, by the people, for the people, shall not perish from the earth."

"The Gettysburg Address!" the bookworm exclaims. "So, it started on that day."

Bookworm is proud of himself. I don't want that. He's ruining my story.

I laugh the way one laughs at a child. It's meant to be worse than a spanking, to make one feel intellectually inferior.

"No, Bookworm. It's not about a day. It's about a person; it's about the people. It always has been and always will be. Step back to the first United States President. Did you know that once they had defeated the British, the American people asked George Washington to be king? To perfectly mimic the very thing they had fought against. No? Well, they did, and he turned down the offer. History books created a fable that he wanted to make sure his country would never have a king. That was not the truth.

The first United States President wanted to make sure that his country would not create a demigod. The first, modern-day demigod."

I open my eyes to soak in the awe that washes over Bookworm's face. His jaw is slack and his irises unfocused. Yes, I had given him and his superiors something new. I will be getting my crab cakes. Oh, and my French fries. I love the crunchy outside and soft inside of French fries. Wait, that was very similar to the consistency of crab cakes. Did I like crab cakes and French fries or just things that are crunchy on the outside and soft on the inside? Would I enjoy eating a beetle? Maybe even a—.

"George Washington? Because he had become a hero, or was it that he had become very popular?" asks Bookworm.

I lean forward and let my stone-like chin jut out of the shadows. My sarcastic smile is even stronger than my insulting laugh as I shake my head back and forth. "Remember movie and rock stars from the twenty-first century? Nah, you wouldn't remember. That was a long time ago. But if you have studied history, then you know just how popular some of them became. Followed by millions, even tens of millions. Some had power that rivaled the dictators in small countries. However, none of them ever became demigods. Why?"

Bookworm shrugs his shoulders as he tries to think of what it is. Then he remembers his job and picks up his pen and starts to scribble down what I've already given him.

"The popularity and even heroism was, and is, a start. However, it's really what happens behind the scenes that creates the power.

"Worship," I state and then pause for dramatic effect.

"George Washington was worshipped in his own country, and in others, because he led our first successful revolution against an empire. Men and women gave their lives for him, and those who still breathed the faith of the older gods burned gifts and sacrificed animals to him. The greater the sacrifice or the costlier the gift, the more powerful he became." My eyes stare off into the distance as I reflect on some of the sacrifices I had received.

"Then, it made sense to cater to the rich as they could give the greatest gifts, and—," Bookworm starts.

"No!" I shout as my right fist lifts and slams into the granite arm of my chair, pulverizing most of the stone while sending out the remaining pieces as shards of rock. The noise from the chains deafens, and the sound of the rock explosion forces Bookworm to cover his ears once more. I regret my action as soon as I hit the granite.

It's my last chair, they had warned me.

I take a deep breath before continuing. "It was the cost to the individual, not the cost of the gift or sacrifice. A rich man barely notices when a gold coin drops from his purse. But a poor, desperate man could kill his family if he offered up half a bag of rice."

Bookworm nods as he writes. "I am truly sorry about that. I misunderstood."

"No. No," I reply, adding in a sigh. "It's not your fault. It just…well, it brought back memories."

"So, you know when someone sacrifices or burns a gift?" asks Bookworm.

"Yes, in a sense. It's not a visual picture, but rather the emotions that come through. With time and experience, it becomes easy to tell not only what was given, but also who gave it and where they reside." I settle back into my chair, worn out from recalling even the little bit of information I have given Bookworm.

"Do you remember your first sacrifice?" Bookworm asks.

I shake my head. "I am done with answering questions for today. But what about you, Bookworm? You're a scientist, no doubt specializing in computers, which are very rare. Were you a First?"

"No, sir. I was a Third," Bookworm replies as he puts away his pen and paper.

"A Third? How unusual. Tell me." I thump my fingers sequentially on the good arm of my chair. I'm aware that the resulting noise is like a hammer hitting the ground.

"I was lucky, really. They came to my town and when they tested me, I was able to wire together a circuit for lighting without having ever seen one before. Within the day, I said goodbye to my family and was shipped to a Second. Within the year, I could build a complex calculator and even a simplified computer. Eventually, I received a full-time educator position at First University, which lead me to this rock." Bookworm relays his story in an unexciting manner. Matter of fact it was, with no sense of pride from starting at the bottom and moving up so fast.

There is more. There should be more. His storytelling is bland, and no one moves from Third to First without a good story.

"Have you heard from your family since that day?" I ask.

Bookworm shakes his head from side to side. "There was only my dad and older sister. They both already had the blisters, so I assume they are gone now."

"Ah. You lived near a hot spot." I have grown too insensitive about death to care about his feelings for a family, which no doubt had suffered greatly from radiation poisoning. However, if he had been near a former metropolis, then there really was something more to his story. "Did you ever see temples in the city?"

Bookworm nods his head and answers what would be my next question. "Most of them were yours, a giant hexagonal column at their entrances with the eagle on top, staring down at all who entered. There were people still worshipping you when I last visited."

Worship. I wonder why they continue after all I did wrong. However, it's not something I will discuss with Bookworm. I pick out the part of his response that I want to expound on. "Yes, the powerful American eagle, with its illuminating single eye watching over and protecting the lands of its people. Perched high above, on a pillar. Do you know what the six corners of the pillar represent?"

"My father had mentioned something about that. One was strength, and another was intelligence. I think he said something about justice, but I forget the rest," Bookworm reflects.

"Strength, intelligence, honor, freedom, protection, and justice. I was the embodiment of those things Americans held dear. But they come from a fool's dream. For no person, no nation, no demigod can sustain such a pure set of values." My voice is raspy now; the confidence in my soul wains. Anger slowly pours over me again. Anger at letting my country down. Anger at causing its downfall.

11

Bookworm must have sensed my change, as he stands up and gathers his belongings.

"Your food will be here when you awake. I will come back again and would like to discuss how the power inside of you came to be, and how it felt."

"How it felt? How about what I feel? All they wanted me to do was destroy and kill. A mindless warrior who did their bidding, no matter how horrible the deed. I was more than that. I am more than that!" My voice rages with pain, and my shouting shakes the walls. The soft-glow lights behind Bookworm's rock power on and off as the sound waves hit them. I want to hurt something, make it feel my pain. My left hand grips the arm of my granite chair and snaps off a large chunk. I lift myself up and charge to the limit of the chains, hurling the chunk of rock at the elevator shaft. The rock shatters into small fragments inside the tube.

It's empty inside, and he's gone. I stare at where it hit; my chest heaves from the effort of running with the chains.

Had I known he had already left? Would I have killed him if he still stood in the cavern? Maybe not. There is something different about Bookworm. Something I like.

I walk backward to my broken chair and sink into the misery that is my comfort.

Maybe it's time to tell my story.

Chapter 2

The next morning a plate of crab cakes is in front of my chair, just as I expected. I had yet to see the person who brought my food and drink. They somehow knew when I was sleeping, and even when I was pretending. The cakes are perfect and satisfy my craving, as I really don't need to eat. My substance is the offerings I'm freely given. The more offerings I receive, the more engorged I become. However, as they lessen, it's like an obese person being placed on a diet—sharp, frequent pains needle my body until I shrink to a size where the offerings can sustain me.

I'm satisfied, and ready to talk.

However, Bookworm doesn't show up for many more days. I become irritable again, and when he finally does show up, I'm not in the mood to talk.

"How were your crab cakes?" he politely asks as he extracts his pen and paper from a leather book bag.

I only grunt in return.

"That good? I'll talk to the chef to see if she can't make them better next time. What was wrong with them? Were they undercooked? Perhaps some spices were needed?"

"It's not that," I respond calmly, although I want to shout.

"Oh. I see." Bookworm replies.

"No. You only think you see. That's the problem with every person they bring down here. You're scribes, not writers. You pen what's said, not what is felt. You're afraid to write with any emotion because you then turn the objective into the subjective, not realizing that the objective is always biased anyway. Scribing is a mathematical problem, but writing is an art. Your writing style will always be biased by who you are. And what is read is biased by whoever reads your scribblings."

I pause to let him think on what I said, but Bookworm replies right away.

"I'm not here to scribe. I'm here to tell your story, if you choose to let me."

I stand up from my chair and pull along the clanking weights as I walk out of the shadows. I don't stop until I'm as close as I can get to Bookworm. I stare him in the eyes, searching for the hanging thread that will unravel his lie. I neither find nor feel anything different from what Bookworm has said.

"Why?" I ask.

"I would like to let people know how you came about and show people who you are." Bookworm pauses and for the first time shows a slight hint of uncertainty. "My father and sister worshiped you. I did not. They surely died because of what demigods had done. I had always believed the demigods were abominations that needed to be destroyed."

He used the word 'that' not 'who,' meaning he saw me and the others as inhuman, nonorganic. Interesting.

"And now?" I ask, as Bookworm's flash of weakness evaporates.

"I'm reserving my judgment until we are done," replies Bookworm. "Although so far, it's not looking to be in your favor."

I roar out sincere and pleasant laughter again. I hadn't laughed for fun in a long time, and now it has happened twice. Like before, once it started I didn't want to stop. I do keep it lower to avoid a cave-in, but continue until nothing is left inside of me except for a small chuckle. I take a deep breath and step back a few feet to release the tension on the chains. I had forgotten they were there while I was laughing. "Okay, Bookworm. Where do you want to start? And please don't say at the beginning."

"When you first felt the power," he responds.

"Hmm. We need to go farther back than that, Bookworm." I walk backward and sit in my chair. "The Americas began with The United States of America, a once powerful democracy from where I root my beginnings.

I watched as it steered and then maneuvered the world away from a global war. It seemed invincible at the time, but the end came quicker than anyone predicted. Like so many governments, it was being crushed under its continuous creation of rules and regulations. Laws that at first snaked around each other soon became intertwined, wrapping over and doubling up until they had become one big ball of yarn. No piece could be pulled without the rest following. Nothing useful could be done, and as a result the country fell into a state of economic despair, as had the rest of the world. That was when I was elected to office. My advisors and I saw no way out. Prices for the staples in life rose above what even the well-to-do could afford. Starvation brought crime, and crime brought death. Death brought despair. Despair was the final signal for total annihilation."

I notice that Bookworm is paying strict attention and furiously scribbling.

"It was then I had an idea, one that I took from an American pastime called football. When collegiate football teams had leveled off, in terms of success, they were in large groups, called conferences. They made a lot of money, but everyone wanted more. Their college presidents could only generate more revenue by growing the number of teams in each conference, which could only be done by poaching. Obviously, he who poached the most won. But that's not my point. This process revived their sport, while also shaking up the stagnancy, creating energy for all collegiate football without bringing in anything external. The United States of America needed to rediscover her strength and power, and that could only be done by adding resources from other countries of the world. So, we signed and established a fifty-year consortium with Mexico and Canada to form The United Americas, or The Americas, and then added in select smaller countries that helped us gain key resources. With rapidly growing success, I relocated the capital of The Americas to Cincinnati, initiating the building of the first megacity that would be known as Entara. We terraformed the land; creating high-speed ground, rail, air, and water transportation that reached out like the spokes of a wheel."

I stop for a moment to search for a good way to continue.

15

"It was a great start, but everyone knew that the Earth had developed to the point where one could not gain without someone else losing. I understood that for the short term my plan would work, but after a while other countries would become desperate, poaching would start, and new enemies would be formed. The poaching would further reinvigorate the economy, but even that would eventually spill over into war."

I take a moment to catch my breath, not being used to such long speeches any more.

"I decided it was time to fund the development of a Mars outpost, and eventually the building of a colony on the red planet. Even with the discovery of vast frozen lakes of water under the surface of Mars, the cost would come at a sacrifice. I decided to cut aid to any country not owned by or aligned with us, while also becoming a banking nation for others. No longer freely handing out money, but loaning money and collecting interest or acquiring the nation if payments weren't met. It worked, and the Mars outpost became a reality.

"During my first two terms as President, we saw an upswing in the economy. But I still had so much to do and no one else to carry my vision forward. I fought for and won a repeal of The United Americas' twenty-second amendment, allowing me to run for office two more times, and then two more times after that. Maybe…maybe that was the beginning of the end."

I glance over at Bookworm as he feverishly writes down what I am feeding him. Hunger. He is hungry for information, my information. I lower my voice a little as I continue. "It was so long ago that I forget most individual events, and only remember the larger pieces. However, one day in particular stands out during that time. We had just completed the building of Entara, and two hundred million people had already moved into the self-sustaining city. I walked out on a master balcony, which overlooked the grand gardens, and stared down in awe at what I saw. Over a million people below me, chanting my name. A thousand times that watching through electronic mediums throughout the world. I leaned into the microphone and spoke one word, 'Hello.'"

I pause for dramatic effect.

"What came back was the feeling that a rock star would receive as he strummed his guitar and stormed around the stage, one light encapsulating his greatness. A wave of praise hit me like a bolt of lightning. I was energized and powerful. Over two decades of toil, wear and tear, pushing my body to give its last ounce of energy was wiped clean in a second. I felt alive, free of pain.

"I spoke to my people about our great nation and consortium, and how it was them who had righted the ship, and it was them who deserved the rewards that came with success. I unveiled my new plan that would reduce work hours while improving living for all. No one cared about the details, only that I was speaking to them. Although I was speaking words that I meant to make come true. Afterward, I went back to my room to be with my wife and two daughters. Their smiles were as pure and innocent as mine. The energy that had rejuvenated me also flowed through them. It was a joyous day."

Memories sweep through my mind and force me to pause.

"However, just like the stage performance of a rock star, the energy was short-lived, and the pressures of the job and pains of an aging body overtook me. I was soon on to the next challenge; that day quickly became nothing more than a pleasant memory. Other countries finally had enough of The Americas' success. Alliances and consortiums began to form all around the world. Some made sense, leveraging natural resources, infrastructure, human capital, or technological superiority. However, many were done out of desperation. Countries with opposing forms of government aligned, and internal conflict erupted almost immediately. Economies collapsed, poverty soared, people died."

I look at Bookworm's face and see that he is saddened by what I say.

"I took on the challenge of being an ambassador to help resolve these conflicts, until…" I stop just before the emotions well up inside me and pour out. I hadn't shed a tear since that day, and won't ever again. Or so I want to believe.

Bookworm doesn't press me. He waits patiently until I'm ready to begin anew. Sighing, knowing I need to go on, I lower my voice again, and from the corner of my eye see him lean closer, off the rock, needing to hear my every word.

"An assassination attempt from one of the consortiums I was trying to help. One that never had any known animosities against myself or The Americas. We had still been cautious, but we didn't expect them to attack my family. It was one small explosion in the room down the hallway, and even before I turned around, I knew what had happened. When I got there, their lifeless bodies were sitting on the tattered couch, blood pouring out of numerous small holes. My legs gave, and I heard the marble floor crack as my knees made impact. The motivation for my dreams and happiness was gone, wiped out without reason."

I stop and wipe my hand across the side of my face. It's moist and dampens my gnarled index finger. Anger once again rises inside me. I take a deep breath, fighting to keep it just below the surface, and continue, yet again lowering my voice to what is now a whisper.

"I carried the bodies to a place I knew from my childhood. Somewhere that no one else would find. I buried the bodies together and mourned them without a care as to how my people were doing. I remember sitting in one spot for days without moving, until a tingling sensation tickled my nose. The tingling turned to warmth and soon enveloped my whole head. It then flowed down my body, comforting me, making me feel stronger. That was the first time I had truly felt it—felt true power. The praise had turned to compassion, and the compassion to worship. My people had seen the human side of me, and with that had elevated me above them. I emerged two weeks later, barely able to fit in the elevator…"

I lunge without warning, quickly making up the ground between Bookworm and my chair with two long steps. His wiry neck is in my massive hand, and I lift him high off the ground. His face turns beet red and his eyes nearly bulge out of their sockets. I'm seconds away from popping his head off with the flick of my thumb.

But Bookworm doesn't struggle; his arms don't flail or make a futile attempt to remove my steel grip. Instead, his bulging eyes look down at the rock he was sitting on before I set my trap. I follow his gaze and stare at the piece of paper that bears his handwriting. Words. A few simple words that weaken me, challenge my motives. I release my grip, dropping him almost four feet to the ground, and laugh as he gasps for air. Not laughing at what I have done to him, but rather because I both hope for and doubt those words.

"You? Really? How are you gonna do that?" I ask with another amusing chuckle.

"I will. You just wait and see," Bookworm chokes out as he massages his neck and gasps for the precious air he nearly lost for good. He then unbuttons his shirt and shows me the wires and the recording device strapped to his chest.

"Very well." I walk backward to my chair and sit down. Bookworm grabs his writing materials and then walks forward until he is halfway between the rock and my chair. I raise an eyebrow. *Is he stupid?*

"Is that where they're buried?" Bookworm points to the opposite corner, where a mound of coal rises from the flattened ground.

I nod before continuing, while Bookworm sits on the ground to listen.

"When I resurfaced and was escorted back to my city, I saw them. My first temples. They were dispersed throughout the parks and streets. Small structures. Some were made from cardboard or constructed from discarded crates, while others were more elaborate, made by craftsmen and decorated with personal trinkets. We drove by a particularly large, open pentagram, and at its center was a short-haired man dressed in nice robes. When he saw my car, he flicked a lighter and dropped it to the ground. Only it wasn't the ground, it was a bowl of oil. I was horrified and confused at the same time. He screamed, but less from the pain and more in anger at what had been done to me. I could feel the difference. As the man burned, the strength and lust for revenge fueled within me. I was compelled to ensure my attackers would know the meaning of pain and fear the sleeping giant they had awakened."

Fury still grips me, but I go on.

"As I stepped out of my car, I smacked my head on the door frame, bending it upward while lifting the car a few inches. Unfazed, I stood and realized that I was at least a head taller than all around me. I had been six feet ever since the tenth grade, but now I was over seven feet in height.

While others were baffled, I immediately understood what was happening, welcoming the power, lusting it, and wanting more. I formed and executed a strategy to gain worshippers, feeding off their pity for my loss and turning it into what I needed. Power flowed into me like underground streams filling a lake. Soon my Presidential staff began to understand what was happening to me. Actually, it was too drastic a change to ignore, even if it defied the laws of nature and physics. I wondered what would happen when the people of my nation and consortium saw the changes. Would they run in fear, cast me aside, or try to imprison me?"

I stop as if questioning myself.

"It didn't take long for the masses to notice and, instead of the negative reaction I thought would happen, even more began to worship me. They needed someone, wanted to identify with something strong and powerful. I was it. I became the embodiment of the six symbols on the pillars of our consortium's capital house and the illuminated eye of the eagle that overlooked the lands. I became the first modern-day demigod."

I pause to gather my thoughts and to decide what more is needed to complete the story.

"Mr. President. When you said you became the embodiment of the six symbols, does that mean you lost free will?"

Bookworm's voice is unusually shaky. Is he afraid of asking too much about my personal life? Afraid of stepping outside the physical world and into my disjointed mind?

"No. I didn't lose my individuality, but it did become harder and harder to separate what I wanted from what my followers prayed for me to do. I think that if they banded together and tried to force me to do something I didn't want to do, I could still fight it off. However, their collective desires and wishes became a part of me. Who I was and what I wanted weren't the same as before, but I wasn't completely what they wanted either."

Bookworm gulps as he forms his next question. "And who you are now, is that a reflection of what they wanted?"

I have to give Bookworm credit. He's scared to death now that he is in striking range, but he still asks the needed questions. "I guessed you're a scientist. Psychiatrists try to get me to talk about my personality in a roundabout way. Hoping self-reflection would be how we got there. That never worked."

Bookworm waits without saying a word.

I rub my face with my good hand. "I honestly don't know. Maybe it's some warped agglomeration of their wants and my desires. Maybe I should have let the other scribes live so we could sort through it."

Bookworm smiles as a result of my sick joke. It's sincere, which worries me.

"Back to my story. Using all the resources I had at my disposal, I tracked down the group who had murdered my family. I brought in my chief of staff for defense, and his analysis was that my revenge would lead us into a nuclear war. One that my nation and consortium would not come out of unscathed. Worse was that the opposing country's people knew nothing about their involvement. An attack on them would unleash their own anger at being repressed for over a century after lost wars."

"Well, you couldn't just let the group or country go unpunished. I bet you kidnapped their leader, didn't you?"

"Close. We apprehended their ambassador, the one who set off the bomb, and let the country's leader know that we wanted him to stand trial. I wanted him dead, all of them dead, but this time I looked out for what was best for my people. It didn't work. They turned it around, showing their people how The Americas was a bully who was now torturing their ambassador. It was a calculated move on their part, as they knew of my growing power. They set up the ambassador, whose last name was Arthuren, to be their demigod. People prayed for him, and their government milked it like a laden cow, then churned that prayer to worship…and it worked."

"How can that happen so quickly when the world hadn't seen something like you for thousands of years?" Bookworm questions.

I only shrug my shoulders, the chains rattling to remind me of my incarceration, before continuing. "Their ambassador grew more and more powerful with each passing day, making it difficult to keep him imprisoned. My cabinet worked furiously to grow my power. They built temples, dispersed propaganda of my benevolence and caregiving so more would worship me, and even whispered in the ears of the desperate on how their self-sacrifice would lead to riches in the afterlife. Of course, I hadn't known about the latter until I felt their sacrifice. But…I wouldn't have stopped it."

"The days grew into weeks, and weeks into months. We were at a standstill—nuclear arms poised for ensured global devastation, armies chomping at the bit to race along red-streaked fields and lend their blood for another paint swath. Neither side blinked, until their ambassador started to break free. We simply couldn't contain him anymore. That was when it was decided that I would fight their ambassador to settle the issue. A loss by either nation would result in the defection of a top consortium nation to the winning side. Such a deal had never been proposed before, let alone agreed upon by both parties. As one can imagine, both Canada and Britain were irate."

Bookworm clears his throat to let me politely know he has a question. "Was it written in the consortium agreement that the joining parties could be traded?"

"No, but it also wasn't written that they couldn't. None of that really mattered though, as he who has the power makes the rules. They had no real power and were like children begging for favors. Anyway, the terms of the battle were set. A grouping of neutral locations was picked by each side and then one was randomly selected by a computer. The peaceful mountains near Hikone, Japan, had been pulled from the black hat. It was a place known for its hot springs and ryokan getaways since feudal times. A place to rest one's spirit and heal a broken body. And we were going to destroy it."

"How would you destroy a whole area with just the two of you, even if you were demigods. It was a physical battle, correct?"

Bookworm is so entranced with the story that his pen rests on his leg. I nod down to the utensil, causing him to hurriedly pick it up.

"A bare-fisted brawl was agreed upon, as that was his strength, and we would fight until one surrendered or was rendered unconscious. Neither side knew if we could be destroyed, but we were anointed demigods, so it was just assumed that we couldn't. Since I had never been in a real fight my whole life, I was given crash classes in boxing, street fighting, and mixed martial arts. It was just enough to make sure I could get out of a really difficult position."

I close my eyes again to try to remember the exact details of the battle. I was sure it was what Bookworm was looking for as he wrote my biography. Fight details were always the most exciting part of a story. When I open my eyes again, I'm alone. I feel strange and can't figure out what happened. I look down at my puddle of water and have the urge to touch it. No, to drink it. I'm thirsty. I lift myself off my chair and kneel to scoop up the refreshing liquid. As I bring the water to my face, I stop and separate my cupped hands, letting the water leak back into the clear, colorless puddle. I examine my right hand and then my left, just to make sure. Yes, my fingers are no longer gnarled, no longer permanently disfigured; the cracked callouses healed and covered with fresh, pink skin. The strange feeling was of being refreshed. My aches and pains that had accompanied me for decades were almost gone. Merely a dull annoyance. Was it something I ate or drank? Maybe Bookworm had given me medicine? Was he tricking me?

The sharp whistling of George Cohan's "You're a Grand Old Flag" flitters in the air. Vibrant and crisp as a freshly plucked head of lettuce. It's then that I realize it was the humming from the elevator shaft that woke me and also made the musical sound. I stare at Bookworm as he turns the corner and nonchalantly walks within striking distance. I have to admit that I don't know what to do. Part of me is ready to hammer my fist on the top of his head so hard that he will be nothing more than a red inkblot on the ground, which I could later have one of the psychologists analyze with me. The other part of me wants to have him listen to me, or is it to talk? As I debate which course I will pursue, Bookworm reaches into his leather bag and pulls out a dishcloth. As he gently unfolds the checkered cloth, the baked smell wafts toward me.

"Blueberry muffins? How did you know?"

I'm suspicious yet again. I don't like being manipulated. I wonder if I can hurt Bookworm bad enough to get my message across without killing him.

23

Bookworm senses the anger in my voice. You never could completely tame a wild animal, and just maybe he has slipped up. "You started to talk in your sleep. Most of it didn't make any sense, but the words blueberry muffins kept coming out loud and clear. I left right after that, as I thought it was improper to eavesdrop."

I let my features relax and unclench my fists. I stand up, then shoot my right hand out toward him with my index finger pointing strongly at Bookworm. "And what about this?"

"Is that the one that was gnarled before?" he asks, not as surprised as I thought he would be or pretend to be.

"Of course it is. What did you do? What did they do!" I shout.

Bookworm covers his ears and shouts back at me. "How should I know? I am a computer engineer, not a blasted biologist!"

The strain of the chains wins out, and I slump to the ground. I don't know what is going on, but things are changing without my knowledge. Am I being manipulated? I don't know.

Bookworm stops glaring at me and grabs a muffin, stuffing the whole thing in his mouth. I decide he is telling the truth, or at least is willing to let it rest for now, and thrust out my open palm. Bookworm grabs another muffin but, instead of handing it to me, flings it at my chest. Even though I'm surprised, I catch it against my chest, the hot bread pleasantly warm against my cold skin. I open my palm and shove the flattened muffin into my mouth. "Hmm. A little more hairy than I like, but not bad."

Bookworm laughs so hard that he snorts, which causes me to laugh back at him. With the tension wiped away, we sit and chat about everything but my story. How the outside world was when I left it and what has happened since then. The challenge of rebuilding after global war, and rumors of which countries have risen from the ashes and which have blinked out of existence. I'm even happy to learn that people have been trying to revive technology. The very thing that aided their destruction is yet again a driving factor for which to measure economic growth.

****

The days go on like this for a while, until the day that Bookworm arrives with a solemn look on his face.

"Sorry, Mr. President. I have enjoyed the discussions we've had, but they tell me that you need to get back to the story."

"Not to worry, Bookworm. I understand, and the extra days have given me some time to reflect on what happened during the battle and the years that followed. I think I've pieced it all together, and it should make for a bestseller." I smile in unison with Bookworm. "And, Bookworm?"

"Yes, sir?" he replies as he pulls out his writing materials.

"Who are they? The ones who sent you down here? Are they part of the new government of The Americas or another country that gained control of her?" I already know what the answer will be, but I have to ask.

"I'm sorry, sir. My contract stated that under no circumstances would I divulge any information that could be used to ascertain who they are. However, I will tell you that the purpose is not malevolent. In fact, I believe it is worthwhile."

I can tell Bookworm is lying, and that he is worried that I know it and will hurt him for the deceit.

"Hmm. In all my years on Earth, I have seen very few acts that weren't selfish. You're still young Bookworm, very young."

"Yes, and full of hope," Bookworm replies.

I wink at him and motion that I need some sleep before we get back to what his superiors want. I wonder how they will react to the demigod battles.

Chapter 3

"The Battle of Hikone," I tell Bookworm at our next session. "That's where we left off. There was a send-off celebration hosted at my largest temple within Entara. I had never been to any of my temples but had driven by several of them. All of those had been simple in design, but this one was beyond excessive. I felt like an Arabian prince, which was not appropriate. How could people pray for help, pray for food, when they walked into a house of opulence; a house that had wealth to share without the need for prayer. As I entered I turned to one of my aides and decreed that all temples be built to stand the test of time, including being less attractive to robbers. I explained that stonework was okay, but expensive materials and lavish quarters would be forbidden. As I was giving my last words, I stepped into a grand room filled with thousands of people, all of whom dropped to the ground and prayed upon seeing me. To be honest, it was the first time I had witnessed the mass worshipping, and I wasn't embarrassed or shy. I embraced it, letting my power grow with each passing moment until it was time for me to board the cargo plane. I felt like a god, invincible and ready to extract my revenge."

Bookworm, I observe, is taking notes.

"The details leading up to the battle are droll, no matter how many times I try to spin the tale in my head. Too many pre-parties, formal meetings, and excessive politics. Instead, I'll start with when they dropped me off for the battle. It was at an abandoned national park that used to house a gondola system to travel between the mountains, and it was located along the eastern side of Lake Biwa. The lake itself was beautiful in its blue purity while also being the largest lake in all of Japan. The trees of the park were plentiful, and I seemed small standing beside them, even though I was now over eighteen feet in height and weighed a couple tons. I had chosen a plaid wool shirt, blue denim overalls, and steel-reinforced leather boots. My rich, black hair was slicked back, and I hadn't shaved for over a week, leaving a thick growth of stubble that spoke to my rugged and tough side. Yes, my goal had been to re-create the look of Paul Bunyan, a folk hero lumberjack who helped shape North America. I was going to reshape the world; straighten out the crooked river this former man and his leaders had dug."

Bookworm looks at my girth and nods.

"I walked up to one of the gondola supports and placed a palm on its cold metal. My giant hand covered almost a third of its width. For fun, I squeezed it, and I watched in self-awe as the metal easily creased and caved in. One more squeeze and I was able to split it in half, as if it had been a piece of Play-Doh. When I let go, the detached support slammed into the ground and leaned forward until the gondola cables were taut. I stood there for a moment, staring at the crushed metal while clenching my fist. It had been too easy to destroy, my shock transferring into fuel for my ego. An inflated ego that I needed for this battle.

"What could possibly defeat me? My skin was tougher than metal, and my strength seemed unmatched. I felt invincible. Well, until I heard the heavy footsteps behind me. I turned and stared at the first demigod I had ever seen that wasn't my own reflection. I expected a larger version of the gray-haired, portly ambassador who had murdered my family. Instead, I was confronted by a blond-haired giant whose shirtless body was stacked with layers of glistening muscle. He was about three feet shorter than me, but appeared so much stronger. It made sense. He was created to fight, while I was created to lead. My first thought was that the world-televised battle would be short, and my second was to wonder just how much oil they had used to make him glisten."

Bookworm is caught off guard and inhales so fast from the onset of laughter that he releases the familiar snort.

I smile before continuing. "I looked him square in the eyes and asked why he had killed my family. What had I done to him or his nation to deserve such a barbaric act? You see, no matter his answer, I was going to use it to spur my attack. I wanted the rage to engulf me and drive my revenge. But his response was nothing I had ever expected, even though I had run the scenario in my head thousands of times. He said it was to help me see that the path I had chosen for The Americas was wrong. That I was seeking to be the king of the world, when I should have been seeking to better the world for all people. His words were much deeper than I expected, and I knew truth lay somewhere in his words. He broke through the surface of my skin with those words. A wound that festered and would eventually lead to my downfall."

I pause for effect.

"The only reply that I could muster was that his actions had only made it worse, made me more than a king. To which he replied that it was unexpected but okay, as he could wipe out The Americas by defeating me. That his goal was still attainable, and The Americas would become an indentured colony. I was no longer out for revenge, but rather fighting to ensure the freedom of my people. I reached out for the gondola support I had sheared off. Gripping it with both hands, I swung it at Arthuren with such force that the thick metal cables snapped and cleaved trees in half on their recoiling flight. I hit him. It was a glancing blow, but it sent Arthuren into and through a huge oak tree. Without even a moment to regroup, he stood up, brushed off the tree chippings, and ran at me. I swung again, but this time he blocked the support and wrestled the mangled piece of metal out of my grasp. I caught his first punch with my chin and the second with my temple.

"The sounds of the impact were deafening, like thunder in my ears, but much worse was the pain. As a demigod, I didn't think I could feel physical pain until Arthuren hit me. With two punches, he made me question my power. My head was spinning until he threw an uppercut to my stomach. My counterattack was to throw up on his cowhide pants and to try to launch my bulging eyes at him. Still trying to shake out the cobwebs, he grabbed my neck and used it as a discus, throwing me into a grove of trees. I flew through them as if they were twigs, snapping them in half before rolling dozens of feet down the hill.

"From the pain that now covered my entire body, I thought that my end was near. But when I regained my footing, the bruises and cuts were completely gone, and my head clear. My worshippers had come to the rescue. Their sacrifices were working. I attacked back, aiming to weaken his knees. However, worshippers were doing the same for Arthuren. He healed as fast as I did.

"We raged in battle for days and destroyed hundreds of forested acres. The land looked as if a tornado had rolled up the mountains. And while neither of us were seriously injured, he was definitely winning each round.

"The days of battle gave me plenty of time to think and learn. I used my recently gained knowledge, that I could feel pain, to my advantage. As we battled, or rather as I was beaten up, I worked my way closer to the broken gondola. When close enough, I grabbed a severed cable and subtly looped it around us as I ducked under and moved around his punches. After a few turns, I stepped aside and cinched the massive cable around his arms and waist. He laughed and spouted something about it only being a matter of time before he broke out. He was right, but I didn't give him that time. I grabbed Arthuren and hurled him the hundreds of feet it took for him to land in the lake. I had won."

Bookworm writes furiously until he has caught up with my last words. A puzzled look crosses his face as he tries to grasp what has happened. It's exactly what I want.

"How?"

I only stare back at him, waiting.

"He didn't die, did he?" Bookworm asks.

I shake my head.

"Oh, wait! He was perpetually drowning so that the healing he received from his followers had to be used to keep him alive, and thus he couldn't break free of the cables."

"Good job, Bookworm. They determined it was similar to a stalemate in chess, yet the only true win for a demigod. Again, there are more details about the outcome, but they're irrelevant to the story. After that battle, I thought I had regained my humanity and had become what my followers wanted me to be. Sadly, they changed more than I did, and for the worse. The ratings and profits The Americas gained from the battle were massive. The former Eastern European country we absorbed had huge coal deposits that were critical for the massive amounts of diamond film required by The Americas. Everyone in The Americas saw their standard of living jump. It was just too much to walk away from, and too much for any country to not get involved in. The demigod battles swept through the world like a virus. First came the English colonies' Prince Robertson of Westminster challenging the Gaul Consortium's Bluebeard after the ugly demigod slept with the prince's wife. We all thought it would be one-sided, and it was."

I pause to catch my breath.

"However, the shifty Bluebeard poisoned the prince before the battle, weakening him so that the fight favored the Gaul. Afterward, the Gaul Consortium gained a third of the underwater colonies, moving it into the top five world powers. Seeing this, my worshippers wanted even more, and in under a year I went from being their president and protector to being nothing more than a mindless gladiator."

I stop and catch the look from Bookworm that I knew would be coming.

"Sure, I could have stopped it as I mentioned before, free will and all. But I guess I liked it enough to not resist their requests, and I was so busy that I didn't have much time to think of a better pathway. A new demigod seemed to pop up every year as countries joined together to form a cult that then spread to become a popularized religion for their consortium. That consortium would then find a way to show they had been slighted, and then demand justice through a demigod battle. It was the easiest way to grow, if you won. Unfortunately for them, I always won. And The Americas and our new Marsian city benefitted from my wins. Until Zofara."

"Zofara? What was that?" Bookworm asks as he munches on a piece of dried jerky.

31

"She. She was a demigoddess for The United African Nations. Although she was a good four feet shorter than me, and easily a third of my weight, she was a feared warrior. She combined a warrior's combative skills with unparalleled agility and a razor-sharp mind. While I had only seen her on videos, I was impressed with her ability as much as I was infatuated with her beauty. However, like me, she never smiled and never had been heard to laugh. She lived only for what her people wanted. You see, she had grown up in an orphanage after her village was destroyed from a civil war. It was a rough orphanage, and she had to fight for every meal. She didn't resent the boys and girls at the orphanage, but rather grew up wanting to ensure that her people didn't need to fight internally to survive. She became a shrewd diplomat before taking on her demigoddess status."

"What happened?"

"The usual. An accusation that we had slighted their nations by blocking a merger with a formidable European power. They not only demanded resolution through a demigod battle, but argued that it take place on their soil." I stop and wait for Bookworm to catch up.

"But you said the battles always occurred on neutral grounds. I assume that was because of the extra power one would have on his or her own soil?"

"Yes, Bookworm. That's exactly why the rule was put in place. However, I agreed to their terms. No, don't worry. I didn't throw the battle because I fell in love. Her worshipper base was paltry compared to mine. I knew I would easily beat her, possibly even permanently maim her, since I was much more powerful. In fact, the only reason I agreed to fight on The United African Nations' soil was because I was afraid I would kill her. I had begun to get a feeling that even though we demigods were powerful, we weren't immortal. I hoped that being on her own lands would give her the added energy she needed."

"But it didn't, did it?"

Bookworm is so naïve. He has not only stopped fearing me, but he's bordering on being rude. I wonder if I've allowed him to get too close. Part of me desires to end the story, end him, and go back to my chair.

32

However, Bookworm is up to something big. I need to see how it will play out.

"Let's not get ahead of ourselves, Bookworm." I growl.

The words and growl are enough for him to understand it's more than his finishing my sentences that bothers me. Bookworm jumps up from his seated position and scoots back onto his sitting rock. After he adjusts his tools, he apologizes.

"Sorry."

I ignore the apology, but stand to loosen my joints.

"They selected a recently abandoned village for us to begin our battle. I looked down at it from the Sikorsky helicopter from which I was hanging, a thick chain with one end centered on the helicopter and the other wrapped around my arm. There were roughly forty thatched huts lining a small road that weaved its way through the desolate land for a few miles until it ended at a muddy river. Sunning crocodiles the size of small boats were resting on its banks, and a large hippo dipped its head under the water upon hearing the chopping blades of the helicopter. I surveyed the rest of the area, as I needed to assess the best spots to finish the battle. You see, I knew they couldn't afford to lose their demigod. A couple other small countries were ready to absorb them if Zofara disappeared. A lost battle through being rendered unconscious wasn't life-threatening to a nation like hers, but a forced submission was worse than losing a war. And it's even worse for the demigod. When one surrenders during a broadcasted battle, about half of the demigod's worshippers walk away within the first few minutes. I never experienced it myself, but I've been told it feels like your soul has been stripped from your body. Most demigods will then lie down to rest, and never wake up."

Disjointed memories flood in, but this time of those demigods who had lost their worshippers. I didn't recognize most of the faces, but one stuck out like a bad earache. Umiak, the Inuit demigod. He and I had battled over a border dispute between The Americas and The Iced Lands. He had been powerful and proud, standing without concern against the relentless winter winds of the Himalayan mountain range that was the neutral battle site. However, he was half my height and held a tenth of my power. I hadn't wanted to harm him as we were in the wrong. Instead, I choked him until he was forced to submit. I walked away, thinking I had done right. Then I heard the thud on the ground behind me. I turned and watched him wither into an old man. His furs slid off to reveal veins barely held against his bones by a thin veil of leathery skin. But that wasn't what haunted me. It was his large brown eyes. They were hollow, lifeless. He never moved from that spot, letting the snow and ice of an entire winter bury him alive.

I will share none of this with Bookworm, and am glad that he pretends to be working while I'm lost in thoughts. My mood is turning foul again.

"Video recorders were everywhere—in the trees, on the huts, embedded in the ground, and attached to dozens of drones flying over my head. A fool's spectacle with billions watching. And somehow, I needed to ensure that I won without destroying a valued nation.

"It was then that I spotted her, Zofara. She strode into the clearing from the opposite end of the village and surveyed the area before looking up at my helicopter. The white markings on her face were neither painted nor tattooed into her skin. Her worshippers had created them, and she wore them with pride. The sun only silhouetted her beauty, transforming the barren landscape behind her into a breathtaking tale of survival. Wiry trees challenging the ever-present winds, thorny bushes attacking any creature daring to come near, and droves of insects buzzing toward their next victim. While still looking up at me, she set the butt of her spear on the ground and leaned against it. I could feel her confidence even from five hundred feet up. I needed to break it, because it would get her killed.

"It was time. I let go of the chain and plummeted to the earth like a rock. I closed my eyes and reveled in a free-fall that only a demigod could enjoy. The air rushed past me faster than the seconds ticked by. It was only five hundred feet up, but the impact sounded like a car bomb exploding in the desert. The hard-packed ground cracked, compressed, and then shot out a cloud of dust that obscured me for nearly half a minute. When the wind finally blew away the remnants, I was staring down at Zofara. She had charged forward during my showboating, and now her laser-sharpened, titanium-steel spear was accelerating toward my chest."

Bookworm was drinking in my description.

"I stepped into her thrust, letting the blade hit me with even more force. The tip fractured and the shaft crumpled without so much as a small puncture in my skin. Yes, Bookworm, it still hurt. But it was worth what I gained, or so I thought. As I predicted, she hesitated. I grabbed her forward arm and threw her at one of the abandoned huts. I waited to turn so she could get back up to her feet, but instead heard a scream. It wasn't one of pain, but rather of sorrow. So deep, like a mother's scream after finding out her son has died in war. When I looked over my shoulder, I saw it. A small misshapen arm sticking out from the broken reeds of the hut. Somehow, when they had checked the village, they had missed a small boy."

My chains are too heavy to hold up, the memory cascades over me and washes away my strength. The pain as fresh as the day the boy died. Time had not deadened it, only allowed a festering scab to cover the hole.

Moisture covers my eyes and I want to stop talking. I want to, but know I can't. I need to get it out. I go back to my chair, letting the shadows hide my cracking façade.

"Up to that point in my life, I had killed tens of thousands, Bookworm. Tens of thousands! I even knew how many were innocent civilians. Thousands that I deemed were necessary casualties. But to me, it had been like a haircut. They were all cleanly removed to make me and my country look better. You know, you never are pained by a haircut. However, grab a single hair and pluck it. Now, there's pain. That was the pain I was experiencing. A single lost life hurt more than all I had done before. The small scratch that the ambassador, who killed my family, had made with his words was now a gaping wound. He was right about me and what I stood for. So, I walked away that day, vowing to never again fight for others and their warped desires."

"That was when the nuclear attacks started, didn't they? I read that the rest of the world was waiting, and when The Americas weakened, they attacked."

Bookworm's voice was humble, even as he recites his history lesson. I peer out from the shadows to look him in the eyes. Sweet, blue eyes. I hadn't noticed before just how much depth they held.

"Oh," Bookworm replies. "It wasn't how it happened, was it?"

"Close. They skipped a few details." I lean back, exhausted, and close my eyes, falling asleep. Falling back down into the bottomless hole from which I had almost escaped.

****

Smells can change one's mood faster than one's sight can absorb a scene. My eyes are closed when I smell the slightly burnt butter and cooked protein that fill my cavern. I keep my eyes closed, trying to determine what meat it was. Maybe a pig or horse?

"Hello, Mr. President." Bookworm's voice is lively, but also filled with something else.

I stare over at his sitting stone. He is holding a skillet with steam still rising from its surface. "Hmmm. What is that, Bookworm?"

"Bacon and cheese omelet. Well, sort of. The bacon is really fried antelope ears and the eggs from the omelet came from a hybrid, bloated chicken that looks more like a legless ostrich." Bookworm takes a bite.

"Are you trying to make it sound less appealing so I won't want it? It won't work." I hear the edge in my voice, surely from the nightmare I was pulled from. I look to see if Bookworm catches it, noticing the growth on his face. "How long was I asleep for?"

"Why?" Bookworm replies as he slides the skillet over to me. It scrapes against the ground and stops in front of the freshly filled puddle of water.

"Your beard. Looks like you haven't shaved for days."

There it is. A quick look of panic before Bookworm casually shrugs off the comment. He is hiding something, just like they all do. Only he has fooled me for longer than any of the others. I'm not going to let on though, as I want to find out more. I take a mouthful of the omelet, chew and savor the sharp flavors of the first bite until it becomes a tasteless paste in my mouth. I finally swallow, and do the same with each bite until nothing is left. I casually grab the skillet and roll it up like a piece of paper, before tossing it perfectly into the elevator shaft. I'm sure Bookworm doesn't need reminding of what I can do, but....

Bookworm pulls out his tools and readies himself. "You mentioned that the history books were wrong. How so, if I may ask?"

"Ah, yes, my fall from grace." I stay in my seat as I speak. "The death was charged against me and my country, which was valid. It hurt us, but not as much as my walking away. Over the next year, I slowly lost a quarter of my followers, mostly the compassionate ones. Yes, those who balanced the anger inside myself and from others. Without it, I was intolerable. However, I was still better off than my country. The Americas weakened as consortium after consortium signed onto a trade embargo, and their cries of our injustices demanded demigod battles. Our congress became desperate, even more so after I ignored their repeated requests to fix the mess I had caused. Within a month the House of Americans had impeached me, and then the Senatorial Statehood had convicted me. The people appointed a new President, Daniel Grayson, and put together the usual roadmap for transforming him into a deity."

I had to stop, recalling the sad events.

"Grayson was nearly everything one would want from a leader and future demigod: intelligent, charismatic, insightful, and war-tested. Unfortunately, they didn't probe far enough into his background. He was politically polished, but also sadomasochistic. As a child, he had tortured small animals, and as a teenager, he had been admitted briefly to a hospital for being a cutter. His adulthood torture sessions and killings were hidden by wealth, but they were there for anyone who wanted to dig deep. No one did though, as the outside coating was too tasty to resist. My country had chosen to hand over the keys of the most powerful weapon arsenal on the planet to a genius who had longed for a final world war."

I allowed myself a moment of reflection.

"They found out their mistake as a nuclear missile headed across the Pacific Ocean. Not just any nuclear missile. It was developed under a special project called the God Bomb. It was developed out of fear of us demigods. Since our power came from worshippers, that is what it targeted. The hypersonic missile followed a depressed trajectory splitting into twenty separate nuclear warheads. Each one aimed at the largest populations of the targeted consortium. It would detonate above the cities, vaporizing millions and slowly killing ten to a hundred million more. However, its true power lay in the long-term effects. A consortium's people would be devastated and lose faith in their demigod. He or she would waste away in less than a month."

"The God Bomb? But to even have developed such a thing would have violated our treaties." Bookworm's mouth hung open, his pen a useless extension of his unmoving arm. "Our own leaders failed us."

"Yes, we did," I reply. "No one outside the Cabinet of The Americas was aware of what had happened until three more detonated over the China-India Consortium. The other nations and consortiums knew that the China-India demigod had slighted Grayson, and quickly ascertained that The Americas had retaliated. Within hours the casualty count was almost beyond comprehension. You see, they were fearful we had more God Bombs, and so nuclear and conventional triggers were pressed. Grayson's world war began and ended on the same day."

Bookworm is genuinely stunned. He knew nothing about what had happened. How could he be lying to me, using me, when he doesn't even know the truth about the group who imprisoned me? I need to test him.

I stand, chains rattling, and walk up to him. Each word that follows is slow and threatening. "How did your beard grow so fast?"

To my surprise, Bookworm isn't fazed by my observation. He recomposes himself quickly after finding out about the God Bomb. He undoes his watch, places it on the sitting rock, and walks right up to me. "You cannot handle the answer...yet."

YET? My anger boils back to the surface of my skin, my muscles and veins strain as I pull the chains. They groan, trying to stretch apart. This is a test of him no more. How dare he challenge me! How dare he walk so close. I decide it will end now. I lift my hand and form a fist to crush him into the ground. Nothing will stop me. It's over.

His eyes stop me.

They glisten right before a single tear falls over each lower lid. I look at his emotionless face, then back at his deep eyes. It isn't fear, yet I can't figure out what brings him such sadness.

The chains pull my clenched fist back to my side. I look over at the face of his watch, studying the time and date for a while before walking back to my chair. I need to sleep and let my subconscious ponder Bookworm's letter, his beard, and his sorrow. I have an inkling that it will be a powerful awakening.

Chapter 4

The trembling beneath my feet disturbs my deep slumber. The dim lights flicker as I groggily watch the ripples in the water puddle fight each other until peace returns to the surface. I reach down and splash the cool elixir against my coal-laced face. I'm thirsty but need something to wake and sharpen my senses. My eyes blink out the water, and I look over at the sitting rock, noticing that Bookworm's watch is still sitting on top at an angle so I can see its face.

Strange.

I stand and take a step forward to confirm what I have seen. It can't be. It has to be wrong! But it isn't.

I fall into my chair, cracking the granite back, and raise my hands to my face. Only four times in my life have I been truly devastated. The first was my family's murder, with the second being my killing of the small child during my battle against Zofara. The third was the release of the God Bombs and my cause of the final world war. And the fourth? It came with the display of a small watch, showing the passing of a month since Bookworm had last visited. I thought only a night had passed; I had tricked myself into thinking only a night passed each time I slept. Now I know the truth, and I know why Bookworm's beard had grown so fast.

How long have I been down here? I need Bookworm to answer that. That, and so much more.

The ground shakes again, but this time the walls and ceiling join in, a chorus that I do not like. Small rocks break loose, dropping all around me, while the lights cycle through dim and bright castings. It's the first time

41

since my imprisonment that I've been truly afraid of a collapse. Most days I had wished it, but now I need questions answered. The thought of being trapped under a couple miles of rock for something close to eternity freezes me in place.

The shaking ends with one large jolt that nearly topples me from my chair. The lights blink off but don't come back on for the first time since I've been imprisoned. It's as if I'm blind, the cavern too far below the mine's entrance for the light to reach. I stand in one spot for many minutes, confused as to what I should do. I'm ready to go back and sit in my chair when a noise in the elevator shaft stops me. It sounds like someone grunting.

"Bookworm, is that you?" I growl.

"Hold on," he calls back in a strained voice.

Shortly, his feet thump onto the ground and a cough escapes his lips. "Where are you, Mr. President? I can't see anything."

"Near your watch."

"My watch?" Bookworm asks, with a deeper questioning in his voice.

"Yeah. The one that has the correct time and day."

He coughs again. There must have been a lot of coal dust shaken loose in the elevator shaft.

"How did you get down here? What happened to the elevator?" I ask.

"The answer is tied to the watch," Bookworm replies in a raspy voice.

I pause to think on this, having many questions I want answered. But one question is the most important. "Can I trust you, Bookworm?"

A low growl escapes me.

"Yes, but you need to understand that if I had told you the truth earlier, you would not have believed me," Bookworm says, coughing again.

"How...how long have I been down here?" I try to ask without sounding afraid, masking my fear with an even deeper growl. It doesn't work.

"I do not know for sure, but the record books upstairs date back nearly two hundred years."

Two hundred years? How could that be? It had seemed less than a dozen. I have more questions to ask than I think he can answer in one sitting. His response plays back in my mind over and over, until Bookworm coughs again. I catch something in those previous words.

"Upstairs? There is an..." I stop as a low rumbling sound emanates from the elevator shaft. It grows louder and louder with each passing second, grows in intensity until it makes the sound of my shifting chains seem mild. Metal grinds against stone, then metal against metal until the elevator crashes onto the bottom of the shaft, crumpling under its own weight and speed. Metal supports bend and then rupture, and welded joints rip apart, briefly lighting the room from thousands of sparks. I'm facing the shaft when the sparks create light, and I get a brief glimpse of the destruction along with my broken chair and my family's grave. When it's over, darkness and quiet return, and I'm thankful that the sparks didn't ignite the floating coal dust.

"What happened?" I ask, remembering the small note Bookworm wrote me many days ago. Or was it many months, perhaps years?

"They figured out my plan to free you," Bookworm replies in a raspy voice.

"I thought you were being metaphorical."

"No, only you can free your mind, and I do hope that will happen. However, we need you to be free, sir," Bookworm says, this time wheezing.

"Why?" I ask, puzzled.

There is a long pause, ending with a sigh. The words that follow are broken, but I don't stop him. The climb down the mine shaft must have been draining for the frail Bookworm.

"It is my turn for the story. Although I assure you my skills are not suited for such a job. I guess the God Bomb is the best place to start. Even though we were lied to about what happened, I do know that in that single day nearly thirty percent of the world's population was wiped out. Four billion lives lost before sunset. Another twenty percent were hit with large-enough radiation doses to kill them within a week. Over the next year, another thirty percent lived a painfully short life as their bodies formed tumors or their organs slowly stopped working. The rest learned to avoid the hot spots, but very few were prepared for the harsh, nomadic lifestyle they were forced to live. Within one decade less than three percent of the Earth's population lived, with most hanging on by a thread. Over the next three decades, small villages began to spring up. Humankind may have many flaws, but their survival instinct can overcome most of them. The small villages began to turn into small cities, and within another decade we looked to be back on a course of rebuilding. But that was when they struck."

"They? What government was left?"

"The Marsians. Remember the colony you had funded during the early years of your presidency? It not only survived without Earth's support, but it thrived. In fact, it grew too fast. They stripped many of the precious resources of their new but limited planet, and needed Earth's. They came back. Well, not them but their machines. They easily defeated any resistance we could muster, and soon we became their colony. We gathered everything they demanded and loaded it onto trains, which transported the supplies to their spaceports. More decades passed, and their demands kept increasing. With all the work it required, we were unable to prosper and slowly began to wither away. Fifteen more decades have passed, and we are now on the verge of a final collapse."

Bookworm coughs, spits, and begins anew with a more solemn tone. "It is not just The Americas that need you. It is the entire world."

I chuckle at the idea of defending Earth against an onslaught of death machines. "Thanks for the compliment, Bookworm. But I wasn't made to fight an army. They may not be able to kill me, but they could overwhelm me."

More coughing from Bookworm. Something isn't right.

"I know, and that is why we need you to confront them in person. On Mars. You see, only you can get there. The launch vehicles are merely space cargo ships operated by their machines. There is no life support system, which means no human could survive the voyage to Mars. Your story about the battle in Hikone proves that demigods can survive without oxygen, although it will surely be painful."

"And if I somehow get there? How do I make it right?"

I hear Bookworm land hard on the ground; his head smacks like a watermelon. He groans and mumbles to himself. My chains rattle as I carefully reach down. Just one of the chains brushing against him would surely bring about his death. I feel his face and accidently burst a large bubble on his cheek. I can't see it, but I know what it means. "Bookworm. What's happened to you? Is there radiation above us?"

Bookworm coughs and hacks, until he settles into a soft wheezing. It's easy to imagine the blood that is oozing into his mouth and is now splattered on the cave's floor.

"No. When I signed up for this job, they had me wear a rad-bracelet around my ankle. If I gave away any information to you or came down to visit without permission, it would inject me with radioactive isotopes. They showed me a rather graphic video of how painful the death was so I wouldn't think twice about disobeying their orders."

Bookworm coughs, then wheezes out something like a laugh. "Attached to my chest is a recorder. Each time I talked with you, I was required to go back to my cave and transfer the conversation onto my computer for upload. They wanted to learn how to create their own demigod."

"You gave this kind of power to the Marsians? Why?" I growl it out, even though I'm worried for him.

"No. I'm a computer scientist. I altered our conversations to make up an elaborate ritual. The first part was to write out a few special symbols in their own feces." Bookworm begins laughing so hard that I'm sure it's going to kill him.

My laughter overrides Bookworm's, like a shark swallowing a flounder. I'm eager to hear about the other things he made them do. I wait for him to continue.

Silence.

I gently pick him up and carry him to my chair. I lay him down on the unyielding granite, still holding his head and legs. My mind is finally clear, and with it I know what I need to do.

"Bookworm. Where's this space port?" I lean in to hear his mouse-like response.

"You are in what used to be Alabama. You need to get to what used to be Cape Canaveral, Florida, by tomorrow night."

"That has to be over six hundred miles. How?" I ask, trying not to sound frustrated.

"I've released your story to the remaining people on Earth. That's why…why your finger healed. They are…all are worshipping you. They know to give you speed, but also I've laid out steps to…"

I laugh a gentle laugh at the brilliance of this diminutive man, even though he couldn't finish his sentence since his end is near. A cloth of sorrow falls over my heart.

"One last thing." The words are drawn out, and at the end Bookworm's head goes limp.

"What?" I ask.

He whispers something I can't hear.

"What, Bookworm?" I ask again.

The words barely come out, but they're more powerful than any I have ever heard in my life. "You imprisoned yourself."

****

I had let two hundred years travel by me without care, but the next few minutes seem like a millennium in the making. Bookworm's words bounce around my mind, only growing stronger with each ricochet. Soon they are loud enough to crack the mirrored walls I had put up. Memories fall out of those fractures, pushing aside the lies I had created. No one had chopped me into pieces and dropped me down the elevator shaft, nor repositioned my body parts to allow the healing to begin. No one had forged the chains and welded them around my arms, legs, and neck. No one but me.

I wonder if the dark coal mine is also my doing. However, when I open my eyes I'm still enveloped by the same darkness, still holding Bookworm. Or rather the husk of the man who had been more powerful than I on my strongest day. He had fought against an entire government, had devised a plan to free his own planet from suppression, and had stood toe-to-toe with a bitter, angry demigod, wielding only a pen and the belief that what he was doing was right.

I stand, and for the first time I don't hear the rattling of the massive chains. They have dissolved, just like my false imprisonment. Turning back around, I carefully curl up Bookworm's lifeless body into my granite chair. He deserves so much more than the seat where I used to wallow in self-pity. He is the one who deserves to be worshipped. He has given hope to an entire world, has figured out how to save that world, and sacrificed everything to save me. I want to give him a proper burial. However, I need to leave.

"I owe you everything, my friend." I turn and walk past the sitting rock, not needing light to pick up Bookworm's watch.

I reach the mine's shaft and press the small button on the side of Bookworm's watch to see what is in front of me. The mine's mangled elevator fills the human-sized entrance. I bend down, reach in with both hands, and grip the largest pieces of the elevator I can find. Turning my hands in opposite directions and applying some force, I easily work the metal into a small ball, the groan of its reshaping sounding like trumpeting elephants. Once done I cast it aside, realizing that I need to somehow fit my fourteen-foot frame into the diminutive hole. How had I done it before?

Diminutive.

Now that is a strong word. It conveys extreme weakness and frailty. Surely that was my persona when I entered the coal mine to begin my self-imposed exile. I need to be humble. No, more than humble. I need to feel and believe that I am less than human. Less important and less deserving than all the people above ground, who for some reason still held onto the hope that I would save them. I'm not deserving of their worship. It was I who should be worshipping them. I should be worshipping the late Bookworm. He gave more to me than I had ever given to humankind. He died believing I would save Earth. He had faith. A faith that embarrasses me.

I had abandoned my people by hiding away. And because of my actions the God Bomb had been deployed, obliterating billions of people. Billions! Two hundred thousand years of evolution nearly wiped out in years, just as so many science-fiction writers had predicted. Worse yet, those few who survived had lived off a hope that things would get better. However, generations died with that hope unfulfilled, again because of me.

The feeling I still hold in my heart for the child I accidentally killed in the hut is nothing compared to the sorrow for the losses I willingly allowed. The air thickens around me, and my breathing becomes labored. My shoulders buckle as an ethereal weight drops on them. I try to breathe and push upward, but fail as my knees buckle and my feet flatten out. A new pain attacks me from the sides, squeezes me as if a vice's handle is slowly being turned. I twist sideways to try and alleviate the intense pressure and pain, only to collapse onto the ground, crumpling inward like the ball I had made from the elevator's broken pieces. My thoughts turn inward; yet again, I am starting to feel sorry for myself. This time I rebuff them, instead imagining the pain of those who survived the God Bombs, only to feel their bodies implode as their immune systems yielded to the radiation's poison. Tears for those who suffered ebb out and onto the floor, creating a small pool under my face.

I lie there, wondering if I will disappear into nothingness.

The pain recedes; the pressure eases. I reach out with my finger and touch the water, watching my disturbance spread outward until it has run its course. I stand up, reborn.

I want to marvel at my metamorphosis, but there is no time. Stepping through the entrance, I look up the ten thousand feet of vertical shaft. Even with my eagle eyes, I barely notice the pinpoint of light that tells me it's daytime, but what time of the day I couldn't guess. I only hope it's morning, as I have to somehow travel over six hundred miles before the morrow.

I stretch out my human-sized arms until they touch the smooth walls. There's no place to grip, so I cup my right hand and dig it into the hard rock, easily creating a small ledge. While I'm smaller in size, I'm still strong. I repeat this move on my other side before scooting myself upward until my bare feet are wedged into the ledges. I do this a dozen more times, feeling skin and nails rip away with each dig and quickly heal before my next dig. I rest and check my pace. I'm probably fifty to sixty feet up, but at my pace, I won't be to the top until the next day.

I need to do something different.

I stop creating ledges, instead placing immense pressure on the walls with my arms, elbows, knees, and feet before lifting myself upward. After a couple hundred feet, and aching muscles, I push out with my right hand, only to find nothing to push against. I lose my balance and almost fall to the bottom of the shaft, but am able to grasp onto the opening's ledge. In darkness, I pull myself up, smelling that this is another cavern, which someone recently inhabited. I sniff again, familiar odors riding along the inner hairs of my nose, onto my taste buds, and down my throat. Bookworm! This must have been where he lived.

The light of my watch briefly lights up the room. I dare not overuse it, as I don't know how long the battery will last. Back in darkness, I meditate to recall what I 've seen, then I walk over to a desk with a computer on it. I carefully reach out, pinching a piece of paper between my finger and thumb. I take one more quick lighting with the watch, closing my eyes to recite what I read.

Mr. President,

I regret that my dialogue from now on will be preprogrammed, and must come with the assumption that you will not only take on a monumental challenge, but also succeed in every step. However, there is no other way. The ePEG watch I left in your cavern is embedded with a holographic chip. If you push on the faceplate and call for me, an image of me will appear, and hopefully it will be able to answer most of the questions you will ask.

Your mission is straightforward in approach, but challenging in execution. You need to break into the Floridian launch site and board a space shuttle cargo transporter. Once launched, it should take you to the Moon refueling base, and then to Mars. After that, you will need to convince the Marsians that you will no longer allow Earth humans to be their slaves. How you do that is well beyond my pay grade, but I believe that you will choose the right course of action once you have assessed the situation.

Regrettably, you will only have one day to get to the launch site, which will be followed by a thirty-day trip to the Moon and four to five more months before you arrive on Mars. Each step will require that your worshippers, those whom I have been updating over the last two years, aid you in a unique way. To get started, I need you to turn on the generator in the corner and then power up the computer. It will run a script and start sending out messages to key people I knew around the world, who will distribute your story to help you along the journey. The first will be a request for unique appendages to climb up the elevator shaft, the second will be endurance and speed to get to the launch complex, and the third will be willpower.

You cannot fail. There is no one left who can help, and only very few left to help.
Your friend,
Bookworm

Willpower?

I wonder why, surely forgetting something Bookworm said, but time is too short for me to dwell on it. I walk over to where I recall the generator was sitting, fumbling with it until I feel the toggle switch. Once it starts, I press the old computer's round button, relieved when the screen casts a blue hue over the room. I watch the computer's startup sequence, stunned for a moment when my image comes up as the background setting. It's from my first oath of office, eyes casting an overabundance of confidence but lacking any depth. A chin that had yet to be cast in iron-willed stubbornness, and a smile that conveyed true happiness and a belief that my country's future was bright. My family at my side, my trusted team behind me, and around us the luscious greenery from my farm. The farm where I had first discovered the abandoned mine, and had covered it up to ensure no one would fall to their death.

It had taken less than two decades for a collapse that made the fall of the Roman Empire seem trivial.

The computer beeps when it finishes the startup. I watch as a file opens and a document is highlighted before a 'sent' message flashes on the screen. I know it's relaying my need to the world, but I wonder just how much of my story it holds. Did Bookworm start from the beginning or pick key points to highlight, attempting to win over more worshippers? Maybe he added in his own comments or altered what I had said. Admittedly, my disposition was rather gruff when I first met Bookworm. If that was his first post, then it may take a while for people to warm up to me. Maybe never. And if I sit here and wait for something to happen, then I might reach the launch complex only to find it empty.

I walk to the elevator-shaft opening, grasp the walls, and lean out to look upward. The pinhole of light seems no closer than when I started my ascent. I know I could climb up the shaft, but at my previous pace it would take longer than the total time I have to get to the transporter.

A shiver begins at the base of my neck before spreading out along my appendages.

F

L

I

G

H

T

Chapter 5

A power surge strikes my brain, emanating from where the demigod device had been inserted. It charges down my spine as fast as my thoughts, growing in power even faster than it travels. When it slams into the base of my spine, the pain is so intense that I think my torso will be blasted away from my legs. Instead, my legs are also racked with powerful convulsions. Muscles pop and sizzle, tightening up as if I had grasped Zeus's lightning bolt.

Involuntarily, my head snaps up and I howl in pain, expecting a beam of energy to be cast out my mouth, hurling my teeth and tongue to the top of the mine shaft. I reach out, pushing my hands into the stone wall, attempting to keep my balance as my feet melt and spread out across the floor. Still filled with pain and blanketed in darkness, I wiggle my floppy feet, which I believe have turned into something I could only describe as gargantuan banana slugs. My ankles jut out the back and my legs pivot sideways as my hips rotate outward. The pain ebbs away, and my curiosity takes hold. The same transformation and pain captures my once-powerful hands, wrists, and elbows. My lower arms elongate to four times their original length, then double in width before overdeveloped muscles grow on top. I flip one over, rubbing the flat surfaces together, which I feel are coated with millions of steel-like hairs.

Bookworm's watch? I thought.

Panic. I hurriedly sweep the ground with my new awkward appendages, nearly launching the watch into the shaft. With no fingers, it takes too much of the precious time I have left to scoop it up and slide into my pants pocket. After that, I want to carefully test how to use my new body, but I have to trust that my worshippers know what they are doing. Realistically, it has to be Bookworm's design, which he must have set up to send out when I rebooted the computer.

Time is up. I stretch my arms out until they firmly press against the shaft walls, and then I step off the ledge. After I push my legs onto the walls, I remain motionless to assess how my new body works. My slug-like appendages grip the walls like an oversized sucker. Also, my joints are hinged and now lock in place so I don't have to use my muscles to maintain the position. The combination is a great design by Bookworm, as the muscle endurance required for the climb is minimized.

Suspended a couple hundred feet in the shaft, I quickly realize I have no idea how to free myself, let alone climb. I wiggle my arms and legs, succeeding in only turning my torso into vibrating jelly. I should stop, but my short temper overrides any sensibility Bookworm had brought back. Screaming in frustration, I pull as hard as I can, successfully ripping all my appendages off the wall in one fell swoop. Even though it's only for a split second, I feel like Wile E. Coyote after he realizes he has run off a cliff.

I plummet back down the shaft. I could have tried to grip the walls during my rapid descent but am more worried about breaking my watch. So instead I prepare for a back flop, as I had fallen much further without dying. Yes, it is going to hurt like…

Boom!

My spine smacks against the shaft's floor with enough force to send newly formed shards of rock and dust into the air. My head plows into the ground, leaving a fossil-like impression to remember how rattled my brain felt as I lay on the ground, gasping for air while my body swiftly heals itself.

As I lie there, small rocks fall from the ceiling of my old room. They are followed by larger and larger rocks, and an increase in the sound and seismic activity of the cavern. The shaft begins to shake as a column inside the cavern buckles. The following roar of the collapsing room signals the end of my self-inflicted isolation. Dust shoots out at me, and rocks rolls against my prone body.

"Bookworm!" I call out when I have enough of my senses gathered to think straight. I reach for my pocket, cursing at my slug arms.

"Mr. President?" Bookworm's muffled voice queries from my pants.

"You're alive," I hack out.

"Alive?"

"You know what I mean, Bookworm."

"I see you fell down the shaft. Perhaps I should explain how to climb up?"

"Perhaps," I grumble, then cough before extricating myself from the ground. I stretch my back, noting the popping sounds as bones realign themselves, and look up the shaft.

"It is simple physics, really. The tiny hairs on your extremities use van der Waals forces to cause adhesion, thus allowing you to climb up the mining shaft. Now, at the molecular level, the van der Waal interactions are miniscule, but when the millions upon millions of interactions are added together, they can support an amazing amount of mass."

"So I noticed, Bookworm. But how do I climb?"

"I'm getting there. Just be patient."

I growl. "Getting pretty bold now that you're dead."

"Well, I admittedly have nothing to lose. Anyway, to release your extremity, you merely need to lift, starting at the bottom. It is similar to peeling a banana. To apply this to climbing, you would lift one arm and the opposite leg at the same time, then reattach them to the wall before moving the other pair. Do you understand, or should I go over it again?" asks Bookworm.

I ignore him as I place my banana slug appendages on the cracked walls of the shaft. I lift my left arm and right leg at the same time before cautiously placing them slightly higher up on the wall, then do the same for the opposite arm and leg. I repeat this several times before hearing the soft sound of two pieces of wood being hit together. It grows louder as I matriculate up the shaft, and after about five minutes I figure out where it's coming from.

"Bookworm, what is that?" I continue climbing as I speak.

"It is a metronome, Mr. President. Used to regulate timing for musicians. I figured it would help you set a pace as you climbed."

"Good idea, Bookworm." I look down and then back up. "However, I'm moving way too slow. Double the timing."

"Okay. I will halve the interval."

The clicks come at me twice as fast, and I fight to keep pace. At first, I fail miserably, forgetting to release the proper way or moving the wrong leg. However, I'm able to find a rhythm after a few more minutes and begin to gloat in my success. Gloat until my right appendage reaches for the wall and misses. I have already detached my other arm and leg before I realize it, and find myself hanging upside down by one leg.

"Are you okay, sir?" asks Bookworm. "I sense you are upside down."

"I'm better than okay," I respond as I realize that I haven't misjudged the location of the wall but rather have already reached Bookworm's room. I pull myself upright. "Let's start again at the original pace of the metronome."

In under a minute I double the pace, and again after another half hour passes. Sweat streams down my body, my heart screams to be freed from my chest, and my muscles ache.

"Bookworm…how…much…further?" I gasp.

"Seven thousand six hundred and thirty feet. You are over a quarter of the way from the top."

Nearly a mile and a half left. "Bookworm, double the metronome."

"I do not think that is wise, sir. Your heart rate is already over two hundred beats a minute, and muscle fatigue is setting in."

"Then let my worshippers know what I need!" I yell out, partly in frustration and partly due to the effort it takes to speak.

The only response is the doubling of the metronome, its individual clicks barely discernable in the echoing shaft; now sounding more like bubble wrap being run over by hundreds of sugar-hyped kids. I quicken my pace to what would have been equivalent to an Olympic runner's, still not catching up to the set rhythm. However, energy flows into me, lowering my heart rate and replenishing my muscles. Loose rock from the walls continuously pours down the shaft, but I'm moving way to fast to be hit by the debris.

My arms slap against the rock, and the locking mechanism in my bones clicks like an automatic machine gun. Blood seeps out my skin from the abrasions, and I'm sheering off more of the steel hairs than could be replaced, which is making the climb slippery.

"Mr. President, you need to slow down," cautions Bookworm.

"I don't have time, Bookworm. I can do this."

"But…"

"Quiet!" I roar. It's then that a pleasant heat soaks into my back, but I'm moving too fast to stop. I shoot out of the hole, flailing like a novice trapeze artist as I fly higher and higher into the air. The searing sun tears into my underground and unadjusted eyes, burning the retinas before I have a chance to close them.

As my ascension is overtaken by gravity, I recall what I saw before being forced to shut my eyes. A vast and thick forest comprised a majority of the landscape, with only three signs of human habitation. The farthest off was a maintained railroad that stretched west to east, the gray rocks of its bedding glimmering in the sun.

Closer, I saw a small dilapidated building marking a stopping point, or train station, and initiating a dirt road that leads into a small town only a few hundred yards away. The town couldn't have more than a couple hundred drab houses, which are spread out in a loosely repeating, rectangular pattern. Two-story wood buildings sat on either side of the road, necking down to a small trail that led to the clearing I shot out from. The clearing itself was barely a hundred feet in diameter, coated with a combination of charred grass and burnt tree stumps. Nearly a dozen opaque domes were systematically located throughout the clearing.

My thoughts make me forget I am falling back to the earth. With a quick mid-air adjustment, I land on my feet next to the shaft, but then stumble on top of a heap of twisted metal. I lose my balance, and the metal groans as I fall on top of it. The dust clears as I stand up and slowly open my healed eyes. I try to locate where a new humming noise is coming from.

A zapping sound, deep in pitch, and a bright green flash from one of the domes is followed by a searing pain in my left arm. I take a step back and fall into the shaft. Reaching out, I grab the edge, succeeding with one arm while I watch a large portion of the other slug-like arm fall down the shaft. It tumbles end over end, a part of me falling back into my prison. Holding onto the edge with ease, I examine what is left of my damaged arm. It has been severed off and cauterized slightly below the elbow. The pain is there, but I don't remember a time when pain hasn't been a primary part of my life. I watch for a little while as white bone and then pink flesh grows out of the cauterized section. I don't know if this is how humans heal, or if it follows how a body part would have to rebuild, but it's working. I look back up.

So, the domes are here to ensure I don't escape. But how did they survive for two hundred years, and how did Bookworm get past them? How can I get past them? It seems to have taken time for them to start up, target, and fire at me. Were they initializing after being dormant for so long? Or was it that they didn't aim at anything unless it was near the ground? That would explain why I wasn't shot at until I landed. Maybe I can hop and skip my way to freedom. Or maybe that would only allow all of them to shoot me. Sure, I'm a demigod, but that doesn't mean I can't die…I think. I could lose part of an arm, which was still hurting, but shooting a hole through my head with whatever took off my arm would probably do the trick.

A slow, aged voice interrupts my thoughts. "Excuse me, sir."

I look up to see an ancient man who could have come right out a medieval movie. A bald crown is surrounded by long, flowing white hair, which also grows out of every orifice on the man's crackled head. His brown robes add to the medieval movie theme, making him appear to be some sort of monk.

"Yes?" I reply in my less-than-friendly voice.

"You are the one we have been waiting for, yes?" He seems hopeful, yet lost.

"Sure." I consider his charcoal eyes, far from impressed. "But, I must warn you that I'm prone to disappointing people."

I'm rewarded with a blank stare.

"Who are you, old man?" I ask.

"Oh, I'm the cleaner." He smiles and raises up a rusted bucket that sloshes over with soapy water, spilling onto my head. "Oh, dear. I'm sorry."

I suppress my annoyance, as I'm sure it would only result in my being delayed even longer.

"Cleaner of what?" I ask.

"The domes. Every day I come out and scrub them to ensure they work properly, just as my father did. Just as his father, and his father did. Five generations of cleaning, and now it's finally over."

I decide not to point out that it was only four generations.

"The same domes that severed my arm? You're my prison guard?" I growl and would've reached up to pop his head off, if I actually had another arm. I mean one with a hand on it.

His eyes water, but he doesn't look away. "I'm sorry. I had no choice. The trains would stop if I didn't."

I chuckle, but not at him. "So, you're also a prisoner. Suppressed by the Marsian colonists, and forced to bestow offerings on them in return for your life."

Wrinkled, white brows show his confusion. "We don't give offerings. We provide lumber, minerals, food, and whatever else they require."

I'm definitely talking to the wrong person.

"Listen, Cleaner. I'm not enjoying our conversation or hanging above a two-mile-deep shaft. So, can you help me?"

His face lights up and he vigorously nods his head. "There's only one way to get past the light guns."

Impatiently, I wait for the answer as he sits down next to the shaft and drops his feet over the ledge. He swings them back and forth, like a young kid hanging out on a park bench, holding the same smile as he counts the rocking of his feet.

"Seven, nine, eleven, thirteen, fifteen…"

"Do you mind telling me?" I growl after he passes twenty. It's then that I notice the band around his ankle. It is like the one that Bookworm wore; the one that killed him for helping me. "The ankle band?"

The old man nods and brings his ankle up to where his hands can hold the band.

"But wait, Cleaner. What about the radiation poisoning?" At this point I place my feet against the sides of the shaft, as this isn't turning into a quick conversation; the old man seems lost in his own mind. I look over at my wounded arm, pleasantly surprised at the pinkish nub that continues to grow from the seared end. It should completely heal in a day or two. Well, only if I don't receive any new injuries.

"This one has no poison, but if taken off it will never go back on the same person. It's passed down from one generation to the next, allowing us to clean the domes." A popping noise emanates from the device. "There it is. Thank you for giving us hope, and please make sure the trains don't stop. Very bad."

He lays the device next to my arm, and then leans forward, too far forward.

I watch, emotionless, as he flips over and over while plummeting down the mine shaft. No scream, no look of horror, or even acknowledgement in his face of the impending death as he tumbles out of view.

I'm sure I'll learn what that was all about a little bit later, but for now I need to get out of the shaft. My legs are firmly secured against the walls, so I reach up and gently scoop the opened bracelet into my elongated hand. I don't think I can attempt to put it on my ankle without dropping it down the shaft, so I take a risk. I climb out, holding it in my alien hand before stretching out and clasping the thing around my ankle. It gives off the familiar hum of an ePEG device, letting me know it was built to last centuries…and already had.

I stand up and walk in the direction of the small town, figuring that a methodical approach to testing the device would only delay the inevitable. Either it works or it doesn't. I also don't consider destroying the domes, because if they have an ePET to relay discharge information, then the

Marsian suppressers would know and not only punish the townspeople, but also shut down the supply launch I needed to board.

I hear a rustling in the dense shrubs and trees ahead of me.

"Friend or foe! Speak now or my next action will be your last vision." I run across the burnt field, determined to crush whoever is hiding.

Spreading apart a group of saplings, I stare down at a frightened group of children, dressed in drab, torn clothes and coated with mud.

"Why did Old Man Gavin do that?" asks one terrified boy.

A little girl, rapidly regaining her confidence, steps up and places her hands on her hips. "Did ya' use mind control to kill him? Ya' gonna do the same to us? I'd like to see ya' try."

I chuckle, which comes out more like an evil laugh. "No, I didn't kill him, and there is no way I'd try and kill any of you. Why are you hiding here?"

"The domes," says an older boy. "Sometimes they go crazy and start firing when being cleaned. Hey, that was junk when it blew off your arm! Did it hurt?"

"Yes," I reply.

"An' it was funny how ya' shot outta the hole like a scared baby," notes the brazen little girl.

I almost yell at her, but instead step over the gaggle of kids and continue toward the town. They follow, hopping all around me like crazed rabbits. The entire way I'm assaulted with hundreds of questions, and ignoring the little rodents doesn't seem to lessen the intensity. In fact, they even hurl insults at me that no adult would have dared fling. "Slug legs," "nub," and even "grouchy fart" soon become chants. My temper flares, but there's no way I'll lash out at them. Well, not in the few minutes it takes me to enter the town.

What I'm greeted with is a gathering of worn-down townsfolk, barely able to keep from running as I walk closer. In fact, probably too worn out to run. To the generations before them, I was a demigod worthy of praise and fear. But with each generation I fell from the exalted, to a fearful ghost, to a childish story that ended with a crazy old man cleaning domes for a purpose that no one remembered. Well, not until Bookworm released my memories into their empty souls, filling them with hope.

Hope.

I stop when I'm sure that another step would send them all running. I bend down on one knee, pretending to bow, but instead pull off the ankle bracelet and chuck it toward the crowd. "Where's your leader? I need to get to the launch site, and fast."

I expect the small group to part and some pompous elder to step out, pretending to be superior to me.

"Well, aren't you full of pleasantries?" comes an elderly female voice from my right. It isn't arrogant, instead possessing a calm assertiveness.

The woman I spot is older than her voice, but younger than the experiences burnt into her hazel eyes. Her layers of brown garments are plain but well kept, as is her gray-black hair. The frame she holds up is straight enough, but beginning to show signs of aged bending. There are signs of neither fear nor welcome.

She catches sight of the ankle bracelet before meeting my gaze. Her tone and pace quicken. "Please come inside. We haven't much time, but there are things you must know before you leave."

The lady walks inside her hut, and I follow without question, only realizing once inside that the children stopped pestering me when she appeared. Now that was true power. The single-roomed wall holds a bed for two, a small stove in the center, a tub in one far corner, and a rickety tan desk pushed against the other. It's all very simple and very clean. She's seated at the desk and motions for me to come and sit next to her. I flop over with my banana-slug feet and carefully place my left cheek on the seat. I seem to have grown a little since my trip up the shaft, though I'm nowhere near my original height.

The woman unrolls a flap of black plastic, which I recognize as a FlipFilm, and taps the middle three times. Aqua-colored lines spin outward from the center, forming a computer keyboard on the bottom half and a relief map on the upper half.

"The one you called Bookworm, he convinced you to take on the mission to Mars?" she asks while working on the FlipFilm.

"His death convinced me," I reply.

She looks over at the bed before returning to her typing. "Motives change with time. And while your anger will remain strong, your desire to complete the mission will weaken. You must have a better reason than revenge."

"What do you know of the power of revenge, Old Woman!" I stand up, hitting my head on the low ceiling. "They killed him, and I will return the favor. You must not know what it's like to…"

She doesn't move, her eyes don't stray from the computer, but I notice how her shoulders slump ever so slightly. It's enough to clue me in.

"The Cleaner. He was your husband. I'm sorry." I right the chair and sit back down. "You heard how he died?"

"No. I saw the sign that he was finally freed," she replies.

"What do you mean?" I ask, my temper controlled.

She ignores the question, taking control of the meeting. "The best way for you to get to the space port is to travel along the magnetic rail. It will be a long, exhausting trip if you are to make it in time for the launch, especially since you must stop at Lake City and convince them not to destroy the next train."

"I'll already be gone by then. What does it matter?"

"Each of the four trains on this continent run by the Marsians holds an ePET, allowing them to instantly assess what is put on the train and what they will distribute."

"I really don't have time for this, Old Woman," I grumble.

She sighs and turns to look at me. "Mr. President, did you see any fencing or sentries to keep us here? No, and you won't. Those who enter this township do so because we are stronger as a group than as individuals. But with that comes acceptance that we must deliver what the Marsians want, which also means that over time we rely on what they give. My husband, from generations of men who have protected your site, learned this the hard way. You see, we were married in our late teens, and had a daughter shortly after that. He had already inherited the ankle bracelet after his father died from a fire, and had worked on the domes for over five years without missing a day. Then he became sick. It wasn't a bad sickness, but he stayed in bed for a few days. When he felt better, he went right back to cleaning the domes. Our daughter caught his sickness, but she was young and it worsened with each day that passed. We were out of medical supplies, but the train was to come soon and we knew it would have our regular shipment if we delivered the grains and wood that they ordered. But when it came, there was nothing in the compartments for us but a folded note. It said, 'Never stop cleaning the domes.'

"Isabelle died two days later. It hurt, and still hurts forty years later. I healed over time, but Gavin couldn't accept the fact that he caused her death. His mind snapped. In one night, I lost my daughter and my husband. But today, you released him from the only thing he could do or talk about since then. It was his prison."

"I'm sorry," is all I can muster.

"I'm not asking for your sympathy, Mr. President. I'm telling you so that you will understand three things. The most important is that my people are suppressed by a force stronger than walls or fences. We rely on the Marsians and always will, as long as that train delivers what we need. However, the Lake City factory workers aren't in the same position. They are big enough to be self-sustaining and thus are fenced in and monitored by sentries. They want their freedom and plan to blow up the train, as it only takes their electronics and mechanical devices while leaving them nothing. However, if they succeed then the launch could be aborted, as the Marsian leaders would surely be worried that something dangerous would arrive that could shatter their fragile ecosystem. This would ruin your mission. You must convince them that they need to give you time to complete that mission."

"Easy enough, Old Woman. What are the other reasons for your story?" I had served as the ultimate politician in the past and can do so again. At least, I hope I can.

"Very simple. You have been sulking in that cave for two hundred years, and during that time a lot of bad things have happened to every good human being on Earth. My story of loss is similar to what most mothers have had to endure, and none of them had the time to let their pain immobilize them. Why? Because we don't have time to live in the past. We strive to give others a future, but we can't regrow humankind if we are kept on the verge of extinction. We need you to do this for our future."

She finishes typing on the FlipFilm and folds it up, wiping away a small tear that escapes her eye. "There. Everyone knows that you need speed to get to the space port. You must go now, and hopefully the change will happen as…"

The familiar numbness and power grow in my skull and flow over my body. I look down as my slug-like appendages mold into new feet, and my legs grow longer. My chest juts outward as my lungs expand, and my good arm remolds while the nub regrows into a normal hand. Unlike last time, there is no pain. I place Bookworm's watch on my right arm, feeling a surge of energy. I nod to the old woman, duck down, and walk out the door. Outside, all the townspeople, including the children, are kneeling on the ground and praying. I slowly jog by them and head for where I had seen the train station.

I wish I could say that her words sank in, but they didn't. I don't need anyone to tell my why to do this mission. Sure, in the cave I felt sympathy and wanted to help humankind. But the truth is, I'm doing it for revenge for Bookworm, and the people of Earth are lucky that they will benefit from my reason.

As I leave the village, I realize that she only gave me two of the three reasons for her story. What is the missing one? I wonder, but there isn't time to go back for an answer.

Chapter 6

Once I pass the train station, I assess the single rail that rises some four feet above the ground on cement-like columns. The rail shines as if it were just built, glistening as the sun's rays bounce off its shiny surface. Its base is shaped like a parallelogram, with another square-shaped part of the rail resting on top of the parallelogram. Nothing seems odd, so I jump on the smooth railroad track to head southeast. I fly off it faster than I jumped on, the surge of electricity still coursing through my body as I spin in the air. I land on my head and shoulder, my frame taught from the thousands of volts I absorbed. My muscles violently twitch, throwing me around like a dog trying to rub its back in the grass. The searing pain recedes, and I flex my hands to ensure my muscles obey. When I'm finally able to flex all my muscles, I sit up and look at my watch, surprised that it isn't fried. I spit out some grass I accidently gnawed on while I was convulsing on the ground.

"What was that, Bookworm?" I ask.

"Sorry I missed that, sir," the newly formed hologram replies. "The bottom part of the rail has a lip on the top that the fifty-foot sections of square rail are slid over. Inside the square rail are evenly spaced ePEG devices that generate electricity for the train to absorb as it passes over. Do you know what an ePEG is, Mr. President?"

"It's been mentioned several times earlier without such a question. Of course I do. So, let's save that discussion for later," I growl, still ticked that I served as an electrical conduit. "From now on if I'm in danger, you will give me a warning."

"Yes, Mr. President," Bookworm replies and then scratches his holographic head. "On a scale of one to ten, to what sensitivity level should I set my warning system?"

"Figure it out," I snap. "If I die, then you'll know it was too high."

Bookworm doesn't reply.

"Now, please ask my worshippers for immunity to electrical shock. That can be done by making the pads of my feet rubber. No, wait, I want the ability to absorb the electrical energy from the rail." I'm pleased with my idea.

After a short while, I carefully touch the rail, expecting a shock. Instead, the electricity flows up my finger and into my body. It feels great. I jump onto the rail again, a small smile curling my lips as the surge of power hits me. I adjust my feet to get a feel for the balance I will need. The metal is wide enough that it shouldn't be a problem. I take a few steps forward and then move it up to a slight jog, not having any balancing issues and surging with the energy I absorb. I pick up my pace until I can barely sustain the run, and then back off a little.

I'm traveling faster than any human has ever done, but I don't know if it's fast enough to make it in time. I'd hate to get there and find out I was too late. The shifting trees and bright green shrubs whip by me, and my bouncing up and down at this speed makes it challenging to get more than a general view of my surroundings. I start to worry about getting to the space launch in time and quicken my pace to the point that I'm gasping for air. My lungs burn and muscles ache as I exceed both the energy from the rail and that supplied by my followers. My mind tells me I can't keep this pace, but my heart, my desire for revenge, tells me to press on. I cough; the taste of bitter iron covered with redness coats my mouth. Gasps escape me faster than I inhale. It's too much.

I have to remember that I'm not a fighter, a climber, or a runner. I was—I am—a leader, and I have to use my brain, not just hope things will happen. I slow my pace enough so that I'm not on the verge of death.

Bookworm had mentioned there was a seam on the rail every fifty feet, so I use Bookworm's watch to time how long it takes me to travel ten rails. It's around twelve seconds to cover five hundred feet, or roughly fifty feet per second. Converting to miles per hour is fairly easy with my rounded numbers, as I need to multiply by 3,600 seconds and divide by 5,280 feet. Rounding again, I have 150,000, which I need to divide by 5,000 to get my speed. So, I'm traveling at thirty miles per hour. I estimate from the map Old Woman provided that I have three hundred miles to get to Lake City, Florida, and another two hundred miles to The Cape. Therefore, I need somewhere between seventeen and twenty hours to get there. Since it's just approaching nightfall, I have twenty-four hours left and surely will need an hour or two to get into the cargo bay. That leaves me less than two hours to convince a city on the verge of revolt to let me help them, when they won't see the results for at least a year. If they attack the train that is somewhere behind me, then the shuttle launch could be cancelled and I wouldn't be able to get to Mars.

Easy enough.

I have a flickering thought as I sprint along the rail. "Bookworm?" I ask.

"Yes, Mr. President?" replies Bookworm's voice from the watch.

"How fast am I traveling?"

"29.56 miles per hour, sir."

Like I said, I need to work smarter, not harder.

After an hour of enjoying the wind whipping by me, I realize it's becoming harder and harder to see the rail in the coming darkness. Clouds block the Moon, and from the looks of it, I am heading into a storm. Traveling at my speed with rain slicking the smooth metal could make for an unpleasant fall.

"Bookworm!" I huff.

"The watch glows, and Bookworm's six-inch hologram emanates from its neon blue faceplate. "Mr. President. I see you are still doing well."

"How long will the battery life...of this watch last?" I ask, gasping for air. I realize I have inadvertently picked up my pace.

"You do not remember that I said it was an ePEG device, sir?" Bookworm replies.

I know I am going to regret my next word. "Explain."

"While the electron Planar Entropy Devices, or ePEDs, were the biggest discovery of the twenty-first century, innovative applications were built upon it shortly thereafter by taking advantage of the timeless plane. One such application was the ability to freeze and slowly time-step nuclear fission at the atomic level. Dr. Michael Benjamin was able to take the reacting atom and partially suspend it in the same plane as opened by the ePEG. Since the fourth dimension—or time—is non-existent in the Saranji—or timeless—plane, one can control the fission reaction by controlling how far into the plane the atom resides. The watch was initially charged by a powerful external energy source, but uses the energy supplied by the temporal fission to not only recharge it, but also to control the field that regulates the fission process."

"So, it will last...a long time. Got it." With my chemistry degree, I could understand the concept, but I had no idea how it worked. There was a reason I escaped the sciences and completed a Master's degree in international policy.

It's getting darker, and I'm squinting to try and see further ahead. "Bookworm, I need you to cast your projection about fifty feet in front of me."

"Glad to be used as a guiding light, Mr. President," replies the hologram as the rail in front of me lights up with a bluish hue.

I can't tell if it was said with sarcasm or sincerity. Based on my disposition and the programmed personality of the mechanical Bookworm, I take it as sarcastic. I focus back on the blue-lit rail in front of me. Over time, the dense woodlands slowly transform into sparse patches of trees with large sections of previously farmed land. Small saplings have successfully begun their hostile takeover of the human terraforming, but it looks like it will need many more decades before the battle is won.

I squint and try to keep my vision ahead of the bends of the rail as it progresses into swamplands. Darkness soon wins out, and an odd assortment of eyes appear all around me, some hanging from tree limbs or fluttering in the air, while others poke out of the swamp water. Most disappear before I get too close, with their warning cries fighting to race ahead of my blistering pace.

A large splatter on my head takes my focus from the tracks to the darkened skies above. Another hits my face, confirming that I haven't been assaulted by some vengeful bird, but rather I'm running straight into a storm front. A few more minutes at my pace and a steady rain pours from the sky, finally starting to coat the electrified rail. I tell Bookworm to have some of my followers pray for sure footing, which turns out to be a good thing. In less than an hour, I'm running through a heavy downpour, with thunder regularly breaking up the rain's drone and lightning giving me brief glimpses of the endless swamplands.

I'm so worried about my footing on the smooth, wet rail that I fail to question the flashing small lights ahead of me. I'm traveling over yet another simple bridge when I hear an explosion to my left, followed by another on my right. Something with the power of a large hammer hits me in the chest, but worse is the small grouping of bird shot that pelts my calf.

The impact on my leg shifts my foot enough that I miss the rail. At over thirty miles per hour, I don't just fall to the ground but enjoy a combination of forward momentum and Mother Earth's gravitational pull. One glancing blow from an auburn tree and my slow somersault transforms into a fast helicopter spin. A few dozen more feet and I tear into a large Cyprus before belly flopping into the swamp water.

Instinctively inhaling, I invite a plethora of foul flavors into my mouth. Stagnant water, rotting leaves, pasty mud, and a dead brine shrimp are those that I recognize. I raise my head and spit out what I can.

Happenstance.

A word that doesn't seem real, but perfectly describes what is happening to me. I happen to have landed next to a full-grown alligator, which decides my leg is easy dinner. Its strong jaws snap down on my already-wounded calf muscle, only irritating me more. Firmly latched on, it attempts a death roll but only succeeds in twisting its lower body into the air. I reach down and pry its jaws apart, hearing a combination of cracking and snapping noises. It hisses and tries to do another death roll, but I have braced my other foot firmly in the muddy earth.

71

Two more shots ring out, with a slug hitting my arm and more bird shot pelting my chest.

Assaults and assassination attempts had occurred regularly after I had become a demigod. People who believed I was an abomination targeted me many times, with the hopes to destroy that which challenged their beliefs. Initially, the attacks were as crude as this one, but over time they became very creative. From dropping a safe from a high-rise to contaminating my food with mutagens and carcinogens. Obviously, none of them succeeded, but their attempts did cause a lot of collateral damage. Confusion had been my first emotion, as I never understood how, even in the most prosperous of times, there was always someone upset enough to want to kill me. As the attacks escalated, I started to develop a sense of compassion, feeling like I had let them down. Finally, the compassion turned to anger. Anger, which was always my final emotional stop…and that hadn't changed with two hundred years of self-imprisonment.

My anger overflows, turning my skin a bright red that glows like a flare in the rainy night. I roar as I fling the eight-hundred-pound alligator toward the last place I had seen the rifle's flash on my left. I charge to my right, growling as I rip through the knee-deep water. A scream behind me confirms that my gator-toss is successful, while a missed shot helps me hone in on my other assailant. I reach the shotgun-wielding idiot before taking any more hits and attempt to lift the weapon away from his grasp. The flannel-clothed Neanderthal refuses to let go, so I raise the shotgun over my head, placing his bearded face at eye level. The glow from my watch lets me see that there is no fear in his eyes.

Surprising.

"Why are you shooting at me?" I growl.

"Yeren't even hurt. Dang!" His southern drawl also holds no fear. "We saw youse were comin' on our computer. Thought we'd take you out, den demand an 'ward from da Marzans. How you not hurt?"

"I'm a demigod, idiot." Something he said comes back to me as I hear a shot in the distance. "You can read?"

"Sho'nuff kin. We ain't dumb. Now gimme mah gun," he says, his own anger growing.

The idiot tries to shake it free from my iron grip, but only succeeds in flopping his legs around. I wait until he stops wiggling to do one more assessment. Yep, redneck.

"You can have your shotgun and help your friend," I reply after deciding that he really is an idiot.

I fling his shotgun—and him, since he refuses to let go—in the direction of his friend. He howls until I hear a splash and a scream, letting me know I threw him near the alligator. I jog back to the rail, smiling more than I should, and climb aboard before continuing a run that would have shamed even the fabled Greek marathon runner Pheidippides. The storm never worsens, and after a couple more hours I'm again in peaceful darkness. I use the time to strategize how I will handle the Lake City Rebels.

Yes, I like to give nicknames. Easier to remember.

I don't know how the city will be guarded, whether it will be with dreaded Space Force Bots or humans paid to suppress their own. SFBots will require a stealthy insertion, as they will kill anything and everything that moves, once engaged. Intimidation might work with human guards, but it's possible that I will have to kill several of them before they give up. Either way, I will have to worry about an ePET being used to notify the Marsians of my attack. I can't let that happen, so maybe stealth for either type of guard will be needed. But how will I find the factory leaders who are bent on stopping the next train?

Diversion.

If I create a ruckus, it will not only allow me in but also force the factory leaders to take some sort of action. I only need to look for those running toward the diversion to pick them out. Wait, that doesn't make sense. My mind redirects to the challenge. What kind of diversion would work? At first my thoughts fall back to my usual course of action…mass destruction and blowing up buildings. However, the recent encounter with the redneck gives me a better idea. Well, I keep telling myself it's better, but something in the back of my mind keeps warning me that it's stupid.

Chapter 7

The rail splits sharply to the right, the bypass letting me know that I'm close to Lake City. The stench of rotting vegetation and sloshing noises of scared animals is a reminder that I'm still in a swamp, and it probably surrounds the entire city.

"Bookworm...turn off the light." I welcome the chance to stop running, even if it means something more challenging is ahead.

"Mr. President, the tree coverage ends in a quarter mile, leaving another quarter mile of receding marshland. The city is surrounded by a rather ominous wall, and it has a slightly acute angle to make it difficult to climb. There is a large gate that must be opened for trains to enter, and on the opposite side resides the main gate, which opens up toward grasslands."

I slow down to a light jog. "Bookworm, give me specs on the walls of the city."

"The city walls are mostly brick, as the high humidity and wetlands would rust away steel fortifications. They are approximately twenty-five feet tall, with no exterior lighting. Interior structures seemed to have been required to be thirty feet from the wall." The simulated voice of Bookworm sounds more robotic than normal.

"Sounds like no exterior threats, so the guards should be looking inward," I think out loud.

"Correct. However, if the guards are humans, then they could be disobeying orders and looking outward."

Bookworm's assessment is valid. History had shown over and over again that guards never perfectly obeyed their orders. Psychologists had refuted the notion that it was a subconscious desire to challenge authority, and proved it was a result of human curiosity and the mind's battle against the mundane. A city on a quiet night would be the epitome of boring.

I slow to a walk before jumping into the knee-high water. It's time to do some hunting, using my legs as the live bait. I hate the thought of it, but I still decide to press on.

****

I drag my two presents along the muddy earth, their bellies leaving a wide trail, which even a half-blind guard would spot in the morning. But that's okay, as I have no plans of being in the area for more than a couple of hours. My legs dig deep into the mud as I pull the half-ton gators along. They offer little resistance, as I have spent the last dozen minutes wrestling with them so that they are worn out. It turns out that all those croc hunter shows on TV had been right in that the species calms down once they are exhausted. Lactic acid buildup was an alligator's only true enemy. Well, that and humans.

I reach the city wall with no one discovering me and see why they didn't need to worry about escapees. The area is littered with wooden spikes, protruding a few inches out of the ground. Even a jump from a few feet would result in enough damage to prevent running away. I'm sure that people could figure a way around it, such as falling on a padded bag. But the point wasn't to prevent one or two people from escaping, but rather to avert a mass exodus while also letting people know they were prisoners. It was an incredibly smart plan, as the most poisonous of prisoners could escape and thus leave no one to build up opposition. But then, why were the inhabitants of the Lake City factories bent on destroying the train? There had to be something keeping their leaders within the confines of the city. Maybe family, such as the young or elderly to care for. Yes, that was probably it.

The noises of the swamp fill the night with enough sound to mask my efforts, but also limit my own hearing. As I walk alongside the fortress, shearing off the pointy sticks with the underbellies of the gators, I strain to hear movement on the wall. I begin to wonder if there is anyone at all, nearly deciding that the entire wall is guarded by sensors until I catch mumblings from a brief discussion. I continue until I hear another noise, and then another. The guards are human, working in pairs, and spaced roughly two hundred feet apart. I'm far enough out that they can't see or hear me as I walk alongside a section of the wall until I can barely hear the guards talking. I wait for their conversation to end, then pick up again, as that is the most likely chance at least one will turn to look at the other.

I let go of one gator and step on its tail, resulting in it turning and locking onto my calf…again. I ignore the discomfort, cursing my plan, and grip the other's tail in both hands. Squatting down, I swing it in an upward arc, like I'm shoveling snow. The gator flies high, spinning and rotating as it clears the wall and then lands with a solid thud.

"What was that?" a curious voice sounds.

A small light appears, pointing into the city.

"It's a freakin' gator, Sal. It jumped right over the dang wall," comments a stunned guard.

I nearly laugh out loud. Am I hitting the lottery on meeting stupid people?

"No way," the other guard replies in a mocking tone.

I don't listen to the rest of the conversation, as I'm busy extracting my leg from the other gator's bite. Once successful, I grab its tail and sprint alongside the wall for another two hundred feet, dragging the grumpy gator with ease. I heave it over the wall, like the last one, not knowing whether either has survived the return to Earth, but also not really understanding why I came up with such a plan. Hearing more startled voices, I sprint halfway back from where I started, angling toward the wall and building up as much speed as possible in the muck. Mud flies in every direction, splattering my back, arms, and face.

When I near my destination, I jump straight up, rising like a collegiate pole-vaulter. The top of the wall is almost within reach as my ascent peaks. I stretch my arm as high as possible, barely catching the lip of the wall with my first two fingertips, but that is all I need. I slowly lift myself to eye level, relieved to see that my ridiculous gator tactics have worked. It turns out I have popped up where the middle guards were stationed, and luckily they have charged in opposite directions to investigate the gator ruckus.

Looking into the city, I see that Bookworm was correct regarding the thirty-foot distance between the interior structures and the city wall. I don't have much time before they turn back around, so I slither onto the top of the wall and leap without any hesitation toward the roof of the one-story buildings directly across from me. I fly through the air with ease, no concern given the power my followers have bestowed me, yet still not understanding why I'm so worried about being caught. I'm a demigod, and they're humans with limited weapons. While I don't want to alert the Marsians, I have never been this cautious before.

I make it! Landing on the roof…and crashing through what must have been a thin sheet of plastic that allowed sunlight into the building. I resign myself to hitting the ground but instead land on a pile of pointy objects inside the building. I also must have hit my head on something because my thinking is a little foggy. I lie there for a while in the darkness to recover, wondering if they've heard me.

"Another just fell en the 'lectronics building. Where the heck are they coming from!" yells out one of the guards. "Sound the alarm!"

My plan had been pretty stupid, almost stupid enough to work. In fact, I hadn't really thought of how I was going to track down the factory leaders if the ruckus hadn't raised the alarm. Maybe my misfortunate fall is a good thing.

I stand up, my eyes having adjusted to the interior darkness, and jog toward the lit outline of a shoddy door. It opens into a break room, and in it sits a small, Asian boy with spiked hair. A colorful, serpentine tattoo rides up his middle finger to his right arm, wrapping around his elbow and disappearing into his white T-shirt. His opposite arm displays a simple inked outline of a small snake. Its scales are the raised markings of a burn scar on the boy's arm. It's odd enough that he is calmly staring at me with a slight smile on his face, but even more disturbing is the assortment of electronic parts neatly organized on the table that separates us.

The parts spelled out *Welcome, Mr. President.*

"Not a lucky guess, I take it, Boy," I say.

His head twitches to the side and his eyes focus on me. It appears that he has been in a trance. He shakes his head side to side as he stands up, wiping the electronic pieces off the table and onto the floor.

"We need to go. Follow me." The voice that comes out seems older than his pre-teen body, and the confident swagger reminds me of a Berkley student twice his age, who I had engaged in a fun debate early in my first presidency.

"I saw an alley on the right side," I say. "We can use that to go to the factory leaders."

"Ha!" comes back an insulting laugh, with a tone in the voice much different than from the first comment. "You're over seven-feet tall and thick as an ox, man. Even the idiot guards would easily spot you. All these factories are connected. I'll get you to where we need to go."

Thick as an ox? That's weird, I think.

The boy slides past me and runs out of the room. Huffing in frustration, or at being insulted, I turn and follow. The maze he takes us through seems to have no rhyme or reason, as sometimes we pass close to guards and other times run away from them. After a half hour, and as the sounds of outside chaos diminish, we step out onto a small alleyway and quickly cross the open area to stand before a grimy house. The boy opens the door and motions for me to enter. I duck down and walk into the front room. The furniture is simple and old, its chipped surfaces crafting a story of being passed down for generations, each scuff a year in its life. The warped floor is made of wood from the swamp, having buckled and lifted in several spots, yet sanded smooth enough to slide along in bare feet without being impaled by splinters. A blackened, brick fireplace lends the room enough light for me to see the faces of the middle-aged man and woman sitting on a couch, both their mouths agape in awe of my presence.

The man jumps off the couch as if a spider bit him and prostrates on the floor, his wife mimicking the movements seconds later.

"Oh, powerful and mighty protector of The United Americas, with the strength to reshape mountains, intelligence to grow our nation, honor to lead our military. Oh, great granter of freedom, protector of your people, and server of justice; I pray before you, waiting for your command." The last words come out as sobs.

Tears flow down the man's face and splatter against the wood floor; each drop snaps a power chord in my chest. The man is sincere, and what I feel is the power it releases into the timeless plane, through the demigod device, and into me. I soak it up, even if it's a minute fraction of the power I possess.

The boy shakes his head as he speaks. "Mom and Dad, we'll be in the back room. Please don't disturb us...and don't tell anyone that he's here."

"If that's what he wants," his mother replies.

"Yes," I grunt as I follow the boy and duck into the back room.

The boy walks over to a round, purple pillow, spins around to face me, and plops down. He then crosses his legs and places his hands on his knees, palms up. The smile he held when we first met reappears, along with my anger at seeing it.

"You're it," I surmise, letting my disappointment show.

"Brilliant. How long have you known?" Boy asks, genuinely excited.

"Only after we left the warehouses, Boy. Maybe even before that, but it was just a hunch back then." I'm becoming angrier as I speak, but don't know why. "I figure that by some freak genetic miscue, judging only by the short encounter with your parents, you're a genius. And you somehow were able to take that genius and craft a persona that led the people to believe in a pre-teen rebel leader, which, you should know, is a dishonorable move. I can already tell that you portray two disjointed sides. One that is a brazen kid and the other a wise leader. But you're not wise. You're this rebel kid who wants to overthrow the Marsians. 'Destroy the train and everything will be great,' you think. Instead you're leading this entire city into a valley of death." I sit down and cross my legs. "Good guess?"

Boy reaches to the side of the pillow and unrolls a FlipFilm. "Do you know how the man you called Bookworm passed along your info? He would feed the information to a trusted few, who would then send it to another trusted few. Only after ten times was it approved for worldwide dissemination. Why was this done? Because of fear of retaliation by the Marsians. Because what little history we've been able to keep in this post-apocalyptic world details deadly consequences by the Marsians when we disobey. But we must disobey, Mr. President, even if I'm leading my city into something similar to the Biblical reference you gave. Humankind is not meant to be suppressed, although history shows us that suppression of the many by the few is easier than one thinks. I could delve deeper into this, but we would merely end in a philosophical debate with no winner. That crap isn't worth my time."

Reluctantly, I have to agree with him.

"Now, do you wonder why you feel so powerful, when the number of humans left on Earth is so small? In fact, I'm confident that the current number is a mere fraction of the number of followers you had at your peak of power. That smaller number is stronger because each and every individual is desperate, and as a unified whole is hoping that you will end the suppression. Just like my parents, people are praying that you'll end the suffering and starvation, and stop the needless loss of life."

Boy stops, surely expecting a question or response from me. However, I'm tired of being lectured by every new person I meet, especially on things I already know. And yes, it really bugs me to be lectured by a brash boy. A vision crosses me where I throw him off the roof and onto a couple of guards. I pull my arm back down to my side. Part of me wants to end him and another wants to make him cry. So I just stare at him.

"Even though I was one of the first trusted with your information, I have no illusion about your odds of saving humankind. You slept in a hole for two hundred years instead of doing your job, so why would you help now? Why would you push through the toughest challenges after the previous choices you made under similar circumstances? Even if you have the desire, you won't be able to handle the lack of oxygen for what will seem like an eternity. You'll slip into a restful sleep like the demigods who lie under nature's blanket."

Now he is making me angry, but he doesn't seem to care.

"Sir, you're here to convince me to not act against our suppressors, and you wrongly assume I'm doing it to prove myself as a leader, despite my age. What if I told you that I was not the genius, but rather that such a title belonged to my deceased older brother?"

Boy stretches out his hands toward me, displaying his tattoos. "That I am the colorful one, and he is the serious one. He saved me from an explosion in the factory when I was barely old enough to walk. He is the one who pushes me to ensure that the small group of people living in Lake City not only survive but thrive. He pushes me to use this city as a spear point for change. A change that needs to be spread throughout the world. Would you believe me if I told you that he pushes me every day, even after death?"

The bland tattoo shifts on his arm, which I want to brush off as a lighting trick. However, it stretches wings across Boy's skin, flapping them into the air as it puffs up and breathes red fire down to his fingertips. It then winks at me. I'm transfixed on the living tattoo as he continues.

"History has taught us that humankind can survive almost anything, hanging on by the thinnest of threads until the bountiful times arrive. Then it thrives, dominating over every obstacle in its path. But more importantly, the species advances, making a giant revolutionary leap during each struggle."

"You want a revolutionary advancement. To what end?" I growl with suspicion. I want to tell him I thought it was to take over the Marsians, but I've already been wrong about him and his portraying two sides to fool folks.

"No, not to take over the Marsians. Rather to save humankind from the asteroid that's headed toward Earth." Boy reaches for the computer, taps on it several times, and then holds it out. "Asteroid 2215RQ36 was named Renella, after it inexplicably was jettisoned from the asteroid belt. While the thirty years it still has before the four-mile-diameter asteroid falls into Earth may seem like a long time, it isn't if you have no technical options for turning it away. Our fate seems to necessitate Earth's rebirth, unless there is another way."

"You think there is another way?" I ask, starting to wonder if I'm going after the wrong set of beings. Maybe the Marsians will need to live in order for humankind to survive.

"Transcendence." Boy's reply chills the air as his eyes lose focus and his body stills. The only thing moving is the serpent. There is no thought of rebuttal or laughter, not only because of what is happening to him, but also because I immediately know what he means…and that he's serious.

"Complete dissolution of one's material existence. They all become spirits like your brother. I assume you have a plan," I reply.

Boy is in a trance. The voice that comes out of him is much older and very serious. "Plan? No, not so much a plan as a movement. I will lead our people through the awakening, but it will take nearly as much time as we have left, and that is why we need to start the revolution. Once humankind is ready, then the cosmic event will be the thing that forces all who have prepared to move into transcendence."

"What if there's another option?" I query.

"No matter. Humankind has already shown that technological superiority is not sustainable. Transcendence is still needed."

"What if I can force the Marsians to help?" I ask, remembering my promise to Bookworm.

Boy snaps out of his trance and a wry smile creases his face. "And now we have the exact reason you're here. You wish the train to continue its suppressing travels."

"Yes," I reply.

"No!" Boy shoots back.

I leap out of my seated position and in one step have his fragile neck in my steel grip. Rage fills me and pours down my arm like poison. "Listen, Boy. With one snap of my fingers I could pop your head off its fragile support, ending your pathetic rebellion. You act old, but you are clearly too young to understand that people will die from your foolish actions!"

Boy doesn't flinch, even as the redness of my slight choking rises up his neck and onto his ears. "No, I do understand. I understand more than you know."

My hand opens and I stagger backward, falling on the ground as a fog surrounds my thoughts. I don't want to hurt the boy; it had been a mistake. I need to listen and see his side, but about what, I can't remember. My anger is subsiding and the blood pounding between my ears transforms into ocean waves, rolling gently on a calm day. The fog slowly lifts, allowing me to assess what is happening.

"You took over my mind outside the city? You forced me to execute that stupid gator plan?" I'm more shocked than upset. How could he have manipulated me?

Boy nods his head, the wry smile coming back. "I didn't think the plan was that stupid. After all, it brought you to me."

"How?"

"Easy. You're a demigod. Demigods subject themselves to the will of their followers. Those followers partially control your actions, invade your thoughts, and are the source of your power. It's the world's most foolproof democracy. Well, almost foolproof. Anyway, I merely jumped ahead of the masses, blocked their wishes, and inserted mine."

"That is not transcendence," I comment, reassessing my belief that my followers can't completely control me.

"How I described it may not be, but how I did it was. I transferred my brother's spirit to the front of the line. It's not the first time I've done it, but with regular people I can only give weak suggestions. With you I can easily force direction. Although I must admit that I don't understand how you receive the power and thoughts of your followers. There's a step I'm missing, and I would like to know as it may help lead people to transcendence."

Quite frankly, I hadn't yet bought into all his spirit crap. Sure, as a demigod I know he can bend my will, but I don't think one needs a spirit to do it. Whether I believe him or not doesn't matter, as I have a bargaining chip, but one that I don't want to use. I hadn't even told Bookworm the whole truth regarding my ascension to demigod status, and I trust him completely. Well, maybe not completely. If I were to give Boy the information, then it could get to the Marsians, and they could use it against me. Was it worth ensuring that the train wasn't derailed?

"If I tell you, then you must delay your attack on the train by a year, even if you think I failed in my mission." I have another thought. "And don't try to force me to tell you using your brother's spirit. It's the one thing I could never be forced to reveal."

A stare-down ensues. I can hear the sobbing of his parents in the front room, still awestruck by my presence. Outside, the wind is picking up, rattling the loose glass windows. My own breathing is heavy and grating, while Boy's is noiseless. I could stare without blinking for hours, maybe years, but that isn't the point. We aren't testing wills; we are weighing needs.

"If I deem it to be a fair trade, after you tell me, then yes." Boy holds his stare while speaking.

I rise as fast as my anger, but this time I don't lunge forward. Not because I don't want to. I figure he will just control me again.

"Ha! Made you blink. I win!" Boy claps his hands as a childish smile shows his crooked and pitted teeth. Healthcare isn't what it used to be.

"What?" I wonder if he has a split personality, even apart from his 'spirit' brother. It would explain a lot.

"The stare-down. I win." Boy's excitement turns to dejection when I don't respond. "Geez. Okay, I will delay it as there's no way you'd hold back if it was lame. Lay it on me."

I shake my head before sitting again. "It should go without saying that you cannot pass this along to anyone. Oh, you neither, Bookworm."

"Yes, Mr. President," responds my watch.

My words are slow, methodical, as I reflect on my early life. "I assume Bookworm released the information about my first experience? The one where the man burned himself alive as he worshipped me."

Boy nods slowly, seeming to have fallen back into his trance-like state.

"While it was a big step, it wasn't the first. Years earlier I was eating breakfast in the State Room, when an aide burst in. There was an explosion at a house in Cleveland that wiped out most of the city block around it.

The fire department ruled out a broken gas line or even a drug lab, as there weren't any signs of a primary fire. The FBI took over the scene once they realized it was the home of a brilliant physicist who had recently been fired from the University of Michigan. He had been studying electron tunneling."

I knew I needed to explain the theory, but I had taken only a few physics classes. "Electron tunneling, or quantum tunneling, is based on the Heisenberg Uncertainty Principle, where the location and momentum of a particle cannot be determined at the same time for particles at the quantum level. This has to do with the fact that a particle is also a wave. Essentially, it explains how electrons can travel through space. Professor Saranji believed that the particle could have a specific location and momentum, but that the location could only be defined in another plane. The tunneling was the electron moving in and out of this plane. He was able to place a tracer on the particle wave and even published his results on a three-dimensional plane where the particle existed."

I paused, admittedly for dramatic effect. It had taken me a few weeks of studying what my chief scientist had presented before I understood it. Boy only stared straight ahead. It was like talking to one of my old cave walls.

"The fourth dimension is time," I went on nonetheless. "The dimensional plane he proposed had no time. He was mocked by the entire community, ridiculed by colleagues and students, and even became the butt of late-night talk shows. It all led to heavy drinking, and ultimately, his firing. He apparently continued the work in his basement, which was also destroyed in the explosion. Fortunately, he saved everything to the cloud."

"Cloud? You can't save things to a cloud," Boy spat out, clearly thinking I was telling him a lie.

"No, the cloud was a name for computer storage utilizing shared online resources. It became obsolete because of what I'm trying to explain." I acted frustrated, but was enjoying being the teacher. "He had built upon the Saranji plane hypothesis and figured out how to make this useful. The second law of thermodynamics states that entropy will dissipate, going to the least energetic state. However, this requires time…the fourth dimension. In Saranji's plane, time does not exist and pockets of energy can be found in vast quantities, similar to oil fields. Professor Saranji had built a device, based on electron tunneling—that travelled into this plane—and pulled the energy with it. Unlike Benjamin Franklin and his discovery of electricity, where he was lucky to not be electrocuted, Professor Saranji had punched into a very dense pocket of energy and what came out was enough energy to obliterate him and destroy his house."

"Was this built into a weapon?" Boy is clearly back in control, as the childish enthusiasm has returned.

I chuckle. "It's humankind's nature to try, but luckily, electronic tunneling can only be done at the quantum level. Once you try and scale it up, the effect is no longer valid since you switch to classical mechanics. However, the important part is that there became a nearly limitless source of energy."

"ePEG," comments Boy.

"Yes, the electron Planar Energy Gatherer and also the electron Planar Energy Transmitter or ePET, which was created from the energy-gathering devices—these were the next technical revolution for humankind. The ePEG is what enabled Entara, my megacity, to be created. The energy consumption required for such a grand vision would have been too much for our nation, but with tens of millions of ePEGs, it became almost too easy. In fact, it also was critical to the colonization of Mars. The ePET was built off the fundamentals of ePEG technology. It allowed instant communication between Earth and Mars, since the Saranji plane was timeless. One could transmit information into the Saranji plane and the ePER, or electronic Planar Energy Receiver, would relay the data instantaneously."

I paused a beat. "Later, the ePER was built into the ePET, and people just called the entire device an ePET." I pause again, but this time because I'm going to reveal my secret. Once I speak, there's no going back. "Let's move forward a few years to when I witnessed the worshipper burning himself alive. It's true that I felt the energy surge, but it didn't result in any physical benefits. No increase in height, no hardened skin or renewed vitality. But the power surge had sparked my curiosity. I had an irrational idea, wondering if there was a way to magnify the energy I had received from my followers, like what an amplifier did for a guitar. My top government scientists and engineers set out to see if it was possible; the biologist exploring biothermal energy patterns and their tie to different parts of the brain, mechanical and electric engineers retuning the ePEG to pick up human energy that had dissipated into the Saranji plane, and biomechanical engineers studying how to integrate the device into a human."

Boy listens raptly.

"The first device weighed over one hundred pounds, but could amplify the energy I received from my worshippers by more than one thousand percent. They found that when connected to it, I grew over two inches and my body reversed its aging by fifteen years. However, it wasn't something I could easily carry, and as soon as I was extracted from it, I reverted back to normal."

"Wowser! I think I see where this is going, but please continue. You are an awesome storyteller."

Awesome? I think it's a bit of an exaggeration, but it's a sincere compliment.

"We had a brilliant electrical engineer who not only miniaturized the device and made it one hundred times more powerful, but also encased it in a nearly indestructible RheTungst sphere. However, his last step was his most brilliant. He perfectly matched the electronic signals to those of the human brain and figured out exactly where it needed to be placed within the brain. Our initial excitement turned to disappointment as every test case deceased within minutes after insertion. It turned out that one needed to already be worshipped to survive the surgery and melding, or else—."

"You're the first cyborg!" Boy interrupts. "So cool, man."

"Bring your brother back!" I snap. I am tired of talking to an excited child. My story has a purpose, and it isn't for entertaining.

Boy regains his composure and is consumed again by the trance.

"It's obvious that it worked, and my only mistake was not rewarding the electrical engineer who built the final device with riches or bringing him in to other government black programs so he would be too engrossed in his work to think about money. He went rogue, selling each new device to the highest bidding consortium. His first sale created the demigod that killed my family."

I stop abruptly, completing my story. The pain of losing my family resurfaces, and I know from the past that the more I speak, the more it will hurt.

"Interesting," Boy comments. "A technological device for spiritual needs. I never would have guessed it, but it will surely help me with the transcendence." Boy stands up and walks to the door. "We have a deal, Mr. President. While I still don't believe you will be able to stop the Marsian suppression, I now hope you'll figure out how to negotiate with them to save Earth from Renella. After all, they can't survive without our resources."

Thanking Boy before I left would have been the diplomatic thing to do; however, he gave up very little while I took on the extra burden of not only saving humankind from the Marsians, but trying to thwart an asteroid that would destroy Earth even if I succeeded. It had been so much easier when I talked to no one.

I duck to pass through the interior door, walking by his parents who were still prostrated and praying to me. I open the front door without hesitation and casually stroll toward the center of the city until I find the raised train rail. Once I jump on, I look at my watch. Over three hours for my visit in Lake City. I head off on a full sprint, realizing that I need to make up the extra hour I lost in Boy's house. Nearly two hundred miles left, and any delay would likely result in me having the best view of the shuttle's launch. I near the other side of the walled city, spotting the closed wrought-iron gates that lay ahead. I'm not in the mood to be careful, and admittedly I'm not thinking of whether my breaking through the gate will result in a message to the Marsians.

I pick up speed; my muscles bulge and my bones thicken with the anticipation of a head-on crash at over thirty miles per hour. I need a release, something to quench my anger; anger at nothing, yet anger at everything. The closer I get, the more vivid my imagination of the bars buckling, then snapping as they are bent beyond their ductility, shattering like a glass window and sending shards in front of me as I continue on my path. I inhale deeply, wanting to roar when I break through the gate. I look up at the guards, who are all sleeping even though it's well past noon. No matter, I'll wake them up.

The wall and the gate near. I start a countdown like ground control during a rocket launch. Five, four...the gate begins to drop into the ground with a surprising quietness. By the time I reach the wall, it's completely submerged and I'm outside the city, on my way to another adventure. I exhale my stored-up anger. Maybe there is something to this transcendence thing.

Thanks, Boy, I think to myself.

You're welcome, Mr. President, comes back a thought in my head.

It wasn't Boy, but rather his brother. I can tell because he didn't throw *dude* or something else like that at me. Heck, the kid probably would've wanted me to crash through the gate.

I don't want to know just yet how fast I need to go to make up for lost time. I'm going to press on, even if it's impossible to succeed.

Chapter 8

An uneventful hour passes on the journey to The Cape; if you ignore that I did ask Bookworm if I could make it and had to increase my speed by another ten miles per hour. I was sucking air like a vacuum cleaner and moving so fast that the newer inland Georgian swamplands swiftly gave way to the cypress swamplands of Florida. I'm sure there is a more vivid way to describe the change from one swampland to another, but I have never been enthralled with ecosystems and am even less so when sprinting with all the energy I can draw forth.

"Bookworm!" I gasp.

His hologram appears in front of my face. "Yes, Mr. President."

"I need…my worshippers…to help inc…rease my speed," I say, wondering if my words were too alien to understand.

"I am afraid that is not possible, sir. They are already helping, and you will need a surge from them shortly after liftoff. It's unlikely they will be able to do both."

"Thanks…for the help!" I gasp again.

"You are welcome, sir," he responds before the hologram disappears.

I inhale deeply, raising my anger to push me on. I will my lungs to expand further, inhaling the precious oxygen that I crave—crave, for I don't know if it's really needed. I push my overstrained calves, aching quads, and stretched hamstrings, willing blood to flow faster than what gravity and my heart can force. I shrug off the weariness of travel, willing my mind to stay sharp and set a pace I shouldn't be able to maintain.

Thoughts creep in my mind, trying to derail my steps. My wife and children, the rise of the megacity, the colonization of Mars, the God Bomb, the collapse of human society, my descent into the mine, my acceptance of failure. Each thought I hastily push away, each new thought stronger and more painful than the last. They keep coming, trying to crush my willpower with hammer fists of doubt, and I continue to deflect their intent.

Finally, I shove aside the past, but a new burden of travel weighs on my shoulders, bunching up the muscles and bending my back. The burden is from what remains of humankind, a hundred times fewer followers than I had before, but a thousand times more in need. They pray not of monetary desire, fame, or well-being, but rather for survival of their children, their parents, their neighbors, themselves. Each day is a struggle to live, and each night a prayer for a better day. Each new day just like the last, yet still they hope and pray. Prayed to me for survival for over two hundred years. Prayed for over two hundred years, without ever an answer.

The pressure, the weight on my soul, becomes too much.

My breath leaves me and my pace slows. I falter on the rail as spasms rack my back. Each step seems to be my last, but I will myself on, even as my legs wade through air thicker than quicksand. The rail ascends and I attempt to go with it, praying to my god that I crest the hill before my legs give out. It was a true god I prayed to, not created by humans to serve humankind. A god who created humankind for the purity of creation, granted free will, and only bound the people by an invisible tether called faith.

I meet the apex of the hill before falling off the end of the rail like a dead man, my face bouncing off the crumbling concrete that once was an overpass. I wonder if this is what Pheidippides felt like right before he died. His heart ready to burst out of his chest, his lungs filling with blood, his feet bleeding as if he had walked over thousands of nails. Not once, not twice, but dozens of times.

At least he could die.

I convulse on the cement like an electrocuted bear, powerful muscles rising and then slamming down with unnatural power. The convulsions hammer the already broken bridge, luckily not quite strong enough to send it into the ocean.

After a few minutes, my body heals enough that the convulsions stop and I can open my eyes. I'm peering through a hole in the concrete of the overpass, gazing not upon another crumbled road but small waves lapping against steel and cracked concrete. It's only then that I smell and taste the salty air, and feel the thick dampness of the ocean on my body. I had ridden on this overpass as a young boy, traveling with my Air Force grandpa to see one of the Space Shuttle's last launches. The massive building and structures on the small island were built not only for the shuttle, but also to launch The United States' military satellites.

I had waited for a half-day in a secondary control room, staring intently at live feeds of the vertical rocket stand, which was holding the shuttle and its two solid rocket boosters. I had watched during the cryo cool-down and loading of the astronauts, which started a tickling sensation on the back of my neck. A sensation itching did not get rid of. The countdown blared on the loudspeakers, and the ground vibrated my feet as the main engines started up, over a million pounds of thrust kicking on. More powerful than a hundred Hoover Dams. The countdown was drowned out by the noise, and the power of the solid rocket motors firing was deafening. I stared at the flaming exhausts from the nozzles on the screens until my eyes watered from not blinking.

When it had disappeared into the upper clouds, the itch had grown into a dream to go beyond Earth. It had begun my desire to colonize Mars.

I stand up, expecting to see the roads crisscrossing the island's greenery, with towering buildings and ivory rocket stands from my childhood.

I shouldn't have been so naïve. The island is now one massive metallic scaffold—multi-layered levels built upon each other as needed, interwoven with train monorails, and other smaller rails wrapping around the whole structure. Rail bots and unmanned cargo carts whip around on the lesser rails in a chaotic pattern that surely no organic brain could comprehend. I watch them for a while, trying to follow their destination, but feel like I'm watching a magician shuffling a deck of cards. The only thing I can ascertain is that they are travelling toward the center of the island. While watching, I figure out something, which disturbs me.

"Bookworm. Steel couldn't handle this salty environment for so long. What's the structure made of?"

"Certainly, what you have already guessed, sir. It's the rustproof iron/titanium/tungsten carbide alloy, six times stronger than steel at one third the weight," replies Bookworm.

"Only one place had that much Titung alloy," I think out loud.

"Yes, sir. It's from your megacity, Entara. Nothing withstood the God Bombs and two hundred years of Mother Nature except the city's scaffolding."

There was no need to reply. The development of Titung alloy was what had allowed Entara to be built to the dizzying heights needed for my vision. The five pillars of the city rose over a mile high, and even more impressive had been that each one's base was half as wide. They were the world's most challenging engineering marvel...now gone. Entara was a wasteland, and my Mars colony was the home of a suppressing government. Were my visions a failure, or was it that Mother Nature and Father Time would eventually lay waste to any of humankind's creations?

I also hadn't expected a newer version of the space shuttle, as it had been built for human exploration and was inefficient for cargo launches, but am awestruck by the three superstructures nested within the center of the island. Each one is nearly five hundred feet in height, with the one on the left holding the spear-like cargo launch vehicle I need to infiltrate. In my early days, I had studied the Saturn V rocket and its journey to land humankind on the Moon. Its five 1.5 million-pound engines, or more accurately it's turbopumps, released more energy than one hundred and twenty hoover dams, which pales in comparison to what my eyes now gaze upon. I had thought that by now someone would have figured out a creative way to escape the Earth's gravity well, but it looks like more power had been the only available answer.

The gleaming metal of the superstructure contrasts with the matte-black vehicle, holding the taxed supplies from Earth—enough to keep a greedy colony happily stuffed. I'm too far away to see where the cargo is loaded, and with no walls to be seen, it's going to be difficult to get much closer without being spotted.

"Bookworm?" I call, my energy having fully returned.

"Yes, Mr. President." His hologram is seated on a virtual rock, the same rock from the mine. "I do hope you're not thinking of recklessly charging onto the island to forcibly board the cargo ship."

"It may have crossed my mind," I embarrassingly reply.

"Based on some rather lengthy and complicated calculations, which include weather forecasts and possible malfunctions, I predict the launch to have a 92 percent chance of occurring on time. And while aborting the launch is proportional to the amount of destruction you will cause while attempting to board, it isn't my biggest concern."

The holographic Bookworm is writing in his little notebook as he speaks to me. It's disconcerting, as there was no need for it other than to provide me comfort. Comfort for what, I don't know.

"And what is your biggest concern? That I throw this watch into the ocean because you enjoy feeding me information piecemeal?"

"Uh. Very sorry, sir. I guess the simulation software may be a little too accurate. I will adjust it, although I have been increasing my emotional programming. Hope you do not mind."

The hologram slides off the rock and bows.

"That would be the Marsian leaders finding out that you are aboard and detonating the cargo, sending you spinning off into space...forever."

"Okay, that would be unpleasant. Any other ideas?" I ask.

"The weight of the launch complex has sunk the island an average of four feet below sea level. With the plethora of crocodiles inhabiting the marsh area and the sharks surrounding that, they wouldn't expect anyone to approach from below. If you swam over, you could then scale the scaffolding and get close enough for us to ascertain the location of the cargo entrance."

"That's it? You and Boy in Lake City should be brothers," I growl back. "I'm not going into the water, so you better come up with a better plan or else I'm charging forward."

"What? Why?"

I stare at Bookworm's hologram, wanting him and his innocent question to leave me. Childish. That's how I'm acting, yet again. I take a deep breath before responding.

"I...I can't swim, and I don't like sharks," I confess.

"Really? Quite interesting, sir. Well, the water isn't that deep on this side, so it's more like wading. And the sharks can't hurt you any more than the alligators near Lake City."

Bookworm tries to rationalize his approach to an irrational being...me, with irrational fears. But, he isn't the one who has experienced two thousand pounds of bone-crushing force biting down on his leg.

"I don't care, I'm not—" I snap back.

"Oh, no!" exclaims Bookworm.

"What now?" I ask.

"They appear to be moving up the launch schedule. See the moisture plume near the fairing? That's the pressure release of the cryogenic hydrogen. You have about thirty minutes to get aboard."

Bookworm's distraught voice, even though computerized, washes over me. Not wanting to be spotted by the bots, I quickly crawl over to a larger hole in the overpass and launch myself into it without thought. I plummet thirty feet before my less-than-graceful entrance into the warm Atlantic Ocean, thankful that the overpass obstructs the large splash. I stretch out my legs, expecting to stand on the sand with my head above water. However, I keep sinking like an anchor, flailing my arms in a pathetic attempt to reverse my direction.

When my feet finally sink into the fine sand, I'm sure the water is leagues above my head and that my air supply is nearly used up. I see a concrete column to one side and half swim, half run toward it. My lungs burn, my ears ring, and my brain orders me to open my mouth, but I ignore it all as I push forward with a speed that wouldn't beat a sloth. I take a few more steps before my vision begins to fade. I know I won't die if I open my mouth, but I also may not be able to extract myself from the ocean floor.

Memories of trapping Arthuren run over me. I take a few more steps before my mouth involuntarily opens and the warm, algae-filled seawater rushes in, over my teeth, past my tongue, down my throat, and out the sides of my neck.

Out the sides of my neck?

I don't find my lungs filling with the salty fluid, I clearly am not inhaling air, and yet a small amount of oxygen is rushing through my circulatory system and reconstituting my cells and organs. I continue moving toward the column, sure that I'm experiencing some sort of underwater mirage and that if I stop, they will find my body with an eerie smile etched on my swollen face. I near the column and reach out to touch it, noticing that my watch has words flashing across it.

You have gills now, Mr. President. Just keep moving and you will be fine.

Gills?

I touch the mushy flaps on the side of my neck, both upset and elated with Bookworm's plan. I'm sure that the cargo ship isn't leaving early and that Bookworm tricked me so I would jump in the water, so I take my time walking toward the island. My steps are slow, yet I stir up so much sand that it's hard to tell if I'm traveling in the right direction. I look down at my watch and smile upon seeing a bright blue arrow pointing the way. That Bookworm is a smart one.

Correction, Bookworm *was* a smart one. Murdered before he was able to change the world. He left a backup, but nothing would be as good as the original. Nothing ever was. Although this backup copy is seeming to be more and more human-like in actions.

A large, ominous shadow overhead slowly blocks my remaining sunlight and curtails my sullen reflection. I hate sharks, and judging by the shadow, this one has to be nearly twenty feet long—enough to give me fits. I inhale deeply, trying to use the odd sensation of oxygen uptake through my temporary gills to dampen my foreboding. I look up, expecting to see the gaping jaws of a great white bearing down on me, its massive teeth desiring to be drenched with pain-gotten red paint.

My dread quickly turns to an odd gurgling chuckle as I stare upon an oversized manatee, otherwise known as a sea cow. Its paddle-like flippers and tail attached to a bloated body make the docile creature seem out of place in the ocean. However, manatees had been found to be way smarter than real cows, able to work in groups much like dolphins. As a new president, I remember renewing a protection act for the manatee, which had fallen once again on the endangered species list. After the signing, I visited Florida and swam with a couple manatees, even touching their rough skin as they swam around me.

However, those manatees were half the size of the one I am now eye-to-eye with. Strangely enough, it seems to be sizing me up, trying to determine my intentions. More shadows appear overhead, and I wonder if the grouping is called herds or something different. As I ponder what to call the gathering, they gracefully sink down to my level, encasing me within their group.

While it's a surreal experience, I don't have much time. Knowing they are harmless, I plod on, kicking up more sand as I move forward. Two of the manatees close in on me, one on each side. They press their massive bodies against me, which doesn't cause me any discomfort but does bring some concern. They could slow me enough to miss the launch, so I push them away. I have enough power even underwater that the two sea cows are propelled dozens of feet to my side. However, they rush back, faster than I thought possible, and crush me between them. I'm quickly lifted off the sandy bottom, but my worry turns to amazement as the manatees drive me in the same direction I am headed, but so much faster. The herd, as I decide I will call them now, encircles the three of us. I look down, and between the manatees I spot a field of domes like those that guarded my previous prison. I understand what's going to happen next, though I'm shocked that these creatures are able to make an intelligent, self-sacrificing decision.

Within minutes I'm in the midst of a gruesome battlefield; numerous flashes of green light turn the sea into a near opaque redness coupled with large chunks of fatty manatee flesh. We keep moving forward, none of the manatees swimming away. The manatee on my left is almost cleaved in half, but another quickly takes its place. They keep pushing me through the battlefield, the taste of iron flooding my gills and overloading my taste buds. More flashes and the manatee herd rapidly dwindles. I fear we won't make it, but then my feet brush against sand. I plant them in the sand and jump forward, leaving the water for a few seconds before I splash and tumble only a dozen feet from the beach, the waves gently lapping only a foot above my head. I'm exhausted, but not so much from the short water trip as from the entire journey. I just need a minute before stepping onto the beach.

Chapter 9

I step out of the water and onto the rocky sand, easily climbing on top of a large boulder that one of the Titung alloy beams was embedded through, my mind still assessing the actions of the manatees. They had gone beyond the documented stories of dolphins saving men lost at sea. Many manatees had sacrificed their own lives so that I would survive, but more amazing is that they seemed to have coordinated their maneuvers through the deadly maze as a tactical unit. Had the already intelligent mammals advanced even further after humankind's fall? Did nature force the rapid evolution of a highly-intelligent species, needing something to ascend to the pinnacle of the mammalian pyramid? In fact, had the manatees already built an underwater society? Maybe I'm overthinking this, and it was Boy's brother guiding them through some spiritual power he had. Once laughable, I now consider it plausible.

I'm deep in thought as I walk, not noticing the lack of oxygen in my body until it's nearly depleted. Breathing is an autonomous function, whether it be through an air duct to lungs or from gills. My gills, which hadn't disappeared when I ascended from the water, flare, reaching out for the water they had been filtering oxygen from a few short moments before. Failing, a signal shoots up to my brain, and animalistic survival mode kicks in. I open my mouth and cup my hands around my neck to shut the gills, but still no air rushes in. My mouth is no longer connected to my lungs, having been diverted when the gills appeared. Still gasping, I solidly tap Bookworm's watch. A bluish light appears, flickers, dims, shoots out a holographic image of strange letters and numbers, and then flickers again before blackness returns. I barely notice the unusual amount of heat emanating from it. It must have overloaded, performing so many functions that it's overheating.

I'm weakening fast, so I grab the massive metal beam in front of me to stave off my body's desire to collapse onto my knees. I'm helpless, and I hate being helpless. Anger rises from my belly, turning my chest and face into a battle between lines of blue oxygen deprivation and splotches of red rage. I attempt to yell out, to scream at the world, but not even a wheeze escapes my open jaws. I've been reduced to a primordial fish, mouth gulping for nonexistent water. The anger gives me strength but not reason; I slam my fist into the metal beam, but it's made of the Titung alloy and only rings out like an unharmonious dinner bell, surely ruining my secret assault on the island. Still fighting the weakness washing over my body, I sink to my knees and then fall backward, splaying across the boulder, ready to be deboned. My eyes stare at the blinding sun, while my mind still races, failing to follow the calmest thread that would tell me to roll off the rock and back into the water. This is the part of humanity that I have refused to release. While we had come from the sea, no human without oxygen would jump into water to be saved. We fear that from which we came.

A rusted worker robot, driving its wobbly wheels along one of the smaller, exterior rails stops suddenly, the clattering of metal parts in its cargo bin resisting the order. Its mesh-like face spins around and aims down at my location, scanning my oversized bulk, which, while the same shape as a human intruder, clearly is not of the appropriate size. The rust bucket rolls cautiously forward, examining me with the curiosity of a hare watching its lifelong predator slowly die, not sure just how close it could get, but too curious to spring away.

I continue to stare at it, even as a haze clouds over my eyes. I ignore the violent twitches my body makes as it fights for the last crumbs of oxygen slugging through the viscous liquid within my veins, but know that I'm soon to fall into the coma-like sleep that my demigod friends and foes took under the heavy water...no...snows of the Himalayan mountains. My rage burns out as the oxygen in my body is consumed, and that which I believe to be my consciousness is only able to focus on the pain of suffocation. I'm perpetually drowning, without the ability to welcome death.

I close my eyes and decide it's time to sleep. Someone else will have to save humankind, as I can't even save myself.

My eyelids have barely closed when my body is jolted by a large convulsion that tumbles me off the boulder and onto the rocky beach. I wheeze and inhale sharply, my lungs burning as if fire courses along their length; my heart fights to find rhythm within the song of renewed life. Instinctively, I reach up and around my neck to clamp down on gills that are no longer present. I exhale to release the poisonous vapors within me and inhale the oxygen-rich air, already feeling as if the traumatic event is a distant memory borrowed from a long-ago friend. My eyes open, and even though I have rolled off the boulder, my first sight is the rust bucket rolling away as fast as its wobbly wheels can travel.

"Bookworm," I cough out gently before remembering my anger. "Bookworm!"

"Yes, Mr. President. Very sorry about that."

The emotion riding along the words seems sincere, but that's probably the programming.

I push my hands into the warm sand; they sink deeply as I sit up. "If you're going to have my worshippers turn me into a fish, please make sure you have the decency to turn me back before I become dinner for the birds."

"I do apologize, sir. I didn't realize that the whole island had a sophisticated passive defense system. As soon as we came within range, it attacked my core ePEG programming, attempting to drive the system beyond maximum power. I was busy trying to create new lines of code to override the multitude of attacks. I barely made it out ali…you know what I mean."

The miniature Bookworm standing on top of the watch seems exhausted and almost scared. I furrow my brows.

"It was that bad?" My growl hasn't completely disappeared.

"I'm afraid so, but while you were being transformed, I was able to override the early launch signal. You now have enough time to scale the scaffolding up to that cargo door, which I remotely opened."

Bookworm's image points up to one of the matte-black shuttles.

My eyes follow the blue finger, watering against the sun's glare. I blink several times before I can make out the small door near the apex of the gargantuan shuttle. I guess I had been wrong, as Bookworm hadn't been lying about the early launch.

"Didn't I mention that I hated being confined?" I growl.

A hollow voice emanates from within the scaffolding of the island. It carries authority within its loud, arrogant depth, but lacks something human. "It seems that you have more fears than one would expect from a demigod. But then again, you are the summation of your followers' beliefs...and weaknesses."

"The Marsian Magnate," both Bookworm and I comment.

Mine is an educated guess, while Bookworm's is surely based on a rapid cross-reference of stored voice recordings. We really screwed up the element of surprise.

A four-foot-wide and six-foot-high screen flickers into existence amidst the scaffolding and floats forward to traverse the hundreds of feet between us. The image it portrays is one of an elderly man with milky blue eyes and puffy cheeks, held in place by nearly translucent skin stretched tight across his face. An old-fashioned Band-Aid loosely sits on the tip of his dough-like nose, nearly disintegrating the air of importance he conveys. A hand appears from out of site and brushes his white hair to the side as the screen nears the end of its journey. In the last few feet, the lengthwise edges fold backward while the unused pixels along the width disappear until all that is left is the ominous head of Magnate. His head shrinks and shifts to the top of the screen, a black-suited man's body filling in where it had been. A nearly translucent white cap rests over his shoulders, with the hood extending halfway up his head, surely being held on by hidden pins. Within moments a very lifelike, 3-D replication of the man stands before me, looking up in disdain, the cape flowing down to the back of his knees.

He mumbles at first, no sound emanating from his lips; then he begins to talk out loud.

"Not the most difficult assessment, I admit. But I had feared that the centuries of solitude had rotted away any deductive reasoning you had remaining after your presidency," he says with a straight face.

I stare back, not saying a word. While it's merely an ePEG reflection of the man 140 million miles away, I can still read his body language to help me during the engagement.

"I must say that I was surprised you were able to escape the confines of your prison, and if not for my desire to talk to you, we would have launched well before your arrival."

Again, he mumbles words before speaking, but I assume it's a glitch with ePET communication between two planets. Magnate walks up to me with the all the confidence of a man who can't be harmed. He looks down at my feet, rolling his eyes upward until he reaches my own eyes. Even though I tower over him, he somehow manages to look down at me.

"And why would you speak with me, Magnate? By now you've surely realized that the info Bookworm fed you was childhood stories infested with complex lies to ensure you didn't gain my secrets."

I watch the corner of his right eye twitch.

"Bookworm? Ah, yes! The poor man who died from radiation poisoning. Who died because of your actions. Was he your pet? The nickname seems to imply such."

I slap my right hand over the watch to prevent Bookworm from rebuking the man. The watch—Bookworm's knowledge—is an advantage I don't want to reveal just yet.

"Magnate—," I start, but I'm cut off.

"Magnate Palmer," he interrupts.

"Magnate. I've lived more years than I care to remember and have taken on the sharpest verbal swords humankind has to offer. Your feints, intended to put me off, will not deter me from my mission. There's only one possible way to turn me back. That being if you agree to stop your oppression of the remaining humans on Earth. They're left with so little that they are not only prevented from flourishing but are dying out. You've bastardized the whole purpose of the Marsian Colony. It was meant to allow humankind to move beyond the limitations of Earth and allow us to eventually slingshot beyond the only planet we have ever known. Considering Earth's health, it's their hope and their future. You were supposed to look to the stars with purpose, not turn back to Earth with the purpose of slavery. You're barbaric. I've seen how you readily kill those in your way and treat children like expendable pawns on a sloppy chessboard to get what you want. I see no hope of change within you, for your eyes and your words tell me that you believe you're doing the right thing. The only solution is for someone to ensure you are wiped out of existence. I can and will do it. You have two choices. Release Earth from your grip now, or live in fear until I walk through your front door and grind you into the Martian soil."

Magnate does not respond immediately. I can tell he's rolling my words, my sentences, around in his head, looking for a fault to take issue on; attempting to find a hole to stab through. There are many holes, but apparently nothing he wishes to lunge at. Instead he throws a grenade.

"And how will you accomplish your goal, if you have no way to reach me, Mr. President? You, you are not God, but rather an anomaly in the bounded laws of the universe. Yes, you are powerful, but not all-powerful. You cannot reach us without help."

Magnate takes a step back as he lifts his arms, palms up, and bows. "I will let yet you aboard the shuttle, and even let you feel the excitement of escaping the Earth's gravity well and launching into space. You will even be allowed to experience the joy of weightlessness. And your hope of murdering me will build with each closing mile. But...," a smile creases his taut skin, popping out dozens of wrinkles that beg to relax as his white cape flutters, "...somewhere along the journey, I will detonate the vehicle, sending your body hurtling into deep space. Now, you probably will not die, but you will float in space forever, having plenty of time to reflect upon your failed foolish mission."

I assess his words, which have been carefully weighed. He wants to convey that every step is his decision, not mine. That he will decide, and has decided, my fate. However, there's a flaw in his speech. Well, maybe not the speech, but the motivation behind it all—Magnate showing up threatening me...to ensure I wouldn't climb aboard the shuttle. But why? I need to hear more of his words, so I can catch what lays beneath.

I step forward, he retreats, and I step forward again. We repeat this game until I'm within the complex scaffolding. Robots dart away and a few red lights swirl to life, their waves bouncing off the varying angles of the metal and sending out a discordant visual effect, not unlike the parking garage of an inner-city triage hospital.

I bring my voice down an octave and slowly create my words from the thick air. "I don't believe you were tracking me this whole time. Remember, I'm a demigod. I have the eyes of an eagle, thanks to those flawed individuals who worship me. I saw the shocked expression on your face when you saw me, even though you quickly recovered. You're still wondering how I freed myself, but will never guess, so I will tell you. Revelation."

Magnate attempts to raise an eyebrow, but his drawn skin makes it look like a small tick. "Revelation?"

"I had imprisoned myself before burying all memory of how or why I did it. But with the help of Bookworm, my memories resurfaced." I purposely stop.

"Ah, and he helped you realize your purpose?" surmised Magnate.

"No. You killing him made me realize that I wasn't the cause of all the suffering and senseless death that surrounded me." I grow in height and width, watching Magnate's milky eyes widen. "I was created by those who are suffering, those who lost loved ones to people like you. I was created to help those in need. I was reborn to destroy you, even if I'm only doing it for revenge."

The last words are a growl, but I'm not consumed by anger. I watch Magnate as little ticks and quivers pit his face and lips, and I smile inwardly as a bead of sweat slips out from under his hairline, dropping onto his indented temple and disappearing behind his ear. In that moment I had figured out his bluff. He won't destroy the shuttle; there's something aboard that he desperately needs.

I stretch out my nine-foot frame, reach up, and grab an I-beam. I stare into his eyes, mocking him. "It's time to catch my ride."

I ignore what starts as objections and then turns into an attempt to engage me in conversation. I climb up another level before moving toward a central beam, which will make my climb easier. I hold onto it as I reach up and grab one of the smaller rails the robots have been using. I didn't realize Magnate had ceased talking until a swooshing sound catches my right ear. Both my calves are punctured by a group of three to four knife-like objects, and a grayish-clawed hand grasps my throat and squeezes. Before I have time to move, a prick in my back quickly expands until my ribs spread apart as a sharp white horn bursts through my skin right below my chest. Blood sprays out as the white horn is driven deeper into my back.

I feel the weight of the creature that is using me as a ladder and realize there's only one way to get it off me before it rips my torso in half. I let go of the beams, asking gravity to do the rest. The claws in my calves release, pain sears my chest, and the horn rapidly extracts from my chest. I land heavily on my back, with my attacker—not wanting to come between me and ground—having jumped to safety.

"Bookworm! What was that?" I gasp as I shake my head to clear the cobwebs from the forty-five-foot fall.

"I can see it, but I do not know yet, Mr. President," Bookworm replies.

Magnate speaks, with his confidence having returned in force. "While I may not have determined how to create one of you, the stories you shared with Bookworm helped me understand how to bring back a hopeless demigod."

I roll over before rising up to one knee. Standing next to Magnate's reflection is a hideous apparition that had once terrorized the children of a divided Asian country. It's slightly taller than me in stature, but its wispy gray hair flows down over an emaciated frame that is only covered by a red loincloth. Its spindly legs step forward as it lowers its head, aiming a jagged horn already dipped in my blood.

"Dokisin," I exclaim loud enough to drown out a warning from Bookworm.

"So, you have met the child killer before?" Magnate queries. "It is a most impressive specimen, the only demigod to feed off the fear of other worshippers. And I dare say, a suitable adversary for you, Mr. President."

"I remember," I growl as memories flood in. "I will never forget. And I'll do what should have been done long ago."

Chapter 10

Dokisin's creation occurred near the end of the demigod battles, a few years before the dropping of the God Bombs. The Asian country he supported was called Sangdan Bando—I forget its post-war name—which had lost two successive demigod battles and was on the brink of a social uprising. The people of the psychotic dictator refused to worship another demigod, demanding to join their southern neighbor in order to prevent economic collapse. The desperate leader acted quickly, driving his scientists to create a new kind of demigod, one that fed off the fears of others.

Attempt after attempt failed, always resulting in a being slightly more powerful than a human but many steps lower than even the weakest demigod. After each failed experiment, he ordered each one terminated, and Dokisin was no different. In fact, his ragged body came out even weaker than an average man, his ribs and spine protruding from a grayish-white skin with a tongue bitten off during the torturous event that created him.

However, Dokisin was determined not to die. He escaped and while seeking refuge found himself inside the city's main orphanage, housing thousands of abandoned children. The dictator's elite military force surrounded the building and began closing in. Knowing the end was near, the small part of humanity he still retained broke—a part close to that which drives one to survive the most desperate situations, but miles apart in the outcome. Humankind often calls it going crazy, but I think it's something more. Some barrier inside that shatters, allowing the most heinous of thoughts to pour out, unfiltered and unchallenged. He punctured his own ears with the long claws that had once been fingers. He ripped out an eye and threw it against the window, then scraped his claws along his body, blood pouring freely onto the hostages.

Once done with the self-mutilation, Dokisin turned his attention back to the world that had created him and let those evil thoughts pour over him like a hot shower on a winter's day. Unfortunately, he was in the orphanage. He walked amongst the cribs, killing caretakers and infants alike. Not only did he lack remorse and enjoy the slayings, but a surge of power also grew within him with each child he killed. However, his madness also grew with each innocent life taken. Hundreds of children were murdered by the creature. Recorders inside had been hacked and were being broadcast to the country's people. So many watched in fear, and that fear fueled his power even more.

By the time the elite force found him, they stood no chance against a new, powerful demigod. Shots punctured his body over and over again, but his smile only widened with each new hole. He impaled them on his horn or slashed their bodies in half with his ever-growing claws. After all were dead, he fearlessly limped out the front door. Yet, in front of him stood an even more fearless individual; the ruthless dictator stood tall and demanded that Dokisin kneel before him. He understood what the demigod had become and promised him not riches, not fame, but more innocent children to feed his specialized appetite.

With difficulty, due to his twisted frame, Dokisin prostrated before the leader. They set out on a reign of terror, using propaganda and embedding his name in horror stories involving children. A mythological creature that murdered children, but one that became much more than a myth. It only ended because Sangdan Bando had been on the edge of a God Bomb detonation, and the children of those neighboring countries he tormented, those who fueled his power, were also killed. Some quickly, others slowly as they had no way to survive after their parents had died from radiation poisoning. He hadn't died from the God Bomb but must have been severely weakened. Afterward, Dokisin surely wandered the world aimlessly until being enlisted by the Marsians, surviving by feeding off the fear of humans he encountered.

I had always said I needed to destroy Dokisin, but my country, my worshippers, always had more immediate needs. He now stood before me, misshapen and still holding the twisted smile and possessing a single red-glowing eye.

"Dokisin only needs to delay you for a few minutes. Just enough time for the engines and boosters to fire so the shuttle can lift off," comments Magnate, shaking me out of my memories.

Revenge, I think.

I say nothing as I take my first step toward Dokisin. My pained anger drives deeper inside me than I thought possible, drilling for the oil that will fuel it. My heart, my soul, tightens as the surge powers through them. With my next step, the creature dips its head further down and charges. I keep my walk steady, the cracking of my knuckles sounding like thunder as I clench and unclench my hands. A slobbering howl bursts from Dokisin's ridged lips as it closes, appearing as if it will meet me head on. It has lightning-like reflexes and will be ready for any sidestep I make, but I'm not going to back down…I have a plan.

Dokisin takes one more step before launching the bloody horn toward my chest, which thankfully has already healed from its last attack. I shoot out my left hand, letting its horn impale my palm. At my peak of power, the horn would have shattered on my steel-like flesh. However, that flesh is now more like softened aluminum, and while the horn slows upon impact, it still punctures through the other side of my hand. I grip the rocky ground with my toes, bend down as my muscles strain from the impact, and push forward, ignoring the pain as the increasing diameter of the horn spreads my ligaments, muscles, and bones apart.

Dokisin, momentum stopped and stuck on my hand, rakes its right claws across my face while plunging its left claws between my ribs. I feel no pain, being too focused on raising my free arm high into the air. I bring my fist down between its head and my stuck hand, breaking off the horn as I spin in a complete circle and thrust the newfound weapon deep into its chest. I hammer it even deeper with my free hand as I stare into its eye.

No blood flows from the wound, but it convulses with pain. I extract my hand from the horn and wrap both hands around Dokisin's neck, squeezing with every ounce of strength I possess. Its hands and feet flail, raking my skin, as the bones in its neck crush under my power. I then grab one of its wraith-like arms and tear it off before tossing it into the ocean. I repeat the ghastly act three more times until it's just a torso and pained head, limply flopping on the ground.

I feel no regret for my actions, even with my anger being exhausted, and the sadness for the past loss of innocent lives returns. I look over at the shocked magnate.

"Dokisin isn't dead, but it will take long enough for the baby killer to recover. I strongly advise you not to use him against humankind, else the dismemberment you witnessed will become your own. I'll start with your fingers and toes, then your nose and ears. Don't get me wrong. You'll die either way, but I recommend the quick out. That's the one where I walk up to you and pop off your head."

"You horrific barbarian," he responds, without any show of fear.

I turn, kick Dokisin's torso hard enough to propel it into the water, and renew my ascent. It's quite easy to grab beams, jump levels, and scale vertical fixtures with the power I possess. It's as easy as a monkey climbing a tree. Within minutes I'm next to the open hatch, and my physical wounds are no longer visible. I reach out, grab the thick door, and then swing inside.

"Wait!" Bookworm yelps.

He'd been silent since I covered the watch the first time I'd seen Magnate. Too late. I assumed the hatch was like a door to a house, with the floor less than a foot below. Instead, I bounce off a large metal crate attached to the wall and fall nearly thirty feet before landing on a cargo net.

"Think I'd learn to be less impulsive," I state to Bookworm, trying to untangle my arms and legs.

"Sometimes impulsiveness is a good thing."

I know he's referring to what I did to Dokisin. Was he worried I'd feel guilty? He's being supportive; another human trait he shouldn't possess.

The hatch shuts, and locks push into their fittings.

"Where do I need to be for the launch?" I ask, feeling as if I'm on a hammock. The slight rocking motion is relaxing, and I'd like nothing better than to sleep after fighting Dokisin. I flex my hand, appreciating how fast my worshippers have healed it.

"It does not matter. Prior to liftoff, the entire fairing will fill with an expanding polyurethane foam. It not only prevents the cargo from shifting, but it also dampens vibrational loads between the shuttle and the cargo, averting a number potential catastrophic events."

I raise an eyebrow as I speak to the diminutive image. "That would seem to be very uncomfortable, especially for months on end."

"Judging by your reaction during the gills incident on the boulder, I predict that you will be more concerned about not having any oxygen during the entire journey," he replies, back to the usual matter-of-fact tone.

"Thanks for reminding me."

"Sorry. I only bring it up because of your reaction and that of other demigods within your stories. However, it does not make sense," says Bookworm.

I close my eyes and inhale deeply, savoring the air. "Why?"

"Well, you are impervious to many forms of damage, can heal from the most horrific of injuries, and seem unable to die. Yet, the lack of oxygen quickly incapacitates you. It is odd."

"While we're demigods, we all started as humans and thus still have some of the same needs in spite of our elevated status."

"But, Mr. President," starts Bookworm, which means he is preparing to offend me. "You survived hundreds of years without food, another fundamental sustenance. Why one and not the other?"

I inhale again, but the air doesn't smell as sweet. "You have a theory?"

"No, a hypothesis. A theory is based upon a preponderance of evidence. I have yet to conduct even a single test. I propose that it is because you—."

I growl loudly, stopping Bookworm from completing his words. "How much time before liftoff?" I ask.

"Four minutes and twenty-three seconds. Oh, and there is one thing we need to discuss before then."

"I thought you got my hint that I didn't want to talk about it," I growl again.

"No, not that. However, it is something related. In space, there is no air and thus sound has no medium with which to traverse. You and I will not be able to communicate through our normal means. I can send messages on the watch's display and even create a small shock on your wrist when I wish to discuss things of immediate importance. I can project a keyboard for you to use, but—."

"If the keyboard is just a hologram, that won't work," I interrupt.

"Actually, it is not a hologram, sir. Before World War III, a Korean Confederation physicist figured out how to embed a stopping wave within coherent light, such as a laser, that could rapidly dissipate it at a predetermined distance. This was advanced by a JapIno Nation's physical chemist who built clustered microlasers in combination with integrated sensors, which rapidly overtook the hologram market, not only because it was contained in a single device but also because of the ability to obtain instant feedback with movement."

Yet again, I catch most of what Bookworm says, but don't have enough understanding to challenge it.

"Hmm," I reply.

"With this invention, police and military drivers went away from the QWERTY keyboard and moved to the SHiP lasense system. Mainly because one could drive with one hand and rapidly type with the other. It disappeared quickly with advanced voice recognition software, but was still used in many situations where one did not want to be heard."

"How does it work?"

"Mr. President, it is easier if I take you through the steps. We'll skip the characters and focus on the concept," replies Bookworm. "Triple clutch your watch hand to activate the keyboard."

Blue lights shoot forth from the watch, creating a mesh-like pattern around my hand. "First, hold your watch hand out as if you were going to type on a computer keyboard. Perfect. That is the first plane, with your four fingers always being used for entering characters and your thumb for switching between three sets of characters. In this first plane, the four characters are alphabetic. Press down your thumb once for the next set, twice for the third and three times to return to the first screen."

"Sounds simple enough. That gives me twelve characters. How do I get the rest?" I ask.

"From the first plane, you have five options. The first is to quickly clench your fist, which brings up the second alphabetical set. Repeat the previous actions with your thumb to scroll through the next twelve. Quickly clenching your fist twice brings you to the last two letters of the alphabet plus caps lock, shift, delete, insert, etcetera."

"Still simple enough," I reply as I practice flipping between the screens.

"Twisting your wrist to the right will enable the numeric keypad, while twisting your wrist to the left will bring up the first set of special characters. Pulling back is the spacebar option and pushing forward is the return key. Pulling back while clenching your fist turns off the keyboard, and pushing forward while clenching moves you into the drawing option. There are another two dozen sets of specialty movements that provide over three hundred thousand options."

"Uh huh," I say, still working on the twisting motions, and clearly not listening anymore.

"You will have plenty of time on the trip to master them all, sir."

I pause and look down at the mini-Bookworm, who is standing above the blue mesh. "I think we both know I might not remain conscious during the journey." My voice was deep, strained.

A valve opens somewhere below the netting I'm still resting on.

"Sorry, sir. I think we should talk about why the lack of oxygen incapacitates demigods," suggests Bookworm.

"No," I reply.

Nozzles throughout the payload bay sputter before spraying out a yellow liquid. Water-size droplets, reminiscent of the soap from an old-style car wash, begin to cover the containers, walls, and cargo webbing within the bay.

"It is the vibration-damping foam. You should close your mouth and eyes, and cover your nose and ears. Also, do not try to clear the foam until it has set, or else it will just keep filling back in."

It takes me a few seconds to figure out how to accomplish such a task. Ultimately, I hold my head like one would set a volleyball, with my thumbs pinching my nose and my middle fingers in my ears.

An uneven coating of the sticky material covers my body, the earliest of the spray already foaming up, stretching my skin as it expands. It continues to expand outward, while rapidly rising from the base of the bay. The pressure as it rides up my chest is very minor, but my skin itches like crazy as it pulls and tugs my hairs. I take one final breath, failing to keep the thought out of my head that it will probably be my last until I reach the Marsian colony. I realize then that I forgot to ask Bookworm how I'll be transferred from the Moon base to the Marsian colony.

The foam continues to expand, creeping behind my ears, between my fingers, and spreading my toes apart. Soon I'm immobile, and I wriggle just to see what will happen. It's a strange feeling as I'm on a hammock, but then the foam dampens the movement and I'm soon completely still. My sight is gone and the outside sounds are merely muffled thumps against the hull of the bay. I hear the flow of liquids pumping through pipes and know that the engines will soon be starting up. I pull my fingers out of my ears and push my hands through the set foam, clearing my face. I open my eyes to the same sight I had experienced when they were closed, pitch darkness. I inhale deeply, but only receive a fraction of the oxygen I need. It's humid and hot from the curing of the foam. I breathe again, shallower, reminded of a combination of the few minutes I stood on the top of Mt. Everest as a young man and my time in the pits of the coal mine.

Another inhale, and a little more oxygen seeps through the open pores of the polymer, but not enough to fill my lungs and replenish that which was depleted while rounding my circulatory system. My heart speeds up and my breathing turns into short, quick gasps. Panic is setting in, against my will. I try to calm my body, breathing slower and slower.

The sound of muffled thunder fills my ears, followed by a sledgehammer hitting my back and a shockwave riding up the cargo bay. Liftoff begins as the powerful solid rocket boosters fight to drag the rocket out of the Earth's gravity well. The dampening foam works, as everything stabilizes inside to the point that I'm able to focus all of my attention on the decreasing oxygen supply. Perspiration covers my entire body, drenching the thick shorts that somehow always fit, no matter my size. Seconds crawl forward as we scale the Earth's atmosphere, the boosters combining with the main rocket engines to propel us even faster toward outer space.

"Bookworm!" I burst out, gasping from the one word.

"Yes, Mr. President?"

"What...did...you...want...to..." The five words drain me, and I can't finish my sentence.

Mini-explosions boom outside and below me, the solid rocket booster attachment lugs exploding from specialized shape charges that cut them in half and propel the spent casings cleanly away from the launch vehicle.

"Discuss? Well, it is about all of you demigods. Why do you cling to the biggest weaknesses of your human side?" The words start loud enough, but lessen as the engines propel us into the upper atmosphere.

My eyes droop and my body twitches as a drunken stupor clouds my thoughts. Soon the oxygen is virtually nonexistent. I writhe from the pain and beg for the return of the depleted oxygen. I fight the desire to sleep, fight to keep in control, to understand the meaning behind the words Bookworm has started. Each one was easy to hear, but piecing them together is difficult; a complex puzzle jumbled in my mind. I bring up my hand to rub my face, but it only reaches my chest before I give up. Fatigue washes over my body as my lungs still fight for oxygen.

Weightlessness arrives, but I'm already absent, floating into a dream state. The pain seeps away as I fall further and further into unconsciousness.

Dreams.

I hadn't dreamt since I became a demigod, as was the case with all the demigods. Even during my centuries holed up within the mine shaft, I hadn't dreamed. Many psychologists hypothesized that it was because of the bond with our worshippers. There were too many dreams pushing into our minds from them, so our brains just shut all of them out. Sleep studies on demigods showed brain activity but nothing approaching a dream-like state. I believe it's because it's the only time we are free from the thoughts of our worshippers; a time to be left alone.

However, during the three days it takes to get to the Moon, dreams fall in and out of my mind like fall leaves dropping onto a pond's surface before sinking. Dreams as a young boy on my aunt's farm, being chased by angry geese who are protecting their goslings. It seems more like a memory until the geese, with their long necks, transform into sea serpents, wrapping around me in the choppy Pacific Ocean. They drag me under the waves, trying to steal my life, but I refuse to drown. Like the stories of Gilgamesh, I bend their bodies around and upon themselves until they're now nothing more than floating knots of a large rope. Dreams of returning to high school even though I had already graduated from college, confused as to why time was linear for everyone except me. They're twisted dreams that hold enough reality for me to believe they're happening, with plenty of horrifying parts added in to fuel my fears.

I wake up once during the trip, my eyes snapping open as I realize I can't breathe. I flail my arms and arch my back, grasping for the absent oxygen, before I remember where I am and where I'm going. My energy leaves me and I settle back into unconsciousness.

I dream...and I remember.

The God Bomb had resulted in a nuclear war, accelerating my fall from grace...and my disgust with what I had caused. At the time, I had been confined to my apartment in Entara, although even the guards knew they were only window dressing, which could be easily spread apart if I wanted to open the windows. But I didn't want to, and I just sat on my oversized chair, watching newscast after newscast of what was happening to the world—wanting to know what was happening, but from a distance.

I was watching a piece about developing countries and experts predicting what new demigods would spring forth when the display froze, turned black, and flicked back on, showing two bewildered news anchors trying to grasp what they had been told to report. Dozens of downloaded images phased in and out, showing the real-time destruction over Asia. Clouds of gray dust covering the megacities, hiding the tens—maybe even hundreds—of millions of bodies whose souls had been wiped away. A retired military colonel excitedly popped onto the screen, explaining the secret God Bomb program he had helped manage and how he believed it to be the only explanation. He began to explain what would happen next with hard-hitting military jargon. I muted him.

I already knew what it meant. It didn't take a genius to figure it out.

I rose and walked to the door of my apartment. When I opened it, the guards were gone. I pressed the elevator button for over a minute, with the digital readouts for all fourteen elevators never coming close to the ninetieth floor I lived on. I could hear people screaming as they rushed down the stairwells, some encouraging friends and family while others cried for help. Entara's emergency sirens began to blare, bouncing off the façades of the superscrapers.

The window wasn't far away, so I grudgingly walked the few steps to get there before ripping the metal frame inward. The heavy alumina-glass crumpled and bent upon itself. Even though I knew it was hopeless for the millions stampeding below, I didn't want to hurt any of them. I searched amongst the crowded streets for a safe landing spot, ascertaining that the white top of an empty yellow school bus was my best option. I sighed and jumped, not caring how I landed. It would hurt just as bad—and no worse—no matter what part of my body impacted the bus first. The freefall would've been exhilarating if I hadn't known what was coming, if the end of our civilization wasn't imminent. The wind howled by me, whistling in my ears, as I made minor adjustments to guide my fall. I closed my eyes right before impact, the sounds of metal groaning and glass bursting outward were nearly lost under the tidal wave of terror emanating from the masses in the streets.

It took a while to rip away the bent metal that surrounded me. When I climbed out, some saw me and begged for my protection, but I had nothing to offer. Most stared at the bright lights in the sky from the reentry vehicles plummeting toward Entara, hopeful that they would somehow be stopped. I stared at the sky with them, hoping it would be my end.

The Americas defense system destroyed hundreds of nuclear warheads in their ascent phase, and nearly a hundred more in the descent phase. However, a couple dozen got through. Los Angeles, San Diego, and San

Francisco were hit first, followed by Denver, Kansas City, and then New York and Miami. Chicago and Detroit took a couple each. With my eagle eyes, I saw a few of the nuclear warheads headed my way destroyed and held some hope that the people in this great city might be spared. But when three of the warheads descended between the tips of Entara's largest superscrapers, I let my pain and my tears flow. It was short-lived, as the heat of the explosion and radiation rippled over my body. The physical pain was like nothing I had ever experienced before, as flesh and bone were peeled away almost faster than I could heal. I didn't scream, soaking in the pain I deserved.

It continued for several minutes, my mind trying to grasp a reference and only finding being dipped in lava as suitable. When it ended I stood alone amongst the fires, collapsing buildings, and what remained of the dead. The pain from the loss was so much...was too much. My nerves were on fire from the lingering radiation, but my mind was numb. I walked like a zombie through the lifeless streets for hours until I was on the outskirts of Entara, ignoring both pained calls for help and angry verbal lashings.

I kept walking, exiting the city's south side, only shifting my course when a body of water blocked my path. Uncaring, I fell off hills and cliffs, hopelessly hoping they would end it all. But I always healed in minutes, not comprehending why some still worshipped me, rising back up to continue my pointless journey. Sometimes I went through small towns, my eyes lowered as I didn't want to see the radiation bubbles littering the surface of dying souls.

After a week, I happened upon an abandoned mine shaft, not realizing until that moment that I was back upon my own property. I wanted to rest with my family. I sized it up after a thought drove through my fog of depression. The surface of the world was sick, and I needed to be rid of it. However, I was nine feet tall and too wide to fit down the shaft. I used a trick a demigod friend of mine had taught me that would temporarily shrink my body down in size. It involved self-humiliation and was easy to execute in my current state. When completed, I was the size of a normal, beaten-down man. I leaned over the mine and fell in, tumbling awkwardly down the shaft. I bounced heavily off the walls, steadily increasing the number of rocks that followed my descent.

I kept falling, waiting for the impact with every passing second so that when it finally came, I was surprised. My shoulder buckled and cracked as it shattered the ground at the bottom of the mine shaft. My neck snapped, and my spine twisted so far back that my feet smacked the back of my head. I lay there, happy to be feeling the pain—to feel anything—as the rocks I had broken free during my fall pelted my body. Unmoving for days, not caring, not wanting to live, but not able to die.

When I finally raised myself, I walked blindly into the cavern and stumbled upon a chair. The chair that would be my comfort during my exile. I grabbed the massive shackles that were spread across the ground and clamped them onto my body before sitting down on the chair and drifting off to sleep.

I didn't deserve to forget the pain, to forget the fear, forget what it was like to be human. As a demigod I had risen to the highest levels of power, sworn to protect my worshippers and all others who needed help. But I had forgotten where I came from and what I was born to do. I had lost my humanity and I wanted it back.

However, my time as a human had long since passed, no matter how desperately I clung to it. While my mind knew it, it would take over two hundred years for me to embrace it. Two hundred years because I chose to forget.

Chapter 11

I slowly open my eyes, finding myself still in pitch darkness. My body floats gently around the cargo hold, as the foam apparently dissolved some time ago. My lungs are unmoving, but their painful need to expand out, to fill with life-sustaining breath is absent. Along the way my circulatory system was frozen, a signal of death for humans but not for me. I stop myself from thinking too much and revel in the fact that I'm in zero gravity. I'm weightless; the weight of the world is no longer on my shoulders. I softly bounce off a container, laughing inside as my body tries to figure which way is up. It's a fruitless activity, just like how I'd tried to hold onto human traits throughout my demigod life. I had been caught up in the individual roller coaster of my life, instead of viewing the world through a bigger lens like corporate executives, although they were often accused of being heartless.

I reach out and tap Bookworm's watch with my right hand. The screen lights up with mini-Bookworm standing on top of the watch face.

Hello, Mr. President. The bold words appear on the screen above the image. There is a pause as his head tilts sideways and stares at my face. **You no longer need oxygen?**

I clench my fist three times and the SHiP keyboard appears in classic green lighting. Like a toddler speaking, I fumble for words. **No. I don-t. I no longr need .**

I have to acknowledge that I did not expect you to figure this out and adapt so quickly. I am impressed, sir. Willpower is an amazing thing when coupled with self-reflection.

I want to ask if he was impressed because of how long it took me to accept other things, but my lack of expertise with the SHiP keyboard leads me to just one word.

Tanks. I meant thanks.

Sarcasm? Bookworm asks.

I ignore the question and decide to press with a question, even though it takes me a while to type it out.

Wher exactly are we? I'm somewhat of a perfectionist when it comes to spelling, and am already annoyed at my own words.

We just landed on the Moon. The jolt from docking with the transfer station is probably what woke you up. According to the station's antiquated system, it will take approximately thirty-two hours to reconfigure the cargo fairing on the launch propulsion bus for interplanetary travel. The interplanetary propulsion system is fueled by a nuclear-powered core, surrounded by an annulus containing two hundred ePEGs. It will sling us into an orbit around the center of mass of the Moon and Earth, which will intersect with Mars's orbit in approximately thirty-one days.

Bookworm provides more information than I need, but I assume it's to help minimize my fumbling with the SHiP keyboard. Of course, he always volunteers more information than I ask for, but this time he piques my curiosity.

Thirty..one days? That is muc less than i remember.

Yes, Mr. President. During the early years of Marsian colonization, we used electric propulsion for our launch vehicles and had to conserve fuel, forcing us to use intersecting orbits that required more time. However, with the nuclear and ePEG propulsion this vehicle surprisingly has, we can continuously accelerate for the first half of the journey and then reverse our thrusters to slow down during the second half. This makes for a much quicker trip.

How much time til we leave?

Thirsty-two hours, sir, Bookworm replies.

Can you open one of the hatch doors?

Yes, but it is unwise to leave, Mr. President.

? I ask, already tiring of this form of communication.

The hands of the mini-Bookworm raise in frustration, right before crossing his arms.

For a number of reasons. First, we are on the Moon, and if you do not get back in time, we will be stranded here for several months, possibly failing in our mission. Second, the station no longer has any human inhabitants and could be hazardous. Third, the Moon's gravity is one-sixth the gravity of Earth. With your strength, you could accidentally launch yourself into outer space, and there would be no way to recover from such a mistake.

I give an airless chuckle. I'm sure it doesn't look anything like what I imagine.

Open the hatch, I demand.

Yes, Master, Bookworm replies, displaying his anger by spinning around and pretending to walk hunched over like Quasimodo, a large hump appearing on the right side of his upper back.

I shrug my shoulders as I try to chuckle again. It's funny to see this computerized image conveying human emotions. But then I stop as I realize I had been doing the same thing for so long. The only difference was that I had done it to ensure I maintained my human half, while mini-Bookworm was programmed to do it in order to aide in communication. At least I thought it was programmed in. However, it did seem to be developing realistic human emotions.

I can't hear the hatch open, but the bright light breaks into the bay with the power of a nuclear explosion. Nearly blinded, I twist, floating and bumping my way to the opening. I climb out of the hatch as my eyes adjust, expecting to see the sun only because I hadn't learned anything about the Moon station. Instead, I find myself in a half dome nearly four hundred feet in radius, yet only six stories tall. Small ePEG lights dot the girders supporting the structure. Only about a third still work, casting a dim lighting to the area, which seems much brighter after being confined to complete darkness for so many days. The girders hold up thirty-foot-long transparent sheets of what must be metallic glass, used in space due its ability to quickly self-heal when a small electric current is applied.

However, large punctures, small holes, and long cracks could be seen on almost every worn panel, indicating that there was no atmosphere within the dome. I fall the twenty feet to the metal floor, landing softly in the reduced gravity. Spinning around, I can see five rails that run outward in a star-like pattern, each continuing past the dome and through an open bay door, ending at an exterior landing pad. One leads to the space shuttle from our arrival, with the cargo module having already been removed and pulled inside the dome for reconfiguration. A fine, grayish dust covers everything, making me feel like I'm in a grayscale painting. I ignore the mini-bots removing the payload bus from the capsule I had been in and take a few steps forward.

By the third step, I realize that I hadn't been compensating for the change in gravity and find myself leaning so far forward that I've no choice but to fall. My nose bounces off the railing, and only with the added pain do I realize it's extremely cold. When I skid to a stop, I triple clutch my left hand, activating the watch's keyboard.

How could is it? I type, not bothering to correct my misspelling.

A much-calmer appearing Bookworm looks up at me. **It is minus one hundred forty-one degrees, sir.**

So now I don't need to breathe and can't feel the temperature unless I focus on it. Am I becoming something more than a demigod? What would that be? I stop this line of thought as I know I'm not a God.

I rise a little too strongly and find myself about ten feet above the railing before floating back down. With the next effort, I slowly stand and carefully walk the couple hundred feet to an open bay door. When I 'm close, the watch zaps me.

You are in for a treat, Mr. President. There is a full Earth right now. With Earth appearing four times as big as the Moon and over eighty times brighter, it will be an amazing sight.

A colored image of what I will see appears above the watch. I push my arm forward and type. **Thanks for ruining it.**

I **do not think I did.**

I catch the sight of the bluish-gray glow of the lunar landscape outside the bay. It's an eerie site, worth its own perusal, but I'm more excited to see the Earth. I pull myself outside and stop. The image in my mind is one taken by a lunar explorer when I was in office. Part of me expects that I will see the deep-blue oceans clashing with the brown wastelands from the nuclear war. However, not only are there no decaying brown areas, but the view is even more stunning than the high-resolution picture I had in my mind. The clouds are pure-white wisps, covering both the vast green lands and large blue oceans. The polar caps look more massive than ever and…and by happenstance, I am looking at The Americas.

I ignore the zap from my wrist and sit down on the glowing dust, looking upon the land that I fought so hard to create and protect. Looking at a land that is doing much better without a demigod's guidance. I stare; no other thoughts enter my mind for what seems like minutes, but I would later realize was hours. When I finally glance down to acknowledge the continuous zapping, I see a smiling Bookworm with a comic-book caption above his head.

I did not spoil it, did I, sir?

I nod my head to acknowledge that he's right. I type carefully. **It didn't need our help. It just needed there to be fewer humans.**

Bookworm nods in affirmation. **Is it time to go back inside the cargo bay, Mr. President?**

No. I want to see if there are clues for why the Marsian colony took control of Earth. Maybe we'll find something in the station that we can leverage when dealing with Magnate.

I take one last look at Earth before heading back to the Moon base, bothered by something I can't quite grasp. Of course, I'm always bothered by something.

The magnificence of the Moon, the radiant surface, and longing Earth fade into gray with every step that takes me deeper into the Moon base. The dome is the only part of the base above the Moon's surface, making my walk an eerie one.

How far down does the base go, Bookworm? I query.

When the Conglomeration of Russian Territories, or CORT, began to build their transport base on the Moon, they discovered that depressurization cracks where not only inevitable but also costly. They lost hundreds of lives before deciding to tunnel into the Moon. The pace and art of their tunneling was so impressive that The Americas struck a deal with CORT; our technology for surface building in exchange for their tunneling technology. It began a prosperous exchange between the Marsian and Moon colonies, but—.

Bookworm, I know all that. It was right before the God Bombs. What happened after that? I type methodically.

Strange. All records have been erased.

Erased records are a clue.

I enter a forty-foot-diameter room with a hatch covering almost the entire opposite wall.

Anything on this hatch, Bookworm?

Yes, Mr. President. It is the main hatch to the base. On the other side is the inspection room, where incoming shipments and people were itemized before distribution to the lower levels.

Lower levels? How many levels? I'm getting the hang of the keyboard.

Sixteen. At least, that is how many schematics I have available.

Bookworm's hologram, or whatever it is, doubles in size—a neat trick. Sir, we do not have time to search through even one level. In fact, we do not even know what to look for. In addition, I cannot tell whether the other side of the hatch is pressurized. If it is and you open it, we will not make it to Mars unless you are blown off the surface in the correct direction.

I'm strong enough to hold onto the hatch during depressurization, Bookworm.

I grab one of the six spokes surrounding the circular lock and push down. It doesn't move. I ignore another zap on the wrist from Bookworm, place my other hand on another spoke, and bear down. It's strange not to grunt and release some air as I strain to open the door, but this is my new life. The muscles in my arms pop, and veins in my shoulders and neck bulge outward with the effort. The metal spokes bend with the increasing force I apply, but I refuse to stop. They slowly bend even more, nearly reaching a forty-five-degree angle when finally, something inside the frame snaps, and the vibrations run through my hands. Freed, I turn the latch a full three revolutions before it stops. I want to say something sarcastic to Bookworm, but that would mean I'd have to stop and type. Instead, I pull on the door. A mixture of relief and confusion fills me as the seal is broken without blowing me and the hatch into the wall. I open it wide enough to squeeze through and then step inside. I fear very little.

The rectangular room is twice the size of the one I stood in and is like an empty tomb. Nothing stands between me and the open, smaller door on the right. To the left is what looks like a control room, with its large windows covered in a thin film of lunar dust. In fact, the whole room is covered in it.

I type without looking, still surveying the room. **Bookworm, this appear strange to you also?**

Yes, Mr. President. If there had been rapid decompression, the main hatch would have been left in the open position. If they had run out of air or abandoned the base, then no lunar dust could have gotten in.

Bookworm displays a puzzled expression.

Exactly, I reply.

I walk over to the window and wipe the glass with one of my massive paws. The lunar dust clears on my side, but the other side is also coated. Not finding a door, I push my hand through the metallic glass sheet and crumple it enough so I can look inside. I poke my head in and am greeted by two grotesquely mummified bodies. I pull my head back.

Slow decompression? I type.

It would appear so, sir.

I have a feeling we're going to see the same thing throughout the base, Bookworm.

Why is that?

I ignore the question, not wanting to get into a debate about the reality of a sixth sense, and walk through the open door.

Dread.

****

Slightly more than two hours later, Bookworm and I exit the main hatch, and I thoughtfully reseal the tomb. Every corner led to another room; led to another gathering of slowly decompressed bodies. Large ones, fat ones, huddled ones, lying down ones, praying ones, children...

Children upon children, all held tightly by their parents, as always happened throughout humankind's history when hope was being wiped away.

Sir?

Yes.

Are we reboarding? Bookworm asks.

Not yet.

I walk back up to the dome and circle the inner structure once, knowing there has to be one more clue but not knowing what it is. Walking each rail out of the dome provides no more help, as they all end abruptly. Well, all except for the one we landed on. It was built specifically for the shuttle that would arrive from Earth. Once landing was complete, the cargo bay was brought inside while the robot worked to prepare the shuttle for interplanetary travel.

Bookworm? I type, as I make my way back to the docking station.

Yes, Mr. President.

You mentioned that the Moon colony served as a conduit between Mars and Earth, but the docking station would be different than the one we landed on, right?

Correct, sir. I cannot believe I missed that! Bookworm exclaims, or at least the words above the mini-Bookworm end with an exclamation point.

132

I pause as I climb into the hatch. **I'm betting that the air handling system was purposely and permanently destroyed by the people who lived on the Moon colony.**

Bookworm interfaces with the base's computer system, shutting the bay door. **I see where you are headed with this, sir. You think an entire base of people would commit suicide to prevent the Marsian colony from taking over them and Earth?**

Maybe, but why couldn't they get to Earth without going through here?

The piece of the puzzle was falling into place, but it wasn't fitting perfectly...yet.

Sir, they could construct a two-stage vehicle, orbit the Earth before separating the second stage, and enter the Earth's atmosphere. The first stage could then travel back to Mars for a new second stage. While it would require a large amount of resources, the Marsian colony has the technological capability, and many of the required materials they had already obtained from Earth. However, they would be manpower limited, as the colony had a maximum capacity of ten thousand people. Accounting for the fact that approximately only ten percent of the workforce could be assigned to such a project without harming self-sustainment, it would take more than a decade to build each system, and then they would only be able to do it a few times before requiring more of Earth's resources.

They needed Earth's resources for something critical and massive, or else they would have blown us up on the launch pad. But it was not for a hostile takeover, or else over the last one hundred and fifty years they should have been able to develop a reliable way to travel back and forth to Earth.

The puzzle piece falls off the table when Bookworm finishes his monologue.

Bookworm's image pauses for a few seconds. **I ran through all possible scenarios, and only two came up as even remotely possible.**

The first is that they believed they could slow down the assault long enough to allow Earth time to prepare.

And the second? I ask.

Bookworm shook his head before the words appear. **They were so afraid of something that they chose death over having their fears become reality.**

The puzzle piece was back on the table. **It's the latter, Bookworm.**

How do you know, Mr. President? What did I miss?

A hunch, I reply.

A noted psychologist stated that hunches are only accurate when based on human interactions, most notably from nonverbal communication. I can only assume that your hunch came from how the humans on the Moon colony behaved before dying, which was displayed in the positions of the dead. Is that how you also knew Magnate would not blow up the launch vehicle? asks Bookworm.

Sure, I reply. Until Bookworm's insight, I thought it was a special sixth sense of mine. His explanation did seem more logical.

We have approximately eleven hours until we take off, sir. Did you want me to do anything?

No, I'm good. I just need time to think.

No, wait. While the SHiP keyboard is working fine, I wonder what happens if my hands are busy and I need to communicate with Bookworm. I don't want to do it, but if I'm going to save humankind then…I need to trust him. Correction. If we are going to save humankind. **5a62power$long2345S6!Save**, I type.

What is that? asks Bookworm.

The back-door code to my god device. It also has an ePET, and I know we'll need it if we hope to save Earth.

My shoulders sink. I have never given the code to anyone.

But sir, that will allow me access beyond mere communication.

I close my eyes…and dream again, reliving a moment I had thought forgotten. Images of death and destruction by my hands close in, and my body jerks in response.

Chapter 12

I sat in the Presidential suite, alone, looking over the plans that my military cabinet had presented me on our stalemate with a small country, which held a dozen of my top officials. Kidnapped during peace talks, they had already killed my Secretary of State and promised to torture and behead a hostage each day until their demands were met. Or until no one was left. They pushed their plans over the Internet like a virus, successfully urging millions upon millions of people to challenge our stance on not succumbing to their demands. They were savvy, sending a private and more horrifying message to me. Once all of my officials were deceased, they would start killing the children and women of their own country. It would be a massive genocide, with the blame to be placed squarely on me and my country. A simple yet effective plan.

Fear.

The primal instinct that triggers fight or flight can also freeze one in space or drive an entire group, an entire nation, into hopelessness. Such fear allows the few to control, oppress, and rule over millions. It was allowing a small group to freeze the president of the most powerful nation on Earth. I feared the death of my friends, the public outcry no matter which direction I chose, and the current and future loss of lives by this radical regime.

Fear, not strategy, had made me waver in sending in a military strike until it was too late. Too late to prevent Ron Stalwart's head from being detached from his body, his eyes wide and mouth twitching, failing to form the words for what he was feeling during his last few seconds of life. I replayed the video dozens of times, until each movement was imprinted further than just in my mind; it was attached to my soul.

I looked over the documents on my table again before sitting down and encasing my face with my hands. I had finally decided my course of action, and it was one that would dramatically change the course of humankind…if I succeeded.

A strong, evenly-spaced series of knocks passed through the wood of my office door. I directed my unsteady hand to the smooth button under my desk and depressed it. As the door opened, my Chief of Staff strutted into the room, displaying as much respect as he could muster for a man he had never seen eye-to-eye with. He walked up to the desk and opened his mouth just as my hand raised for him to stop. I looked past the overdecorated uniform, the stern face, gray mustache, and creased lines of his tanned skin, and stared into his eyes. I had always seen resolve in those eyes, but for the first time I delved further into them, feeling the storied hatred he possessed for me built from a stairway of decisions that always went against his recommendations. Today would be no different.

"General," I said as I stood, stretching my frame to its full height so that he was forced to look up. "I have made my decision, and we will not send our soldiers in for a rescue mission. The regime's location makes it impossible to enter without being noticed. I believe they will kill the hostages before we have a chance to get close. Also, while we could take out a significant portion of their leadership with a single bunker buster, we would also kill our own. I will not authorize that."

He let out a steady sigh as neither of us lowered our gaze. His deep voice captured and commanded the air. "They are not stupid, sir. They will start to disperse after they realize you won't meet their demands and that you don't care about the lives of the hostages."

I ignored the last words, as they were said in anger.

My words came out as if I were chopping vegetables: crisp and exacting. "I've made my decision, General."

He finally looked down as he spoke. "Very well, I'll inform your cabinet and media relations."

"No!" It was my turn to look down. "I've decided to move out on the Alpha project. Please have the medical team prepped and ready in one hour…in my plane. Not the touring one, but the one with the rapid-escape module."

"A plane, Mr. President?" He took a step back. "They can't do brain surgery while flying."

"Agreed. As soon as the procedure is done, the plane will take off and head to the hostage location." My decision verbalized, the shackles of fear unbound.

"You'll need time to stabilize after the surgery, Mr. President. In addition, the changes in pressure on a plane could result in your death." His warning came with less conviction than I had hoped.

"If this is successful and works like they've told me, I won't have to worry. However, if it doesn't, then you are authorized to execute your plan." I waited for a smugness to overtake his face, but none came.

"You may not believe it, but your death would not bring me joy, Mr. President. The Americas can ill afford to lose one of their greatest public leaders." He stood at attention, weighing his next words. "It's a stupid action, sir."

I held in my shock from his lack of joy, and sternly replied, "That will be all, General!"

After he left, I placed all my personal belongings except my phone on the table before leaving through a side door. I told my aide the plan and ensured she would execute each step at carefully timed moments. Once done I took a shower, shaved my head—which felt even odder than it looked—and put on a pair of very loose khaki shorts and a plain white T-shirt. Barefoot, something new and quite enjoyable to me, I walked to my waiting underground limo and was driven to the plane. Ensuring I was alone in the backseat, I recorded a video, wondering if it would be my last. As I boarded the plane, I handed the phone to my aide, only then noticing that the gaggle of doctors and nurses looked more nervous than me. None of them wanted to be known as the one who killed the President.

"Relax, it's only brain surgery," I commented, enjoying the forced chuckles my words produced. "Now, I wouldn't worry about the sterility of the room or anything else for that matter. It will work, and then I won't have to fear infections."

They all nodded as if my words made sense. It had to be the title, as I had no clue what to expect after the surgery.

The lead physician, a thin, beak-nosed man, stepped forward as I spread myself comfortably on a table that had replaced a few of the plane's plush chairs. To my surprise it was sturdy, despite the short notice the maintenance crew had been given for its installation.

The words from the lead physician were precise and quick, and as nasally as I expected. He also enunciated every fourth or fifth word, even if it made no sense to do so. "Mr. President, you must remain awake during the surgery to ensure I don't negatively affect any of your higher functions or motor skills. We will apply a local anesthetic to numb your skin before opening your skull and manipulating the gray matter to fit the device. You will feel no pain and will be able to engage in normal conversation during the procedure."

I wanted to make a joke about normal conversations with a brain doctor, but the queasiness in my stomach overpowered my desire for humor. So, I carried on casual conversations with the doctors and nurses during the entire three-hour surgery, using it as a way to not think about the initial smell of grinding bone as they cut through my skull and the Slurpee-like noises as they moved my brain around. At one point my vision blurred, and at another my speech slurred so badly that I thought I was having a stroke, but the doctors quickly re-glopped things together until they had created the perfect spot for the device.

Using a series of mirrors, they showed me the golf-ball-sized black sphere before settling it within my brain. I stared in awe at the object, even though I knew it was just the protective sheath for the ePEG device that lay within. With this small sphere, I would become the most powerful being on Earth, perhaps in the Universe. The powers from my worshippers would be enhanced, possibly to the point that I would be like the immortals of ancient lore, their heroics still found in so many fables. I would no longer be human.

Human? I thought.

Did I want to lose my humanity? Part of me said no, despite the power I would possess. I wanted to feel, wanted to keep part of who I was. I didn't want to become exactly like those deities of lore, so detached from humankind that they eventually lost their followers before casting all aside. I determined right then that I would ensure I would fight to maintain my human identity. I couldn't know how to best serve humanity if I wasn't human. It was a lofty goal.

The device's position was fine-tuned over the next hour, with the doctors using ePEG readouts and my physical responses to the power to maximize the effect. It was like tuning the signal of a satellite TV, but with some pretty nasty side effects when the signal was lost.

Later, they said I went into cardiac arrest twice, but I don't remember that. What I do remember is drifting off to sleep as the plane departed for the rogue nation. At that point my aide informed only the most trusted of my advisors and followers of what I had done, and then asked them all to perform one act. They had to pray, not for me but to me, to worship me. I had transformed, or bastardized, my presidency into one where there would no longer be separation of church and government. I would be both. The direction of humankind would be altered as faith became more than an abstract thing.

There was some hesitation at first, but my aide explained why I had done it. Only then did they agree and obey. I was awakened by their prayers, awakened by the power that resulted. The two doctors who came with me were excitedly stunned. My wound had nearly healed in minutes, and my color returned from ghostlike to a normal pasty complexion. I stood up a few minutes later, feeling no ill effects, and prepared for an exit using the emergency pod. A few hours later I was sliding inside the pod, and I signaled my aide to release the previously recorded video.

All TV stations and social media were ordered to directly send out my video to hundreds of millions of viewers. In the video I thanked them for my presidency, explained the challenges I had faced and the one I faced now, and then described what I was doing. I didn't explain how—although others would learn later—but implored them to help us through this crisis, to help put an end to the decades of senseless killings, to help me save the hostages. I asked them to pray, not to the gods of their beliefs, but to me because I was now their demigod. I was prepared to protect and answer to them. I would become the first modern-day demigod—their demigod.

It was a race of social media's lightning speed to raise my power versus the terrorists getting word of what was happening. However, I was also betting that if they did get word, they wouldn't believe it. I silently counted the seconds as I watched the impassioned video play across the small video screen in the escape pod. My words were far from perfect, but the passion within my plea was strong enough to make me stare in awe. Yes, in awe of myself, which I know sounds conceited. My charisma had always been discussed in the media, noting how I could sway even the crotchetiest despondent. I had always attributed it to my logic and careful research, but after the video, I had to acknowledge they were right. I knew that if nothing happened, it wasn't because people didn't try to obey my orders.

I couldn't feel the device, which was now firmly entrenched in my brain, but something was happening, as my scalp itched and my nose felt as if a small battery had been shoved inside it. It was heating up, and the my held a static charge, the skin buzzing with energy. The cartilage in my ears began to ache, and my throat constricted as it dried and tightened like a belt on a horse saddle being cinched down for a long ride. I swallowed, surprised as a ball of electrical energy coursed down my throat and landed with a thud in the pit of my stomach. It was stranger than butterflies of nervous energy, yet comforting in the power that was now stored there. I exhaled, and that ball of energy exploded up my spine, racking bones with pain, as they tried to expand out of my skin. The energy shot up to the base of my brain. My head snapped back and my mouth opened wide as the invisible ball expanded and encased my entire head. My eyes were open, yet all I could see were small crackles of white in a bowl of blackness.

"Mr. President? Are you okay, sir? What's going on?" queried a concerned voice from my thin headset.

I must have vocalized my pain without knowing. I had needed to calm down lest they decide the plan was a failure and take more drastic measures.

However, inhaling deeply only brought in even more of the unfamiliar energy, and with it, stronger pulses of pain coursing up and down my body. My muscles seized up, ripping my arms from the glider's controls and smacking my clawed fingers into my face. Trying to manage the pain, I turned to short breaths similar to my wife's previous Lamaze training. My vision slowly returned as the pain became manageable, but my skin was stretching beyond its limits. I was still prone, facing forward, however my shoulders and head were squashed against the canopy. In fact, my whole body barely fit into the cockpit, whereas moments before there had been plenty of space.

"Mr. President?" came the voice again.

"Yeah," I groaned, the pain jumping from one body part to another. A trickle of liquid seeped out of the remaining unhealed sutures in my head and slithered down my cheek.

That couldn't be good.

"You are one minute out from initiating descent. You will need to start with an eight deg—"

"I can't reach the controls. The cockpit is shrinking," I replied, before cracking of the composite airframe was followed by the ripping of my shirt.

"That's not possible, sir," came the quizzical reply.

No, it wasn't shrinking. I was growing. In the soft glow of the control panel, I stared at my hands to make sure they weren't turning green. My pale fingers were much thicker than before, and Popeye-like forearms emanated from my torn shirtsleeves. My skin was stretching in response to some type of accelerated body growth, which had to be from those who were praying to me. I started to smile, but then popping sounds near my face halted the exhilaration. I couldn't locate where the noise emanated from until cool air blew past my ears. The canopy's attachment points had begun to fracture under the pressure from my increasing size.

"Mr. President, you need to initiate descent, or you will overshoot your target."

"Oh, I don't think overshooting is going to be a problem," I replied.

Another popping sound and the canopy lifted nearly four inches, air rushing in at over eighty miles an hour. I grabbed the canopy as the drag flipped the nose of the vehicle upward, causing the strained composite frame to rupture, rapidly disassembling the entire glider. My body squirted out and up, my face slamming into the canopy I still held. I expected lots of pain and my neck to snap, but the only issue was that my body was suddenly spinning violently out of control, nearly five thousand feet above the ground.

"What is going on—," were the last words I heard as my headset dislodged and took its own trajectory back to Earth.

After a dozen or so dizzying flips, I grasped the canopy with my other hand and used it to straighten out and guide my descent. I stared upon the darkened landscape below, trying to compare any lighted areas to the dimensions of larger buildings my officers had shown me on the map. A large temple caught my eye, and I scanned forward and to the right until I saw the masonry of the palace where the terrorists resided. I yelped to no one in particular before trying to guide my canopy-craft toward the palace.

Foolish.

I spun around, flipped, dove, and vomited, synchronizing all four actions in just a few seconds. After some fumbling, I straightened out my descent and pulled in line with the palace. I could see shapes on top of the corner of the palace where I was told the hostages resided. Staring even more intently, I somehow zoomed in on two armed guards, even noticing a gold necklace worn by one of them.

A few more seconds passed, and then I realized I was going to overshoot my mark. I released the canopy, turning my fast fall into a screaming descent. The palace's walls were a speeding car, and I was a frozen rabbit, or more appropriately, a frozen bear. I didn't even think to put my arms over my face as I plowed into the palace's side at nearly 150 miles per hour. The impact jarred my body, and the resulting explosion deafened me as chunks of masonry shot outward like the release of a monstrous grenade. I must have blown right through the outer wall, as I experienced a temporal moment of free space before I slammed through what must have been the floor. I landed on my head and chest, my back arching at a painfully odd angle that resulted in my feet smacking the back of my neck, for the first time but not my last. The pain wasn't the excruciating kind that made one wish for death, but it definitely wasn't what I thought a demigod should feel.

Silence, mimicking the dust from my collision, briefly hung in the air as I grabbed two larger chunks of debris and hauled my battered frame into a kneeling position. The rounded piece of debris in my right hand squeezed under my weight, but my curiosity was redirected by the dozens of machine-gun rounds that partially pierced my exposed shoulders and chest. Instinctively, I threw the squishy boulder at the attacker peering down at me from the first floor, hitting him in the chest with what was actually the head of a fellow soldier. He fell out of sight and screamed, giving me enough time to brush off the slugs that had barely penetrated my skin. I was starting to feel like a demigod.

I grabbed a real chunk of concrete in my empty hand, glancing down to ensure it wasn't a head, and jumped through the gaping hole and back onto the first floor. I landed with a loud thud, sending more concrete dust into the air. I was much heavier, in fact too heavy, as if I were denser. Luckily, my weight was offset by the tremendous power coursing through my body. I raised my right arm and prepared to unleash its burden.

The dusty haze was less than that below, but my ascension resulted in a nearly exponential increase in the sounds and chaos within the building. I had never been part of a battle that included more than two others, so I struggled to make sense of the screaming in multiple languages, the shouts of surprise and anger, weapons firing at me, and the cries for help. What was I to do? Was there a best option for helping the hostages?

I tossed my first rock at a screaming idiot who was calling me the son of Satan, ripping his leg and part of his hip from his body. The rest of him spun backward and crumpled to the ground. Semiautomatic gunfire and the subsequent smacking of rounds against my head and neck ensured I didn't dwell on the horrific death I had caused. I threw the other piece of concrete at a column, which the firing soldier had ducked behind. The rock broke through the column with enough force to fling the soldier into another column, knocking him unconscious. I looked down for another weapon, and that's when I spied the carcass of my Secretary of State, my friend Ron, his head connected only by an overstretched-strand of skin.

143

The pooled blood had already dried before my grand entrance, as evidenced by the dust coating its surface as if it were a glaze on the tile. The severed body seared into my memory.

I roared as the rage burst out of my body.

Anger boiled through my skin, and blood dripped out of my eyes as my blood pressure rose beyond what my closed circulatory system could handle. I snatched up a long piece of rebar, squeezing it tight as I charged past the remaining hostages and confronted a group of armed reinforcements. I tried and failed to blink away the blood, the images in front of me too hazy to determine their intent. It didn't matter, as the first row only had time to gawk at my inhuman frame before being cut in half by the swinging metal bar. The next row fired a few rounds at me before they joined their fellow soldiers. The two in the last row spun around to run before I severed their spines with a quick snap of my wrist. I huffed in short breaths until my anger lowered enough for rational thoughts to take over. I wiped my eyes again and then looked at the quivering hostages. They feared me. No. They were in awe of me.

"Follow me if you want to get out of here alive." None moved until I screamed out an order. "Now!"

I led them into a long open space with two rows of marble columns supporting white archways and torn golden tapestries. We were behind the left columns when automatic-machine-gun fire rang out from the other side, cleaving one of the hostages in half. The columns were too thin to offer any real protection, so without having time to think, I charged the right row of columns, rounds ricocheting off me the entire way. The first column I encountered cracked loudly from the impact, not impeding my progress at all. The next half dozen went down just as quickly, barely slowing my progress and only causing a small amount of pain. The next few presented me with a little more of a challenge, with the tenth one stopping all my forward momentum. My body bounced off and I spun behind it and right in front of a grouping of soldiers who had their machine guns aimed at me but weren't firing. The ceiling groaned, the men having almost no time to look up before the entire right side of the hallway collapsed on us. Tens of thousands of pounds of marble and stone rained down on my body, forcing me to my knees. Screams from the soldiers were short-lived, while also being drowned out by the hall's collapse.

The weight on my shoulders and back was immense, but if I went to the ground, it would take too much time to get back up. I roared and rose, blocks from the ceiling running off me like water. To my relief, the left side of the hall was still intact, but then I was annoyed to see the hostages cowering. They should have run. Caked in a sweat of white dust, I motioned slowly for them to follow, not wanting to turn but forced to look behind me to ensure they were obeying. I kicked down one more door and we were outside. Only one solider blocked our escape. He was on a building across the street and was taking shots at me. I ripped the broken metal door off its hinges and flung it at the man. He ducked, but the heavy door ripped through the roof's lip and carried the solider away. I ran the hostages about a quarter mile to two waiting trucks without another encounter. Once I had handed them off, I turned and headed back to the palace.

The rest was a blur that I still prefer to leave hidden in the far recesses of my mind. While I didn't torture anyone, nor create a gruesome scene, I did kill everyone I encountered who wasn't a child or unarmed woman. They met swift deaths, but it still was a killing spree that I'm not proud of. In the end, I was praised by my people and appropriately villainized by the region I had invaded. I was ashamed at what I had done, not realizing for a long time that I was fueled by the prayers of my followers.

That rescue, that night, began both my ascension and my downfall.

Chapter 13

A light radiates from the wall across from my resting place, drawing me back to the reality where my deep, awakening inhale immediately halts because of the absence of air. The stagnant liquid in my veins and the useless organs in my body serve as a reminder of what I really am. Only cargo being delivered to extract revenge. I blink a few times, and it seems the light is doing the same thing. It starts as a circle, no bigger than my hand, but with each blink it grows until it's the size of my head. Then it spins in a circle, rotating counterclockwise as it expands until it's half the size of a human. The bright white light is washed over by a blue electricity that crackles, snapping lines as jagged as lightning strikes across the wall. Then, as if by magic, a face appears, creased like a piece of failed origami paper, returned to the box in a hopeless attempt that no one would notice. Over-dilated, milky eyes stare at me with lips that quiver in an attempt to release words. As I wait for the words, I realize that the gaunt face and tufts of white hair poking out of the odd helmet are familiar. It's Magnate of the Marsian colony.

He looks older, which I didn't think was possible. The eyes more bloodshot, the proboscis pronounced, and the cheekbones now like jagged rocks above a concave slope that ends with a frail jawbone. I had called his bluff on blowing up the spaceship, and now I'm approaching Mars. He must be watching the clock count down to the end of his rule, a slow, gut-wrenching event where the only end is his and mine. The anticipation hadn't been good for him. His loss will be others' freedom.

I had been dreaming of freeing the hostages during my initial transformation into a demigod. And I will end it all, finish my story, with freeing a world from the same future.

The lips part and silent words are stuck in the screen. I slowly remember that I'm in space. Light can travel in space, but sound waves need other particles, no wait…molecules, to travel. They need a medium. Surely, he realizes the problem. Or could he be so distraught that he…

Words appear at the bottom of the screen. Emotionless words, coincidentally matching a strangely emotionless face.

You should not have come. People will die.

The ship must have an advanced ePET, allowing Magistrate to video chat. I hold no anger, as the advantage is clearly mine. He doesn't realize that over my time as President I have grown to acknowledge that there are always acceptable losses. Acceptable lying somewhere between zero and the number who would die if I did nothing. It's not an easy lesson for anyone with a heart to learn, but over time one either accepts the reality or becomes an impotent leader. Dictators, rebels, terrorists, and even friendly nations knew they had the advantage if a leader was fearful of losing lives. However, one couldn't be reckless or perceived to be ruthless. There was a balance, and bluffing was always risky.

I pull up the keyboard on my watch, then shut it down and think my words.

Bookworm, can I respond?

Yes. All you need to do is think what you want to say, and I will transmit your words via the ePET, replies Bookworm.

People will always die, but I'm here to ensure that those who live are no longer suppressed by you and your Marsian regime. You are driving Earth's humans to extinction. Surrender now, vow to free Earth from your stranglehold, and I will only kill you, I reply.

There is a pause, which one might have assumed was from a transmission delay. However, the ePET allows for near-instantaneous communication. Something is not right. I stare at the drawn face, but find nothing as I wait for a response.

Nothing.

That in itself is strange. He gives no sign that he is talking with others or mulling over his options. He is a mannequin, not quite staring in my direction. Even a little off-center when he finally mumbles more silent words. He then mouths them again.

Your request is not possible.

Not possible, I reply. *No, your word choice is poor. It's possible, but what you're saying is that you won't accept my solution.*

Hesitation again before his lips move without any facial emotion, and the words appear on the wall.

Yes, you are correct. Your solution will not be considered. We realize you cannot turn around as the shuttle's course is set. However, you can surrender now and people will not die.

His words are calculated, also holding no emotion.

The strange threat comes again. Strange in that he won't say he will kill people or who the people who will die are. I had assumed it was the Earth humans, but what if he means the Marsians? Would he kill his own people, and why? They are the ones who need the supplies, the supplies that are draining the Earth humans. I refocus on the screen, analyzing the cold, expressionless face once again. No, he has to mean that he will use every means possible to kill the Earth humans. The trains won't deliver medical supplies; the laser fields will start firing at everything; the robots will be ordered to kill. The Marsian regime will bring the Earth humans to their knees, and then expect even more from those who survive. That's how dictators think and act. One had to exercise unyielding power to keep people suppressed. That always involved killing people.

*Thanks for the offer, but I despise backtracking. I've travelled all this way to...*I pause as the word 'travelled' struck me and expanded into the deeper meaning of my personal journey. I had started the journey as an angry, blind man who couldn't see that he had crafted his own fate. I tried to hide behind revenge, but now I'm fighting for others, exactly what I was created for...*travelled to save Earth humans, and more importantly to ensure their enslavement will never happen again. Yes, people will die, but not on Earth.*

I look up after Bookworm types the last word, letting an old-fashioned maniacal smile cross my face. Unfortunately, it's lost on the emotionless dictator. I'm essentially smiling at a wall.

The image slowly fades away, leaving me with only the blue glow from Bookworm's watch.

Bookworm?

Yes, Mr. President?

Can you disable the propulsion system whenever you want?

You want an entrance like when you first became a demigod? Bookworm asks.

How did you...never mind. I forgot that you have access to everything now. I mentally huff.

Do you wish me to stop, sir?

I don't take long to answer. This would all be over soon enough. *No,* I reply.

Good, because even though your dreams are something that even a practiced psychologist would not be able to assess, watching them does help pass the time.

Bookworm's wry humor resonates in my mind.

Maybe that is why I still allow it. When it's just words through the watch, Bookworm has lost his humanity. But knowing that his words came through my implanted device, the emotional side lunged out at me. Maybe it's something I do in my brain, but I like it. Of course, I still don't appreciate how brazen he has become after dying.

Yes, just like that. I want a grand entrance, but I also want to destroy the landing pad and everything on board this shuttle.

I imagine the look on their faces and the hopelessness in their hearts when they realize their precious cargo shuttle isn't slowing down as it prepares to enter Mar's atmosphere. All their work as slave masters, forcing others to gather their supplies even when those people were on the brink of death, soon to be part of a massive crater. They will be waiting with drooling mouths for their dark delivery shuttle to land. Instead, it will turn into a kinetic bomb.

Wake me up when it's time to disable the propulsion system, Bookworm.

Exhausted from the discussions with the Marsian leader and the mental imagery, I try to yawn. My lungs involuntarily seize again, failing to suck in the nonexistent air. My human side awake, fearing death, my heart races, my eyes bulge, and my muscles tighten as my body tries to go into convulsions. I have to remind myself that I'm a demigod, that I'm not human, and that I don't need oxygen to survive.

It takes several minutes before my demigod side wins out; all the while the small hologram of Bookworm on my wrist takes notes in his journal. I know that it's just a symbol of information gathering by the watch, but part of me is still trying to understand how he could write while I was jostling around, struggling for breath.

Once under control I ask my question. *Bookworm, what were you writing? Or rather, why did you make a point to write during my struggle?*

The small image adjusts its glasses as it looks into my eyes. Again, another symbolic gesture to make it appear more human. *Oh, that? Well, to be honest I was trying to be respectful while you gasped for air. I thought it impolite to stare, and decided pretending to take notes was like looking away when someone had to zip up their pants.*

Not what I expect at all. I give a soundless chuckle, my shoulders jumping up and down before closing my eyes and drifting off to sleep. No dreams this time, as I've made my decision and have accepted what I am.

Chapter 14

A sharp electric jolt shoots into my wrist, and I immediately awake to see Bookworm's hologram holding a classic American flag in his hands, which he has just embedded into my wrist.

I claim this land as my own, discovered through nameless perils that have cost me my life. I shall call it Brashland, home of the impetuous people, Bookworm declares as he lifts the banner again and drives it into my wrist. The electric jolt comes again.

I'm awake, you garish actor, I growl in my mind. *And yes, I still plan to make my point by driving this shuttle full speed into Mars's surface.*

Bookworm sighs, the banner disappearing as he crosses his arms. *I was hoping you would change your mind about the crash landing. In fact, while you were sleeping, I thought of a few other options that are far less drastic. The first would be to modify our flight trajectory so that we land far enough away that they can't visually estimate our location. Combine that with my recent infiltration of their AI system, and you'll have the highest probability for reaching the Marsian colony. The second highest probability is to jettison the cargo during our descent. If I time it correctly, the cargo will land in front of the colony, creating a large dust cloud, as the surface near the entrances has not been eroded away like the landing pad. The last option—*

Hold on, Bookworm. Why are we worried about probabilities? I'm a demigod. We'll crash-land, and I'll emerge from the crater, striking fear in their leaders. I smile as my thoughts are transmitted to Bookworm. However, it fades as the diminutive figure crosses its arms again and taps his foot.

I swat at the figure, hoping it will fly across the room and scatter into more pieces than a large bowl of M&Ms. Of course, my hand passes through the hologram. Bookworm just continues to stare, causing the anger to rise again within me. What does he want me to do? Shall I casually walk in, smile pleasantly like some diplomat while humankind is dying? Well, I won't do that. I'm not created for that!

I swat at the figure again, but this time the little guy flies end over end, slamming into the opposite wall and shattering into hundreds of pieces. The little blue pieces spin in the zero gravity, and as I watch in surprise, they turn into small spheres. No, they turned into M&Ms. Little blue M&Ms.

What the...? I think, confused.

After a few seconds, the candies begin to slowly spin in looping circles. The looping forces each one closer and closer until they coalesce into one dark sphere with blue light crackling through miniature fissures on its surface. The fissures grow, as does the blue light, until they burst in a bright flash, revealing Bookworm standing there again, crossed arms and stare unmoved. A stare that could stop a charging elephant.

However, in the confined cargo bay there was no immediate reaction from me. It was a vacuum, devoid of everything but the visual rippling of my body, jolting of my shoulders, and the strain on the holding straps that kept me in place, which signal the end of my anger.

Bookworm, I forgot that you have access to all my thoughts, and that was a funny way to remind me. I stretch my index finger and thumb across my chin and rub my aching jowls. *Okay, tell me why you're so upset with me, and I promise I won't be angry at you.*

Bookworm lowers his arms to his sides and then reaches behind his back and clasps them together before speaking. *I highly discourage you from making promises you can't keep. You are not campaigning for the Presidency again.*

Ouch! Yeah, that is a valid jab, but not for the reason you think. I was naïve when I ran for office, thinking that what I wanted would become reality. Not knowing that I was relegated to a figurehead in so many aspects, as agendas became pieces to a complex, ever-changing puzzle. Too complex for me to put together on my own, and thus forcing me to rely on others...and thus losing the potential power of my office. I give a long, airless sigh.

While they may not be able to inflict permanent damage to you with any of the weapons available to the Marsians, they don't need to, thought Bookworm. *What would be the easiest way to dispose of you?*

Hmm. Let me think. I don't need to breathe, so that rules out taking away my air supply. I can deflect most projectiles, and with Earth humans' prayers, I quickly heal from damage. I inadvertently glance upward as I think. *Upward. Aha, Bookworm! They'll try to use a weapon that launches me off Mars.*

Bookworm nods slowly. *And that is why one of my three solutions, one which you still haven't heard—.*

No. I want the shock and awe of creating a crater. I rub my cheeks again. *What if you alter the trajectory so that we skip on the landing pad, destroying it, and are at such an angle that the shuttle explodes closer to the base. Then I can quickly appear, but I'll be too close to the domes for them to attack me with such a weapon.*

Bookworm nods again. *That is possible, and admittedly has a higher chance of success than option two or option three. Did I mention that I had not yet briefed you on option three?*

Okay, let's do it. I assume you're already slowing us down in preparation for the correct maneuvers required?

Bookworm ignores the question. *Mr. President, why do you sometimes refer to me as an 'it' and sometimes as a living being?*

Truthfully? For the exact same reason that at times I'm an emotional, reactionary demigod, and at other times a reflective, thoughtful human. My mind is split into two distinct parts, one for my worshippers and the other for me. However, unlike the way I'm able to control my body now, I can't do the same for my mind. I operate in the gray area between the two parts, no pun intended. That gray area is a swirling, chaotic middle ground.

Bookworm stares at me for a long while before pushing up his glasses and smiling. *You are screwed up just as much as the rest of us. As with all humankind.*

I appreciate his comment, but I don't feel like reciprocating the compliment. *How much time before we arrive?*

A couple of hours. Do you want me to wake you when we are closer? asks Bookworm.

No. No, Bookworm. I think I'm going to stay awake this time.

I visualize the impending battle, running different scenarios in my mind and assessing how I'll handle them. Sometimes there are images of the shuttle missing its mark and crashing into a dome, killing thousands of people. Other times it will be of me missing a specialized weapon that then propels me into outer space. As with all battles, there will be good things that happen and bad decisions that will hurt me. However, no matter what, there will be a new set of horrific memories to relive. There always is.

My thoughts stop as a rectangular white box bumps into me. Actually, I realize I have been floating in the cargo bay, so I reach for a strap to retighten, finding that it has been ripped apart. In fact, all of them have. I haven't drifted away from my resting spot. Rather, I've been growing and reached a point where I'm almost too big for the free space in the cargo bay. It's only then that I recognize the immense power exuding from my entire body, like a teenager trying on cologne for the first time. The once-lost stream of energy coming from my worshippers is as intense as at the height of my power. I feel like I can crush a building, jump miles in one bound, or win the fight for humankind's existence.

Bookworm?

Yes?

How? How so much? There are so few left on Earth. I stare at my iron-like hands that are swollen to a size the Hulk would have been proud to own. I flex my fingers, feeling the layers of shoulder muscles also flex and brush against more cargo boxes.

You said it yourself, Mr. President. It is not the number, but the need of your followers. They have been fed your journey like a daily radio show from the past, and have been pulled in. They understand the gravity of the situation and that you are their only hope. You have their hearts and souls.

Bookworm stops and does his usual stare into an imaginary corner when he is processing data. *The Marsian dictator wishes to converse with you again. I have blocked it this time, but I can let him through if you want.*

I nod yes, turning my gaze to the wall where the aged man appeared last time. This time only words appear on the wall.

Are you insane?

Yes. Yes, I very well could be. I rely on Bookworm to transmit my reply before signaling him to cut the communication. It's time for my grand entrance.

F

I

G

H

T

Chapter 15

Impact in one minute, sir, calculates Bookworm.

I turn toward the dark wall and rest my massive paws on it, then grab the metal struts running along its side. I squeeze as if I were extracting juice from a lemon, and it's just as easy. The struts buckle as my fingers embed within them. I don't want to be thrown from the crash site upon impact as it would ruin my grand entrance.

Thirty seconds until impact, Bookworm warns.

I push down the human thoughts of pain that I know will rack my body upon impact. Sure, I'm nearly indestructible, but even I can't easily shake off what is going to happen next. A horrible thought crashes into my mind, and I release my grip, quickly unstrapping the watch.

Ten, nine, eight, seven, six, five...

Bookworm's loud countdown softens as I shove the watch in my mouth. I regrip the struts and brace for impact.

Four, three, two, one.

A powerful jolt attempts to tear me away from the metal strut I'm gripping, and it's quickly followed by the buckling of the shuttle's belly as it rips through the landing pad's metal supports before slamming into the hard-packed ground. Jagged metal rips through the hull even as it collapses from the impact. I hold onto the strut, feeling it tear away from the shuttle as the buckled skin splits apart and folds into the cargo bay. Sharp fragments puncture the boxed supplies as we flip end over end. I still hold onto the strut, although it's been ripped free from the shuttle, as I slam into the walls and grit away the pain from the multiple metal fragments that find homes in my body. I know we have just skipped into the landing pad, and it's only a matter of moments before the real crash landing. I try to gain my bearings using Mars's gravity to aide me, but the spinning shuttle and the plethora of shrapnel are too distracting.

The shuttle hits the ground to my right, flinging me into what must have been the forward dome with such speed that I'm sure I hit solid rock with my face. Everything that has still been whipping around the cargo bay comes toward me like knives from an entertainer's circus act. Some bounce off, some stick, and a few find their way into and out the other side of my body. New pain registers just as the entire shuttle explodes in an orangish-yellow fireball. The shock wave hits first, harmlessly rolling over me before the searing heat scorches my body and sets nearly everything on fire. I hold onto whatever has hit me in the face to brace for the series of explosions that propel pieces of the shuttle in every direction. The pain is more than I expected, and I roar as my vision narrows before being overcome with darkness.

****

I blink my eyes, awaking to a mixture of billowing smoke and red dust hanging thickly in the thin air. Fresh pink skin covers my exterior, and the gaping wounds running through my body are now mere scratches, outlined with splatterings of oven-cured blood. I extricate the watch from my mouth and lock it back onto my arm before rolling onto my stomach and slowly crawling out of the crater the crash landing has created. As I emerge from the wreckage, I smile, as my struggling crawl out of the damaged, billowing womb is exactly what I want. The grand entrance is a success.

Mr. President, there are two unmanned cargo exoskeletons approximately one hundred meters ahead of you. Their posturing suggests they are aiming weapons in your direction.

Are they armed with the weapons that could launch me into outer space? I think.

I believe one is, but the other seems to be employing a laser generator like the ones outside of the mine shaft. It is called a WeL or Weaponized electron Laser, using a concentric arrangement of ePEGs to draw the 30 kilowatts of power needed to miniaturize laser technology to a rifle-sized weapon. It is not as powerful as the domes surrounding your prison, but it will melt your skin and more depending on the dwell time. Anyway, they are still scanning for your location inside the smoke and dust, as the IR sensors are having a hard time with the fire from the crash, Bookworm continues.

Perfect. Time to act. Well, not really perfect. Those laser cutters hurt, and I really don't want to have my first minutes on Mars ending quickly in an exodus to outer space.

Bookworm, project a larger image of you about five feet to my side, I order before leaping up and forward with all my strength.

As I draw closer, I can make out their hazy outlines, which must have been nearly the same time they saw me coming. Luckily, Bookworm's blue image to my side is too enticing for them to pass up. A red pulse of light rips through Bookworm's enlarged image, quickly followed by a blob of green light that hits the ground but then takes a ninety-degree turn straight into the air. I definitely don't like the look of that one.

They don't have time for a second shot, as I'm already on them and almost by them before they have time to reset their aim. I grab the shoulder of the exoskeleton holding the gravity weapon as I fly by, crushing the metal in my hand. I spin in the air and place the weapon between myself and the other exoskeleton while using my free hand to rip off the arm that has been holding the weapon. We skip on the ground once before slamming into the framework of one of the biodomes. The exoskeleton in my hand shears away, leaving me with a cluster of metal and wires. I brace for a shot by the other, but it doesn't come.

Bookworm?

I was able to scramble the incoming signal that was directing the exoskeleton. It has a lock on you and is merely waiting for the fire command, replies Bookworm, somehow inserting a smug tone into my mind.

How long do I have?

The receiver on the exoskeleton is extremely primitive, only being able to accept a single inbound signal at any given time. I have sent a continuous stream to block out the other signal, and could continue to do so for hours.

I stand up, brushing away some of the red dust with my free hand before looking behind me at the biodome that had halted my flight. I expect to be staring into a glimmering metal scaffold with pristine transparent inserts that will allow me to peer into the lavish interior. Perhaps even seeing a gathering of pretentious, yet horrified, Marsians who just now realize that their opulent lifestyle is soon to end. I want to lay my hand on its surface and stare deep into their souls before turning away to finish off their remaining defender.

Instead I gaze upon a pitted, bent, and broken framework with holes the size of my fist accentuating its façade. The red dust layers the structure and has built up within the crevices and coated the sharp ridges of the holes. That is expected in this barren wasteland; however, when I brush one of the transparent frames, my view is still blocked by a heavy layer of red dust that also coats the inside. I take a dozen steps back to get a better view of the massive structure, amazed that my first glance is actually at one of the less-damaged portions of the biodome. Whole sections have either been blown outward or crashed inward; some the size of a human and others large enough to drive a train through. Memories of a dilapidated greenhouse from my youth come to mind as my eyes comb over the uninhabitable structure, slowly moving up the hundreds of feet to the top and then scanning what must have been over a mile sideways for the single dome.

There's a large bay door a few hundred feet to my left, which stands wide open. By the looks of it, it hasn't been closed in a very long time. Large footprints exit from the door and lead back to the remaining exoskeleton. I ignore my static attacker and continue my perusal of the Marsian colony. Another dome is situated on each side of the center one where I had landed, their appearance being no better than it. No signs of life.

Foreshadowing what I will surely see very soon, I had thought that all the Marsians were feeding off the workings of the Earth humans, but my assumption is clearly wrong. The drawn, old man who was trying to stop me had to be a dictator or leading a small group who even used Marsians to support their extravagant lifestyle. It turns out that I'm not here to stop the entire colony, but just a select few who are in charge. A few who feed off the lives of others without care.

This is going to be so much easier.

I turn back around and stare at the exoskeleton, knowing that the onboard camera has been transmitting my actions. I walk forward with power. No, not stomping with weight that causes the dust to stir around my feet. Rather, the confidence of one who will not and cannot be stopped. That body language also speaks louder than any words as I step up to the robot and sneer. I take the weapon from its waiting arms, wanting to crush it in my hands but luckily not angry enough to do so. It might blast me into outer space, so I just toss it aside. I then wrap my hands around each of its arms and slowly squeeze, wishing there was air so that the groaning of metal could be heard. I have to settle for ripping both arms off at the shoulder. I bring them together and start folding them into each other, easily reshaping the metal as if it were clay.

When I finish, I hold a somewhat round agglomeration of metal, wires, plastic, and blipping lights. I toss the mess aside and grasp the robot's neck before reaching down with my other hand to its waist and twisting it to the side, feeling the metal supports snap. I pull it up, showcasing the lower body to the camera before dropping and grinding it into the ground with my foot. My last action is to wink before I wrap both hands around the head and squeeze with all my might. The force causes small pieces to shoot off in various directions as the head compresses as far as it can go. Electricity surges through my arms as the last lighting inside the exoskeleton's head snuffs out.

I'm sure my message had been transmitted. He…they are not powerful enough to stop me.

Bookworm, how many domes are there?

The blue figure appears on my wrist, sitting at a small desk and typing on a computer keyboard. I don't understand why he did this. Was it so that I will feel like I am talking to something more human, or had he programmed it before he died to try and retain a semblance of his humanity?

The detailed drawings, layout, and purpose on the colony have been lost over time. What I have been able to retrieve is a compilation from thousands of sources, resulting in numerous overlaps of conflicting data.

That wasn't my question, I reply tersely. *I want to know if it's like we planned in the beginning.*

It appears to be a three-by-three grouping of biodomes, able to support ten thousand humans, not including livestock and crops. However, many of the historical documents I pulled data from seem to suggest almost twice that many had been living on the colony during its peak. Of course, I think it is much less now.

You think, I reply with a little sarcasm.

I stare out and over the three connected domes that are visible. The other six are hiding behind the dilapidated ones, and I wonder if they're just as broken down. Although most of my demigod battles involved me crashing on site from high above, just like this time, another advantage was that I could survey the site as I made my dramatic descent. It was a quick, yet effective way to do reconnaissance. Unfortunately, I had forgotten to do it this time. Sure, it wouldn't have been possible using my own eyes while inside the spaceship, but I'm sure that Bookworm could have tapped into the shuttle's sensors. It was a novice mistake. One that could result in a painful surprise. I decide to blame it on being trapped underground for a couple hundred years. Time away from battle could rust the senses of even the most battle-hardened warrior. Still, I need to see which domes are being actively used in order to estimate how many Marsians still live under the suppressing rule of their magnate turned dictator.

I walk over and peer into a larger hole of the middle dome, then assess its scaffolding that provided both easy climbing while building the dome and a sturdy, long-lasting framework for human inhabitation. I have three options in front of me: go around, go through, or go over. Going around will give the dictator plenty of time to reposition his defenses for my next assault, while going through will make me an easy target if there are any more exoskeletons waiting for me to make a mistake. I also will be an easy target while climbing, if the exoskeletons are waiting inside for me.

However, I have a big advantage when scaling the dome as I can use the power in my legs and the 40 percent less gravity of Mars to make it to the top in just a few leaps. It's a faster way to move than running, even with my heightened speed.

I squat down and look at a triangular section nearly five stories up, guesstimating the angle I need to land on it. I release the coiled-up energy in my legs, springing upward faster than I thought possible. I have even more energy than I predicted and find myself shooting past the point I want to land on. As I travel past it, I realize that my miscalculation in power also means my angle is off...by a lot. I am too far away from the biodome when I reach my apex, probably about seventy feet too high with twenty feet separating me and anything to grab onto. I reach out with both hands in every direction possible, looking all the more foolish as the reduced gravity presents me with even more time to aimlessly flail. I quickly descend, crashing into one of the undamaged panes with a surprising jolt. I expect it not to be able to bear my weight, but it easily holds. My relief turns into even more flailing as I slide off the panel and toward the ground. I find my grip on a jagged piece of scaffolding and pull myself around so that my feet are firmly braced on the framework. After a few seconds, I surmise that no more exoskeletons are inside the dilapidated dome, as they would have surely shot at me as I hung from above.

I'm wasting precious time!

I crouch down and launch upward with all the power I possess in my legs. I soar beyond even where I think I'll reach, and I watch in amazement as I approach the top of the dome. I reach out and grab the rounded peak, redirecting myself toward the next set of three domes as I start my descent. These domes are in better shape, with no visible holes, but the exteriors still appear not to have been kept up in a very long time. The panels are nearly opaque from the red dust that has weathered into their surfaces. As I near a landing halfway between the first and second set of domes, I notice tracks from the dome to my left. The exoskeletons must have come out of that airlock and walked through the other domes before I encountered them.

My landing is soft, barely requiring the flexing of my knees before I absorb all the energy. What little dust had stirred, slowly drifts back to the ground as I stand and turn left. I take my first step toward the airlock, knowing that the confrontation with the ruthless dictator is nearly at hand. With my next step, I dwell on the pain of the Earth humans, of my people who have suffered and died because of his greed. Each step that hits the ground drives into my core the pain this feeble man has caused to others. I will spare him no mercy; I will not heed his pleas or words that will attempt to justify his actions. He will receive death as swiftly as I can bring it forth, for him and his cabinet of henchmen. Only then can I deal with the Marsian people and help rebuild their society through negotiations and collaborations, which will also start the rebuilding for the Earth humans.

I reach out my shaking hand and grip the wheel that will vent the inside air of the hatch and allow me to enter. Turning it, the metal wheel begins to yield to my strength, the nearly uncontrollable rage I'm building almost buckling the wheel before I turn it. I relax my grip and spin the wheel counterclockwise a full turn before releasing it, stepping back to watch as the series of colored lights spring to life in a pattern not discernible to me. I've only done what Bookworm had coached during the journey to Mars, and it's taking much longer than I care for. My rage makes patience a lost virtue.

Not able to wait any longer, I place both hands on the door, ready to crush it, when it silently releases inward. I duck my head through the fifteen-foot-high entrance and storm to the other end of the large holding area, knowing the hatch behind me has already shut, then pause. I'm angry and ready for battle, but I still care for the life of the suppressed Marsians. There are hissing sounds from multiple small vents. The sweet taste of oxygen inflates my lungs, blood courses through my veins as my heart beats anew, and a cacophony of small, yet powerful sounds fill the air.

The compression of my chest as I release my first breath since I left Earth calms some of my anger. I inhale deeply, muscles unused come to life, skin stretching uncomfortably as if pulled beyond taut. I revel in it only briefly as the feelings are drowned out by the hatch opening, sound of air fluttering around buildings, the distant ticking and clacking from unseen rooms, and the rhythmic soft breathing of thousands upon thousands of sleeping beings.

Yes, I hear them, but not because of any enhancement to my hearing at that moment. I hear them because they are breathing together, in perfect rhythm. No strain in the amplified sound, no evidence of sickness that rasps with each breath. Just, perfectly matched, relaxed breathing. I duck and step through, the sound adds to what I see in front of me. Buildings run unevenly up the sides of the dome, some only a few stories, most nearly halfway to the apex, but all interlocking and connecting at odd levels. There is no rhyme or reason to the chosen colors of the buildings; some are gray, others steeped in earth tones, and still others coated with vibrant yellows and oranges. I remember the designs for the colony, how the buildings were attached to the dome's scaffolding to serve not only as structural reinforcement but also as thousands of airlocks if the lower half of the dome were damaged by the colonists. Also, every housing dome was split into quadrants with each segment representing a country's most beloved city. I'm standing on a street that leads to Puerta del Sol, the city center for Madrid, Spain. For this dome, Paris, France; London, England; and Berlin, Germany, fill the remaining three quadrants. Reflexively, I turn my head toward the first dome, even though I can't see it.

"Bookworm," I speak out loud, although in a quieter voice. Not because I'm afraid of what will happen if the Marsians awake, but because it seems like the right thing to do. As if I'm in a library or a church.

No. As if I'm in a mausoleum.

His blue image appears on my wrist.

"Yes," replies Bookworm, his soft voice mimicking mine in tone.

"Can you extract only the original designs of the Marsian colony?" I ask.

"Yes, Mr. President. However, as I mentioned before, they are not complete."

"I understand," I whisper to him as I look down at his image on my wrist.

Bookworm is replaced by a blue drawing of nine domes in a three-by-three matrix. I reach down and expand the map, then zoom in on the first dome I peered into upon my arrival, using simple hand motions that Bookworm is able to interpret and execute. The gaps from missing data are massive, but after turning the 3-D image a few times and rotating it several more, I can see what I need. There are supposed to be buildings inside, just like the one I'm in now. However, all the buildings are gone. Deconstructed some time ago. Long enough in the past for the Martian dust to conceal any evidence of the removal. I close my eyes for a few seconds, attempting to recall my quick view into the first dome. However, I can't tell if the interior's deconstruction has been done methodically, hurriedly, or destructively.

Interesting assessment, sir. Bookworm's voice emanates from the device embedded in my brain.

It isn't expected or wanted.

"Bookworm. Let's not use that method of communication unless absolutely necessary." I give a guttural whisper, topping it with frustration.

"Understood, sir," is all that comes back.

I resurvey the dome's layout, noting that it's neither meticulous nor in sore need of a deep cleaning. The mixture of granite, cobblestone, cement, and asphalt pathways on the ground hold a smooth cleanliness from people walking about, but the sections outside of the traveler's patterns display signs of neglect. Buildings, with colors slightly different in hues and shades, haven't been cleaned or repainted but also don't seem in need of repairs. It all seems wrong. I scratch my chin while thinking. Everything is existing and aging exactly the same, but why this bothers me I don't know.

I walk down the center road, expecting a stray child to peek out from one of the central buildings. They always did whenever I entered a battle. No matter what parents ordered or how they tried to stop them, there was always a child whose curiosity was stronger than the fear of punishment. However, halfway down the street I still don't hear or see a single Marsian, not even a spying child. I continue my massive steps, easily reaching the replica of Puerta del Sol in minutes and gazing upon the mounted statue of Palmer III of Spain. The building to my right lets me know that I've travelled upon Calle Mayor and now am stopped at Calle Carrettas. When I had visited this exact spot in the original Madrid, I was amidst protests of using demigods to settle disputes. The real city center had a rich history of protests, and plenty of policia ready for action. But on Mars, it's barren. I realize it could take days or even weeks for me to find the Marsian dictator, so I release what is left of my anger. I'm very good at calling it back up on a moment's notice.

"I wouldn't call that a talent, sir." From my wrist comes Bookworm's whispered voice.

"I told you not to listen in," I growl lowly.

"Yes, I know. But it is very boring waiting for you to call on me."

Right before my terse reprimand, I hear shoes slapping against the cobblestones, followed by the skipping of loose rocks as they slide along the path. The strides are long, too long, and the destruction of the street can only mean one thing. However, that's impossible.

Chapter 16

Impossible.

A word overused, even by me. Very few things are truly impossible, and most of those are based on the laws of physics and founded in mathematical calculations. But we demigods proved that even those could be broken. And as far as I know, no one had been able to explain how. They tried, but every time their mathematical calculations and quantum mechanics had to enumerate the power gained by worshippers, their equations incorporated a complex polynomial that could fit a line drawn by the worst of drunks. Of course, only a handful knew the secret to magnifying our power, and even then, the origination of the power still came from the energy of our worshippers. It was still labelled as impossible.

Those shoes, that stride. It could only be one being. The impossible had happened again, as it always did.

An enormous shadow plays onto the ground from an alley across the plaza just before the being steps out and faces me. He is at least seventeen feet in height, dressed in a workman's brown leather lederhosen with the matching Bavarian shoes that had signaled his approach. The hunter green socks and Tyrolean cap with a quail feather adds a boldness that matches the sneering smile on the demigod's face. He is the embodiment of the German working class. I'm too stunned to react.

"Guten Tag, meine fruend," comes out a baritone German voice, which switches to thick English. "It is good to see you, John."

He flexes his thick chest muscles, which ripple in multiple layers, a visual display of his ego. It's an ego that won't let him admit failure or defeat, and one that let him go far beyond what his homeland had ever wanted.

"Arthuren," is all I can initially muster forth.

I swallow deeply at the demigod who had killed my family; whom I had defeated at the Battle of Hikone. The blond, muscle-bound warrior had been a better fighter than I, and I had won only by outwitting him. Now, judging by his size, he is even more powerful. But this makes no sense. I have nearly all Earth's worshippers who believe in demigods, and there aren't enough Marsians to give him even close to the power he appears to possess.

"I don't understand..." My last word trails into nothingness.

"Ha! Of course you don't, and of course you are surprised. You have sulked in isolation for hundreds of years, failing to protect your precious worshippers from deserved oppression. Yet now that you have opened your eyes, you wish to try to save the day at the last minute. However, you cannot stop what you still cannot see." Arthuren crosses his arms, barely able to do so as his biceps attempt to impede any progress.

"So, you know about how the Earth humans are being treated and yet you do nothing? They are your people also, Arthuren. They are the ones you represented as an ambassador and who made you a demigod." My anger is building as I speak.

Arrogant, cutting laughter bellows forth from Arthuren. "No, John. No on every account. I was cast aside by the Earth humans after you tricked me in Hikone. Unlike the other lost demigods, I wandered the world until I was rescued by those that want what I want. I never represented the humans. As an ambassador, they were tools to ensure my leaders got what they needed, and as a demigod, they were there for the same reason."

"And is that what your new worshippers are now? A tool for the Marsian dictator?" I growl.

"What? Oh, I see your mistake now. Yes, they are a tool for my new leaders, but unlike the humans, they have no issue with this. They are there to serve the greater need, without question." Arthuren restarts his strong gate. "The time for talk is past."

"And I'll defeat you just like last time!" I yell, keeping my place so that he will meet me in the center of the plaza. If I move to meet him halfway, we will battle in the middle of the narrow street, damaging the apartments and surely killing many who sleep. Many who still sleep even after the noise we have already created.

"I doubt it!" Arthuren yells as he closes the distance.

His fist thunders toward my face, just as I predicted. I shift my neck, which moves my head, and step to the side as I sink on the same leg. His fist whistles past my ear, followed by the cracking of my fist into his nose. It isn't powerful enough to send him backward, but I hear a grunt of pain. I continue my wind movement, spinning another full turn so that I'm out of his range.

Arthuren wipes his bloody nose and then wipes the smeared blood on his hand against the lederhosen. "I see you've learned a little about fighting," he states.

I respond by moving into a defensive stance, my closed fists halfway between those of a boxer and a mixed martial artist.

"I have a few tricks myself," Arthuren says as he moves into an old-school boxer stance, one arm extended out and the other bent, with both fists up.

He takes one step forward and I one step back, both waiting for the other to fully commit. A red and gold blur flits from my left side, followed by an incredible pain piercing my lower back. I grunt as I'm forced to one knee, so focused on the pain that I miss the forward step and uppercut by Arthuren. My jaw cracks and my head snaps back as I'm lifted from the impact and flung backward. Whatever had been stuck in my back impales even farther as I land, protruding through my stomach before snapping against the stone street.

I lay on my side, trying to fight off the pain and catch my breath. A trumpet blares out eight long notes, then more as maracas blend into the fold. The music dances boldly across my ears and familiarity chimes in. El Matador! I look across the plaza at the tight red pants and shirt, overdressed with gold lines and insignias. His posture is stiff and bold, as straight as the black cap that covers his hair. In one hand he holds a banderilla, a pointed flag whose brother is surely what I am skewered on. His other hand holds a simple, red-hilted sword that is designed for quick, puncturing strikes. However, his signature red cape, always flowing much slower than the demigod's quickness and creating a confusing illusion, has been replaced by a pulsing white cape. The cape not only wraps around his shoulders, but extends up and under his black cap. It's very similar to Magnate's, surely signifying the Marsian regime.

A foot breaks through my ribs, sending me skidding across the plaza to rest at the feet of El Matador.

"You were good, El Matador," I gasp out, finding it hard to breathe now that my ribs have punctured my lung.

I look up at his face, noticing little familiarity in the motionless face.

His bright blue eyes, ones that once charmed every lady—and many men—are coated in a milky haze. Ill-focused and uncaring.

I let my guard down and pay the price as the second banderilla slides through my side, piercing my spine and sending my lower body into a pleasant, yet horrifying numbness. The bone-crushing grip of Arthuren envelopes my shoulder as he lifts me up. He turns me toward El Matador, allowing me to look down at the nine-foot, slender demigod, and see that he is not the friend I once helped. It's only his body.

My end is near, and disjointed thoughts solidify to that of Old Woman and the second of three things she wanted to convey. She said humankind needed me, but failed to let me know the third thing. In the moment I realize the third thing, that I need humankind. Without them I have no purpose, and from them comes my power.

"Watch your death, John. Watch as his blade slides through your neck, right before I rip your head off and throw it into outer space." Arthuren grips my head with his other hand as El Matador raises his elbow so that the blade touches my neck and is perpendicular to my body. I can't help but admire his posture even as he prepares to kill me.

The blade pushes forward a few millimeters but then stops. El Matador pushes harder, his force equally opposed by something intangible. He braces his angled feet against the cobblestone and lunges with all his strength, the sword bowing to the point that one could have tied a string to it and shot an arrow.

Renewed life fills my legs as I support myself. Arthuren is behind me, but I can imagine his surprise without seeing his face. I reach out and grab El Matador by the neck, then spin while sinking down so that Arthuren loses his grip on me. Now free, I leap back down the street, dragging the Spaniard along.

"Impressive, John. I see you have some sort of instant communication with your worshippers. They know what you need and pray to give it to you," Arthuren correctly guesses as he also leaps toward me.

I leap down the street again, this time throwing the Spaniard at Arthuren. He swats away the lesser demigod and makes a huge leap forward, hitting me squarely in the chest. As I fly backward, I pull out both banderillas, keeping the unbroken one in my left hand. I drive my feet into the ground, kicking up broken cobblestones, before charging forward, swinging wildly while barely avoiding another uppercut. However, the next straight punch to my face sends me hurtling backward dozens of feet and landing on my side. Dazed, Arthuren jumps on top of me. A couple blows slam into the back of my head before I spin around, grabbing the straps of his lederhosen and scissor kicking him off me. He flies down the street before standing up and assessing his surroundings.

"Ah, I see your plan, John. You hope to keep sending me toward the airlock and then trap me inside as you depressurize it," he says as he slowly comes forward. "It won't work as I can hold my breath long enough to get back inside."

I huff, seemingly out of breath. "Was hoping you wanted to relive old times, Arthuren."

I sidestep a straight punch and his follow-up jab, but mistime a side punch that sends me crashing through the first-level door and wall of an apartment. The lights flicker on as Arthuren walks into the room. I stand up, fully healed and refreshed.

"Arthuren, looks like both of us can do this for a very long time. How about a break." I look at the vibrant man as I speak. "No? Okay."

I rush forward, ducking under his straight punch and hugging him around the waist. An elbow crashes down on my spine, the booming crack against my back not nearly loud enough to signify the pain the hit evokes. I'm driven down to both knees but manage to hold on. Another hit and I'm on my stomach, grasping the ankles of his shoes. I yank with all my might, hearing the gratifying noise of his back smacking into the apartment floor as I quickly rise to my knees. I pull back to keep him off balance as I stand up.

"This is child's wrestling, John! You aren't even hurting me. Let go and let's fight like true demigods!" shouts Arthuren.

Without a word I squat down and leap back one last time, crashing into the back wall of the apartment, which happens to be attached to the dome wall. I fly through it, carrying Arthuren with me. Carrying him out onto the airless Martian desert.

Airless.

I have learned that I don't need air to live, that pain is a mortal person's way to know that his life is in danger. I'm not mortal; I'm an impossible being, one that also doesn't need a spine to walk. Arthuren could reach the same point, but he's lost in himself. Lost like I had been for hundreds of years.

We skid along the ground, with me climbing up his body until I'm wrapped around his waist. Arthuren claws at me with his hands, kicks with his legs, and tries to wriggle free as he holds his breath, but I play a child's game. I torque my body and kick my legs, rolling farther away from the dome. With each strike, we roll, the Martian dust coating our bodies. I wind up with my back on the ground, but with Arthuren's back on my chest, both my legs and arms squeezing around him in a jujitsu back mount.

I can do this all day.

I stop rolling when we are halfway between the two domes. A blue light appears above us, followed by the appearance of Bookworm. He looks at us, nods affirmation, and his body transforms into letters.

I hold no anger toward you anymore, Arthuren. Not even pity. You're misguided and always will be. You will always seek to be a

destructive force, but that causes me no concern. I have beaten you twice, and I will always be able to defeat you. Why? I could explain, but you would never understand.

I wedge Arthuren's neck between my forearm and bicep, then squeeze my vice-like grip until his powerful struggle turns to weak, frantic pulses. Even after his arms fall limp and his legs spread out like a flayed fish, I hold on for another half dozen minutes. Afterward, I stand up, dust myself off, and begin to walk calmly back to the airlock. I stop and turn around. My mind tells me I shouldn't, that I've already won. However, my heart remembers the pain he caused me and will always try to cause. I walk over, grab him by the torso and launch him into the air with all the strength I can muster. I watch him travel so high that he appears a fraction of his size, but then he starts to grow in size. I keep watching even after I realize he's coming back to Mars. I step to the side as he lands with a disfiguring thud, unable to move as he continues to suffocate without oxygen. Unable to heal the broken neck and twisted leg.

Sir, I should have told you ahead of time that it would not work. You are not on the Moon, Bookworm comments. *Sorry you wasted your time.*

Oh, it wasn't a waste of time, Bookworm. Not at all, I reply as I walk back to the airlock, noting that the hole I created had already been sealed over with a black substance.

I attempt to turn the handle, but stop when I hear hissing sounds within the antechamber.

Bookworm, I think. *Looks like they're trying to stop my entrance.*

On it, Mr. President, comes Bookworm's reply in my head. *And done.*

I open the latch, walk inside, and relock it, this time taking no pleasure breathing in the oxygen-filled air. Once inside I retrace my steps to and through the central plaza, and then confidently stroll between the English and German quadrants. On my left are Westminster Abbey and Buckingham Palace; Big Ben is about half the size of the original. The clock sits still, at least three hours earlier than it should have shown. To my right and in the middle of the street is Brandenburg Gate, facing to the north and south of the German quadrant to represent the former East and West

Germany. As with all the other areas, the only sound seeps out of the apartments. The noise of the sleeping Marsians.

I travel through the passageway to the next dome, the one that should contain the Marsian dictator. In this dome, the first two quadrants contain some housing and businesses, but the back half is set up with government office buildings, ranging from electric and power to judiciary.

"Bookworm, guide me to the place where Magnate would conduct business."

"Yes, Mr. President," Bookworm replies. "One hundred and seventy-two feet ahead and fifteen feet to your right is a series of steps that lead to heavy steel gates. Behind the gates is a one-story white marble building. That building is merely a guardhouse to the elevator of the seven-story building behind it. His office is on the seventh floor."

I turn right when I reach the stairs, finding El Matador in front of the closed gates. He points his sword in my direction while assuming a defensive stance, sinking on his legs with one knee forward and the other to the side. His weight is on the back leg so that he can quickly lunge forward or retreat. I'm not afraid, as our previous encounter showed he could no longer hurt me. My only concern is the lack of any expression on the face that holds the recessed, milky eyes. Something is wrong, and I don't know what. Of course, something was wrong with this entire journey.

With two steps I clear the stairs, whereupon El Matador lunges and attempts to impale me. I step into the attack, pleasantly relieved when the top few inches of the sword snaps off, pinging as it skips across the ground. While I'm confident in my new invulnerability, the painful memories of his first attack haven't yet faded away. Of course, it happened less than an hour earlier.

As fast as his lunge was, his post-attack pause is just the opposite. He is a statue, as if waiting for another command. I grab his arm and forcibly throw him behind me and past the stairs, noting from the sound that he crashed into a wall somewhere on the English side. I wonder if it's the London Bridge he hit, and if it's falling down.

In front of me stands a pair of interlocked gates. I place my hands on each of the thick, wrought-iron frames and pull in opposite directions, the only protest being the groan of the metal. After some snapping sounds, I grip the one on the left with both hands and rip it off its hinges, throwing it over to the English side. Dust drops down from the ceiling and falls on me as I proceed to walk through and to the other side. However, I stop before I reach the shorter, white marble building, as I have an idea. Instead of walking in, I jump on top of the smaller building and stare up at the higher gray building, which rests behind the one I'm standing on. I'm sure the man I sought isn't up there, but I still need to check. Also, I might be able to gather some clues on all the weird things that have been happening. The emotionless Magnate and El Matador, the Moon base, and now Arthuren's quizzical comments.

Chapter 17

I squat down and launch into the air again, this time missing the seventh floor by only a dozen feet. Only. I tear through the roof's small wall and skid to a stop a few dozen feet away from the roof entrance. I walk over, rip off the door, and then realize I won't be getting in, let alone walking around the inside of the building, at this size. I'm nearly twice its height and at least four times too wide to fit in. I slowly shrink as my needs are conveyed from Bookworm to my worshippers, and then I enter and proceed to the first door, which is easy to spot with the stairway lights having been left on. I rip that door off the hinges and follow a few more of Bookworm's prompts until I'm standing outside an office door with an engraving that reads:

Magnate Palmer
Mars Colony

The single-door entrance is made from a polycer-extruded material, which had been a relatively new discovery during my first term as President. It was a hybrid organic/ceramic nanomaterial made from the copolymerization of plastic precursors with functionalized silicates (clay), and it had been developed by military scientists. While cheap and easy to make in multi-ton quantities, it was discarded because accelerated aging studies revealed that the two materials would phase separate, losing many

181

of the advanced physical properties required for military strike systems. However, artists picked up the material and when they added dyes, found that over time the phase separation created unique, stunning textiles that were perfect for breaking up the décor found in monotone government-constructed housing projects. We had used it extensively in the creation of Entara. Obviously, the material had also been great for the government-constructed Marsian colony. I reach for the doorknob and stop short. While the lacquered hardwood knob is a sign of a foolish lavishness that any respectable leader would shy away from, it isn't what halts my entrance. There is a fine layer of reddish dust barely visible on the dark, cherry wood.

"Bookworm." I pause until the hologram appears. "Based on the ventilation system, how much time would it take to build up this level of dust on the doorknob?"

"Hmmm," Bookworm replies slowly, a sign he is accessing databases and running calculations. "I calculate that it's been between one to two months."

"So, they've been prepping for my overthrow of their dictatorship since we took off from the Moon. That's great news."

"Why is that, sir?"

"It means they're scared, that they know their end is near." I look around the large waiting room as I speak. The admin desk is to my left, and a dozen chairs are spaced around the room, some with small tables and others positioned to give access to the video wall, which also has a fine layer of dust on the screen. "I can't count how many times I've seen this during my life as a demigod. So many rulers puffed out their chests, spouted off how they were going to end my life, and claimed that I caused them no concern. However, each and every one—well, except for the truly maniacal ones—lied. They all hid well before my infiltration of their lair, but it didn't matter. Their realization that it was over happened way before the end. The dust is a sign that the regime may be ruthless, but not crazy. We have the advantage."

I reach for the door again, and pause again.

"What's wrong, Mr. President?" asks Bookworm from my wrist, looking at the doorknob and then back at me.

I switch hands. "Often, they would trap the entrance, hoping to blow me up. It never worked, but I lost a lot of watches."

"Thanks for your consideration, sir."

"No problem. I don't have time to go back to Earth and get a suitable replacement," I reply with a smirk on my face.

This time I grab the handle with my other hand, brace for the worse, and turn the doorknob counterclockwise. It turns without fireworks, so I push it open and walk in, noting that I had started to lose my focus on controlling my height as I'm barely able to walk under the eight-foot door frame. While the waiting room had been tastefully decorated, focused on providing just the right level of comfort to ease the nerves of anyone waiting to be seen, the even larger office was clearly meant to satisfy the eccentric, expensive taste of the Marsian Magnate.

The doorknob foreshadowed what to expect, starting with the cherry wood floorboards that singularly run the length of the forty-plus-foot room, each also being ten inches in width. A wooden, built-in bookcase of the same grain fills the entire left wall, broken up into three large segments. The middle houses leather-bound volumes with titles such as *Grimm's Complete Fairy Tales*, *The Iliad*, *Hans Christian Andersen's Complete Fairy Tales*, *Dracula*, and *Frankenstein*, all at eye level. Below these are an organized assortment of business management, leadership, and government regulation books, while the top shelves house a complete set of The Americas Constitutional Law, Volumes 1–60. I cringe at that last set, remembering not only commissioning their writing but having to review parts of them for release every day for nearly a year. The section of the bookcase furthest from me appears to be government-approved log books, barely holding onto the bright-green covering that makes their identification so easy. I turn my attention to the closest section of the bookcase, which contains an assortment of framed pictures of Magnate with other people. The middle row appears to be reserved for family and close friends, while the top and bottom rows are the usual handshake pics with dignitaries, the working class after speeches, and award handouts. Magnate looks happy and healthy, but all dictators were good at presenting an image of caring and being loved by the people they destroyed to stay on top. They'd pull out the devoted followers or make others pose and tell them that if they didn't look happy in the pictures, their families would be punished.

Disgusted, I scan past the large picture window to the right side where an oversized, cherry-wood table with a leather chair is situated, along with a meeting table made again of the same wood. I look up and am unsurprised to find that the same wood is covering the ceiling too. It must have cost tens of millions of dollars just to import all that wood from Earth. Of course, there isn't any real cost when you force others to do whatever you want. I stroll over to the desk, which has nothing on it except the usual layer of fine, red dust. It's then that I notice something odd about the green government books now directly across from me. Getting closer, I read the written numbering on the bindings and pull out the last one, flipping it open.

"Bookworm," I call out.

"Yes, Mr. President?" He reappears as his usual blue holographic image.

"Please scan this book," I ask as I flip the pages quickly from the beginning to the end in a matter of seconds. "Was there anything strange?"

Bookworm's image grabs his chin and rubs a finger up and down it for a while before he speaks. "Most of it is Magnate's daily logs, containing details of shuttle arrivals, important meetings, and future efforts."

Bookworm peers up at the bookshelf before continuing. "It looks to have started when the first magnate took over, more than two hundred years ago. However, it stops nearly one hundred and sixty years ago."

"Nearly a decade before the Marsians turned all Earth humans into slaves," I thought out loud. "But...what caused it?"

Bookworm shrugs his shoulders.

"Great to have you along. Remind me why I keep you around?"

"Comic relief," he says as if unoffended.

I ignore him and stare out the window as I think. "Bookworm, scan the room and point out anything that appears unusual."

"Done," he quickly replies. "The room appears to have been tidied up before they left, indicating that this was a well-planned retreat. Other than that, the only oddity is that one of the leather-bound books has a noticeable tear along the binding. It is strange because all the others appear to have never been opened."

"Which one?" I ask.

"Dracula."

"Just great," I reply as I walk over to the middle section of the bookcase. "As if suffering through three decades of zombie movies and TV shows wasn't enough torture when I was younger, we have a ruthless dictator who may believe he's a vampire."

I walk over to the large picture window and lean against Magnate's desk. The English quadrant is stunning, with Big Ben appearing just like the original and Westminster Abbey's architecture enhanced as it captures the golden rays from the fake moon. While the dome's panels are nearly transparent, they only reflect what little light Mars receives from the sun so that daytime appears more like a permanent overcast. I remember how we planned an exterior bot connected to a damn bright light that would make its way up and over the dome, mimicking the sun's pathway on Earth. It then would rush back to near its starting point, adjust its light to hold an appearance of Earth's moon, and begin again. People adjusted better when they first arrived, and their biorhythms were fooled enough that sleeping issues were no worse than on Earth. I look down at the London Bridge, noting that El Matador still lay where I had tossed him, body cozied up against a large block of the bridge, pointless sword in hand. I wonder how they were able to bring him back without his mind. He is a zombie now, or maybe he is soulless. Seeing Arthuren had been much less of a shock, probably because his festering pit of a personality hadn't changed. It's easy to believe that he was revived through some secret process, fully intact.

"Bookworm?" I ask.

"Yes, Mr. President." Bookworm replies.

"Assuming we have three or six domes where Palmer could hide, how long would it take to track him down?" I cross my arms as I wait for a response.

"I have an answer, but it is irrelevant," Bookworm says.

"Really?" I reply, as I raise an eyebrow but don't move my gaze from the window.

"Really, sir. We have no way of stopping him from moving. If we search an area and move on, he can always take up a hiding spot in the searched area."

"Mmm," I reply. "I'm not much of a detective, but I do know that people don't tend to hide that way. They try to pick the best spot available, holing up for as long as they can. At least until they feel their discovery is imminent."

"If that's the case, sir, then we might be able to track his whereabouts in as little as a day or no longer then a couple weeks."

"Not fast enough," I reply. "We have to hone in on a couple of the most likely spots and attack them as fast as possible."

I scan the apartment buildings behind the scenic foreground of the English quadrant. Just like on Earth, the rows of buildings are in various states of their life cycle. Some are brand new, some are old, and there are even a few holes in the ground where new buildings were to be built.

Holes.

I look back at the polycer door, its red striations striking. Yet I had failed to catch the unique nature of the door because of the excessive use of cherry wood for everything else. I walk over to the entrance and with my index finger create a deep gash in the door. I hold up the sliver of polycer and rotate it in front of my eyes.

"What do you see, Bookworm?"

"The polycer is made of a low-grade polyethylene and a local silicon oxide material. The impurity that has imparted the color is just ordinary Martian dust."

"That means they mine some of the materials, which also means there's a local mine," I surmise.

"Do you think that is where he is hiding?"

"I don't think so. But, if they have mining equipment, it also means they have the resources needed to create elaborate underground living quarters. I'm betting that's where we'll find him cowering."

I unfurl my arms, taking a step forward so that I'm right against the window. I watch the street as El Matador pulls his sword arm behind his head and flings the weapon in my direction. The broken sword takes a wobbly, end-over-end trajectory, heading my way. I don't move as it closes in, somewhat surprised when the broken length hits the window perfectly and embeds in the hardened material. A small part of the blade penetrates all the way through and is now sticking out inches from where my heart would be—I say would be because I don't know whether I truly have one. Unlike traditional glass, the window doesn't crack, and if I had pushed the sword back out, it would have sealed the hole even if there was a vacuum on one side. I place my index finger on the protruding sword and rub it as I think out loud.

"So, nine massive domes with a tunnel complex that could be hidden under any building—heck, any space—within one of these domes. It's likely there's one under this building, and that's one of the targeted areas that makes sense. I guess we should start with scouring the basement."

"Sir?" says Bookworm.

"Yes?"

"There are exactly seventy-three satellites in orbit around Mars. Thirty-four are no longer operational, seventeen are in a state of limited capability—meaning they only have active propulsion systems ensuring station keeping—and of the other twenty-two, I can gain access to twelve. Of those twelve—."

"I assume this is going somewhere other than you demonstrating your ability to subtract?" I interrupt.

"Yes. I have accessed a satellite with penetrating spectroscopic capability, which will fly over the Marsian colony in exactly thirty-six minutes. I have already repositioned its camera to scan the area, and we should have a map displaying any subterranean voids."

"Good. But in the meantime, I'm going down to the basement to dig around."

"Very well. I'll go with you," Bookworm replies.

I stop my walk toward the door, look down at him, and shake my head. "Funny. I don't have to take you. Also, you used a contraction for the first time. You feeling okay?"

No reply.

I find the stairwell next to the elevator and proceed down the steps until I reach the basement level. The door is locked, so I snap off the doorknob, peel back the metal plate, and stick two fingers into the hole. I pull the door and door frame away from the wall, which doesn't require a lot of effort. Like in the stairway, the lights are still on, and it takes me less than twenty minutes to do a quick walkthrough of each room. The entire basement appears to be dedicated to the civil engineering and maintenance staff, along with a small area posting a sign that reads, "IT Customer Support." Always great to deemphasize IT help. I wonder if they had sourced out most of the work to the Moon base.

"Now, that is funny, sir." Bookworm says.

"I told you to stay out of my head unless it was critical," I growl.

No response.

"Bookworm, how much more time until you have the map?"

"The satellite finished its scan of the colony a few minutes ago. It is now compiling the data and should be rendering an image in less than five minutes. It does have an ePET, so I will receive the file as soon as it is sent."

"Good, because I came here to overthrow this regime, not play hide-and-seek," I say. Sure, I was logical when first assessing how to find Magnate, but emotions are meant to change one's mood rather quickly.

My temper is rising even faster than my impatience. This time I decide to stomp around the cement-like floors to see if there are any hollow spots, like a carpenter looking for studs in the wall. About two minutes into my Neanderthalic dance, I hear a hollow reverberation beneath my foot. Excitedly, I bring a fist down, the impact sending shrapnel in all directions as my meaty paw drives completely through the six inches of flooring and bounces off a flexible material. I extract my hand and pummel my other into the ground next to the hole. I picture the look on Magnate's face as he hears and then sees my inevitable entrance into his hiding place. I wonder if he will wet himself or just start crying. The end is near.

Four more hits, a mixture of white floor dust and red Martian dust swirling in the air, and I have created a man-sized hole. A few more hits and my smaller demigod body can squeeze inside, or maybe I can jump in the air and crash through the ground/ceiling for another dramatic entrance.

"Mr. President!" shouts Bookworm, halting my next strike midair.

"What?" I snap.

"For the third time, that is a small tunnel for the building's plumbing," Bookworm says.

I place my closed fist on the ground and peer into the hazy hole. One of the plastic pipes I accidently hit has cracked, and a brownish liquid is dripping out the bottom onto the ground of the tunnel, which is only about a foot below the pipes. The liquid flows slower than molasses, but the aroma hits me faster than a jet fighter. I inhale without thinking, like when someone passes gas and you smell something bad, but your brain involuntarily demands confirmation.

"Good gawd!" I gasp.

"It's a plumbing return line," Bookworm chuckles.

I quickly stand up and walk out of the room, shutting the door behind me and hoping that we'll be leaving this building very soon.

"So, can you pull up the map now?" I ask Bookworm.

"Yes, it's done now, but can you please go back to the open area next to the stairway? It will be easier to display the needed details in a larger room."

Without affirmation, I wind my way back to the stairway, take off the black watch, and lay it in the center of the floor before stepping back. A hologram of the Marsian colony stretches out from the watch, expanding to a twelve-by-twelve-foot topographic view of the planet. Each dome is about three feet in diameter, with my impressive crash site to the right of the first three domes I had encountered.

"Do any of the first set of domes have people living inside them?" I ask.

"The satellite has a very broad range of instrumentation and software, including thermal and stop-start imaging. The stop-start imaging allows tracking of the movements of living beings and even things such as the opening and closing of doors and windows. Using both tools, I was able to see that those domes are not inhabited, and there was no sign of movement over a five-minute period. However, there was something very interesting."

I know he wants me to ask what was so interesting, as he has been playing this game ever since I put on the watch. So instead, I walk to the left and scan the last three domes.

"The setup of these three is interesting. The middle three have the quadrants we had originally planned for, even the parks and other recreational areas so that the colonists would feel more at home. However, these last three not only look the same but also have just rows and rows of the same buildings inside," I say.

"Hmm. Let me check something." Bookworm opens a fake book and pretends to read. "From what I can piece together, it looks like the original plan was scrapped when the contractor, who was awarded the building of the colony, realized that there was not enough housing for the number of required personnel to make the colony self-sustaining. All three of them are low-income housing for those who have limited specialized skills," says Bookworm.

I sigh. It looks like no matter how one tries to create a classless system, something always forces it back to the unwanted.

"Sir, can we get back to the interesting thing I found out?"

"Oh, sorry, I must've missed what you said," I reply, feeling better now that I had a little more control.

Bookworm glares at me, but I pretend to also have missed it as I walk back over to the first three domes. I step on the one closest to me, watching as the hologram tries to adjust around my foot and leg.

"Watch the crash site as I use the hologram's time elapse capability," Bookworm says.

I watch as a group of five exoskeletons exit the dome my foot is on, walk to the crash site, and pick up different items scattered around the

190

crater. They then walk toward the dome that is furthest from my foot. Before they enter the dome, the five minutes of satellite oversite have passed and the hologram has been reset.

"It's just like an old kidnapping movie where the money case blows up as the kidnappers make the exchange, and they run around trying to catch as much of the money as possible, even as the police are chasing them," I say. "Also, whatever was inside the shuttle was more important than trying to stop me with all the exoskeletons they had available."

"My database doesn't seem to have a movie like that in it. Can you be more specific?"

"No," I reply. "Their retrieving of items seems a little odd, unless they really need the supplies right away. Hmm. Anyway, what about the subterranean map? Can you overlap with this one, but just raise up the surface map?"

In response, the holographic image of the domes lifts off the ground by almost three feet, and then a massively complex series of tunnels and caves grows from the ground of the building up to the bottom of the imaged domes. Below the now-abandoned domes on the right side, the larger tunnel entrances slowly angle downward to allow vehicle access. They go deeper and deeper into the ground, with large caves opening up at various spots. The caves aren't very high, and columns within the caves are abundant. It reminds me of my prison, and I know it had to be for mining. Whenever ore or precious-metal deposits were found, they would mine the area and keep columns in place to prevent cave-ins. Unfortunately, when the all the larger deposits had been depleted on Earth, smaller mining groups would go in and play the dangerous game of extracting columns. In this case, it appears there is still a lot of good mining to be done. Also, judging by the depth of the hologram, they had excavated almost a mile into the Martian crust.

"What is the composition of Mars's crust, Bookworm?"

"It's largely volcanic basalt rock, containing mostly silica. It also contains sodium, potassium, and magnesium, but not much else. There are larger pockets of metal, enough for a colony but not for an Earth-like civilization. The crust extends down almost thirty miles, followed by the mantel and…"

"Thanks," I say to cut him off.

I then look at the three domes on the left, which have hundreds of very small, individual subterranean caves and tunnels.

"I'm guessing that these," I point, "were made by individuals who wanted a little extra storage space. I bet that it's not worth looking for him there, as the fortification of those smaller units can't be better than a locked door. I do see one particular tunnel that is four to five times larger than the others. Interesting, but not worth pursuing at this moment. Probably worth a look if we exhaust our other options."

"Agreed, sir."

The organization, alignment, and overall build of the subterranean network under the middle three domes clearly points out that they must have been designed and approved by the colony's civil engineering staff, completely opposite of domes four through six. The network is orderly, and almost all are interconnected, even if there are many interlocks present in case of a breach that could suck out the precious oxygen. After I stare at the hologram for almost ten minutes, the monotone blue lines become more like a bug zapper, drawing me in so close that I'm sure there is going to be a loud snapping of electricity. I rub my eyes and step back.

"Bookworm, do you see anyplace that would be suitable for hiding? Such as a long, narrow, fortified tunnel?"

"Yes, there are nine such tunnels. The most obvious one is below the public services building, which is now used primarily for welfare and government employment. When the colony was built, it was originally the headquarters building, but the headquarters were moved when the building we are currently in was finished."

"Bookworm, did you know this while I was staring at the map?" I ask. My blood was beginning to boil again.

"Yes, sir. However, I did not want to interrupt your thought process in case you were able to figure out a hiding spot that I could not. Your dominant, emotional disposition is something I cannot mimic."

Still upset, I grunt to acknowledge that he might have a valid point.

"Where is it?" I ask with my continuing growl.

"Turn left when you exit the building and walk across the street, then enter the second building on your left. It has a single set of steps leading up to the three-story building. You will not miss it because, uhhh...it has a statue of you at the top of the stairs." Bookworm's voice conveys embarrassment.

Finally, the confrontation with Magistrate is imminent. He can neither hope to defeat me nor run away as he's stuck in the dome like a hamster in a plastic ball.

Chapter 18

I don't know how long I've been standing in front of the statue, but I'm sure it's much longer than what's healthy. The white and black polycer statue was crafted as a reenactment of my Independence Day speech, where I announced the trillion-dollar plan to colonize Mars. Three billionaires had attempted and failed before my unveiling. The first hadn't even made it off Earth, as his company's risk-averse approach was sound but fraught with schedule delays because the most creative minds in the aerospace industry had not been attracted to his company. When technical issues naturally arose, their solutions were fraught with mistakes.

The second billionaire came from a famed Korean mining company. He had driven his vision all the way to the Moon, the same colony I had visited on my way here; the one that was now a house of horrors. He had abandoned his vision when a number of metal-rich asteroids had let loose from Orion's Belt and traveled in close proximity of the Moon. He set up a mining colony and over the next two decades made hundreds of billions from the precious metals he hauled in. When no more asteroids were predicted to fly by, he abandoned the entire base. The Americas had bought the base at a tenth of its original cost and then mothballed it.

The third billionaire had made her fortune on artificial-intelligence networks before throwing it all into accessories for ePEG devices. She had decided to skip the Moon base, using a low Earth orbit docking station, and shoot straight for Mars. Her first, second, and third crews made it safely to the inhospitable planet. They were well prepared for the massive dust storms and absence of oxygen, but the planet's lack of a dense atmosphere made its inhabitants susceptible to radiation damage. One incredibly powerful solar flare, and all three crews had been wiped out after a short battle with acute radiation sickness. The worst part was that their slow radiation poisoning was fully documented by the private company's feed. Sure, the company had tried to bury it, but hackers will always get what they want, especially when money is involved. They made millions and she lost billions before losing something even more valuable: her will to live. It wasn't the loss of money but rather the loss of life that ravaged her spirit, then her mind, and finally her body.

I described my vision for our colonization of Mars earlier, and nothing has changed even as my memory grows stronger. Yet I stand in front of the statue, unwilling to move. I had never been to Mars, had never been to outer space before this journey to right wrongs. In fact, I had never seen the initiation of the project, let alone its completion when on Earth. Yet here is my image, noted as the first to put a human colony on another planet. The plaque below my name compares me to President John F. Kennedy, who in 1961 stated that we would put a man on the Moon. He was assassinated two years later, never seeing his dream come true. I almost didn't myself, yet more than two hundred years later, here I am. I am standing in front of my statue, not gloating, but rather humbled by those who took my vision and turned it into reality. It's almost perfect.

Almost.

A word often used to describe near success or near failure. With it one conveys the pain or joy of a near miss. I think someone should write a book about 'Almost.' Should it be a philosophical one? No, too boring. Maybe a leadership book, where one analyzes great leaders and their near misses and then looks at failures that were so close to being successful. Now that would be interesting.

"Mr. President?" queries Bookworm.

I close my eyes and shake my head. The blanket of darkness that always covers me when I reflect and brood has almost completely enveloped me while standing on the steps. Bookworm is successful in shaking part of it off me, but not enough. My anger, oh so easy to rise, is with me again. The Marsian colony—not Martian colony—my vision, had been successful.

However, the power of leadership had corrupted the current Magnate. He has almost destroyed Earth humans, and it looks like the Marsian colony is also almost on the brink of failure. He has to be stopped, and I'm going to stop him the same way I stopped all those who led through suppression.

I open my eyes, red prevalent again as the blood vessels dilate proportionally to my anger. I now look at eye level with the twelve-foot statue. I'm not as tall as I was when I landed, but any taller and I won't be able to go into the building. I take a deep breath and shout at the top of my lungs.

"When I find you, and I will find you, I'm going to wrap my hand around your aged throat and squeeze until your head pops off and rolls around the ground!"

Bookworm's hologram disappears, and I storm past the statue and up to the solid polycer doors. Without slowing down I shove my arms out, hurtling the doors into the room and embedding them into the far wall. The wide stairwell down to the basement is behind the counters on the left. I barrel into them, sending splinters spraying forward. Each step I take down the stairway cracks from my weight and anger. When I reach the bottom, the lights briefly flicker off, then come back on.

Thanks, Bookworm.

Turn right and head to the wall. The wall is on rollers, and will slide to the right when enough force is applied.

As I storm forward, a hologram of Magnate appears in front of me, moving at my pace. His frail frame is covered by a white and purple robe; a tight necklace with his office symbol rests against his throat, covering the veins and wrinkles that were so pronounced earlier. Unlike before, his glazed eyes shoot out rays of rage, trying to push back my assault.

"You cannot comprehend what you are up against! You will not win. You will not be helping the Earth humans. You must stop!" he orders.

I think about not replying, but I was never good at keeping my mouth shut. "You and your round table will feel my justice for a brief few seconds. Enjoy the last minutes of your rule."

I place my hands against the wall and push to the left. At first the wall buckles slightly and groans before it begins to move. I push harder, hearing metal snap, feeling polycer splintering. With one more push, the wall flies sideways and flips end over end across the room.

It opened to your other right, came Bookworm's voice in my head.

I step into the long hallway, barely noticing the roughened, red walls. Five steps in and an interlock door slams down behind me, immediately followed by the sucking sound of air leaving the area. I keep walking forward, not understanding how they think this could stop me after I survived the trip without oxygen. As I near the end of the hallway, a flash of red light escapes the wall and strikes me in the chest. It cleaves through me, creating a hole the size of a human fist, which quickly seals back up. Another hits me in the abdomen and another strikes my shoulder, tearing through my body faster than I can heal. The light of the laser pulses fills the air as I struggle to maintain my forward progress. I place my hand on the cold metal interlock door as parts of my body evaporate. I wonder if I have enough energy left to push the door open.

Remember Arthuren, comes Bookworm's voice.

I understand, but the problem is that when emotions dominate me, I don't seem invincible. Far from it.

Emotions drive me back to my desire to be human. No! I want to be human when emotions take over. But it doesn't need to be this way. I keep my anger but remember what I really am.

I stand up, ignoring the dozens of lasers, which now pass through me as if I don't exist. I kick the metal door in and am thrown back as air explosively fills the room. It doesn't hurt, but I feel stupid for not realizing it would happen. I stand back up and barrel forward, setting my sights on the safe-like vault door at the end of the next hallway.

"You cannot win. Even if you kill me, it will not change anything," challenges Magnate's image, still no sign of fear on his face.

So unusual, but it doesn't matter. When I reach the circular door, I put one hand on each side, gripping the metal so tightly that my fingers dig into it like with the gondola support in Hikone.

It is a bank safe door. It must have been brought here on one of the first cargo shuttles. It has a dozen three-inch hardened steel rods that, when locked, are held in place by the steel-reinforced concrete surrounding the door, says Bookworm.

And? I growl.

And, I can't figure out why you haven't ripped it out of the wall yet.

I grunt, seeing the veins on my hands, arms, and legs rise up like skyscrapers on a granite surface; hearing the popping of my muscles as I pull backward, feeling the balls of my feet sink into the floor as my toes grip and rip that same floor apart. It starts to move, I hear the metal groan, feel the concrete popping, but it isn't enough. I scream so loud that the building shakes and pull so hard that blood is seeping out of my skin as vessels, arteries, and veins burst. It's not what I want to do, but I don't stop. I scream louder and I pull harder. The entire wall gives way all at once. The sound of destruction outweighs my yell of triumph, hundreds of pieces and parts flying across the room in a mini explosion.

I find myself on both knees, gasping for energy, barely keeping myself from splaying out on the rubble I have created. I don't have time for this, but I can't stand. Not yet. I just need a minute.

You almost succeeded, comes Bookworm's voice.

Almost. Almost? Almost!

My quivering legs somehow find the strength to lift me up, or maybe it's my willpower, or the hope and faith my followers have in me. Whatever it is, it guides me into the innocuous cave behind the vault door. The decrepit, robed being, my nemesis during this journey, stands in front of me as a hologram, with the real one positioned behind the red polycer desk at the back of the cave.

"Stop!" he orders. A hand points out at me, with the index finger extended. "You will not succeed!"

Again, no fear. Only anger.

I take one step forward, pause, then take another. I do this again, staring at the real Magnate as I pass through the hologram. My own blood coats my body, smeared from the door's explosive removal.

More words shoot out of his wrinkled lips, but I don't hear them.

"You're dead!" My rumbling voice seems to emanate from the walls.

I step up to the desk, letting his frail, bent finger rest against my chest. I'm reduced to his height now. I want to create his death scene, not just be a part of it.

Without a word I lean forward and wrap my hand around his neck. I will myself to slowly grow, staring into his eyes to see if my demonstration of power is enough to finally strike fear in him. Continuing to grow, my hair brushes against the cavern's ceiling, and Magnate is now suspended more than four feet off the ground. He flails and helplessly strikes at my hand, trying to free his neck.

"And now it's time for your reign to end." I squeeze slowly, watching his flushed face turn an even deeper shade of red.

And then it happened.

The white robe that clung to his neck—covering the back of his head and shoulders and wrapping around the outside of his arms—lifts up and spins away with a sucking sound emanating from the back of Magnate. He screams, the painful scream of a dying human, tortured while he releases his last breath. For the first time during our many conversations, Magnate sounds human. Though shocked by Magnate's scream, I keep my eyes on the now magically flying cape. It's somewhat translucent, with odd hues of red and green spreading out from its center like cracks on a windshield. It flips in the air, folding and unfolding its shape to slither upward, until it is nearly touching the rough ceiling. It curls up into a sphere, then blasts of air whistle out from the bottom of the cape. It jets out of the room in a straight line, almost faster than my eyes can follow, before disappearing up the tunnel.

"Hmmm. That was odd," I state as the piece of the puzzle I had tried to place when on the Moon finds a perfect fit. I then look at the limp Magnate, who I still hold by the neck. I raise my other hand to evenly balance his weight, and gently lower the frail frame carefully onto the desktop. A small cross on a leather necklace falls out of his shirt. I deliberately cross his arms like a Catholic receiving Communion, and roll him over so I can examine his back.

"Very interesting," Bookworm says as his diminutive form bends over for a closer look.

Magnate's purple and white robe has been altered so that it exposes his entire back, somehow hanging onto the back of the shoulders and slowly tapering down to the tailbone. Even though Magnate is coated in fresh blood, I easily spot four sets of gaping holes the size of quarters riding up his back, slightly increasing in width until the last one, which is positioned just below the shoulder blades. They all ooze a deep red gel, except for one smaller hole at the base of the neck, which is oddly off center, shifted to the right by more than an inch. I peer into the hole, which seems to go straight up into the brain stem.

"He is alive, but barely," Bookworm says. "His blood pressure is seventy over forty, with a heart rate under thirty beats per minute. You need to plug the holes so he loses less blood."

I rip off pieces of the robe and stuff them into the holes, noting that Magnate flinches more and more with each filled hole. When finished, I stand straight and then turn around and look back toward the tunnel exit.

"Do you think there is a med kit in the area?" I ask.

"Yes, but none have the supplies needed to help him. The trauma from whatever that thing did is simply too much for any human to survive." Bookworm pauses, seeming to weigh his words. "I need more time to assess Magnate's body."

"Not yet. He needs to hold on long enough so we can understand what's going on and hopefully have him tell us what that thing was. I have a feeling there are many, many more." I turn my attention back to the peaceful Magnate. "And something tells me that things are even worse than I feared. We need to talk to him."

"Do you think all the Marsians are infected?"

"It makes sense. How else would you get tens of thousands of people to sleep in unison?" It's a rhetorical question, and I'm glad Bookworm realizes that. He is learning and growing each day.

"Then the chances of us finding a doctor, nurse, or medic to help us will be impossible."

"We don't need one of them, but we do need the impossible," I reply.

I place my bloody hands on Magnate's bloody back, the warm, slippery syrup still oozing out like Thanksgiving cranberry sauce. One of my fingers finds the raised ridge of a hole, and I close my eyes. When I'm angry, when I feel at my best, the rage has an energy that pulses out of my skin. I had never thought of it until now, but it is energy. I wonder if I can use that same energy, the one I call forth to kill and destroy, to heal others. It has never been done, never been thought of by any demigod, but it has to be possible. If only because I and all the other demigods are impossible. We shouldn't exist; we shouldn't be able to do what we do. But we do exist, and we do the impossible.

I don't know what to do, so I just focus my thoughts on healing and imagine pushing the energy in my body down my arms and into the dying Marsian. I stay that way, breathing in air only because it helps me imagine pushing the energy out of my body, until I hear a weak cough. When I open my eyes, I stare into deep reddish-blue eyes connected to a slightly-bloodied smile. I pride myself on being able to accurately read people with a simple first impression. In that instant I saw compassion and caring, a person who had been born to help others. I only wonder when he had been abducted. Had it been in the last few years, or was all that he would have gladly given to others unrealized due to a lifetime of being the host of some alien race?

"I knew…" he coughs, and begins anew with a voice that I can barely hear. "I knew you'd come, no matter what the aliens, the Wyndelaces, tried."

"You planned the whole thing?" I ask.

"No. No." More coughing. "They are too good for that. I just…tweaked what they were already doing. And…and it worked. Impossibly grand."

"What do they want?" I ask. "What is their plan? What are they?"

The happiness in his warm eyes is fading like paint after years under a blazing desert heat, but the smile would not. He looks at Bookworm's hologram before closing his eyes. "In my office…in the beginning."

The silent exhale pounds on me like a large, Japanese Taiko drum. It signals the end of the act. The final act for one Marsian, but only the signal for the beginning of the third and final act of my story.

Or so I think.

Chapter 19

I ignore the new stench that nearly always follows death, no matter how horridly or how peacefully a life has ended. His sideways position, looking like he was getting ready for his back to be cracked by a chiropractor, was not dignified enough for someone who had found a way to fight an all-controlling alien race, knowing the only sure thing was his own death. He had killed Bookworm—maybe not of his own volition—inciting me so that I would come for him, which would lead to me finding out the truth. The truth that the Moon base and Marsian colony had been overrun by aliens. Aliens who seemed set on wiping out any trace of humanity. However, I still don't know whether that wiping out meant genocide or some sort of permanent parasitic control.

I thoughtfully roll him onto his back, crossing his feet before strengthening the previous crossing I had done of his arms. His palms lay flat against each sunken breast, one finger bloodied after resting on the desk. His eyes have opened slightly, so I pass my hand down his face with a small amount of force to close them, then pull his long white hair down his sides. The streaks of blood blend with the red dust and red polycer table, seeming to signify his being absorbed back into the entropic universe. That energy will then flow back into the timeless plane, naturally gathering in pockets where the ePEG devices extract it. A true circle of life.

Looking out across the room reveals that no others are present. It's as hollow as it is empty, the lone sacrificial table jutting out from the floor.

"Bookworm," I ask, waiting for the image to turn toward me. "Is that creature still around?"

"I do not think so, Mr. President. Once we found out it was a creature and not a fashionable cape, I was able to use a few spectroscopic techniques to analyze its physical characteristics before it shot away. Unlike humans, it is silicon and sulfur based, most likely getting its flexibility from polysulfone networks. However, when it made decisions on how to move, there were no centralized outputs similar to human brain activity. Rather there was a general increase throughout its entire structure."

"Are you telling me all of this stuff I don't understand to make me feel stupid, or is there a purpose?" I ask.

"The purpose is to begin understanding these aliens, so that we can figure out how to stop them," he replies.

"But right now you have nothing?"

"No, not yet," he replies rather grumpily.

Having achieved my objective, I move to thinking about Magnate's last words. Something was in his office, and it was at the beginning of something, like his life, his bookcase, the room. Hmm.

"Why do people always say cryptic things when they die?" I ask, rhetorically.

"In this case maybe he was afraid that the alien would discover what he had hidden," hypothesizes Bookworm.

"Makes sense," I reply, not bothering to let him know that I hadn't wanted a response. It had been a good answer.

Walking slowly away from the desk, I try to clear my mind. I don't want to think; don't want to reflect on my mistakes, numerous bad assumptions, and how easily I had been manipulated for and along this entire journey. Thinking about it and the manipulations during my whole life will sink me again into the pool of anger that I had called home for so long. I let the thoughts shed off me, each a drop that runs down my body and soaks into the Martian rocks.

By the time I reach the cave entrance, where I pull off the vault door, I'm at peace. I look down the entrance and see that the sealing lock was activated by the alien as it fled. A futile move, showing its desperation. I don't hesitate, don't even close my eyes as I walk through it. The polycer and metallic glass break away, the polycer shatters like glass—many pieces held together by tiny polymer fibers—while the metallic glass fractures and pops before embedding into the walls of the tunnel. I keep walking, breaking the other seal before heading into the basement of the public services building. Still none of the Marsians are up, making me wonder if the aliens have some form of telepathic communication, warning all the others to flee from me.

When I'm back in Magnate's office, I analyze everything: the wood floors, the three columns of the bookshelf, the gaudy desk, the window with El Matador's sword still stuck in it. None of it makes a bell cling in my head. No, wait, none of it rings a bell. That's better.

"Bookworm, do you have any ideas?" I'm wondering where the alien has gone and if there is some sort of time-critical event I'm not aware of.

I open every drawer of the desk, the first time rifling through the papers and the second time dropping each piece on the floor after analyzing it. Nothing!

"Bookworm, any hidden compartments in the desk?"

"Unfortunately, my limited analysis capabilities are unable to penetrate the surface of most dense materials. Judging by the geometry and the drawers you have already taken out though, I can confidently say that that if there is a hidden compartment, it will be very small," replies Bookworm in his analytical voice.

"Yeah, and I bet that is just the size of what we are looking for." I almost pound the table apart, but hold off and go over to the left side of the bookshelf, then walk over to the right. "The bookshelf is not only too obvious, but also probably somewhere the alien would look if it had a hint something was going on. I'm betting it would be somewhere where Magnate could drop it quickly, such as...."

I look over at the door and the classic wooden doorknob, with the screws and outdated keyhole.

Keyhole.

I focus on what I need as I step over to the door. I raise my index finger and can't help but smile when seeing the overgrown nail that is now shaped like a flathead screwdriver. Before using it, I shake the door back and forth, clearly hearing something rattling inside. It only takes a minute to remove the faceplate and pull out the quarter-inch metal disk that is inside. It's oblong in shape, being thicker in the middle than on the sides, with the overall dimensions being just small enough to fit in the keyhole. I hold it up between my finger and thumb, looking over its shiny metal surface for any marks. There are none.

"It is a PMD, personal memory disk, which usually is placed in a circular case behind the ear by those who have an external connector embedded in their skull. He would have needed only a second to remove it and drop it in the keyhole," Bookworm says.

"Maybe another clue about the aliens," I comment. "They don't seem able to read the minds of their hosts and sometimes aren't aware of their hosts' hostile actions."

"Albeit briefly," adds Bookworm, who must have been thinking of the sleight of hand required by Magnate.

"How do we read it?"

"Place it on top of your watch. Unless it is ePEG encrypted, I will be able to abstract whatever is inside."

I do as he suggests, waiting for it to light up or spin. After a few seconds nothing has happened, so I raise an eyebrow at Bookworm's image, which is hunched over a laptop to signify he's doing work.

"Anything?"

A sigh escapes the hologram's lips before he pulls off his glasses and places his head in his hands. "Yes. It's worse than I could have predicted. In fact, it's nearly unimaginable."

"If it's time critical, I suggest you tell me," I growl, almost missing that Bookworm used two contractions for the first time, and when he is also acting upset. He's becoming more human, or is becoming human again.

"The PMD contains a series of video catalogs, and…maybe it is best if you see for yourself," replies Bookworm, regaining his analytical composure.

Bookworm disappears in a slow blip, which is followed by the watch face display lifting out toward me, expanding until it's a six-by-three-inch color screen. It's another holographic image, but it seems real.

A fuzzy, round face with dark hair appears on the screen. The image zooms out, clearing up the picture. A man in his mid-years of life is wiping the sweat away from his receding hairline, while at the same time disheveling his bushy, black eyebrows. His round head looks out of sorts perched on his skinny frame, and he's breathing in deep gasps, as if he just finished a sprint. He's standing in Magnate's office, which is obvious from all the cherry wood furnishings and the familiar bookcase.

"Magnate...Palmer," he huffed.

"Go on, Stanley," Magnate said in a comforting voice.

"It's just as the Earth tracking system—and the Moon base—reported a few hours ago." Stanley placed his hands on his knees before coughing so heavily that I feared he was going to birth a lung.

"It's okay, Stanley. Take your time," Magnate replied.

"That's the problem sir, there is...no time. The spaceship that appeared out of nowhere will soon enter our atmosphere. They're saying that it will either hit the colony or come really close. We must evacuate, sir!"

Stanley's voice was no longer winded, but it was now replaced with panic.

The image raised up before refocusing on the panicked man. Magnate must have stood up.

"And go where, Stanley? Sure, some of us could abandon our positions and leave with the land vehicles, and even a few others could board the escape pod and return to Earth."

The image walked over to the window; the same window I had stared out a short time ago. Over one-hundred and fifty years separated our actions. How had he lived so long?

"However, what about our people? Do you wish them to see their leaders fleeing at the first sign of danger? What if the ship misses us? Surely we would no longer and should no longer oversee this amazing colony." Magnate turned to look back at Stanley.

While the scene continues, I can't help worrying about the escape pod. Did the aliens use it to send some of their kind to Earth?

Stanley huffed and lowered his eyes before speaking. "Of course, you're right, Magnate Palmer."

"I don't know about that. If the ship hits us, then no one will be alive to tell me what a fool I was. If it misses, though, I will look like a soothsayer," he chuckled.

It wasn't an arrogant chuckle, just one of mild amusement.

"Sorry to bother you, Magnate Palmer. I'll send out the word for everyone to resume their duties," Stanley said, now able to look at his boss.

"What? Let's not be silly." The image focused on the room's door. "I'm not going to miss this, and neither should anyone else. Everyone can go outside their buildings and stare out the dome. In fact, I'm heading to the roof, Stanley."

The image faded briefly, reappearing as in the previous video file with a first-person view of someone looking off in the direction of domes seven, eight, and nine; the ones I hadn't visited yet.

A door shut behind the person wearing the video recorder.

"Come to watch our imminent death, Colonel Lync?" came Magnate's voice, from the video recorder he was wearing.

"Well, I do like a good show, even if it involves my own annihilation," came back a calm, deep voice.

Footsteps signaled the approach of the colonel and ended when speckled black hair and the end of a large nose on a very short, pudgy frame could be seen on the right side of the video.

"It sounds funny to say this, but any contact with the spaceship?" asked Magnate.

"Nope," replied the colonel, which was followed by a sigh. "Nothing since we spotted it. Damn thing is blocking all our outgoing signals, but allowing us to still receive. And Sergeant Rinch just let me know that the analysis team says it's coming in too hot for a smooth landing."

"You mean based on our technical capability," replied Magnate. "If it truly is an alien spaceship, then it may have the technology to stop faster than we think possible."

208

"I can't deal with things that defy the physics of our known world, Case. Heck, I'd have an ulcer the size of my nose," Colonel Lync said.

"Like the demigods?"

"Abominations," was all that came back.

The video shifted slightly and Magnate's hand could be seen on the colonel's shoulder, which was a good foot lower than his own.

No more words were exchanged for a few minutes as they watched the sky. A white pinpoint of light appeared at the top of the video and in seconds grew to the size of an onion. In another few seconds, they could see its oblong shape, with the center jutting out much farther than the top or bottom of the white spaceship. The closer it got, the stranger the structure appeared.

"Heck, looks like white Lego pieces a kid stuck together to make a spaceship. It's not smooth at all," commented the colonel with no hint of fear. "Without disobeying the laws of physics, it has to be interstellar."

The door behind them opened and closed again, and the spaceship continued to grow in size on the screen.

"I have emergency response teams ready, your Magnate. Some folks elected to go underground and...oh no!" Stanley's voice moved rapidly from reporting to panic.

"I'd say relax, Stanley. However, even I'm feeling unsettled. I don't see how this can end well," said Magnate.

Magnate's video feed never faltered. The ship grew until it blotted out about a fourth of the video screen, nearly the diameter of a single dome. The flying structure now looked much less like Lego blocks and more like a central hub pierced by a thick spoke. However, it did not spin.

The colonel's hand could be seen reaching up to his ear.

"Sarge says that it will fly over us and land greater than two hundred miles to the southeast," the colonel said.

"So great to—,"

The video feed stops and Bookworm's image appears.

"I'm going to slow down the video and tune out the human voices for the next part, sir," Bookworm says.

I merely nod, but focus more intently, as if I were trying to find a kid wearing a red-and-white-striped hat amidst a horde of people. The video feed played on as the spaceship began to pass over the Marsian colony. The sheer size was almost too difficult to grasp, but I didn't see anything out of the ordinary, except for the video feed bobbing as Magnate turned his head in an arcing motion. Then I caught it.

"Pause," I say. "Can you expand that area on the central stick below the hub?"

Bookworm complies, zooming in on the central spoke to reveal that a large cube-like section of the stick was missing. Furthermore, it was the only part of the white ship that was marbled with black lines and burnt-like splotches.

"It's damaged."

"Yes, sir. And there is more," Bookworm says as he zooms in on the section even further. "It does appear that the entire spaceship is modular. Even I couldn't have picked it out without the missing, damaged section. It is like an assembled puzzle from a distance. But see how symmetrical the hole is and the lines that run along the ship."

Bookworm zooms back out and lets the video play at regular speed. No sooner had it passed over the Marsian colony than its forward momentum nearly ground to a stop. It did keep moving, but with more of a controlled crash landing. It slammed into the surface of Mars only miles away from the colony, shaking the group and sending a billowing, red dust cloud rushing toward the domes. The video feed stops again, with Bookworm reappearing.

"It was aiming for Mars and the colony the whole time," I say.

"Again, at first I would have thought it was happenstance. The video provides a different perspective, and I would hypothesize that these aliens do have technology for inertia dampening, but it isn't strong enough for it to risk a landing on Earth. Or with the damage it couldn't survive entry into our atmosphere. It must have chosen Mars to increase the odds of surviving the crash and—."

"Because it had humans on it," I finish.

Bookworm disappears, and the video of the crash landing plays for a few more seconds before fading out. A good ten seconds pass before the screen brightens to reveal a new scene. The video feed wearer was bouncing up and down, tightly gripping a steering wheel, as the vehicle they were inside plowed blindly through a Martian dust storm. The center of the windshield was oddly transparent, the way it transmitted light being similar to the material used on the domes. The right and left sides provided a panoramic view around the vehicle from external cameras. Underneath the screens were infrared, ultraviolet, and an assortment of other spectroscopic readouts. Above the driver were telemetry and health management displays. Anything that wasn't glowing was wrapped in a matte-black coating.

"—yes, your Magnate," came Colonel Lync's strained voice as he corrected the vehicle after hitting a large rock. "I know this may seem stupid to you, but think about it. I'm the only colonel who volunteered to be the senior Americas Space Force officer of the Marsian Colony. All I got is a few dozen soldiers and a pathetic crew of grudgingly trained militia; they aren't soldiers. I'm not putting civilians in danger, period. You can be upset with me, but in truth the blame lies squarely on the former President of The Americas. He made the law, not me."

I chuckle at the reference to my contentious decision. After seeing how poorly civilians had been treated at the military-run Moon base, I had decided to ensure that the Marsian colony had no choice but to be an exploratory outpost, limiting the number of military assigned to Mars.

The exasperated sigh of Magnate came over the video headpiece. "Yes, Colonel. He made the rule, but you didn't have to so stubbornly follow it to the letter. We have several mercenaries who would have gladly taken the trip with you."

"I think I just vomited in my mouth," Colonel Lync rebutted. "Last thing I need is a couple oversized egos wearing surplus store pajamas backing me up. I'm glad you didn't think of it until I was already out the door."

"You left without notifying anyone, Colonel," Magnate said stiffly.

"And now your reinforcing what a darn good decision I made," Colonel Lync retorted, which was followed by the smacking of a rock against the vehicle's window.

A female Russian voice cut in, her monotone voice signaling that it was the onboard computer. "Destination 0.3 miles ahead. Recommend reducing speed to five miles per hour."

"Time to start prepping for my solo adventure, Magnate. I'm gonna be cautious, surveying the area before I step out, so it may take up to an hour. I'll click back on before I venture outside. However, if you don't hear form me in two hours, then prepare for the worst."

The screen darkened without another word. It reappeared as the colonel grunted, staring down at his bright yellow boot.

"You'd think that the custom spacesuit required by my stature would mean that everything would fit better. Gotta love 'lowest cost, technically mediocre' government purchases."

"It appears the storm is almost past. Were you able to see anything on the screen as you approached, Colonel?" asked Magnate.

"Not visually, and the IR signal looks like one evenly hot blob. Now that my boots are on, I'm gonna mosey up a little closer before I get out," the colonel said as he spun back into the driver's seat.

The vehicle lurched forward with the screens showing only a red haze of fine Martian dust. The gears slowly hummed, which was the only way to tell that it was moving forward. The dust seemed to part as a white light grew in the center of the windshield. The closer the vehicle got, the brighter the light became. The colonel's hand reached up, pressed the windshield, and then slipped the fingers on his suit downward. The light outside dimmed to reveal a shadowy image. The screen twitched, a mixture of green and blue lights twirling in a complex pattern, blurring the image before it refocused to show the entire spaceship in vivid shades of white. The top of the central core was the brightest, and was slowly rotating counterclockwise. Pulses of white light shot up from the center of the hub and disappeared into a small lip below the rotation point, each one followed immediately by a grayish light falling much slower back to the hub. A maze of duller grid lines crossed the entire ship. The hub itself seemed to be broken down into rectangular segments that were slightly curved.

As pristine and majestic as the top sections of the ship were, the bottom of the core had been sheared off, leaving a jagged maw like that of a great white shark. The ground had been scraped and scarred by the crash landing; white pieces of the ship spread out like massive shark teeth washed up along the beach. The Martian dust, which permeated everything on the colony, was somehow thwarted by even the broken pieces of the spaceship.

"Colonel, I can't see the readout for the spaceship's size," Magnate commented. "Can you help me out?"

"Even broken, it's well over two hundred feet high. The center core is nearly three hundred feet in diameter, with each rectangular segment being fifteen feet high and forty feet in length. I can't tell if the segments reach all the way to the inner wall, and I sure would like to find out what's in 'em." The colonel's voice seemed unimpressed, merely factual as he read from the display.

"Disappointed?" asked Magnate.

"Yes," the colonel sighed. "I'd expected an interstellar spaceship to be much larger."

"And why is that?"

"To store the massive lizard-like warriors that are going to pour out and swarm me when I exit the cab," he replied matter-of-factly.

"Are you really looking for a battle?"

"Despite my appearance, I joined the Space Force for that reason only. Sadly, a never-ending onslaught of paperwork became my battle."

The video feed shuddered as the vehicle came to a stop.

"I'm forwarding to when he is closer to the ship, Mr. President. It takes about an hour for him to get in position," Bookworm says.

"Thanks," I reply.

The feed shifts from inside the vehicle to staring into one of the jagged sections at the bottom of the spaceship. It was too dark inside to see, and the colonel shifted his view to look at something close to his feet.

"What's this?" he asked.

A small gray shape the size of a tennis ball was wobbling lightly in the rusty dirt.

"Not good, Bookworm. If we hadn't already encountered one, I'd think that thing is just part of the ship that broke off when it crashed," I say, trying not to respond to the colonel since I was decades late to his question.

"Yes, sir," Bookworm replies. "Although we didn't see the alien in this shape, it's light and flexible framework could fill that volume if compacted."

"Please don't touch it," begged Magnate in a more passionate voice than I had ever heard.

"I've seen enough sci-fi horror movies to know that every good one starts with some idiot doing more than he should. My finger is on my blaster and it ain't leaving it." Colonel Lync's voice held a touch of arrogance in it when he replied. "Just getting a good visual scan."

As Colonel Lync leaned in, the wobbling turned more circular in motion. I could also see more details of the sphere: faded yellow and green lines covering its exterior, small lighter ridges rising from the surface, and a small fold running along half the diameter. The circular motion stopped, the colonel kicked the ball to the side, and his view went back to the broken underbelly of the spaceship. He stepped to the side of where the ball had been before walking forward, scanning his surroundings in a well-trained pattern. A light switched on, probably from his weapon, pointing at a gaping hole at least ten feet high and nearly as wide.

"Seems to be very little free space inside, just tons of broken small tubes and rectangular open spaces that are smaller than me." Colonel Lync continued to scan the area. "Guess that means our alien attackers are midgets."

"Maybe they were all killed in or before the crash. Or this could be a cargo ship," said Magnate.

"Could be. The hub does look like stacks of cargo containers," Colonel Lync said.

He raised his weapon, which brushed against the outer hull...and moved it. The video feed showed the colonel deliberately repeat the movement, with the same result. His hand reached out, which created a reaction from Magnate.

"Lync!" he shouted.

The colonel ignored the shout, and after touching the outer hull, rolled a small section around in his gloved hand.

"Geez. It's like a mix between thick aluminum foil and canvas. No way it could handle space travel," Colonel Lync said authoritatively.

"The inertial dampeners?" I ask Bookworm.

"Would make sense," Bookworm opines. "Also, it may explain why they couldn't land on Earth. The aeroheating from entering the Earth's atmosphere would create a superheated plasma inside the damaged spaceship. The rapid expansion and heat would destroy the entire ship."

The video went on, with the colonel tearing off a piece of the hull before placing it in a Velcro leg pocket. He then walked around the exterior of the spaceship, where about half the hub was touching the ground and the other half was raised high enough for the colonel to walk under. He turned to walk back, stopped, and went over to the cargo-shaped sections of the hub that were resting on the ground. He poked one with the barrel of his rifle, the dull ringing dying quickly in the Martian atmosphere. The colonel tapped it gently one more time, then hit it harder with the barrel of his weapon.

"The central spoke is fragile but the hub is made of a thick metal," the colonel reported.

He walked around the crash site for another ten minutes before heading back to the vehicle. Once back in the seat, Colonel Lync removed his helmet and spoke.

"I don't think anything happened to me out there, but let's play it safe. Soon as I get back, throw me in quarantine inside the mini-dome used for truck storage. Get a doc to remotely watch me, as my vitals can be monitored from inside this vehicle," Colonel Lync advised.

"We'll be ready. Safe travels," Magnate said.

"Anything else on the video feed, Bookworm?" I ask.

"Yes, sir. A lot more."

"I was afraid you'd say that."

Chapter 20

The video forwards rapidly through most of the trip back before slowing down. The colonel appears to be driving comfortably and at a cautious pace. I watch for about a minute, looking at the landscape and the movement of the video feed to try and catch anything amiss.

"Did you see that, sir?" asks Bookworm.

"Obviously not," I grumble.

"I'll rewind," he replies.

"You could tell me," I grumble again.

"Yes, sounds like that is best," Bookworm acquiesces. "Look at the health monitors up top."

I watch as the scene plays again, seeing the colonel's heart rate lower, his body temperature increase to a severe fever, and other mysterious readouts move slightly.

"What are those other ones for?" I ask.

"Basically, every conceivable diagnostic method possible for assessing the health of a human. After analyzing the data, it is apparent that a small amount of additional weight was slowly added to the back of the colonel's spacesuit, and then a local anesthetic was applied to his neck, followed by infiltration of a foreign matter into his neck and along his back," Bookworm says.

"Like the holes on Magnate's back?"

"Yes, and the next part is even more interesting."

Bookworm forwards the video feed by another few minutes.

"Gentlemen, an onboard sensor is not working correctly. It appears to be used for assessing the barometric pressure. I do not want to miss a storm heading my way. I need to stop and see what is wrong," said Colonel Lync, after mumbling to himself for a while.

"Hmm. We aren't reading anything wrong from our end," Magnate replied in a concerned tone.

More mumbling came from the colonel before he answered. "Good to hear. Then it should be an easy and timely fix," replied the colonel. "I need to take the headpiece off to get under the console, but will turn it back on when I am done."

Without time for protest, the screen went dark and came back on a little over thirty minutes later, with the colonel driving again. Bookworm froze the screen.

"Let me guess, that was enough time for the colonel to go back to the spaceship?" I ask.

"Yes, but piecing it all together is the interesting part," Bookworm argues.

"Okay, go ahead, Bookworm," I say.

"The second sign that something was off occurred when the colonel turned back on the video feed. There are vehicle tracks in front of him, meaning he doubled back."

"What was the first sign?"

"His speech pattern. The colonel, like every other human, has a distinct way of speaking. Dialect, word choice, and enunciation are all unique pieces of an individual's speech pattern. However, after his vital signs displayed significant differences, the colonel's speech pattern shifted. Enunciation was classical, dialect disappeared, and his word choice shifted. Especially noteworthy was the disappearance of contractions."

"Oh, yes, I caught that," I lie with an exaggerated wave of my hand. "Wait, don't you ignore contractions?"

"When we crash-landed earlier, I had already infiltrated the colony's main server. On the server is stored everything that has happened on the colony since the first crew landed. It is...it's a massive amount of data, but Magnate's government was extremely well organized. The hierarchical structure is nearly perfect, allowing one to easily navigate to what is needed. I just finished reviewing the vehicle's 360-degree video capture data and an interior camera had been set up, which I don't think anyone was aware of. Now, when Colonel Lync exited the vehicle to look at the spaceship, the first strange thing he saw was the small ball wobbling and then moving in a circular pattern. I had hypothesized that it was the alien that attached to him. However, I was wrong."

The video from my watch played a new view taken from the vehicle's exterior cameras, looking at Colonel Lync, dwarfed by the spaceship in the background, as he stared down at the wobbling ball. When it changed movements, a white cloth-shape dropped softly from above him onto the upper back of his yellow spacesuit.

"Classic distraction technique," I say.

Next the video showed the inside of the vehicle as the colonel opened the side hatch and stepped inside, dipping down to place his weapon on the floor. The white shape slipped off his back, floating in the air for a short while before it sank into a crevice behind a panel to the right of the colonel. Not seeing it, he went about pressurizing the vehicle before removing his helmet and gloves. He walked over and sat down on the only chair at the front of the vehicle and pushed a series of buttons to start the motor before activating his video feed. The screens lit up, and system check readouts scrolled across the screen.

"Colonel Lync," came the voice of Magnate. "Please run a full health scan before you leave. I just want to make sure you're okay and that we have a baseline reading for when you get back."

"Of course, Magnate," replied Colonel Lync. He reached to his right, pulled out a recessed touchpad, and punched four yellow-glowing buttons. Without waiting for the health analysis to complete, he began driving slowly back to the colony.

"Without a camera facing the colonel, they can't see his eyes. I'm betting they have the same milky coating we saw with Magnate and El Matador," I comment.

Bookworm fast-forwards again until I catch a glimpse of the white shape. Once back to normal speed, I can see a twelve-inch square crinkling up like a discarded candy wrapper before uncoiling as it climbed unnoticed up the back of the colonel's suit. Its eerily slow climb nearly gives me goosebumps, like watching a really good horror movie for the second time. You know what's coming, but it still puts all your senses on high alert. It reached the lip of the metallic O-ring where the helmet attached before stopping its ascent. Although the camera was directly behind the driver's seat, it was high enough that I could see the space between the creature and the colonel's neck.

Without a verbal request from me, Bookworm zooms in on this region as white microfilaments grew out of the alien creature, swaying unevenly with the motion of the vehicle's bumpy ride, like living coral as the tide rolls in and out. A few of the filaments grew longer than the others and stopped swaying, instead reaching out toward the colonel's neck. A liquid beaded up on the end of the filaments then drizzled onto his skin.

A few seconds later, the larger filaments slithered onto the colonel, appearing to attach where the liquid had been dropped. More filaments grew in length, emitted more of what must have been an anesthesia, and attached themselves lower and lower on the colonel's neck until the entire alien had slithered into his spacesuit. Once complete, Bookworm's new video feed stops.

"The total time for the parasitic attachment was less than five minutes, and one must assume it took that long only because it was trying to be subtle," Bookworm concludes.

"And I'm guessing we'll know the minimum time shortly," I forecast.

The video feed switches back to Colonel Lync's first-person perspective, with Domes 1, 2, and 3 in the foreground. They were pristine hemispheres, reflecting the sun's much more distant rays as if it were an overcast day on Earth. As he drove closer, one could see clearly into the domes, where large mining vehicles dominated Dome 2; multi-tiered crops rose to the top of Dome 1; and moving machinery spun, lifted, and dropped in Dome 3. Just as we had set out during the planning phase of the Marsian colony, Domes 1 through 3 were for staples needed to keep the colony functioning. If they kept to the plans, over a thousand people worked each of the three shifts required to maintain all necessary production.

Outside of the domes, a few dozen spacesuits milled around while five exoskeletons went back and forth between temporary mini-domes spaced randomly in front of the biodomes. The colonel connected up with a well-worn path, following it like a medieval road leading to a castle. He turned left toward one of the small domes before the vehicle lurched forward and then stopped.

"Sorry. It looks like the sensor issue was a sign of things to come," Colonel Lync said, not sounding worried at all. "I am glad it made it this far before it broke down."

"I really don't like the sound of this, Lync," came Magnate's beleaguered voice. "I recommend you suit up just in case."

"Yes, your Magnate," came a reply, but only after a barely discernible mumbling of words.

The colonel carefully extricated himself from his seat, heading to the back as he put on his helmet and gloves, and then proceeded to flip, turn, and press a few switches on the vehicle's wall opposite the exit. "Sir, it looks like the vehicle is dead. I am going to walk to the minidome. Can you get the doctor to set up a hazmat bed since I cannot use the vehicle? Also, recommend you get a maintenance lead out here to retrieve and repair the vehicle."

"Sir, this is Captain Sandine," came a firm voice from the same location as Magnate. "Margaret is already suited up and headed out of Dome 2. I'll redirect her to your vehicle."

"Negative, Captain. She is our best field electrical engineer and wasted on something this simple. I recommend you send out Jasper or Sergeant Narmo," Colonel Lync said.

"Roger that, sir," the captain replied to his superior.

Colonel Lync exited the vehicle and proceeded toward the minidome about a quarter mile down the tire-packed dirt path. Once inside the minidome entrance, the headset video feed turned off.

"I'm switching back to the inside of the vehicle, Mr. President," Bookworm replies. "That is Sergeant Narmo."

"What's that, Bookworm?" I ask. "Zoom in on the dashboard."
A small note was placed over the speedometer readout.

Sergeant, when fixed please drive directly to Dome 2, tunnel
entrance 4 as they need the vehicle to extract a crew.
-Col Lync

"First bait and switch, then perfect redirection in suggesting a military member that won't question a senior officer's written order." I pause to think. "This alien race is extremely smart. I'm betting it has to be, as it's not a classical predator that can overpower its enemies."

"That does make sense, sir. I wonder if—," Bookworm starts before I cut him off.

"Rewind to the video feed right after the alien slid into the colonel's spacesuit," I say. "Something's been gnawing at me, and I think I know what it is."

The video quickly rewinds and then slowly plays forward until Colonel Lync again states that there is something wrong with one of the sensors.

"Pause, Bookworm," I snap. "Rewind another twenty seconds, then increase the volume so we can hear his mumbling."

It rewinds to the exact spot before I finish my sentence, and the crackling from the volume increase reverberates in my ears. What plays back is exactly what I had been hoping to hear.

The colonel's mumbling voice is strained but monotone. "Tell them that a sensor is not working and that you need to stop."

"I cannot believe I missed that," Bookworm states, sounding shocked.

"You know what this means?" I say to bait Bookworm.

"That the aliens can manipulate the vocal chords of their hosts," he replies.

"Something deeper," I smugly say. "The aliens can't force their hosts to speak, or if they do use their host's vocal chords it must sound strange. Too strange for them to use unless they want to blow their cover."

"I hadn't thought of that," Bookworm says in an even more perplexed voice.

This time I'm glad he has the emotional setting on. I smugly cross my arms.

Bookworm gives a slight bow of acknowledgement before moving on.

"Mr. President. I think the final series of scenes are better viewed playing in your mind. They are much larger in required viewing area and highly complex. Is it okay if I transmit them?" Bookworm asks.

"Hmmm. I didn't know there was a limit to your power," I state while continuing my smugness. "Very well."

I close my eyes and reach backward in my mind, as if falling toward the device implanted in my brain. I find a calm and relaxed point before a rainbow of colors plow over me and swirl up into a free space I hadn't known to exist. Colors blend, shapes coalesce, and sounds barely discernable from when and how I watched the previous video feeds buzz all around me. It's as if I'm watching everything as it happens. I can see the first three domes, the minidomes stretching out on the plateau, indented tracks crossing the entire area, and vehicles driven slowly around the site. Inside the dome hundreds of shapes moved about in random patterns, far less like an ant colony and more like a home for wayward cats. The colonel's vehicle, now driven by Sergeant Narmo, is lit up with a green icon as it headed toward Dome 2. It slipped into the largest entrance hatch before the door shuts.

Take me inside the dome, Bookworm, I order.

I find myself looking across the dome from a ceiling cam. The vehicle exited the interior hatch and made a right turn onto a well-worn red road. It jerked in awkward forward movements, not flowing well with the pedestrian workers who mistakenly assume the vehicle would stop for them. While there were several near misses, most of the people just glared at the vehicle before going back to their jobs. The vehicle passed two large tunnel entrances and a dozen smaller ones before it headed down a tunnel wide enough for three vehicles to enter. After it disappeared, I looked around the Dome 2 complex. The main external vehicle entrance was closest to Dome 1, along with one personnel-sized hatch on each side. The primary causeway between Dome 1 and 2—and 2 and 3, for that matter— was two hundred feet wide and five hundred feet long. That is, if I correctly remember the original designs. Temporary housing cubicles, machine shop floors, enormous sheds, and the safety building took up most of the southern section of Dome 2. The massive center section was taken up by the tunnels and machinery, while butted against the dome's walls were the ore extraction, smelting, and separation mills. The northern face was reserved for the temporary mineral and rock piles that would eventually be transferred to Dome 3 for final refining and eventual fabrication into whatever was needed for the colony.

Bookworm, how many people work in the dome? I ask as I watched the cats chasing laser pointers. Only a few of the workers had spacesuits on, preferring heavy-duty work clothes that offered more comfort. However, I did notice about a half-dozen bald individuals in well-creased Americas Space Force uniforms, their ASF logos of the same original design I had approved when in office.

Each of the three shifts in Dome 2 has approximately 650 personnel working, with another three hundred personnel split between Domes 1 and 3, Bookworm replies in my mind.

I had another thought. *Bookworm, how many of those aliens could Colonel Lync have stored in his vehicle?*

Sir, assuming they were only placed in storage compartments on the vehicle, which is highly probable considering we didn't see any when viewing the interior camera data, I would estimate a little over one thousand.

I don't think it's any coincidence they targeted Domes 1 thru 3. Their strategy may be to completely overtake one area before moving on to the next area, I think.

Yes. With the limited number of access points between each set of three domes, it would make sense, replies Bookworm.

I'm going to skip the next thirty minutes, sir. I didn't detect any unusual activity but am assuming that a number of the workers in the tunnel were overtaken by the aliens.

The video fast forwards in time, stopping as a tunneling truck, with massive, rock-pulverizing sonic cones perched on the front, lumbered out of the first tunnel, pulling a few eight-wheeled beds full of Marsian rock. As the convoy turned to the left toward a milling station, a series of muffled whistles emanated from tunnel 3. The sounds grew rapidly, causing nearly all the workers to stop in their tracks and turn toward the mining tunnel. The sounds rose in volume, the doppler effect marking what Bookworm and I know as impending doom, with only one of the half-dozen ASF military having lumbered over to his vehicle and pulled out an old-school ablation rifle. It would send a heated pulse of air that burned anything it came in contact with, while also having enough velocity to rip off the resulting char layer. It's a very painful way to die, with the burnt skin peeling away to leave behind raw nerves. It's also very effective for crowd control since when switched to 'spread pattern' it would cause first-degree burns to a larger grouping.

The sound of a thousand soccer whistles filled the air, signaling the beginning of a lopsided match. Out from tunnel 3 shot a spinning white tornado, rapidly spreading out like a gigantic white bedsheet that had been lifted into the air to lay over a bed. As it grew, with everyone still gawking, it became apparent that the single sheet was actually the thousand, separate alien rectangles. They hovered in the air for a brief second and then shrunk in unison before high-shrieking whistles deafened the colonists. As they covered their ears, the outer aliens shot toward the perimeter of the dome while the others descended in a dizzying aerial show. The aliens that hadn't headed to the exit points weaved in and out of the largest groups of colonists, while the smaller groups of colonists and individuals were held in check by fear.

Pause, Bookworm, I snap, garnering an immediate response. *Zoom in on the group next to tunnel 2. There! See the white figures crawling into the back of their collars? They're using the movement as a distraction technique so they can attach onto some of the colonists.* I think for a short while. *Proceed.*

Bookworm zooms back out, right before a sharp drum-like noise is followed by two of the flying, white aliens turning into a confetti of black ash. A burst of three drum sounds and another three aliens went down. Finally, people realize what was really happening, and their voices rang out. They started as screams of fear and horror.

Who's shooting, Bookworm? That sergeant? I ask, receiving affirmation. *Zoom in on him, please.*

Yes, sir. It's Master Sergeant Timothy Dillen. I'm also turning on his mic.

"4th Space Force, Group 1! We're under attack! Get armed and shoot the damn white pillowcases, now!" Sergeant Dillen shouted, as he somehow still managed to sound calm and collected.

Another series of deep drum sounds and a couple more aliens are seared and blasted into ash. One of the shots missed its mark, hitting the dome wall but only blackening it. An alien turned toward the sergeant, curled inward, and shot toward him with a high whistle. Its body fashions into a closed umbrella as it dove toward him. He barely stepped aside in time, his eyes widening only slightly as it hit and penetrated the side door of his cab. It unfurled, trying to extract itself from the door, but is turned to ash before it finished. Drum sounds reverberated around the dome, and an ever-increasing amount of ash filled the air.

Once the aliens realized that they were being attacked, groups redirected their aerial assault toward the ASFs, who were easy to spot in their military uniforms. A couple sharp whistles and two of the military were impaled by the aliens, the creatures' bodies sticking out the backside of their skulls. A female ASF ducked an initial attack, slamming the butt of her rifle into the creature before spinning around and slicing it in half with a knife that seemed to appear out of nowhere. However, no sooner had she finished the slicing than another one impaled her foot, pinning her to the ground. She yelled in a mixture of pain and anger, spinning her rifle up just in time to blast another pair of incoming aliens. She hollered at the other two ASFs next to her, but her warning was too late, as they fell to a barrage of alien lawn darts. She lasted a few more seconds before becoming an overused bull's-eye.

"Home base, this is Sergeant Dillen. Immediately seal off all entrances between Domes 1 through 3 and 4 through 6."

Sergeant Dillen paused a second before continuing. "Damn. They're attaching to people's necks, and the infected are then attacking their friends. It's like the zombie apocalypse movies without the eating flesh crap."

"Sergeant Dillen, this is Captain Sandine. All remaining ASF personnel are being activated, armed, and sent to Dome 2. Can you, uh, fight them off for another fifteen minutes?"

More drum-like thwumping sounds filled the audio feed, but now they were coming from a single weapon.

"Negative, sir. I'm all that's left," Sergeant Dillen reported.

He then grunted after an alien whistled in and impaled his leg to the vehicle's frame. There was a groan of pain before the sergeant looked back up to the sky, regained his composure, and rapid-fired at the dozens of inbound aliens. He ashed a few more before being swarmed and hit by so many that it was hard to see his body. However, his face was still exposed, and it held a smile that refused to be erased. It reminded me of the words by Colonel Lync to Magnate. Sergeant Dillen signed up to fight, not to push paper. It's clear he died doing what he wanted.

Bookworm, zoom back out and rewind to where the initial attack began, I order.

The image dropped back to the cloud of white shapes. The first wave blocked off all exits and the others swarmed the confused colonists. It's pre-calculated and well coordinated. A group would distract with darting movements while a smaller number of aliens dropped in from behind and slipped into the shirts of the Marsians. They also searched under or in open vehicles, but ignored any vehicles that were sealed. Apparently, they didn't have the ability to open doors. Marsians who were in the process of being infected didn't show any visible signs or even show awareness of what was happening to them. As the attack replays, the thwumping drum sounds filled the air as the half-dozen military personnel opened fire. None of the ASFs were as calm as Sergeant Dillen, often firing in crazy patterns before quickly and painfully being speared by the alien lawn darts. Right after the sergeant's death, the screen froze again.

Mr. President, Bookworm says. *I didn't notice before you asked me to rewind, but it appears that the whistling sound isn't always the same. I just ran a scan, and there is a significant modulation in pitch that occurs. In fact, it was only after the first attack on the aliens by Sergeant Dillen that they focused on killing the military.*

Language? Can you make out what they were saying?

No, at least not yet, but it seems to suggest that they don't use telepathy for communicating.

I turn my focus back to the image in my head, and Bookworm unfreezes the screen. Within fifteen minutes the attack was over with the only fatalities being the few military who had presented a real threat. The aliens had been very creative in how they took down the military, with some impaling and others slicing off body parts. It was the only sign that a battle had taken place—a small, gruesome sign. The aliens had complete control of Dome 2 and were pushing their Marsian hosts through the entrances of Domes 1 and 3.

One-third of the colony was already lost. What was next?

Chapter 21

Magnate hadn't sealed off Domes 1 and 3 because he assumed some of the aliens had already infiltrated the area, I check with Bookworm. *He accepted losses and preserved what he could. I would've done the same.*

I just ran an analysis of the colony's life support system, Bookworm said. *The power supply for isolation of the Domes is all run on the same system, which requires a significant electrical draw. By ignoring a third of the domes, he increased the power available by forty percent, thus speeding up the isolation procedure.*

I like my explanation better, I grumble. *How long did it take to overrun the other two domes?*

A little under thirty minutes, replies Bookworm.

Play it one more time, but speed it up by a factor of two.

Yes, Mr. President. What are you looking for?

Patterns. Something's still gnawing at me, I say.

The attack plays forward for only a couple minutes before Bookworm stops it. Instead of challenging him, I wait somewhat patiently.

Sir, I was able to find something close to a pattern. Three times different groups redirected their attacks in unison. It also didn't correlate to any of the whistling sounds. Bookworm's voice in my head comes across with true puzzlement.

Hmm. I thought about some of my battles against insurgents, avoiding the gory sections. *Did you look for any external signals such as radio frequencies?*

The audio file has a limited frequency range, but I might be able to access the satellite data from the same time and extract the electromagnetic spectrum data from its recorder. Hold on, sir. A few seconds tick by. *You are correct, Mr. President. There was a small, highly dense pulse of photonic energy from the alien ship before each pattern change.*

As always, there's someone or something in control. I guess we need to get to that ship and find out, I say.

Mr. President. You need to see the last part of the transmission from Magnate Palmer before we go.

I nod.

Colors explode in my mind again, shifting and coalescing until I see the familiar office of Magnate. From the angle of the camera, he is behind his desk with the backs of three men and two women partially blocking the view of the bookcase.

"Could you please pull up the monitor, Stanley?" Magnate asked in a weary voice.

"Yes, Magnate Palmer," came back a high-pitched reply as Stanley quickly tapped something on his tan utility belt.

A blue light swirled behind the figures, expanded to half the size of the wall before solidifying into a screen. A scene of Dome 2 from what appeared to be Dome 5 filled the screen. Red dust swirled lazily between the domes, making it hard to discern what was happening with the aliens.

"Please filter out the dirt particles, Stanley." Magnate's hand reached up to his own video feed and appeared to rub his eyes.

The screen switched to a clearer view of the triangular framework of Dome 2, where three human-sized shadows could be seen behind one of the bottom triangular windows of the structure.

"Your Magnate, one of our audio channels from Dome 2 just opened up. She is asking for you," Captain Sandine said.

Magnate nodded approval, and the tiredness on his face was instantly painted with a dignitary façade.

"Magnate Palmer," came a stoic female voice.

"Angelica?" Magnate uttered, his composure bleeding away upon hearing the voice.

There was some muttering, followed by her reply. "Yes, and no. We have overtaken one third of your domes and will shortly have the entire colony under our control. We do not negotiate; we only offer you a painless option. Please look at your screen that I am told you have opened."

"What do you mean, yes and no?" Magnate Palmer asked, his composure regained.

On the screen, bright lights shot out from the left and right of the three figures, vaporizing the shadows. Two miners, with red dust coating their faces, stood behind a smaller woman with brown hair pulled back in a ponytail to reveal sharp features and a red welt on her face. She wore a red jacket and held a small mic in her roughened hands. The two miners were about the same height, but the one on the right had straggly blond hair while the other's was a neatly trimmed brown color. All their eyes had a milky glaze to them. I couldn't help staring at those eyes through the uncomfortably long silence.

The woman's pursed lips fluttered, stopped, and then moved freely, out of sync with the voice coming through the audio feed. "You have five minutes after our deaths to open the hatches."

The straggly-haired man stepped to the side and screamed out, "I don't want to die! Oh God, no. No. No!"

Screams of pain filled my brain, stopped only by deep gasps. He fell to his knees, trying to claw at his back, but his arms stopping before they got close enough. A white sheet extracted itself from under his collar, flowing up to the top of his head. There was one more wail as the alien leapt off, spread into a thin sheet, whistled, and shot to the sky. The man released a small sigh before closing his eyes. Without time for reflection, the neatly groomed man stepped awkwardly to the side, grimacing with pain. He clinched his teeth so tight that I could hear teeth cracking. He fought for control of his body, grimacing as he lost the battle. His mouth opened but refused to let words come out. There was a loud whistling sound and his thick jacket was ripped from his body as the alien flew away. Blood shot from his back and continued to gush outward as his eyes rolled back and he fell, dead before he hit the ground. The girl took a small step forward and whispered into the mic.

"I'm sorry, Daddy," she said as a tear rolled down her cheek, landing on the mic as she dropped it to the ground.

Her shoulders slumped and her body shook as she lightly sobbed. The shaking and sobbing were interrupted by spasms of pain that grew in waves until they overtook her. Angelica closed her eyes for a moment, then opened them as the milkiness disappeared. A brief glimpse of terror shone before they gazed far off, forever distant. She fell back, a puff of red dust shooting up around her. After an eternal moment of silence, a bloody-tendrilled alien crawled out from under her and launched into the air with a ghostly whistle.

The lights in Dome 2 turned off, the screen disappeared after Stanley tapped his utility button, and Magnate's head dipped down so that I only saw the desk. No one dared speak, and the slow breathing of the Marsian leader was all that could be heard for a while. Finally, he lifted his head and spoke with determination.

"We have less than four minutes before they kill more of my people." His right hand ran across the lines of his desk as he spoke. "Captain Sandine, how long will it take to execute Kill Order Delta 3 using our ASF and the militia?"

One of the men, wearing a khaki ensemble and sporting a handlebar moustache, spun around to face Magnate. "Are you serious? You think killing a thousand people is a viable option?"

"No, I don't see it as a viable option, Charlie. I see it as the only option. We surrender and they take us over; we refuse to surrender and they either painfully kill everyone in the three domes or use them to attack us." There was no anger in Magnate's voice, only sadness. "They're somehow controlling their victims, and we don't know the extent of that control. How much time do we need, Captain?"

"Twenty minutes to get them prepped, armed, and in position, your Magistrate," the captain said with complete confidence.

"Give the order, but tell them to double time," the Magistrate commanded.

"I'm not going to watch another round of their despicable killing!" Charlie shouted.

"Yes you will, Charlie. We all will. It will hurt like hell, but we can't let them know what we are going to do. Watch, feel, and remember that we are servants of our people. Most of the time it means making decisions about budgets or working on city planning, but today it's about bearing the pain so they may not have to."

Magnate's words were like a huge block of ice, cold enough to freeze anyone who challenged him.

Stanley clicked the screen back on, and after a short time the dome lights lit up to reveal nine Marsians lined up, their emotionless faces all showing signs of tears having recently trailed down their faces. Magnate's video recorder looked at each one, moving from left to right. Another two miners coated with red dust stood on the left, next to them a man in something like a crossing guard uniform gripping his plastic whistle so tight that blood was trickling down from one finger, a frail elder with recently ripped jeans, two women in overalls with bulky gloves, another miner with a grizzly beard, and younger twins who couldn't have been more than sixteen years old. The twin boys each placed one large shoe forward in unison and held out the same chubby hand to point in the direction of Dome 5. In unison they spoke without emotion, a hollowness that one would think of coming from a robot.

"You can see that we do not make threats. We execute a plan and give options as to how and when you can surrender. Surrender now, and no more than these nine will be killed. Keep up this wasted bravado, and we will kill every Marsian we have enslaved. We will then focus our efforts on infiltrating your other domes. We have time, and we will be successful."

Magnate's team watched without movement as the twins sobbed until their bodies fell, followed by a timed series of pained deaths for each of the other victims. The lights blinked out, the screen faded away, and still no one moved. Time ticked away in agonizing seconds, silently screaming the emotions that none could convey. Finally, a beep from the captain's earpiece invaded their catatonic state.

"Your Magnate, they're almost in position," said Captain Sandine.

More seconds ticked away before an answer came.

"Screen please, Stanley," came Magnate's distant voice.

The view was from the same angle as before, facing Dome 2, but zoomed out so that over a quarter mile of the dome's side was visible. Into sight walked three dozen rust-colored spacesuits holding unwieldly black rifles. They trudged toward the dome, each step seeming to push the large barrel of the rifle closer to the ground. The lights flicked on from Dome 2, and another twenty-seven Marsians were lined up, facing the oncoming group of soldiers and militia.

"They're hailing us on feed 3, Magnate," Captain Sandine said.

"How much closer do they need to be, Captain?" Magnate Palmer asked, preferring not to acknowledge the alien's attempted contact.

"Another hundred feet and they'll be well within range, sir," Captain Sandine replied. Something rang his earpiece. "The aliens are saying that we're making a mistake."

Silence had sucked the air out of the room as the team watched the spacesuits plod on, only adjusting their rifles when they threatened to scrape along the ground.

What are those weapons, Bookworm? I ask.

MB-24 Buster rifles, sir. Each one weighs 21.25 pounds and can fire single or multiple delayed explosive rounds. They were designed for infiltration missions where one needs to remove enemy targets from reinforced fortifications. When fired, a round will penetrate up to an inch into its target before releasing a supersonic detonation that can generate a two- to five-foot hole in the object. According to the Marsian database, they had three dozen of these weapons, which were never used until this event.

"They're ready, Magnate," Captain Sandine said.

Magnate tapped his earpiece. "Fire until all rounds are spent. That's my order."

The limited Martian atmosphere quickly dampened the first volley's sound and the subsequent explosions. However, the visual display in my head more than made up for the lack of sound effects. The first explosion blew a smaller hole in one of the triangular walls of Dome 2, which was followed by a series of larger holes being ripped open. Air burst out of the dome, sounding like a pride of lions roaring on a cloudy day, echo upon echo bouncing off the thick air inside the dome. Automated emergency drones launched into action, flattening out like large Frisbees right before they hit the dome wall. In seconds, the holes were covered and the dome was resealed.

"Keep firing!" yelled the captain into his mic. "All three domes!"

Volleys shot out, hitting the walls and exploding faster than the drones could patch the damage. It continued for over a minute, rounds exploding and dome triangles bursting. Rounds even travelled through burst triangles and exploded out sections of the wall on the opposite end of the dome. The devastation continued until the spacesuits had emptied their weapons.

The rapid decompression caused small objects, dirt, and infected Marsians to fly out of the holes, launching into the sparse Martian air up to fifteen feet outside the dome before skipping along the ground. The Marsians, who were ejected from the dome and still conscious, clawed at the air and their throats, hoping beyond reason that oxygen could be squeezed from Mars's unwelcome atmosphere. They crawled, rolled, and writhed on the ground, but within minutes all found their peace. Red Martian soil that had shot out of the mines and from the dirt piles at the far end of Dome 2, created an encapsulated dust storm that obscured the view into the three domes.

"Please bring the soldiers and militia back to the decontamination hut connected to Dome 6. There's no need for them to wait around to see the carnage. They'll have to live with what was done for the rest of their lives as it is," Magnate said sadly.

The captain nodded and gave the order, which turned into hand signals by the spacesuit leader to pull back. When they had walked out their heavy weapons had made the trek difficult, but now the consequences of their actions weighed their walk more than that of a thousand weapons. The team of five standing in Magnate's office, and surely thousands in Domes 4–6, watched them trudge through the soundless evening to the sonic showers to decontaminate that which could not be easily cleansed away.

"How long before we can see inside the dome, Captain?" Magnate Palmer asked.

"Hard to tell," interjected a female member of the team. "The filtration system surely kicked on right away, but it's used to pumping in an Earth-like atmosphere. Right now, it'd be pumping at one percent of capacity, which it wasn't designed for. Heck, it might not even work."

I'm going to fast forward an hour, Mr. President, says Bookworm in my mind.

The screen reset to a view of the domes, where only about the bottom tenth of the dome was filled with a thick layer of suspended dust. However, it wasn't just hanging like a fog, instead swirling from what was probably the suction of the filters. It was still too high to see any carnage from the depressurization.

Bookworm, the swirling isn't uniform.

Before he could reply, reddish-white wisps of smoke rose from the haze. As they lifted higher and higher, the red toner fell back, exposing the sheet-like aliens as they rose into the thin Martian air.

I didn't know if they had died and more infiltrated the other domes over time, or if they could thrive without oxygen and the same ones had continued the attack. Now we know, I say.

Yes. Also, the whistling is a result of them compressing the air and releasing it to propel themselves. They are extremely fast in an Earth atmosphere, but are moving much slower in the reduced Martian atmosphere.

My perspective changes again, and we're watching the screen in Magnate's office through his video feed. The aliens continued to slowly rise above the mist, then in unison exited the dome through the hundreds of holes created by the military assault. Once outside, they hovered a couple hundred feet in the air until all of them were free of the dome. By that time the fog in the dome was down to less than a foot, swirling around the mausoleum where every body, every face, every mouth was stretched in a unique, horrific pose, compounded in horror by the red fog reaching in an out of orifices like tentative snakes. Nothing moved inside the dome except for the fog. Nearly one thousand stilled bodies.

The video on the screen expanded to capture all the aliens, who had now created a formation hundreds of feet wide and at least fifty feet high. They hovered imperfectly, having to compress and expel the carbon dioxide atmosphere within their bodies several times a minute.

"What are they waiting for?" Magnate Palmer asked to no one, as he lowered his head to stare at the top of the desk for the second time that day.

"I really don't know, sir," Captain Sandine replied, not realizing Magnate hadn't wanted an answer.

"It appears they don't have a way to get to us. Looks like we have some time to develop a plan and deal with the nine thousand scared colonists. Lucky for us, every day they deal with the possibility of dying due to a faulty filter system, or a leak in the wall of their apartment, or a radiation surge. This is just a new, although more in-your-face, way to die. They will be…"

On the screen, the fading white of the pinpoint sun cast a long twilight that could extend for hours due to the red planet's dust. A long shadow rose up beyond the destroyed domes, causing the twilight to dim just enough to be noticed. They all watched as this off-white shadow crept closer and closer, until one could see that it wasn't a shadow but rather thousands, maybe millions, of the flying aliens descending on their colony. No one spoke, no one moved…again. The day continued to throw one hopeless challenge after another at them until their emotional bank account had nothing more to withdraw.

The aliens merged and swallowed up the small group from above the destroyed domes before floating over to the middle three domes. They slowly descended, surely millions, like sheets on a bed until not a single inch of the dome's transparent surface was exposed. It was simple, yet horrific to the Marsian colonists; the aliens showing them that there was no escape. Magnate's staff watched for another painful hour, waiting for something to happen.

Bookworm, if the hub of the spaceship contained those aliens wrapped up like tennis balls, how many could it hold?

That is an easy calculation, yet results in a surprising number. During Earth's computer revolution, middle- and high-school classes repeated that calculation thousands of time, usually for a 20- to 30-foot-long, 20-foot-wide by 10-foot-high room. Most people guessed that it would be tens of thousands, but the actual number was closer to a million. Assuming the hub's only purpose was for transportation of the aliens in the tennis-ball shape, neglecting their misshapen surface and slight compression, then it would hold 30 to 50 million.

I want to snap at him for the long-winded answer, but know my anger is from watching the masterful takeover of the Marsian colony by the aliens and at the sheer number of aliens. They had used deception, misdirection,

237

and complex strategy, indicating that they were solely focused on a hostile takeover when encountering any other race. They didn't seem to kill for the sake of killing, but that was only because they needed their victims as hosts. And the most important part…they had studied humans. They knew humankind was an emotional race and had attempted to use that against the colonists by torturing their victims.

No, Bookworm did nothing wrong. Well, besides never getting to the point and making me watch each blasted step of this video when he had already scanned the entire thing. So, instead of berating him, I grunt just enough to acknowledge his answer and still convey a mild annoyance.

"Oh, dear God," exclaimed Stanley as he rung his hands. "We're doomed. We're gonna become their slaves. Oh, God!"

"Captain, make sure all of our external hatches are not only sealed and passcode protected, but that any attempt to breach is met with swift, unwavering force," Magnate Palmer ordered.

The captain nodded, pulled out and unrolled his FlipFilm, and then began typing on its lower half with his free hand. He froze mid-execution and looked up with wide eyes.

"Captain?" Magnate Palmer snapped to unfreeze the man.

"Sir, I had locked and sealed the domes when the aliens first attacked hours ago. I used the lockdown system that can only be overridden by senior leadership." Captain Sandine looked down at his FlipFilm and slipped his index and pinky in small, circular motions.

"And?" Magnate Palmer asked.

Captain Sandine looked up, astonished. "Personnel hatch 7 of Dome 9 was opened over an hour ago."

Magnate sighed before speaking. "It was Colonel Lync."

"Yes, sir. It was," Captain Sandine confirmed.

"Can you track him?" Magnate Palmer asked.

"I normally can track anyone, but Colonel Lync overrode that function after he entered." Captain Sandine looked up again, with another expression of shock. "Sir, all the hatches to Domes 4 thru 9 are filled with the aliens, and the inner doors are opening. I can't reseal them."

Magnate, who I still couldn't see since everything was recorded from his perspective, turned to his wall window and walked over. White shapes had already taken flight in the dome and people were running and screaming in fear. The other five in the room had followed him and were watching the assault, finally vocalizing their shock and dismay. In minutes thousands of aliens blanketed the skies, purposely creating chaos and confusion amongst the Marsians to give others time to assimilate their hosts. They continued to watch until a hard, single knock came from Magnate Palmer's door.

"Colonel Lync, I presume," Magnate Palmer said. He walked over to the door and reached out for the handle, but paused. He touched the small keyhole in the door with his index finger before reaching up to his headpiece.

The screen went dark.

So, he had placed it in the keyhole before the Marsians had been enslaved, I thought.

Their freedom had ended, and now it was time to see if I would suffer the same fate.

Chapter 22

"Mr. President, you're not going to like what is happening outside the building," states Bookworm.

My concentration is broken, thoughts of the aliens and why they had crash-landed lost, so I turn toward the glass wall that still has El Matador's sword lodged in it. All I can see is the sword as the entire landscape is blocked from my view.

Hundreds of white shapes float outside the window; some are stationary, while others swirl or dart around. I step up to the window, as it's only my second chance to get an up-close look at the aliens, the first having taken me by surprise. While all are roughly rectangular in size, each has distinct edges that can be ribbed, rounded, or concave. I study the closest one, which has concave edges with small ridges on two of the four sides. Its center is thicker and opaque, and the transparency increases radially until it's nearly see-through at the edges. Copper-green and light red veins spread out in uneven patterns throughout its body. It shifts upward by two feet, allowing me to study the dozen thicker pads the size of human fingers that are integrated into its bottom edge. Another two pads are evenly spaced on each of the other three edges. As I watch the alien, the dozen bottom pads swell to twice their normal size. Loud whistling rings out as the air is released, shooting it away.

"So, I don't have a lot of choices, Bookworm," I say as I play my index finger along the jagged edge of the sword. "I can surrender, run away, or fight until every alien is dead, which would have to include all the Marsians.

Up to 50 million, right? That last one may be slightly beyond my endurance."

"Sir, if you do not want to kill any of the enslaved Marsians or feel you cannot win the battle, then I suggest we remove ourselves from the situation. We should take time to study the aliens until we figure out a weakness or how to abstract them without killing the Marsians."

"Uh-huh. Good analysis, but…" I quickly squat and then launch myself into the hardened window.

Metallic glass isn't really glass at all, and it isn't really metal. The major composition is metal, but functionalized ceramics are smelted into and evenly dispersed throughout the original bimetallic framework of iron and titanium to create an incredibly strong material. The ceramic creates spacing greater than the wavelength of light, thus allowing light to pass through. Not being glass, its breaking is more like when a bullet hits aluminum.

As I go through the metallic glass, it rapidly unfolds like a flower to the morning sun. I shoot my hand to the left and snatch the hilt of El Matador's sword before gravity takes over. The weight and balance of the sword are near perfect, even broken; so light in my massive hand, as if it were a large knife. And I know I'll need it as I stare into the sea of aliens that block my view. I execute a quick upward strike at an alien that has gotten too close, carving off a quarter of its sheet-like body. I roll my strike into a downward swing that cleaves another in half as I start my gravity-induced descent.

The aliens react quickly, already moving to attack. I twist from my midsection and swing the sword behind me, cleanly splitting in half three more. My spinning attack throws off my balance, so I curl up and shoot my legs straight out to redirect my angular momentum downward. I hold the sword upward, the blade symmetrically dividing my face. The ground rises up to greet me. Even at 40 percent of Earth's gravity, I hit the marble roof of the building's entrance with enough force to break through its thick center. I'm like a hammer on a cinder block, the impact not only splitting the spot I land on, but sending fissures along it and the supporting walls.

White dust swirls up and moves sharply sideways in harmony with the cacophonous sounds of pieces of the walls slamming to the ground.

The rows of aliens stop and hover, surrounding me on all sides. I don't know why they wait, and I don't care. I think of their assault on the Marsian colony, and how they never had any intention except for a hostile takeover. I relive the sorrow when the first three Marsians died, including Magnate's daughter, and grip the sword's hilt tighter as the memory of the painful way the aliens killed their hosts floods my emotions. I reflect on the brave sergeant who fought on, knowing his death was imminent. It drives me to anger and fuels the rage I need to fight. I will not win this battle against so many millions, but I will make them pay.

I take a single, slow step forward, signaling my intent. In my beginning years as a demigod I barely knew how to fight, but I also hadn't needed much more than bare fists to beat anyone. However, as more demigods arose, I tired of having to always resort to brute strength to beat them. During a calm time, I read a simple yet powerful book on the life of Miyamoto Musashi, the greatest swordsman of all time, and it started me down the path of a samurai. I learned of samurai history from books on Feudal Japan and studied the art of the sword before delving into the lifestyle change Musashi chose when his soul yearned for more than violence. It had started to change me and I tried to follow The Way, but my followers wanted nothing to do with it. Eventually, I succumbed to their prayers and their compounded will. I had lost the path and doubted I would ever find it again. I enjoyed my anger too much and the way it coursed through my body when I needed it. Yes, I may have forgotten that path, but I now remember how to use a sword again.

I cup the bottom of the sword hilt with my left hand and rest the middle of the hilt between the thumb and index finger of my right hand. I bring the sword to my side as I raise my right elbow. I squat slightly, letting my right kneecap bend while slipping my left forward. I bellow a war cry that blows back or flutters every alien in my line of sight.

They attack in response.

Three from behind, three from the side, and three from above all fly in at once, the high-pitched whistles giving away their positions. I slide back while turning my right foot and swinging my left around. The sword follows effortlessly in an upward arc, taking out the first three before swiping a foot-long gash in the three above. They flutter downward, life spent, as I spear the center of the one in front of me and then swipe the final two in half. I extract the impaled one using my foot and then rub it into the ground, while a maniacal smile creases my face. I revel in the idea of battle.

I remember challenging Boy and reprimanding him for wanting to take on the aliens, wanting to fight when others might suffer because of his actions. He was a straightforward fighter, just like me. I criticized him for wanting to do what I was doing right now. Taking on those that oppressed, and not worrying about the cost. The alternative was to be like Cleaner, placating the suppressors out of fear for what they'd do to others. I will fight to the end.

When facing an insurmountable force, one must reduce the number of attackers by ensuring most are obstructed, whether by a physical, mental, or spiritual barrier. In this case I can only count on the physical, but I'm hoping I can crush their spirit over time.

Twenty-seven come at me this time, and I move my blade in a defensive spin that prevents any attack, while striking whenever I see an opening. After a few minutes, they all lie unmoving at my feet, my anger still full with no sweat evident on my brow. The aliens swirl around me in interweaving patterns, and beyond the swirling groups is still a wall through which I will not be able to penetrate.

Eighty-one next, sir, comes Bookworm's voice in my head.

Eighty-one rain down like a scene from *The Matrix*, and while I have become proficient at using the enemy's group attack against itself, they are too many and thin enough to stack on top of each other so they can easily dart in. I cut down a dozen before the first one rockets past my defense and hits my arm. It wraps around my forearm, tiny tendrils writhing as they try to dig into my skin. I have to choose between ripping it off and letting dozens hit me, or ignoring it and continuing to swing. I execute a figure eight and follow it by taking a knee and swinging my sword behind me as the attacking alien's tendrils search for a grip.

Ensure my skin is like steel, Bookworm, I order, hoping he has already given that direction to my followers.

Another wraps around my knee, and a third loosely holds onto my chest, while nearly fifty of the eighty-one are dead. They are unable to get through my skin after more than a quarter of an hour of trying, and that's when they switch up their attack. A mountain of aliens drops from the sky onto me. Each one must have weighed no more than a pound, but together it feels like the mine from my previous entrapment had collapsed and miles of stone and earth pressed against me. The weight is immense, would have suffocated me if I needed to breathe, would have crushed me if I were human. Instead, it's as if I'm immobilized in a casing of ice.

Thousands of small tendrils and hundreds of larger ones fail to break through my skin, although they do dive into my nose and ears. Large movements fail me, so I wriggle my fingers and toes, then move my hands and feet, and continue to gain some room until I can move my sword. I shake it slowly back and forth, like carving a ham, first clearing my orifices before digging into the meat of the alien mass. I keep carving, sawing, and stabbing for minutes, which turn into hours. I never stop moving, not even for a moment, and Bookworm keeps my follower's up to speed on my dilemma and my needs. I decide that I will keep going until my followers can help no more, and only then will I rest. Rest just like the demigods who still are entombed.

Bookworm lets me know when another day has passed, and tells me that I have killed more than ten thousand aliens. He wants to tell me how long it will take to kill all the aliens, but I mentally yell at him before he finishes his sentence. Time is an irrelevant constant. It's then that the unrelenting mass of aliens begins to lighten, and over the course of an hour, more and more aliens fall back, until above me is a glow from a faint light. I swing upward and use my fallen foes as stepping stones, very slippery stepping stones that drain me to climb, making one last push and crawling on top of the hundred-foot-high mound of dead aliens.

It's only then that I want to rest, but there's no time. Unlike when the battle began, the aliens have retreated a fair distance, far enough to make room for the thousands of milky-eyed Marsians standing on the street across from the federal building. The Marsian cattle fill every free space in the city section behind the street. It's my first time seeing them since the video feed, which itself was recorded over one hundred and fifty years earlier.

When we planned the colonization of Mars, there were many debates as to how the reduced gravity and lack of sunlight would affect the humans who lived on the distant planet. In the end, leading biologists, anthropologists, and biochemists presented their data showing that the effects would either be negligible or easily overcome with supplements and exercise, and that it would take hundreds of generations for any noticeable effects to occur. Even then, they still debated whether it would mean heavier or lighter bones, paler or darker skin, or even larger or smaller eyes.

Yet, nearly nine thousand stand in front of me only seven generations later, and it's clear they are no longer human. It appears neither side was right, but what won out is hard for me to put into words, other than to say that it appears the extremes dominate. Tall, lithe bodies with creamy white skin stand next to squat, darker-pigmented bodies with eyes slightly larger than those of a normal human. Body postures are all strongly erect, which may be due to the white capes all of them are wearing. In fact, the aliens may have been manipulating genetics to try and determine what traits were best for life on Mars. Yet with all the differences, the milky white eyes haunt the faces of every Marsian. And in front of them all stands El Matador. A perfectly postured giant, his bright clothes and curved hat are a strong complement to his sharp features.

I try to gracefully walk down the mound, but it turns into more of a slip and slide due to the layered sheets of aliens. I do manage not to fall as I reach the bottom, which is a major accomplishment given that grace isn't a strength of mine. I take one step away from the mound and look across the street at El Matador before eyeing the sword in my hand.

"Well, that was fun. But I thought you'd be smarter than to fight a lost cause for days on end," I say as I take the sword in both hands and snap it in half.

I chuck both pieces at the feet of El Matador, his alien cape fluttering in the breezeless air of the dome. El Matador's thin lips move ever so slightly for a while before he speaks.

"We Wyndelaces can afford the losses, as we required time to consolidate information on how to proceed next, Mr. President."

El Matador's voice isn't what I remember. His words are as hollow as those of every infected person I have heard speak. However, the Spanish accent still comes through.

"Wyndelaces?" I query, vaguely remembering the word from the dying Magnate. "That's what your race is called."

He nods, so I move on to my next question regarding his statement.

"Consolidate information?" I ask.

"Yes, we determined that it was highly improbable we could physically defeat you, as you demigods somehow defy our understanding of the universe. Therefore, we searched for another approach, which required experimentation on our hosts."

I'm calm after nearly a week of fighting, but I have an endless supply of anger, and the fuse is getting close to being lit again. I'm ready to call them on what they did, but I decide to suppress my anger for a little while longer.

"You and humankind have a weakness, Mr. President. Actually, you have more than one. We will start with the first," says El Matador.

He takes a graceful step forward, raises his hands with the palms up, and speaks as if to an audience much larger than just me. The thousands behind him echo his words, not in perfect unison but in such a controlled fashion that I find levels of chanting within. It's right out of a horror movie. Or rather, I'm in a horror movie.

"When your race works together, it is strong, but rarely does everyone work together. You are individuals with individual needs, wants, desires, and weaknesses. You are individuals, who protect only yourselves. Except when love is involved, but even then it rarely extends beyond two people. That will never defeat us, but love will be your defeat."

An elderly couple steps forward, holding hands. The man's thin strands of gray hair poorly cover his long ears, which seem mismatched with his stubby nose. The woman's white hair has a black tint to it, and she wears a conservative blue dress. Both have dark skin and thick bodies. The milkiness retreats from their eyes, and they turn to look at each other, knowing it's for the last time. Both let out an elderly moan as the aliens rip away from their bodies and fly away, dripping blood from their retracted tendrils.

I cross my arms.

"Just a start," El Matador says with an actual hint of a smirk. "Next."

A couple in their twenties steps up, holding hands just like the elderly. The man is powerful in physical stature and the woman athletic, both wearing exercise clothing. When the milkiness leaves them, he wails as he stares into her eyes. She lifts her hand to his face, caressing softly, not quite finishing before the aliens rip away. His pain is already so intense from knowing he is losing the love of his life that he merely collapses and releases his last breath. Her pain comes with a long shriek as she falls on top of him and passes.

"I know what's next, and while I won't surrender, I will not watch," I say while gritting my teeth to hold back a waterfall of anger.

I hear the tiny footsteps, feeling the tears push out of my closed eyes as I wait. The young screams drive into and through my heart, even though I've steeled myself. After a few seconds, I open my eyes and look at the sleeping blond-haired boy and brunette little girl, both of whom have fallen backward. Small pools of blood expand outward from their backs.

"Wait," said El Matador as he raises a finger. "There is more."

He motions, and the crowd moves aside to reveal another elderly couple, followed by a couple in their fifties, and then a younger couple who are trailed by a boy and girl.

"The results of the studies we performed verified that the worst pain is a parent watching their child die. We were pleasantly surprised that this is compounded by the number and the generational sequence of those who died," El Matador goes on.

"The needs of the many outweigh the needs of the few." My voice is strained, on the verge of cracking. "I have done far worse with my own hands."

They murder the children first, pulling back far enough from the family members so that I can see their grief, watch all the different ways they grieve. Then they kill the next and the next, until all four generations lie in a circle. I want to fight again; I want to battle them for weeks, years, or even decades until every last one is dead. But I don't act. I look back at El Matador and wait.

"Yes, our research concluded that you would be pained but wouldn't surrender," he says.

"Then why'd you do it!" I yell, again seeing my energy shoot out as a gust of air that blows over the crowd. I can't control my anger anymore. I try to hold it in, but the feelings from my repressed memories seep through. Tears stream down my face, my muscles strain from being pulled taught with anger, and the veins on my face and forehead nearly burst. I have made a journey—a long, arduous journey—and am right back where I started. I'm ready to kill them all and…and then I see her. One little, darker-skinned girl with brunette ponytails is looking at me different from all the others. She has the same glazed eyes, but they are focused on me, and her face isn't frozen like a mask. I pause and look at her, whereupon she whispers a word that I don't understand. I blink, and she's gone.

El Matador takes a step back but hides any fear in his voice. "We did it for the next step."

Mr. President, a large pulse was just released from the alien spaceship, Bookworm lets me know.

I barely hear him, but in seconds I know what is happening. Rather, I feel what is happening.

Chapter 23

El Matador places one foot in front of the other, bends down on one knee, crosses his hands on the knee, and lowers his head. The first row of infected Marsians behind him drop to their knees and lean forward with their arms outstretched, their hands and knees touching the ground. A few seconds tick by, and then a small tingle emanates from the center of my brain. The next row sits on the ground with their legs crossed and hands together, pointing to the sky. The third row sits on their knees and hold hands while lowering their heads. Each Marsian prays in some way and some form; prays to me, directing me in the same way. Nearly nine thousand worshipping me, asking for me to surrender. The power is growing, and the single command flows through me, but it's still a fraction of what my human worshippers on Earth are doing.

"It won't work, El Matador," I say. "You've failed physically, emotionally, and spiritually. If it takes a decade, I'll wipe your kind from this planet."

El Matador looks up with wide eyes and a smile. No, it isn't his smile, it's an evil emotion conveyed through El Matador.

"We have only begun," he says before resuming his prayer.

And then it happens.

By the thousands, the aliens who were floating in the air lower to the ground and cover every free inch of space. They mimic the Marsians in their own sheet-like bowing, over three hundred thousand strong. I know because I can always feel every person—or it looks like thing—praying to me. It still isn't enough, but then the next calculated chess move by the

251

aliens occurs: the power of 42,363,131 aliens praying to me overrides the humans who are aiding my cause. Their single prayer, single desire rips through humankind's desire and battles against my free will, the fight like two rams in full spring glory. I want to destroy the aliens, want to fight until only one is standing. However, in moments my knees give way and my head bows deeply in defeat. I try to raise my hands, but don't even manage to shake a finger. It had never crossed my mind that they could do what they did. I want to talk with Bookworm, to speak with someone about what is happening. When I try, there's nothing but emptiness in my mind. I can't connect to Bookworm. Checkmate.

El Matador rises and strides confidently up to me. His hand reaches out, cups my chin, and raises my head. He examines me like I'm his prize thoroughbred.

"Almost…impossible. We had not believed it possible. We did not believe that you and the others were more than a trick. Technology cloaked in parlor tricks and grandiose stories meant to fool humanity. However, the spiritual is as real and even more powerful than we thought. The spiritual makes you even more powerful than the demigod I now possess and the German you defeated. It is something we shed long ago when we left our solar system. It looks like it is something we will have to reexamine."

El Matador raises his opposite hand high. "Now for the final step."

Four of the aliens float down to my level, easily hovering behind me without any sign of jerky movements. On a silent cue, they move closer to each other, two on top and two on bottom. They move in so close that they're touching, their edges becoming blurred and soon indiscernible. One single, the larger sheet drops over my head and settles on my shirtless back. Large groupings of tiny tendrils writhe against my back and neck, trying to invade my body.

The alien worshippers pray to me; pray that I allow the alien tendrils to penetrate my skin…and I obey. They wiggle on my skin and then vibrate as they bore inward. The odd sensation disappears as they release their topical anesthetic and numb the pain receptors. There's a small pushing force until they pass beyond my epidermal layer, travelling along the nerve bundles to my spine. Others wrap along my muscles, even my larynx, and wriggle to test their control; a thousand worms growing into my body. Organs, tendons, and ligaments twitch and shift inside me, but on the surface I appear completely relaxed.

The worst part is when something drives up the base of my skull and grows around different segments of my brain. I can feel the tendrils' pressure around my skull. My breathing becomes labored, my vision blurs, and colors fade to gray before disorientation takes over. My heart rate and body temperature increase because my body thinks it's fighting an infection. It's correct, but not the type of infection it's used to. I remember suffocating during the first part of my space trip and how awful it was, but this is worse. Every part of my being feels as if it's shutting down, and my mind says I should be screaming in pain, but I can't react. I wonder if this is what people in the latter stages of multiple sclerosis feel—trapped in a space smaller than what your body could fit into. It's claustrophobia at its worst. Locked in. That's what it's called.

After a few minutes, things start to return to normal, except that normal also comes with the added bonus that I'm no longer in control. My vision is still blurred, and I remember the milky haze in those that are possessed. My larynx twitches and flexes, and strange syllables whisper from my mouth as air is forced out of my lungs. It happens dozens upon dozens of times until I speak in a mumbling voice. Or rather, it speaks using my voice.

"You are now controlled by a singularity created by the merging of the four of us, Mr. President. We Wyndelaces normally tell our hosts to only say what we want—to listen to what we ask of them first—or else we will make them feel pain so deep that they will wish for death. We give a single example that only lasts a few seconds, but has convinced greater than 99 percent on the first pass."

"And for me?" I ask.

"One second of pain for every Wyndelace you have killed," El Matador says coldly.

That adds up to nearly three hours. This is really gonna hurt.

Every pain receptor in every part of my body rapidly fires at the same time. My skin runs the course of burning, cutting, and bludgeoning sensations from head to toe. My hand feels like it's inside a fire, my back like someone is slicing it open with a sword, and my legs like they are being crushed under a car. My joints are beyond inflamed, while my fingers and toes curl up as the nerves tell me I'm on a torture rack. My organs are experiencing multi-g loads from a car crash and are shutting down. My right lung collapses and my heart stops beating for seconds. The sensations come crashing in like waves, roll back for a brief second, and then slam me with the same sensations but to different parts of my body. I want to scream but can't; I want to attack El Matador, but all I'm allowed to do is stare into his milky eyes.

The waves of pain roll over me at increasing speeds. I hope I pass out, beg mentally for the aliens to stop, even though they can't hear me. It keeps coming, and just when I think it's at its peak, a new pain strikes. I'm burned alive, torn limb by limb; then beheaded, drowned, stabbed a million times. If it can be imagined, I'm feeling it.

I barely hear El Matador's words, but when I piece them together they nearly break me.

"One hour down, Mr. President."

And then, I pray. I pray to whatever being has created me. At first I pray for relief, then compassion, and finally I pray that no matter what happens to me, humankind will be spared from what I'm experiencing. I deserve what's happening to me, deserve it for turning my back for two centuries, but they don't. Boy deserves to grow up, the children in Old Woman's town deserve to be free, and the dark-skinned girl in the Marsian audience deserves so much more. They deserve a chance to try again.

Then it's over.

"Now, Mr. President," El Matador says. "We have you under control and can make the pain even worse if you attempt to disobey us. Although resistance is futile"

"How is that possible?" I ask, my voice weak from the torture session.

"The tendrils are not only wrapped around your muscular structure, but—" replies El Matador until I cut him off.

254

"Not that. How can you make it even more painful?" I ask, being slightly sarcastic. Luckily, it goes unnoticed.

"What you have experienced so far is physical pain. While we can't control your thoughts or read your mind, we can reach into your brain and alter its chemistry," states El Matador. "For example, you surely have high concentrations of glutamate, as evident by your propensity for violence. GABA has the opposite effect. Do you feel it?"

My anger, which I'm holding back, dissipates, and I immediately want to sit down and relax. I'm at peace with my surroundings and my current state. My life is complete and I'm ready to surren...rage bores through me like a bullet, tearing apart my peaceful state. I will kill the aliens who have not only tortured me but purposely killed small children just to prove a point.

I clench my fists, glaring through El Matador's taunting eyes. I try to raise my hand, try to pound him, but it won't budge. I growl and strain against the alien's control; my own muscles—wrapped tightly by alien tendrils—rip and separate as I lift my quaking arm. My arm is only raised a half foot before it drops back to my side, bruised as evidenced by the pools of blood forming beneath the skin. El Matador's facial expression gives away his surprise at how close I came to attacking him. A small crisp whistle from his white cape and calmness flows over me like a bath of warm water.

"Extremely reduced levels of dopamine and serotonin led to a state of depression so low in our Marsian experiments that every individual committed suicide. Endorphins control pain, and noradrenaline affects your levels of energy. You know what happens if we randomly shift the levels around?" El Matador asks.

Yeah, that'd be worse. Much worse, but I really have no clue until a wry smile crosses El Matador's face. These Wyndelaces are getting better at human emotions and definitely aren't the logical, highly-intelligent aliens devoid of emotion portrayed in most sci-fi movies I've watched.

Emotions.

My mind courses through thousands of mixed emotions: hatred, love, questioning, challenging, anger, pain, loss, joy. They switch quickly like gateways on a circuit board, thousands of mood swings in under a second, which continues for several minutes. Then they hit all at once. It's an indescribable feeling, something close to not being an individual anymore and more like a mashed agglomeration of thousands of individuals fighting to use one brain to express one extreme emotion. It's thankfully fleeting, and only after it disappears do I taste the blood in my mouth from nearly biting off my tongue. Not figuratively, as my tongue lops around inside my mouth before it begins to heal.

"You see what we can do to you and what we are capable of doing to all humankind? Do not worry, as we rarely use more than a gentle reminder to reinforce who is in control."

"Are we done with your displays of power? What will you do with me?" I ask. I'm exhausted from the mental maelstrom.

"We will discuss that when we reach our ship. We will need you to reduce your size down to less than four feet once you arrive," El Matador says as he turns and walks away.

He stops and turns his head, still maintaining perfect posture, as if waiting for a bull to attack. "Do you require a ride?"

I wave him off as I stare at my surroundings in Dome 5. The infected Marsians are dispersing and the Wyndelaces are moving back toward the airlocks, although I can still feel their prayers controlling and directing my strongest urges. This place had been the last stand for both the Marsians and for me, and I wonder if it'll also be a landmark for humankind's fall.

My mouth mumbles, "Time to start moving."

I obey and walk toward the hatch, preferring to suffer an unbreathable atmosphere over a ride with my captors. As I enter the airlock, I'm crammed in with hundreds of Wyndelaces and my anger begins to rise. Then there is an unusual pressure on my brain, and peace flattens my anger. This is not going to be easy to accept.

Once outside, I follow the millions of Wyndelaces as they awkwardly float toward their spaceship. I walk for nearly an hour, slower than them, trying not to think; enjoying the fact that the aliens can't talk to me nor I to them. There's nothing but silence. The direction of the travelers leads down a larger crater, which luckily has a gentle slope. I start to veer off course to test my caped captor's ability, and find out just how easy it is for it to redirect me. I'm soon back on the path to the spaceship with a bowed head and a darkened heart.

I walk for nearly another half hour, trudging up the other side of the crater before taking one big step out of it. I'm on a downward sloping plane, full of swirling iron-oxide dust, and less than a quarter mile away is the alien spaceship I had seen in the video. The view is enough to make me stop walking, my captor thankfully giving me a moment of independence.

The spaceship is no longer resting at an awkward angle on its hub, the center spoke absent of its previous jagged surface. Rather, the entire hub is flush on the ground with only the upper half of center spoke showing. Despite decades of large storms and sand blasting by iron-oxide particles, the bright white exterior remains unblemished. The hub does resemble a stack of cargo containers with a slight curvature, like Colonel Lync had stated, appearing to result in nine concentric rings with the smallest attached to the center spoke. The top of each container is open, with the rows of Wyndelaces advancing until over a container, rolling themselves into a tennis-ball shape before dropping out of sight. The spoke is like a beacon shooting light straight upward, reflecting even the small amount of sunlight that Mars receives. It's segmented, which I hadn't caught on the video due to the combination of the distance from the colony and its near-blinding brightness.

I find myself walking toward the spaceship and wonder if it's my desire to see the spaceship up close or the Wyndelace cape pushing me forward. When closer, I can see lines and ridges crisscrossing the surface of the containers, while only vertical lines scale the center spoke. One of the ASF's exploration vehicles is parked next to the hub, with El Matador waiting for me in his usual bull-fighting pose. I'm grateful that I'm not required to be in a constant pose as my followers and I would have had long talks if that were the case. When I'm within a dozen feet of him, he raises a hand to stop my progress. He turns and jumps on top of an already-filled container, freezes in place, and his nine-foot frame appears to shrink before it disappears from my view.

I walk up to the container and touch its side, using the opportunity to feel the surface's texture. The Wyndelace cape tightens its grasp on my muscles, preparing to stop me if I try to destroy any part of the ship. I wonder how fast it can react but decide not to test it at this time, as the two-hour pain session is still fresh in my mind. The container has an extremely smooth surface; even the ridges and lines blend so perfectly into the frame that it feels like a single unbroken structure.

I reach up and grasp the edge of the container with two fingers and easily pull myself onto its top. There are no seams for entrance into the containers, even though I had seen the Wyndelaces drop into them from above. I glance over and watch as one of the recently filled containers begins to grow a ceiling from the four sides, which then merge to form a monolithic piece. It wasn't like a door shutting, more like water from different angles flowing over a surface and coalescing when they make contact. Another advanced technology they had, and I wonder how many more there are. All the rows on this section are sealed, with El Matador having used them as a floor to walk to the center spoke.

I hurry to catch up, which clearly isn't my own doing; I'm rarely in a rushing mood. I'm almost behind him when El Matador touches the surface of the spoke and walks through the white wall, the area darkening as he enters and then returning to white once he is through. I take the chance to look at the segments of the spoke, guessing they are roughly six feet in height and running dozens of segments upward.

Walking toward where the entrance had been for El Matador doesn't work, as my body refuses to move. I growl, noticing a tingling in my skull before I find myself relaxing. I wonder how the Marsians have been able to take this enslavement for decades. I try to move forward again, and again my muscles freeze before I can twitch even a toe. Since I can't use anger to force their hand, and there's no air for them to mumble their desires with my own voice, I look back at where I started and then up at the towering shape.

Finally, I look back at the segmented wall, realizing I am too tall to enter. Yes, that's what El Matador had told me back at the colony. I work on reducing my size to the height that's needed, and with the Wyndelaces worshipping me, it happens so fast that I become lightheaded.

Once finished, I'm allowed to step forward, and I reach my hand out toward and into the white wall. It darkens as my hand slips past, then I find myself stepping into and through the wall. The feeling of passing through the semi-solid object is like walking through layers of plastic wrap. It stretches across my skin—forming a film around my mouth, eyes, and ears—but completely releases as I step out the other side. The film over my orifices falls away, and air rushes in and fills my lungs. It tastes different than on Earth, but I can't ask Bookworm for its composition. I breathe once more in the pitch darkness before mumbling emanates from my lips.

"We do not need air to live, but it makes moving and communication much faster for us," the Wyndelace on my back says, tingling my vocal chords due to its manipulation by the tiny tendrils. "We do hope you like your home for the next few weeks."

Soft lighting emanates from the ceiling, and a yellowish-brown blob grows from the white floor. It flows upward and then begins to solidify, forming a flat surface, a backing, and two rectangular arms. It's a granite chair and not too far away from it is a black rock with a notepad, pen, and a small lantern. Behind the chair is a pillar with a heavy metal plate and two sets of chains welded to it that lead to the metal loops embedded into the chair. The white floor and walls turn as dark as my last prison—the one I inflicted upon myself—whereupon the transformation is complete.

If I could feel anger and rage, I would have. They are mocking me. When rage is absent, insight flows out instead.

"You were able to get the downloads that Bookworm sent to the Earth humans?" I query.

"Yes, but not early enough to stop you from travelling to Mars, which became a good thing," the Wyndelace mumbles back through me.

"What do you mean?" I ask as I involuntarily sit down in the cold chair.

"We had travelled from our solar system to yours over the course of twenty-seven Earth years, but our primary propulsion system was damaged before we could make a final trajectory adjustment toward Earth. We were not able to perform the maneuver required for our mission using the inertia reactionary drive, and we barely made it to Mars before both drives went offline. The crash landing ripped apart the bottom half of our spaceship, destroying the primary propulsion system and partially damaging the inertia reactionary drive."

In my mind I relive the landing from the Magnate's video feed.

"The type of Wyndelaces who took on this journey are not suited for physical activities, and thus we had to use the Marsians to rebuild our spaceship. It took a very long time because we had to first dig a hold deep enough to allow the rebuilding of the lower half of our spaceship as there wasn't the resources available to lift and suspend it for repairs. Also, Mars did not have the necessary elemental materials to fix the propulsion systems. Earth did have all the natural resources we needed, but it took a century and a half to get the required materials delivered while still ensuring the Marsian population remained at a suitable population level to continue the rebuilding of our spaceship. The space shuttle you were on—the one you destroyed—carried the last parts that were required to rebuild the remote startup for the reactionary drive. The remote startup is required because of the very dangerous conditions that are created within the control room during initiation. And while you did thwart our plan, you also gave us an alternative approach. You are that approach, and we will use you now because a powerful being might be able to survive. More specifically, a being that has incredible strength, near imperviousness to damage, and an unmatched willpower could survive the startup sequence."

"So, the startup is deadly?" I ask, somewhat rhetorically.

"Correct. The inertia reactionary system is similar to the ePEG devices the human race developed. We use the same plane, the one that is absent of time, to both dissipate and retrieve the energy for the millions of integrated inertia drives on our ship. During startup there are multiple transient disruptions in space and time that degrade any organic being near the drive."

"And you think I can survive the effects of these transients and finish the startup sequence?" I ask, but continue when there is no answer. "So why not El Matador, and how did you bring him to Mars?"

The mumbling was still annoying me, along with hearing answers to my questions in my own voice. It felt as if I was Two-Face, Batman's nemesis, with two personalities trapped in one body.

"We did not bring El Matador here. The Colonias de España snuck him aboard one of the last colonization ships. He had long ago reached the catatonic state that you described in your discussions with Bookworm. They packaged the catatonic being, then buried him under their central square. When we finally found out, we overtook his body quite easily, unlike yourself."

The Wyndelace pauses for some reason, but then continues. "Unfortunately, we already require El Matador to execute the direct drive startup for the main propulsion system."

I really don't care about this direct driving thing, so I continue down my strategic path of questioning.

"What about Arthuren? You could have used him."

"Arthuren willingly came to us, but those details are not your concern other than knowing that he showed us how to control demigods. We could have used him but at the time, we did not know the level of damage to the cargo you had caused, or else we would have pulled him back from trying to kill you," the Wyndelace replies.

"So, I help you start this reactionary drive. Then what?" I ask.

"You do not help us. We direct you to do what we want. If you survive, then you will serve as our ambassador to Earth. We will signal your arrival and let you show all humankind how beneficial the takeover will be. There will be little resistance when their most powerful demigod explains how the process will finally allow them to flourish."

"Beneficial?" I ask. I was full of questions.

"Yes. While we control your body, it is important to each Wyndelace that the host be healthy and operate at an optimal performance. We—"

"Yeah, I get it," I cut him off. "You optimize your hosts for you all to live—"

Pain racks my body as if I'd been hit by a freight train running downhill. I fling my arms wide, my head snaps back, and I open my mouth to scream, but no sound emanates. Just silent agony as I slide to the floor. As fast as it started, it's over.

"Obviously, your conditioning will take some time, but you will learn."

I say nothing, and instead pull myself off the floor and back onto the chair. I silently wonder if I could be conditioned. I'm willing to bet that I'd take the agonizing pain until I died just to prove a point. I didn't know what point that was, maybe that I'm the universe's most stubborn being. I swallow a little foam and a lot of my ego before I speak.

"When do El Matador and I get the drives going?" I ask.

"In eleven hours. By then we will finish with extracting what we can from your space shuttle crash and will have loaded everything we need for our journey. Until then, you will sleep," it says.

"What about the signal that was sent out from this spaceship to the Wyndelaces when they were in the domes? Who sent that out? Was it your leaders? I'd like to meet them," I say.

"You may after you finish your job."

Suddenly, even as I fear what my job will mean for humankind, my head lowers and my eyes close for sleep.

Chapter 24

My eyes raise like the metal gate of a feudal castle, screaming in both deep and shrill pitches as it grates against the chipped inset that had been created by people far less artful than a true mason. I fight to bring them back down, shutting out the external, but they easily open against my will. My granite chair is positioned so that Bookworm's charcoal outcropping stands directly in front me, signaling the reality I'm in.

"You know, this re-creation is wrong," I say.

The chords of my vocal chords tingle, my cheeks twitch, and my lips do some sort of tune-up as the Wyndelace prepares me for a conversation.

"The purpose is to create an environment that is calming, not to let you live in a false reality," the spokesman says.

"Well, that's unfortunate," I quip, then quickly follow up to avoid an onslaught of punishment. "But it does make sense. Is it time?"

"Yes. I will walk you to the reactionary drive."

"Don't I need some training or directions for how to start it up?" I ask.

"No, I will be manipulating your body to perform the startup sequence," the Wyndelace replies.

"But won't you be affected by the transient issue?"

"No. In this form we can withstand it, but we need you because we cannot physically perform the steps. Also, the descendants of humans were shredded apart before completion of the first step, and the other demigod would have a much smaller chance of success than you."

I pause, realizing what it's saying. They have already tried with the Marsians.

I stand up and am walked to the wall that is opposite the one I entered. As I pass through it, I experience the same plastic-wrap effect a when I first entered the ship. I pass through walls, floors, and even equipment as the Wyndelace navigates me to the inertia reactionary drive. Of course, I don't even know what that means.

"Do you know for sure that I will survive?"

"The probability is extremely high that you will survive even the last step. However, it is possible that the trauma caused by the needed repairs will have long-lasting effects," come back the words in my own voice.

I want to ask what that means, but I'm stopped from forming the words. I'm beginning to think that this is worse than enslaving myself.

I walk up a strange set of steps, each forming right before my foot lands, that carries me through a ceiling into a cramped circular room. A central bank of small pipes protrudes from the floor, travels up to a central dais, and then radiates outward into the walls. The pipes are broken out in a series of three segments, visually apparent not only by their groupings but by the three black lines on the floor. Rising out of the floor, I would have smashed into the pipes if I were my normal height. But as it is, I pass easily underneath them.

I want time to assess the room and ask questions, but my hand reaches up, cutting off my thoughts, and wraps around one of the white pipes. It vibrates, but not in any sort of rhythm. It wants to; I can feel it trying to be consistent, trying to have a pattern, but it keeps cutting out like a car with a bad timing belt.

"Wait!" I shout.

My hand pulls back a few inches and hangs in the air.

"What?" asks my Wyndelace cape.

"What if during the sequence, you can't control me? You need to tell me the steps so I can finish this."

"I doubt you are eager to aid us in overtaking humankind. However, I have proved that you cannot alter what we are going to do. We control every aspect of your being. The answer is no. We will proceed as planned."

My hand moves back up to the horizontal pipe and grips it. The harder I grip, the stronger the noncoherent vibration. I pull it down a foot, and the shaking is like a steel cable jump rope attached to a rapidly spinning motor. The muscles in my legs swell and my shoulders tense as I adjust my grip on the tube. It's then that the undercurrent of a smaller, yet powerful vibration attempts to pulverize my bones. The sonic wave rides along the back of the larger vibration, and the two are crashing against each other. The Wyndelace tries to have me move the pipe into the correct position, but each time my arm pushes toward the location, the larger vibration sends it off in a different direction.

"I have an idea, but you need to let me control my arm," I grunt as the sonication pulverizes my teeth as they come together, white dust emanating from my mouth. My teeth rapidly regrow. "Now, you moron!"

I regain control of my arm and immediately pull the pipe away from the dais, whereupon the larger vibration pushes it in the opposite direction. I swiftly jam it into place next to a different vertical pipe. Instantly, the pipe transforms into a black space with small, twinkling lights. I'm holding a cylinder with no measurable volume; holding the universe. One moment it's pulsing with all the power I can imagine, and the next it's sucking my power like a thirsted vampire. My other hand grabs another pipe and moves it in the opposite direction. When it connects, I gasp. One side pulses power while the other takes it just as quickly. I become a conduit, more like a relay switch for a vast amount of energy. I know it would have fried any human who tried what I'm doing.

The Wyndelace makes me let go, and I'm both relieved and disappointed. So much power and so much loss of power. I hadn't even been shocked at how the pipes grew and shrank as I pulled them out and into the connectors. Nor surprised at how they detached and reattached, melding into the fixed pipes without welds. The switching back and forth of the power was painful, while also fascinating. I really want to ask how the things work, but the Wyndelace gives me no time to ponder what has happened. I walk in a counterclockwise fashion to the next set of pipes, this time simultaneously grasping two, one almost laying on top of the other.

"El Matador has put the propulsion drive back online," I mumble. Well, the Wyndelace mumbled using my vocal chords.

I pull on the pipes.

Heat so hot, so full of energy, burns through my skin and melts my bones. I watch my hands flow over the pipes like a thick syrup and begin to drip. Nuclear radiation, or ionizing radiation, not only produces enough heat to cause cement to crack and burn, but also ionizes the electrons of DNA and cells. My organs scream out and warn of an immediate shutdown. Then I feel the tens of millions of Wyndelaces praying to heal me, surging energy down my arms, working to reform my hands; healing the damage the radiation is causing to my body. The nuclear radiation and the healing energy push against each other, with my hands as the innocent bystanders. The energy from the worshippers begins to win, and I pull the pipes out of their current location. The blast of radiation ripples over my body, and I close my eyes as the corneas burn away. Anger, forced in by the Wyndelace, fuels me on as I roar while detaching and reconnecting the pipes in a different pattern. I lock them in place; the radiation drops off significantly yet still burns my body.

I collapse to the floor, my body twitching and my organs burning from the radiation. Although I heal quickly, I want to lie on the ground for a while as the mental anguish is still a very vivid part of my reality. However, within seconds I'm forced to get up by my alien master.

"How is El Matador?" I ask, my voice cracking like the first time I had spoken with Bookworm in my cave.

"El Matador completed his task, but will not make it. He is still in the propulsion drive room." Even though it's my voice, I can hear the strain of the Wyndelace.

"Thought you said the startup sequence wouldn't hurt you," I say with a little venom in my voice.

"I said we could withstand it, but it is not pleasant."

I turn to walk to the final section.

"Is this the final step?" I ask. I want to talk about how the three segments power the inertia drive, how the whole thing actually works.

"Yes, the last tube must be attached to the center of the dais. It will be the most difficult because it is the conduit to the timeless dimension," replies the Wyndelace.

"Are you sure? My scientists had let me know that the portal to the timeless plane could only occur at the atomic level."

"If we had a couple days and I cared to educate you, I'd show you why your grasp of quantum mechanics fails when reaching into classical mechanics. There is no separation, merely laws your humans missed. For now I will say that you are right, but also very wrong. You are looking at scalability from small to large and large to small, instead of from the timeless fold that connects the two."

I don't bother telling the alien that this is as helpful as telling me, 'because I said so.' I'm also really glad their race can't read minds. I would be in a lot of pain.

My steps are slower and my breathing laborious, which is strange since the Wyndelace is controlling my body. Fear fills my mind and my hands shake as I reach up to the single tube in the third quadrant. Touching it brings no ill effects, and then the alien forces me to pull it away from its current connection. I no longer know where or when I am.

I float just below the surface of a sea of utter blackness with pure white light filling the space above the sea. Thoughts come to me without linearity while I hold the pipe. I try to think, but nothing will come forth, and I try to wiggle my body, but I can't even remove my hand from the pipe. I'm motionless, frozen without the existence of time. I stay that way for what could be seconds but seems to stretch into infinity. Then a small ripple plays across the black surface, then another and another, one building upon the other until they become waves. The waves reach up into the white light's domain before dropping back into the black pool. One time my mouth lifts above the pool and my Wyndelace mumbles: "Move the pipe up when your hand is exposed."

I wait the eons required for another series of waves, and this time my hand crosses the film between white and black. I manage to move the pipe a small amount before my hand slips back into the pool. Eons pass again before another series of waves arrive, but this time only my head is briefly exposed. For that brief time, a thousand emotions play over me, not horrifying like what the Wyndelace did to me, but rather a complex, undecipherable agglomeration.

I fall back under until another ripple exposes my hand. I continue this for no time at all, but for what could have been the lifetime of the sun. Time is a constant, and our minds have evolved along the linearity of a timeline. We can't comprehend a timeless world, so I still frame what is happening to me using 'time.' I must frame it, or else I am—or will go—insane. Another wave, and one last push. I make the connection I cannot see.

I'm back in the room, my hand holding the tube on top of the dais. That's when the timelessness I have just experienced hits me like a bomb going off within my body. The cells of my body both grow anew and die at the same time. My thoughts leap forward to things I have yet to experience while also delving back into a past I have hidden. The non-linearity tortures my mind as thoughts travel in no particular direction, have no timeline, and flow out over each other. Nothing makes sense, and I make no sense. I'm without purpose, yet without need.

"It is done," the Wyndelace interrupts.

I don't react, can't react, won't react, but the Wyndelace does. I let go of the pipe, and it walks me back to my cell, sitting me down on the granite chair. I close my eyes to the senseless world, hoping my mind will heal so I can question the Wyndelace leaders. I was told I could meet them after I started their drive.

Chapter 25

"I'd ask where you're from, but the answer would mean little to me," I say with my eyes still closed.

I have no idea how long I've been out, and no recollection of what nightmares haunted me during that time. If my words shock the white cape on my back, the Wyndelace does a good job of hiding it.

"The propulsion and inertia reactionary drives are up and running at near peak performance," the Wyndelace says, using my vocal chords. "The ship has been travelling for seven Earth days."

Only seven days. Much better than the years that would pass when I slept in the mine. I had feared waking only to find Earth had already been taken over. I have time but need to do more than ask random questions. I need background, to learn using what appears to be innocent dialogue.

"How long until we reach Earth?" I ask, still not opening my eyes.

"Eleven more Earth days."

It's much shorter than the space travel humans could do, even when the orbits of Earth and Mars were close. Not a lot of time for me to work my plan.

"Can I meet with those who are controlling the ship?"

"I said you could after your mission, so we will go now."

My eyes open. I rise and step up to the rapidly appearing white stairs that will take me through the ceiling, a hole opening as I approach. The path is as convoluted as when I was taken to the reactionary drive. I have a feeling they're trying to confuse me with the rounded rooms, and stairs that go up, sideways, and even down. None of the rooms have any distinct markings, no signs of being lived in. Maybe they are also created just for the purpose of confusion. The Wyndelace stops me in another nondescript rectangular room that has a ten-foot-by-fifteen-foot perimeter with the usual six-foot-high ceiling.

The white wall in front of me darkens until it completely disappears, revealing a room holding a dais like the one in the reactionary drive chamber, but nearly four times the diameter. Around it stand—or sit— three feathered beings with the claws of their wings tapping away on the dais's top. Each is distinctly different in look and shape. The closest one is barrel-chested with gray feathers, a thick neck, and a head that looks like the end of a broken branch. Its gray-speckled, jagged beak juts out, and its black eyes are swept back, nearly covered by the plumage around its neck. Each stout leg ends in a perpendicular talon that is as black as its eyes. The creature to my right has an ostrich-like neck, lanky legs, and an emaciated-looking body that towers over the other two, surely regal if not for the numerous patches devoid of brown feathers.

The last creature's sharp features are strengthened by piercing eyes, a sharp beak, and winged arms that move deftly as it focuses on the console. Black and red feathers cover most of its body, except for the chest that holds a faded yellow teardrop shape. While I don't know anything about their race, they all appear to be approaching the end of their lives.

The lanky-legged creature turns to face me while the other two pick up the pace of their tapping on the dais. It patiently watches me, tucking its arms under chest feathers. I size up all three again, wondering what type of control they have over the Wyndelaces. Were the Wyndelaces slaves from another planet, captured and now forced to do their bidding? Maybe they evolved together and had teamed up to overtake other planets.

"What are you?" I ask, trying to not sound subservient but also not disrespectful. I imagine that my Wyndelace cape will cause me unbelievable pain if I offend one of its leaders.

A quick series of chirps and squawks are let out by the creature, and then the room fills with human words.

"I am a Wyndelace. I thought your floater already gave you the name of our race," replies a female-sounding voice.

"Um, yes." I look over the three before proceeding, trying my best not to offend the leader. "You're the same race, or does Wyndelace mean you all come from the same planet?"

More chirps and squawks, before the words emanate from the walls.

"Each planet's creatures evolve differently and have very unique capabilities. We three are juvenile Wyndelaces from a planet having about forty percent of Earth's gravity, covered with massive mountains and spiraling flora that reach high into the sky. With our planet's environmental makeup, it was natural that flying creatures were the ones that evolved the fastest and dominated over other species. However, there were two ground-based predators that were not very far behind our evolution. One is so quick that if we fly too low it has enough speed to launch itself in the air and catch us. The other was a furry, legless animal no bigger than my leg that could silently climb up our trees. It would release a sticky poison on the tree trunk and branches, and when we contacted it, we would both die and be stuck to the branch."

The elderly bird-like creature turns back to the center dais and clicks away on its display.

"You use present tense for one and past tense for the other," I assess, figuring the history lesson was to eventually explain how the birds and the white sheets were related. "You exterminated the snake-like species?"

The bizarre creature spins back around to reply. "For centuries we were the victims, and the Caslylaces grew to such high numbers that there were entire mountains devoid of our race. Even as our technological capability increased, we saw them as a limiting factor. We believed our species couldn't coexist, so we developed a biological weapon that only killed the Caslylaces. Like you have experienced on your planet, the imbalance we placed on nature was catastrophic. There is a parasite that exists at the base of our trees, which, when it reaches the leaves, kills a tree in weeks. The venom a Caslylace extruded as it climbed prevented the parasite from traveling up the tree. With the Caslylaces extinct, the parasite ravished our world. We lost over half the trees and more than 20 percent of our population. It was a harsh lesson to learn, but shaped who we are today."

"How so?" I ask. "You still take over other species, and you have no issues with painfully killing those that get in your way."

"True, but we do not exterminate races," it says. "We control their behaviors to suit our needs. Horses, dogs, chickens; do humans not do the same?"

Well, that was a good point, I think.

"You say it shaped who Wyndelaces are." I left the rest hanging.

"Yes. Our planet, like yours, has an abundance of silica. During our evolution, we incorporated elemental silicon into our basic structure for life. Carbon-silicon bonds are part of who we are; thus, our feathers are more rigid and rougher than birds on your planet, and our bones and organs are much tougher. More importantly, it changed how the core of our central nervous center would evolve. Our brain, as you would call it, is at our center of mass. It requires flexibility and even movement because of its location, so muscle fibers are interwoven with the brain's dendritic structure. Because our brain is at our core, it is the last thing to cease existing once we die. It would live for almost an hour, fighting to survive at the expense of the body."

I was being educated, but not as straightforward as I would like.

"When our biogenetics had become advanced enough, we found we could sustain it for days, then even longer. As we did, it continued to fight for survival, excreting useless cells and thinning out to maximize transport amongst the remaining cells. It took more than a century of scientific research, but eventually we were able to successfully extract it from the dead body and create a second life for the Wyndelace."

It points at my alien cape.

"They are sentient beings, but limited in the physical world because of what they lost upon rebirth. They desire having a body to work through, so it was only a matter of time before we were able to modify their rebirth so they could take over a host body. But that is enough words for today," says the Wyndelace.

I think the session is over, but I'm not walked out of the room. Rather the bird-like creature turns back around and taps on the dais while making clicking noises with its beak. The white walls transform into three-dimensional relief maps, painted with life-like colors. I find myself virtually plummeting down to a planet similar to Earth in surface area, whose blue oceans shade to a slight pink hue wherever they touch land. However, there are many more smaller land masses than on Earth, perhaps hundreds, and more large islands than I can count. Nearly all the land masses are textured with spiraling mountains. A very light green coating of flora and fauna covers everything but the highest of the mountains. As I "fall" into the atmosphere and am spun toward the largest continent, I can see that the mountains reach tens of miles into the sky. In a few seconds, I'm no longer falling but standing on what has to be a tree branch. Their trees are nothing like ours, massive trunks that start as domes then rise from the ground in star-shaped patterns. The branches are sometimes round, sometimes flat, and more often a mixture; seeming to connect from one tree to another, merging perfectly whenever they run into each other. This created huge domed areas that are shown to me to be used by the Wyndelaces for social gatherings.

I'm also shown a few battles between the Wyndelaces and Caslylaces, which were amazingly fast at climbing the trees. I thought them to be like snakes, but no snake moves like that. The scene lurches forward, and I watch as an industrial revolution takes place that teaches me how to advance technology when living hundreds to thousands of feet above the ground. I witness the metamorphosis of a Wyndelace, hearing its first whistle and following its first flight out of the trees. After gaining control of its new body, it quickly stalks the other ground predator until it has captured the host. This happens dozens, hundreds, then thousands upon thousands of times. The movie increasing in speed with each capture, nearly impossible to follow, until the ground predators all possess white capes.

From there on, the juvenile Wyndelaces spend more time on the ground, and the race makes huge technological strides, while the transformed Wyndelaces have taken over every living species they could attach onto. But over time there are too many of the transformed Wyndelaces, which makes sense since their population is no longer dying. They are stored as tennis balls, waiting for hosts. However, the number grows at an amazing rate, and it's clear that the race has an overpopulation issue that rivals humankind's. They build spaceships and set out on many failed missions, which I understand is a desperate move due to the overpopulation of their planet.

Near the end of the show, I'm looking from space onto the entire planet, red dots showing the overpopulation slowly retreating as thousands of spaceships set off in the same direction, then others in different directions. They have found habitable planets, and more importantly, suitable hosts.

The holographic movie ends, but the room doesn't transform back to the three Wyndelaces around the dais. Rather it just freezes as a picture of their solar system. I'm then walked to my room, sat in my chair, and forced to sleep.

I wake up with a lot more questions on my mind, but the time to get answers is dwindling.

"How long ago did you identify Earth as a suitable planet?" I ask groggily.

"Approximately one hundred and ninety Earth years ago," my own voice mumbles back. "It took nearly thirty Earth years to reach your solar system."

"It was after the apocalypse; you brought just enough of your race to take over what was left of humankind, not the other animals of Earth," I assess.

"Yes, our strategy is always to take out the dominant species, followed by the most threatening, if those are different. In Earth's case, they are the same. Earth will become a breeding colony, until we reach the theoretical limit for sustainability. It will take centuries, as we have to decontaminate most of your planet from the radiation damage, but during that time more Wyndelaces will come. They will use lesser creatures as hosts until new humans are ready."

Another piece of the Marsian puzzle popped up in my mind. "Do Marsians live longer once you are attached?"

"We extend the life expectancy of all creatures we inhabit; in their case, they have an increased life expectancy that exceeds three-hundred years," the Wyndelace mumbles back to me.

That explains a lot about the Marsian colonists, and helps even more. But I need to find out about their society.

"Do you Wyndelaces have individual names and a way to talk about the two different stages of your lives?" I ask.

"Yes, and yes. The first is not relevant to your position now. The second involves a slight change in our speaking of the word. You cannot mimic it with your vocal chords," it says, and then its tone changes. "It is now time for the juvenile to ask you some questions."

I stand up and am walked in a different convoluted path to the control deck. The three birds are working on the dais, and the same lanky one that spoke before turns to acknowledge me.

"Do the others talk?" I ask.

"There are many different genus and species of our race; some cannot vocalize, while others would merely find you of little interest. My species is very social, so you get to talk with me." It extends a feathered claw, motioning me to sit in a newly formed chair. "Now, how are you able to survive without oxygen when humans die in such an environment and other demigods become incapacitated?"

I raise an eyebrow at the question before speaking. "How can the transformed Wyndelaces survive without oxygen or food? I assume you can't."

A small whistle and clucking emanates from the lanky, bird-like creature.

My fingers and toes curl inward like bent forks and my legs and back stiffen, sliding me out of the chair as pain courses over me. At the same time, feelings of utter hopelessness and uselessness ravish my mind. I'm a slave and will be for the rest of my days, never being able to bring humankind back to the great species that it had once been. I have failed.

It's over quickly, and I lift myself off the ground and collapse back into the chair. All three of the bird things are looking at me, the stocky one seeming able to show a look of amusement on its beaked face.

"I…I don't know. I was like the others before this journey, but somehow during the trip I no longer needed oxygen. You've read Bookworm's messages. It had to be the prayers, but how is beyond my understanding."

The same whistle and clucking, and I find myself on the floor again, wiping foam from the sides of my mouth when it's over.

That really sucked, I thought.

"What was that for?" I ask, trying to remove the edge from my voice.

"Reinforcement," replies the lanky Wyndelace through the translator, extending its hand again but this time revealing a large black marble. "We extracted this from the other demigod, and we know it is the source of your power. However, there was no apparent connection to the demigod's brain. Also, there is no energy of any kind emanating from it that we can discern. How does it work?"

"You killed El Matador?" I ask, wanting to be angry but currently voided of emotions by the Wyndelace cape.

"No. Not yet. This is from the German one".

Well, that isn't so bad, I think.

A deeper clucking crawls out from the broken-neck bird creature at the dais. The translation emanates from the wall. "Answer the question."

"No one knows for sure. Our scientists suspected that it amplifies the prayers from our followers by pulling energy from the timeless plane."

The usual whistles and clucking from the lanky Wyndelace occur. "We tried to use it on transformed Wyndelaces, and it killed each one. But again, it emitted no energy, even as it killed our own."

"I have no clue. I didn't invent the thing."

All three of them study me before the other two go back to work. The gray-speckled one with the broken-branch neck keeps one eye on me as it works.

"How does the watch you are wearing, the thing you call Bookworm, not get damaged? You crashed on Mars with it, and we saw El Matador slice into the same spot it is worn."

"You ask a lot of questions that I can't answer," I say, and then quickly raise a hand to hopefully stop another excruciating body massage. "I don't understand how my clothes don't get damaged, how they grow and shrink with me; how my fingernails, beard, and hair are immune to these things; or how my body parts reform. Listen, our scientists tried to study the powers that we demigods were given, tried to rationalize how the prayers create an unknown pulse into the timeless dimension that is then extracted by the black sphere, but each explanation they came up with had some sort of hand-waving involved. That thing you call the inertia reaction drive, or whatever, uses the same timeless plane. I bet you don't even know how it works. Am I correct?"

The Wyndelaces are now all looking at me, and I then put together two pieces of the universe's vast puzzle.

"Let me guess, a brilliant scientist figured it out, but then died as he, rather it, tried to develop an application for the discovery."

"Yes!" shoots out the black and red feathered Wyndelace in an excited English voice. The others use some sort of translator on the ship, but its words come without the need for translation.

"What does this mean?" asks the lanky bird.

"I don't know," I sigh. It's the first clue about my demigod existence, but I have no way to follow up on it.

My alien cape turns me, and I travel back to my room to sleep on the granite chair.

Chapter 26

My mouth moves as I wake, mumbling to me. "Why does your watch not talk to you anymore?"

I open my eyes and stare at the silent watch.

"Maybe…maybe it's not really part of the man who died in the mine. Maybe it's some part of me I created to not be lonely," I say as I shrug my shoulders.

"And now that you realize this, it does not appear or you do not need it?" the cape asks, tickling my vocal chords.

"Another question I can't answer."

"Today you will be able to answer the questions the juveniles have for you."

I want to ask why, but it freezes my vocal chords and is already taking me back to the three juveniles. When we arrive, yet again using a different path, all three juveniles are facing the chair I'm sat in.

The gray-speckled bird, who kind of looks like an owl, hoots for a while, staring deeply into my eyes. Its translated voice is deep and sage-like. "When your followers worship you, can you sense where they are located?"

My vocal chords are released for me to speak.

"Not exactly. I get a general feel for where they are, but not…you're going to use me to track down humans that are hiding once you take over." The horror at realizing what they are going to do comes out in my voice.

"We have been able to detect where the major gatherings of humans are, but those less than a few hundred are too numerous and constantly moving. The limited instrumentation we could carry on this journey will not allow us to continuously track such a large number of groups," it says. "Unfortunately, our estimates predict this accounts for over thirty percent of humans. Your history has revealed to us that humans are more resilient in smaller groups. This could cause a serious delay in our plans."

"How do you plan to overtake all the cities spread throughout the world with only one ship?"

"Our spaceship will skip along the outer atmosphere, strategically releasing the insulated pods. Once protection from aeroheating is no longer required, the pods will open and millions of Wyndelaces will float down to their pre-coordinated locations. We will arrive during the night, when most humans are asleep and when darkness will make it impossible to see our arrival. The first step will be to concentrate on the large cities to capture a majority of humans while they are in their sleep. The second step starts in the morning, when we reveal you in the biggest city and across all communication avenues. You will welcome us, and those we miss will come forward without a fight. We will tour all the cities around the world, using you to convince many more in the surrounding areas to come forward. Still not all the humans will obey. The third step will be for you to track down the smaller groups. Within two Earth years, we will have over 98% of the humans under our control."

I try not to show my dismay.

"Do you have to walk toward the follower to get an exact location?" asks the lanky bird.

"No," I sigh, feeling the Wyndelace cape's warning in my tightening muscles. I'm compelled to tell the truth. "I have to focus for a few seconds and can use a map to point them out."

"Preposterous!" snaps the English-speaking one. "Prove it!

"We have placed one of our Wyndelaces in a small room aboard this ship and it is praying to you. It is asking for a delectable fruit from our planet that it loves to eat," states the lanky one as it unfurls a digital map of the spaceship. "Where is this Wyndelace?"

I close my eyes and let the Wyndelace prayers pour over me, searching for the strange request. There are millions, but it's almost like a search engine within my soul as I look for the prayer regarding a fruit. When I find it, I open my eyes to survey the ship's map, pointing at a spot two-thirds down and to the left. It's in one of the cargo containers. I smile in satisfaction and then wink at the argumentative bird.

"Make him pay! Make him pay now!" it shouts.

I'm beginning to wonder if it isn't very bright. This bird is always angry, always wanting to attack. I stop that thinking, as I'm describing the old me.

"He gave us vital information that will help our takeover. We will not punish him for a slight infraction, this time," speaks the lanky one. It adds more words once the other Wyndelace juvenile starts jumping up and down. "But, we will give him a warning."

"How many planets have you taken over?" I ask, not expecting an answer.

"Three are completed and are ours, with five others in the reconstruction phase. This does not include your planet, which is hours away from our initial assault."

When I show little surprise, it replies, "You do not appear concerned."

"You already gave me a warning. Those shock treatments and the mental torture sessions are not fun," I reply.

"Yes, nothing you can do!" Argumentative clucks.

Yes, Argumentative is a good name for it. I need to give these aliens names. I'm losing my touch.

"One more thing," says Lanky. "Where are the other demigods? In your stories to the humans, you said they would travel to Everest to...rest. We checked, and they are not there."

"I thought you couldn't track small groups?"

"I said we could not track so many smaller groups with our limited capability. However, narrowing in on a single area of Earth is easily done," Lanky replies.

"Maybe they decided to awaken to thwart your assault?" I propose.

I drop to my knees and involuntarily slam my own face into the floor before looking back up. Argumentative seems to be doing some sort of happy dance, while Lanky remains composed.

"Where are they?" Lanky asks again.

"We demigods love McDonalds. I heard they finally reopened one in Moscow," I say, adding another wink of my eye toward Argumentative.

The stabbing pain starts in my stomach, doubling me over, before the monster of all migraines strikes my head. My blood pressure soars, each beat of my heart pushing the red fluid so hard that my capillaries explode. Blood seeps out my eyes, and spider-like splotches of red coat my skin. The floor of the spaceship reaches up, grabbing my arms and legs before lifting me high and stretching my limbs out wider than I thought possible. Through the pain and blood, I see two sharp points form out of the floor. I'm leaned forward until they're touching the skin between my ribs. They slowly press forward, failing to penetrate my steel-like skin, lurch back and lunge forward, only to ricochet off. I would have smiled if the internal pain from the Wyndelace cape wasn't increasing.

"Oh yes, I forgot. We need your worshippers to pray for soft skin," Lanky says.

Lanky clicks away on the dais and within seconds the prayers flood me. My steel-like skin melts into something like marshmallows. The points move forward again, stopping at my skin for a few seconds before puncturing through. The pain is minor at first, far less than what the cape is causing, but as it presses in farther my ribs are forced apart, eventually cracking from the force. I growl in anger, then howl in pain, and keep howling until both tips have pass through the skin on my back. The internal pain lessens to a dull throb. I hang limply, still stretched out as Lanky walks forward on legs that don't seem quite stable.

"Where are the demigods?" Lanky asks.

My eyes close and fill with a fuzzy image of deep blue waters, serving as the foreground to a single building consisting of multiple concrete shells layered on top of each other. Pink granite covered the bottom floors of the opera house. On the dock in front of the opera house was a single demigod, dressed in leather chaps held up by a worn gun belt, standing on top of a mound of bloodied bodies. His hair curled on top of itself, and he wore a brown beard that stretched down his chest. It was the notorious Ned Kelly, or at least the New Australia demigod version. Ruthless, lawless, and willing to do anything to ensure his worshippers won. He had defeated the Kiwi nation's and Philippine Islands' demigods with ease, using unethical tactics without remorse. However, on this day he had been forced to fight a civil war—killing his own followers, winning yet losing.

Head hung low, he boarded a large fishing boat and set sail on a new course, one that would be followed by nearly every other fallen demigod over the next few decades. He sailed east, then north, not resting until weeks later when the metal boat floated over Challenger Deep in the Mariana Trench. Ned had found his spot and now stood in the middle of the boat, preparing for his final stand. He stared directly into the sun before raising his arms and pointing his middle fingers to the sky. He then bent down and drove both hands onto the wooden planks of the deck, easily crashing through and landing on the metal hull. Ned pounded against the ship's metal, first denting it, but not stopping until he fractured it. He dropped his hands to the side of his fatigued body, unmoving as water invaded the ship.

Eventually, the bow of the ship lifted upward before all ten tons of steel slid under the water's surface. It would serve as his coffin, thirty-five thousand feet below the water's surface. Unlike my lie about the demigods resting on Everest—which was to protect the fallen—there was no way to come back from that depth without assistance, even if one desired. The lack of oxygen was crippling, and the weight of the ocean ensured the demigod's body would neither move nor surface on its own.

I snap awake, forced to do so by the cape on my back. Two spikes are inches from my eyes. Slowly twisting and moving forward.

"Where are the demigods?" asks Lanky again.

"In the Mariana Trench," I gasp, blood seeping out of my mouth. There's no point in continuing to fight as they will eventually win. I also fear that with their followers controlling my will, they can now extract the demigod device. That would surely be their next step. I don't want to die...yet.

"Find them!" squawks Argumentative to anyone that would listen. "Dozens of powerful beings. They will all be our servants!"

"Go back to your room until we call you," Lanky commands.

The sharp points retract, my wounds heal, and the seamless shackles holding me meld back into the floor. I'm walked back to my room and set down in my chair to sleep.

But for once, I don't sleep. I don't want to sleep; I want to stay awake so I'll know when the time has come.

Minutes turn into hours, and those too pass. I wonder if they've already entered the Earth's atmosphere and begun the assault. I don't think so, but maybe my timing is off and they're already descending. It will be hard to tell with the inertia reactionary drive. I don't understand how it works, but I know that it's able to affect how the physics of momentum occur onboard the spacecraft, allowing for dampening or redirecting so smoothly that the structure and beings inside aren't affected.

I ponder the not-so-coincidental fact that both humankind and the Wyndelaces discovered the timeless plane, but used it for very different purposes. Humans applied it to individual devices to help with communication and powering small electronics. The applications seemed trivial, but they had significant impacts on society as a whole. The Wyndelaces coupled millions together for powering their spaceships, and it was also the basis for the inertia reactionary drive. Completely different uses.

Wait!

Both races had needed it to address overpopulation, or rather for reaching beyond their planet's natural limitations. Th ePEG had allowed humankind to gather in mega cities when energy limitations had prevented it, while also allowing them to settle on Mars. The Wyndelaces' tree homes had become overburdened and couldn't bear the weight of the bird-like creatures' society, while the transformed Wyndelaces had grown so rapidly in numbers with no sign of any dying. They had needed the planar device to leave the planet.

If a sentient being had visited both planets and provided the planar technology, I doubt that the being is something akin to God. No greater being would sacrifice the lives on other planets for domination by one, nor allow the creation of blasphemous demigods. No, this new being's purpose is yet to be revealed, but I'm sure it isn't born out of kindness.

My vocal chords tingle and my lips mumble, "The juveniles need to talk with you."

I don't ask why since the question would not be answered. My body rises, and I follow the ever-altering maze back to the spaceship's control room. I enter from the side, seeing the three bird-like creatures standing in front of the dais and staring angrily at me. Between us are rows of sharp pillars drawn from the ceiling and floor, barely creating enough space for me to peer back at them. The pillars are not static; they move slightly to let me know that the juveniles can repeat what was done to me during the last visit. Clearly, it's a defensive posture. They want to talk, but for the first time seem nervous, possibly wary of my power.

"Your most recent exploits aboard our ship, including how we plan to take over Earth, have been transmitted to all of humankind. The only possibility is that your watch, which you call Bookworm, released the information. How do you control it?" Lanky asks.

"Or…maybe you have an Earth sympathizer onboard the ship?" I say.

"Explain," Lanky orders.

"It appears that information is being sent, yet you have full control of me. Therefore, one of the Wyndelaces could be trying to save Earth from takeover. As I see it, only you three Wyndelaces have the authority to do that since you run all communications for the ship. I'm betting it's the quiet one."

"Preposterous!" Argumentative snaps, flinging its wing arms widely in the air.

"That's an interesting redirection," Owl hoots. "You're clearly stalling."

A blue image of a nerdy young man in glasses appears above my watch, the same watch that had appeared dead since we left Mars. He held a small tablet in one hand while sliding two fingers across it with the other. When done, he looks up.

"Mr. President, stage one is complete," Bookworm breaks in.

I impatiently say nothing until the sharp pillars between us melt into the ceiling and floor. However, watching the Wyndelaces' shock as it happens is worth holding my silence for a little while longer.

"What is stage one?" Lanky asks, the confidence receding so fast from the translated voice that by the end it's desperately whining.

I take a step forward to explain, but then the pain from my caped Wyndelace hits my body and mind. Easily putting it aside, I reach over my head, using one hand to grasp the cape wrapped around the back of my neck and the other to grip its top. I carefully begin to pull, feeling the tendrils inside my body tightly gripping my muscles, voice box, and spine.

"If it doesn't let go," I grunt, "I will rip the tendrils right off its body. Trust me when I say it won't kill me like it would a human host."

Argumentative—the red and black juvenile with the yellow teardrop—jumps back and curses, while Owl stoically speaks using the translator like Lanky.

"Your challenge makes no sense. If you could have done it before, then you would have. The pain you suffered from the Wyndelace embedded in your body was unbearable."

"Alright," I say.

I pull the cape quickly over my head, at first feeling the tendrils digging in to hold on, and next hearing the popping of the tendrils as they rip off the Wyndelace. I hold the fluttering cape, whistling and buckling in my hands as it tries to escape. Folding it once, I rip it in half, shutting up the shrill whistles I had evoked. Looking up at the bird-like creatures, I fold it again.

"And you're right, the pain you caused me was near maddening, but it was worth it in order to get your plans and give Bookworm enough time to take over your spaceship's control system." I smile and rip the folded Wyndelace in half again. I'm not going to let them know when I was able to overcome their control.

Lanky spins around, faster than I thought his aged frame could move, and taps on the dais several times before shrieking loudly at Owl. There is no translation as it was more a scream from fear than of words.

"We never had control of you?" Owl asks, incredibly calm compared to the others.

"Oh, you did, but I worked to develop the ability to override it at any time," I say as I continue to tear the Wyndelace into smaller and smaller pieces. "And no, most likely no other demigod could've done this. I'm different, as I'm the first and last modern-day demigod. I've regained the free will I had when human and can thank you for the journey that forced me to fight for it."

"Impossible! This makes no sense," Argumentative shouts, still jumping up and down. "Impossible!"

In two steps, I'm standing in front of the three juveniles. I look at Argumentative before punching it in the midsection so hard that it flies across the room, smacking into the wall with enough force to puree its central nervous system. It flops onto the floor, red stains dripping down the white wall.

"Sorry, but that was necessary before we talked anymore."

"Necessary?" Lanky asks, translated voice quivering.

"Yes, that damn bird was worse than a parrot." I pause, wondering if that was what kind of juvenile it had been. "Another word out of it and I probably would have killed you all before revealing my plan."

Chapter 27

"And what was stage one?" Owl asks, seemingly unfazed by the loss of the screeching juvenile.

Lanky looks unnerved, staring back and forth from me, to the bloodstained wall, and to Argumentative's stilled body.

"Stage one was to have Bookworm hack into your spaceship's computer system and override your ability to control transforming its shape, while also eliminating input from the central dais. Can you explain the rest, Bookworm?" I ask, lifting my hand holding the folded and torn Wyndelace into the air before letting the pieces flutter to the ground. Well, I wanted them to flutter to the ground, but they are heavy enough that they fall more like a deck of unwrapped playing cards.

"Gladly, Mr. President," replies Bookworm, who then turns his holographic image toward the remaining juveniles. "There actually was a pre-stage section where I recorded every interaction of yours with the President, including the torture you inflicted on him. This was saved until we were confident that releasing it could not result in the stopping of our plan. Now, stage one required me to break into your spaceship's neural network, which I must say is drastically different than any computer system we have or had on Earth. Not only is the language different, but the fact that every atom of this ship stores information and works in a nearly cerebral-like style made it extremely challenging. I almost gave up, but then decided to do exactly what you do to your victims. I infused myself into your system and then worked to gain control. Once done with that, I moved on to stage two."

Neither juvenile bothers to ask what stage two is, knowing they would be told.

"And what was stage two, Bookworm?" I ask.

"Thank you for asking, sir," Bookworm says. "Stage two, which I only completed a few minutes ago, was to disable both the primary propulsion drive and the inertia reactionary drive. You can neither accelerate nor slow down the spaceship. It will be entering Earth's atmosphere in less than fifteen minutes."

"But that is exactly what we want," Lanky mutters.

"Yes, except for when you add in stages three and four," I say. "And that last stage is a real whopper."

"Stage three is to open the life support and access pathways from the containers to the central hub," finishes Bookworm. "Stage four, the final step, is based off your ability to manipulate the spaceship's structure. We'll create a series of holes in the hull, allowing for the formation of a superheated plasma as it enters the Earth's atmosphere. That plasma will expand, ripping apart the spaceship and incinerating everything inside the containers."

There's a lengthy pause before words are returned.

"There is nothing we can do but watch our own deaths?" Owl asks, unconvinced.

I take a step forward and grasp Lanky and Owl by the neck, lifting them off the ground. They are extremely light, although their feathers are coarser than any bird from Earth. If I were human, they would have sliced me to the bone. There definitely is something to this hybrid silicon-carbon body.

"No. I will not let you live to watch it unfold. You came to our solar system and our planet to imprison humankind. You went to Mars and Earth's moon, ruthlessly killing innocent beings. Killing not only to take control, but killing for fun. You took over my body, bringing me physical pain beyond anything I had ever experienced before. I will kill you now, but not out of anger. Rather, I will kill you so that you cannot find some means to stop Bookworm and me from destroying your ship and your plans."

"Thank you for the ePET technology!" Owl squawks as I begin to squeeze.

I relax my grip, ignoring Lanky's flailing and weak attempts to break my lock on his neck, and focus on Owl.

"What do you mean?" I ask.

"We didn't have the capability to instantly communicate with other planets ruled by Wyndelaces. However, decades ago we transmitted the specifications for creating the devices. Before we left Mars, we received the first communication from our home planet via the ePET. In fact, they've been listening to this entire conversation. Soon they will send an army to battle you and the weakened humans. We're merely a first wave, one that isn't meant for battle. But they're ten times stronger. You cannot win," Owl hoots.

I look at Lanky, who is quieting down, and then back to Owl. Closing my eyes, I squeeze until I hear their neck bones crack, then squeeze more until their rough skin becomes powder. I drop the limp bodies on the floor and then step on their midsections, driving my heel into their 'brains.'

"A battle for survival is something that humankind has always been good at. They will win. Somehow, they will win."

"Sir?" queries Bookworm.

"Yes."

"I'm having difficulty with stages three and four of our plan," he stammers.

"Having problems?"

"The neural network of the Wyndelace spaceship is built upon spherical layers, the shells exponentially increasing in security protocols and AI control the closer it is to the center. Opening the containers is going to be a challenge, and creating holes in the exterior hull nearly impossible since it resides within the core," responds a despondent Bookworm.

"Bookworm, if you don't break through the security system, then we just helped the Wyndelaces take over Earth." This time my anger is rising.

"I understand, sir, but we only have minutes before we enter the upper atmosphere."

"Drop me to where El Matador is being kept, while you work on solving the problems," I order.

The floor opens and I plunge over seventy feet, landing hard and sending ripples across the malleable floor. I reach over and rip the metal-like harnesses off the unmoving El Matador, realizing only then that I am back to my semi-normal size of nearly twelve feet. I tuck him under one arm as the spaceship pitches and groans. It's the signal that we're nearing the point of no return.

"Bookworm! You aren't some limited replica of the man I knew. You started that way, but you've grown. You are him. I know it, and it's time you pushed beyond your self-imposed limitations. Now!" I yell with a passion absent of rage.

In seconds the diminutive shape appears above my wrist.

"I was able to execute stage three, Mr. President." Sweat and exhaustion coats his holographic image. "However, there is no way to morph the spaceship's hull as its security protocol is at the center of the network. Without stage four—"

"That's okay, Bookworm," I say, looking upward. "Looks like it wasn't meant to be done with cunning and technology. But it must be done, as we still have another mission to take on."

"What do you mean, sir?"

I don't respond, the image of the future from activating the reaction drive refusing to fade away. I look up. The seventy-foot hole didn't look as daunting in my normal state, but it's also no longer wide enough. I guess that it really doesn't matter. I squat down, covering El Matador, and launch with all my might, hoping that equal and opposite forces will be nearly negligible during my jump since I weigh much less than the spaceship. My shoulders rip through each six-foot section, not slowing my ascent. When I fly past the control room, I think my head will be crashing through each ceiling, but Bookworm catches on to what I'm doing and is opening holes to pass through until I reach the hull. I slam into the hull with my shoulder, having ducked my head. There's a loud cracking sound, then creaking of metal, and finally an outward explosion as I burst out of the spaceship and hurtle into outer space, whirling wildly.

The dizzying spinning is more unsettling than readjusting to the lack of oxygen. I catch glimpses of the spaceship, the Earth, and a few other flashes of light as I spin out of control. I shut my eyes, which only makes the rotations seem to speed up. I start losing hold of reality, slipping toward unwanted sleep.

E

V

O

L

U

T

I

O

N

Chapter 28

Bookworm, I think, using all my willpower to string together my words as I continue to spin out of control. *I remembered that you can generate a small amount of thrust through the watch. Can you use this to stabilize me?*

Yes, Mr. President.

Can you also adjust me so I can watch the alien spaceship? I ask in my mind, wondering if I can throw up. I haven't eaten anything in months, so probably not.

No, sir. At its speed and trajectory, it will be passing around the other side of the Earth before I can get you stabilized, Bookworm replies through the ePET in my brain.

A miniature burst of light shoots out from my watch, followed by several more. My uncontrollable spinning slows but has a long way to go before I'm righted. That is, whatever 'righting' is in space.

Are you still tied into the spaceship's network? I ask.

I was connected until a few seconds ago. There was a large thermal flash, which based on the timing, I estimate to have been from the plasma formation and subsequent explosion within the ship.

Bummer. I really wanted to watch it blow apart, Bookworm.

Me too, sir.

Really?

Yes. As you said earlier—or rather yelled—I'm more than an image of Bookworm. I would have enjoyed watching that evil race be incinerated, Bookworm says.

Wait, you believe you are...?

Actually, more than believe, sir. I ran a diagnostic check, capability analysis, and overall capacity for learning. It turns out that I'm not only functioning at a higher level than seemingly possible, but also have exponentially increased my overall capacity.

Oh, I thought, somewhat disappointed.

One more thing, Mr. President.

Yes.

I also found that I now have what I believe to be true emotions, such as the ability to annoy or disappoint you when I think it's funny to do so. Bookworm chuckles in my mind.

I laugh out loud.

How did you do that, sir? There's no air?

"I'm as shocked as you are, Bookworm." I say out loud.

I realize I'm no longer spinning and that I still hold El Matador in my arm. The demigod isn't moving, and I can't tell if it's because of what the Wyndelaces did to him or because he's without air.

"Bookworm, can you tell what's wrong with El Matador? I mean, is it permanent or from lack of air?"

I cannot, but was able to extract information on his status from the spaceship before we exited. He has very distinct brainwaves, which for humans are often tied to a catatonic state. I believe it fits with your description of what demigods do when they no longer wish to live.

"That's what I feared," I say, before changing the subject. "So, you know what we're going to do next?"

Travel to the Wyndelaces' home planet and blow it up? Bookworm replies.

"More of your newfound humor?"

Yes, Bookworm replies. *Actually, we're going to try and redirect the asteroid that's headed toward Earth?*

"Partially correct. I have a feeling that it was kicked out of the asteroid belt after the Wyndelace spaceship collided with it. I want to fix their screw-up. We're going to fly into it with enough speed to blast it into thousands of little pieces. Do you know where it is?"

Yes, sir. I just ran a calculation, and the total impulse I can generate, your current mass, and the need to redirect us will fall well short of what is required to destroy an asteroid of its size.

I look down at El Matador, knowing he would want to pass into whatever place we demigods go when we die. It seems Arthuren was the first and he will be the second.

"I can redirect us, and what if I increase my mass to ten thousand pounds?" I ask.

The probability of asteroid destruction would be greater than 85 percent.

"Good enough. Can you give me the direction I need to throw El Matador to get us moving?"

Yes, but you will have to keep your watch arm fixed and only throw him with one arm. It doesn't have to be perfect as I can use the watch's energy pulses to gradually place us on the required collision course.

Extending my watch arm, a blue holographic grid unfolds before me with a red trajectory line curving along a path that leads directly toward the sun. Until this moment I hadn't thought about the great view I had of Earth, let alone the Sun. The Sun is perched above a cloud-covered Earth, its pure white light a stark contrast to what I had seen thousands of times before. The Earth's clouds are swirls from a paintbrush, revealing pockets of blue from the ocean and brown ridges from the highest mountains. It's beyond gorgeous, a beautiful planet that is healing over time. Hopefully, humankind will find a way to help. Sighing, I heft El Matador in my hand and pull my arm behind my head.

"Soon you will find peace, my friend. You will be remembered for the great things you did for your people, not for what the Wyndelaces made you do."

El Matador launches rapidly away from me, from the strength only I possess. It will take years for him to reach the sun, just as it will take me a very long time to reach the asteroid.

"Bookworm, how long before I collide with the asteroid?"

If everything goes well, we should reach the asteroid in eleven years, three months, and five days.

"Huh. That's a long time, and I'm exhausted, Bookworm. Wake me up when we are a day away," I order.

With that, I let the lids of my eyes relax so I can sleep, not worried about the nightmares invading my sleep. I've done what was needed, and

I've done it the way myself or my followers wanted it done. Fighting, battles, and war are horrible things, and horrible acts are done by those in them. But most of those who have been in the trenches understand their role and accept their own horrible actions as being required in the moment. To survive both during and after, it has to become a part of them. Not an evil part, just a part of their story, their life. Right or wrong, that is how I also view my story.

Chapter 29

Mr. President. Mr. President, it's one day away. Mr. President.

"I hear you, Bookworm. How can I not? You're in my brain. It's just taking a while to wake up," I say as I look around the vast emptiness of space. "Where's the asteroid?"

You cannot see it, sir. The asteroid is traveling at approximately 52,000 miles per hour, and you are on a direct course to intercept it at a speed of approximately 35,000 miles per hour. Impact is twenty-four hours away, which means we are over two million miles away from the asteroid. Even with your eyesight, you will not see the eleven-mile wide asteroid when it hits you. I rounded the numbers, so if you want a more exact answer or an explanation of my calculations, just let me know.

"Looks like eleven years of solitude and you lost your human side."

While eleven years is a long time if you are not sleeping, I can pass the time as rapidly or as slowly as I wish by adjusting my internal clock speed, Bookworm replies. *However, I did spend a number of years putting together your biography.*

"My biography?"

To be honest, it only took a few hours to search available databases from Earth and then integrate them with the story I had already compiled during our journey together. After that I worked on rewriting and editing until I could not make it read any better. I believe that is what you are referring to as the human side.

"Indeed. You didn't send it to Earth, did you?"

Yes, but encrypted so that no one else can open it. It is purely for archival purposes. I then spent the remaining time helping humankind. I started by cataloging all human sites and other life that had survived the nuclear war, then worked through their ePETs to get as many groups to consolidate into larger groups to not only increase survival chances but to help rebuild a technological society. They have only started, but they are moving in the right direction.

"So, you decided how humankind should progress? That's mighty god-like of you, Bookworm," I chuckle.

Actually, that was not my intent, sir. When I infiltrated the Wyndelaces' neural network, I found a file for their plans for extraction and remediation of the nuclear radiation impregnating many of the large cities from the God-bombs. However, to execute the plan, humankind must advance to a specified technology readiness level. The Wyndelaces had engineered a super-plant with an incredibly broad root system that naturally absorbs radioactive biomass and concentrates it into a single point on its stem until the rad dose is so high that it kills the plant and leaves a pile of radioactive material. They then use rad-hardened, robotics ships that gather the concentrated radioactive material and launch it into a star such as ours. Both the plant replication and spaceship creation will require a significantly higher technology level than currently available.

Now that makes more sense.

I also catalogued all your worship sites around the world, which number over ten thousand. Would you care to see them, sir? asks Bookworm.

"No," I growl.

It's quite amazing, really. The biggest change is that humankind has given you a name, which you never had before. I'm assuming because you refused one.

"What is it?" I ask as curiosity gets the best of me.

Lohannes, the Protector of Life, came his voice in my head, along with an undertone of amusement.

"Lohannes?" I queried.

It's Latin for graced by Yahweh.

"Hmm, that's a little blasphemous," I reply.

It's fitting as you are the epitome of blasphemy, Bookworm chuckles in my mind.

"Okay, let's get back to the asteroid. You said it's eleven miles wide, not four. What is the chance that no significant pieces will enter the Earth's atmosphere after our collision?"

Unfortunately, the original estimate for the asteroid was based on spectroscopic data when it's short side was pointed toward Earth, and I confirmed that it was travelling toward Earth horizontally. Since then it has flipped on its long edge and does not seem to be changing. After collision, the probability of a piece large enough to wipe out a continent or two is approximately fifty percent, Bookworm says with a sudden, sullen mood change.

"What? That's not acceptable!" I rack my brain for solutions. "I still haven't increased my density yet. What if I double or triple it?"

Bookworm shakes his head. *The increase from your original mass is crucial for the collision, but adding more mass will shoot through the asteroid like a bullet, without breaking it up. If you increase your size, you'll spread out your mass even more so that your collision will have a less than optimal effect. There is nothing physically possible, sir.*

"Let me think about this while I increase my density. Can you let my worshippers know what I need?"

Of course, sir.

Even in the vastness of space where nothing seems to be moving, time passes quickly as I try to work out scenario after scenario of what can be done to save humankind. However, unlike the Wyndelaces that I could overpower, no amount of brute force will solve this problem. Bookworm is right; it's physically impossible.

Impossible.

I am impossible. I'm not supposed to exist. I am an abomination. I have time and again done things that defied the laws of physics. It's time for another impossible feat. The asteroid and I will be traveling toward each other at nearly 24 miles per second; even I could do that math. When one second apart, I might get lucky and see a rapidly increasing object, but I wouldn't be able to time my action. Doing what I hope can be done means that I need Bookworm's precision to perform the countdown.

"Bookworm, give a countdown to impact starting at one minute."

Yes, sir. We are currently only a few minutes from impact.

I really want more time to ponder life, not that it will matter. So, I wait uncomfortably for the train wreck that's about to happen. This is really going to hurt; most likely it will annihilate me…and Bookworm. I take off the watch and shove it in my mouth, surprised that Bookworm doesn't protest.

One minute, Mr. President. His voice isn't dampened in my mouth, since it comes into my mind.

I start to draw forth my anger, then stop. I'm not truly angry. In fact, I feel compassion for humankind. They need me to save them, and I need to have the willpower to do it. I will the energy from their prayers into every ounce of my body, drawing as much as I can as fast as I can.

Thirty seconds.

I keep drawing the energy in, my body shaking as if I'm holding a powerline in both hands. My neck muscles bulge and I grind my teeth as I pull it in even faster, straining to keep every ounce inside me. If I'm going to die, it will be grand.

Ten seconds.

Nine.

Eight.

Seven.

Six.

Five.

I think I see a blip.

Four.

Three.

Something is coming very fast at me.

Two.

I release every ounce of energy, expanding it rapidly outward right before the collision. In seconds, the soundless explosion creates a flash of light so bright that my eyes burn worse than from the rad poisoning on the Wyndelaces' spaceship. Searing pain rips through me so fast that my thoughts stop and darkness takes me.

****

My arms and legs float above my torso, as the sensation of being alive slowly returns to me. With the sensation comes discomfort, but nothing compared to what happened during the collision. It's now a dull throb over my entire body, with sharp pains in my right ribs, arm, and leg. I slowly roll my eyes to stare at my broken body, knowing that being so far away from the sun means it should be too dark for me to see. Looking down, I guess I've also developed the ability to create my own light. The right side of my ribcage is missing, as is my right hand and my legs from the knees down. I can see new flesh forming, but it's growing at a very slow pace. My mouth also feels strange, as if there's something inside it.

My watch.

I reach inside with my good hand and pull out the watch, with Bookworm instantly appearing. The look on his face is one of pure joy, with a smile that nearly engulfs his ears.

Welcome back, Mr. President.

"Uh-huh. How long was I asleep?"

Asleep? No, you were not asleep, sir. Your body was nearly incinerated during the collision. While I was trapped in your mouth, I performed a scan of you and it was quite disgusting. All your skin was absent along with more than forty percent of your musculoskeletal system. I don't know how you are even alive. In fact, I thought it was your end, but I still sent out an update to Earth about you destroying the asteroid, and it appears your worshippers' prayers have been rebuilding you over the last few months. It is not as quick for you to heal when you are unconscious, but I do not know why.

"And the asteroid?" That should have been my first question.

A 99.97 percent probability that there were no pieces of the asteroid large enough to survive atmospheric entry. Humankind will have a beautiful meteor shower in about six-and-a-half years, and word is that they will be calling it The Lohannes Shower.

"Huh," I said, not really caring for having a meteor shower named after me. Or, well, with my new name.

Looking down at my body again, I see the healing is now progressing at a much faster rate. I pull even more of the energy from the prayers and redirect it to healing my injuries. In less than an hour, I'm renewed in body, but exhausted in spirit. It appears that when conscious I can draw forth my followers' prayers much more efficiently and now can use it whatever way I wish. Or is it that I'm really just a soul that manifests in physical form when I chose? Maybe there's something to what the brother of Boy said about transcendence. I spin my head around, trying to focus on something close but instead find myself assessing the vastness of outer space. I was going to ask Bookworm how close the nearest object was, but I was sure the answer would be hundreds of thousands to millions of miles. I also don't want to know what direction I'm floating, especially if it means I'm traveling out of our solar system.

Sir, I have some options regarding what we should do next.

"Bookworm, we stopped an alien invasion and obliterated an asteroid that was twice the size of the one that wiped out the dinosaurs. I've been far from good during my time as a demigod, but I'd say that's a nice way of ending my story."

But sir, what about the Marsians? They're still hosts to the Wyndelaces that were left on Mars, and surely are working toward suppressing humankind again. Also, the juvenile Wyndelaces said that they developed ePETs and sent messages back to their home planet. If this is true, we could also have aliens from the other planets they took over coming to Earth for war, Bookworm pleads with his contractions coming back as emotions overtake him.

"And where does it end? I go back to Mars and cause untold deaths when the Wyndelaces extract themselves from the Marsians? I stand tall against an alien invasion on Earth and survive while the human population is wiped out? Do I watch young children being mercilessly killed, again? I don't want to go back to that."

Why not? In fact, you may not have to travel back. Your power has increased every time you have pushed yourself. You started this journey needing strength and special appendages to crawl up the mine shaft. You were transformed to run quickly along the train rail. You stopped requiring the need to breathe, shrugged off the parasitic takeover by an alien race, and then you blew up an eleven-mile-wide asteroid. Each time you test your limits, you grow. Maybe that thing that gave us and the aliens access to the timeless plane has a plan for you. What are you afraid of! Bookworm yells at me for the first time, his anger ringing in my mind, but I'm far from being angry at him.

"Limitless."

What? He asks.

"Limitless, Bookworm. You said it. Every time I push myself, I find out that I have even more power. Power beyond what any being should have. What if I'm able to obliterate an entire alien armada? Or worse yet, what if I can destroy an entire alien planet? Bookworm, what if I can do anything I can think of? What if I'm immortal or even omnipotent? That would mean I have no one to pray to, to have faith in, to drive my hope. I would be my own god, and that's something I can't accept. I need a higher being to exist." My voice turns into a near-whisper at the end.

There's silence for a very long time before Bookworm speaks.

But they need you. They are so precariously balanced between life and death as a race. Without your help, they may fail and…they would no longer exist.

"I can't!" I bellow with frustration rattling my bones and tears coating my eyes.

This time the silence expands from seconds into hours, and hours into days. Me just floating in the vacuum of space, and Bookworm refusing to shut off his hologram. He just sits on a replica of the black rock outcropping from when we first met. I don't think about our argument or the needs of the human race. I stay awake but refuse to think for a very long time. Finally, memories creep into my empty mind.

There is Cleaner at the mine who gave me his safety band and then calmly ended his life. Old Woman, who showed me the path I needed to travel to reach the Launchpad and why humankind needed me. Boy, who communicated with the spirit of his brother to warn me of the deadly asteroid. The weight of a city was on such a young one, and he knowingly accepted his fate. Magnate fought every step of my trip to Mars, but secretly hoped I would succeed in saving his people. El Matador, once a friend, but turned into a pawn for the aliens. Oh, and that little girl who stood out amongst the rows of Marsians, when the Wyndelaces killed those children. Something different about her, as if she wasn't the host of a caped alien at all. The word she mouthed that I couldn't understand at the time, but was able to now as it replayed in my mind…fight.

"Bookworm. I won't go back, but I can still help."

How is that, sir?

"I don't feel like discussing it, but you can trust me that they'll not only survive but thrive. I have faith in humankind, Bookworm. And so should you."

That's great to hear, sir. Thank you, says Bookworm, as his hologram slowly melts into the watch face.

I close my eyes for what will surely be the final time, sending a surge of power along three lines of prayers before drifting off to sleep.

I do have faith in humankind, but know they'll need a new set of demigods to help fight for their survival. It's written in their mythology and embedded in their souls. The demigod creates the ripple, and they follow behind but with a ferocity that I would even fear.

Epilogue

Fanley Rin polished the booted foot of the marble statue, struggling to hold onto the thick brush as his gnarled fingers spasmed in pain. The beginnings of a red and blue tattoo covered his middle finger, and when Fanley raised his hand to wipe the sweat onto his robe, the bland serpent tattoo on his withered arm was revealed. He continued his cleaning for several minutes before dropping the brush into the wash bucket and standing upon wobbly legs.

It had taken days to clean the seated statue, and in truth it probably hadn't needed it. He even doubted people would notice the difference when they came next hour to begin morning worship at the seated image of Lohannes, chains broken and the one-eyed eagle perched on top of the chair's back. Words were scribed into the base of the statue: Strength, Intelligence, Honor, Freedom, Protection, and Faith. Faith were justice had once been.

All cleaned for one reason, the same reason Fanley had been cleaning it for the last half decade. Lohannes was the demigod Fanley had helped along his journey, and whom his brother had met to discuss the asteroid and the how enlightenment could save humankind. But instead of enlightenment, Lohannes had set out to destroy the asteroid, successfully obliterating it only months earlier.

However, during his own journey, Fanley had received a trinket box from a city scavenger that had unknowingly been radioactive. He had nearly died, and his body had never fully recovered. As a teenager, he had spent most of his days in a wheelchair and the rest in bed. Over the years

307

he had fought and dragged his body back to walking, and now he worked for the temple that had provided for him when he was sick.

Needing a break from the physical work, Fanley squatted onto his knees and prayed to Lohannes, asking for removal of the oppressive robots that still imprisoned his city. When finished, he placed the bucket in a side room and cautiously stepped out into the bright morning sunlight. Pulling his hood up with his ever-shaking hands, he limped along side streets, avoiding eye contact at all times. Wearily, he walked through the city gates and continued walking even beyond the limits of what his frail legs should have been able to manage. The sun beat on his sweating body, his vision was cloudy, and he fell more than once, but he always got back up without complaint. He didn't brush off the dirt, as he didn't have the energy to do so.

It was a journey he made at the beginning of every week, always ending as it did today at the battered container. The top and a smaller side were splayed open, and the entire object was coated with soot from entering the Earth's atmosphere. Inside was a mass of blackened sand, the remnants of the alien Wyndelaces that once inhabited the container.

For Fanley, it was the reminder he needed every week. He had helped change the course of humanity, and the constant pain he felt paled in comparison to what could have happened to him. Exhausted, he sat down, closed his eyes, and began his usual meditation routine. He went in a trance to call up his brother, who had entered the spiritual world more than fifteen years earlier. The tattoo on his arm itched, a signal of the connection, but then a growing surge of unusual energy grew deep within his skull.

Fanley shook out of his trance, barely having time to open his eyes before a powerful jolt of electricity lifted him into the air and launched him into the field to his right. He hit a small sapling and fell unconscious, his body left wrapped around the broken branches like a bad game of Twister.

Fanley woke up, recalling what had happened and expecting splintered bones and numerous cuts and bruises with blood still seeping out. With his already weakened physique, he was sure that there was no way he would find the energy to get up and walk back to town. It would be the death of him. Raising a hand to wipe his brow, he froze and stared in amazement at the tattoo on his arm. More specifically, he was awed by the thick blue veins protruding from the layers of muscle underneath the tattoo and the lack of the scar. It couldn't be his arm, as he would've seen the white bones barely hidden under his sickly, pockmarked skin. Moving his whole arm again, a powerful bicep flexed and popped up the sleeve of his robe. He rubbed the rest of his body, each touch hitting muscle where only bone had been before. When he realized that he felt good—no, great—he stood up. The big toe that had been lost from the rad poisoning was defiantly wiggling on his sandaled foot.

He squatted and playfully bounced up, leaving the ground at least two feet behind. He giggled upon landing and then laughed before squatting as low as possible and exploding upward. He leapt higher than he was tall, something no human could do. It could be a dream or a gift from Lohannes. As soon as he had the thought, a familiar tug pulled on the scarred skin of his arm. Surely a confirmation from his brother of where this gift came from.

The cocky boy from so long ago came back in that instant. He was no longer frail, no longer just trying to survive the day and endlessly giving thanks for how others had been saved. Confidence rippled across his soul and unfulfilled dreams roared through his mind, just as powerful as the muscles he now possessed. He cared not if others noticed, as it had been a gift. For what purpose he didn't know, but for now he didn't care. The sun was barely above the western trees, and he wanted to get back to town before the guards dropped the gate. Steps thrice as long and twice as fast carried him back to town before the sun had set. Fanley couldn't believe that the crash site had been so close to town, as it always took him hours to reach the alien container.

Fanley walked up to the familiar guards. They recognized his robes, but his previously bald head bore straight, jet-black hair. Had his eyes not been familiar, they would've thought him an intruder.

"Fanley?" a pudgy guard asked.

"Yes, Harl," Fanley replied.

"What? How?" Harl stammered, taking in Fanley's odd appearance.

"Lohannes, that's how," Fanley responded in a matter-of-fact tone.

"Impossible. Shut the gate!" Harl ordered.

The gate rattled downward. Curious, Fanley reached out his hands. He was sure he couldn't stop it, but figured he could see just how strong he was and let go when it hurt too much. But it didn't hurt, and he found himself holding it up. Trying not to look surprised, he scooted under the gate before releasing it, casually walking away as the gate slammed into the concrete floor.

"And Harl, remember when we used to sneak out of the house to the beer hall when we were only nine?" Fanley said without looking back.

Usually, Fanley was fearfully cautious when he walked around town, avoiding the guards and robots by limping in and out of alleys or doorways. However, he had been careless on his way home tonight, reveling in the wonder of his new body, and paid the price as he ran headlong into one of the modified ASF Bots. Obviously, Harl had reported him because the robot's hand was wrapped around Fanley's arm and it had used it to lift him off his feet.

"You have been arrested for disorderly conduct, Fanley. Please admit your guilt so we can proceed with the appropriate level of punishment," replied a deep and somehow malicious robotic voice.

"What?" shot back Fanley. "I merely tried to walk into the city, and they shut the gate on me. I've lived here most of my life, rotbot."

The ASF Bot captain gripped his arm with even more force, which surely would have crushed his bones prior to his new gift. Instead it felt more like a deep tissue massage. Fanley reached up with his free hand and gripped the robot's arm. Electricity crackled around the metallic appendage, and the hairs on his arm stood at attention as much more than electrons flowed into his body. At that moment he knew how the robot worked; the wiring, logic, control boards and ePEGs were laid out in 3-D relief within his mind. He was able to rapidly flip, turn, and expand the diagram until he had honed in on where his hand now rested. Fanley dug into a seam in the robot's arm, watching the metal easily move aside, and reached his index finger and thumb into a fiberoptic nerve. Without understanding how, he mentally commanded the robot to power down, and it did, releasing him butt first onto the ground. Fanley stood, brushed himself off while staring down at the ASF Bot before continuing his journey home. He wondered what other abilities he had gained.

He kept walking at a brisk pace, and made it home before the solar-heated water tank cooled down. He soaked his body in the steaming water, still amazed at how he felt but starting to wonder why he had been given this gift. He stepped out and stared at the steamed-over mirror. The writing made it all fall into place. Three lines, six words, were all it took.

Alien War
12 Years
Build Army

Fanley smiled. This was the destiny that he'd always prayed Lohannes would grant him. He would start by taking out all the suppressive ASF Bots.

No, you are not, my brother. You will be leading the building of the army, not trying to be a one-man wrecking machine.

The voice in Fanley's head held a distinct Asian dialect that confirmed the identity, even if he had called him brother.

"Wait! You can speak in my head now?" Fanley shouted out.

Looks like I can, which is a good thing because you will need someone to temper that ego.

"Man! No gift comes without strings attached," Fanley said, but the words couldn't hide the happiness from the reunion.

****

Cynthia walked silently with the crowd, returning home from their shift at the farms. Her face was expressionless, and her eyes had the same milky hue as all the other Marsians. The door to her building was open, and she methodically walked to the stairwell and descended to the only below-ground-level apartment in the dome. She rigidly opened and shut the solid, soundproof door. Once inside she let out a sigh, flipping her white cape to the side with a hand before flopping down on her ratty couch.

"I don't know how many more of these days I can handle. So boring. Right, Jimmy?" Cynthia tapped the back of her head.

Her own voice mumbled in response. "Yes, Cynthia."

"At least I have you to talk to, Jimmy. I'd go crazy if I was stuck in this colony without a talk buddy."

"I am not your talk buddy. I am your slave," the Wyndelace replied.

"Complain, complain, complain. Always complaining, Jimmy. How many times have I told you that you can't guilt me? You aliens have enslaved every person in this colony except me, and you expect me to feel guilty that you failed?"

Cynthia stretched as she stood, groaning from a long day of working the fields. She tapped on the closest wall, ordering up a sludge of a meal with a side of unidentifiable greens. She took one bite, faked gagging, and dropped it on the foot-rest to eat later.

"Well, I guess it's time to start my second job. Do you want to go with me, Jimmy?" Cynthia stopped, pretending to wait for an answer. "Oh yeah, you don't have a choice."

Snickering, she moved back the couch and squeezed through a small hole in the floor. Once her feet landed on solid ground, she clapped her hands, and a series of bright lights clicked on, charged by their individual ePEGs. The carved-out room was filled with red benches supporting various semi-repaired biology instruments spread out over their surfaces. Cynthia walked over to a cracked PCR machine and stared at the manual for nearly a half hour before dropping it back on the table.

"One day I'll be able to make you work, Mr. PCR. And then we'll be able to exponentially amplify Jimmy and my DNA for studies." She sighed before speaking again. "But for now, all I can do is simple experiments to try and see why Jimmy can't control me and why I can control him. Once I figure that out, the whole damn race will be in trouble."

"You have not been able to figure out much in more than a decade," the Wyndelace mumbled.

Cynthia sighed. He used that line every night, and it was such a mood killer. He was right, as she was working with broken equipment and a formal education that stopped at the third grade. She'd taught herself biology, but having to hide everything from the aliens meant she had been able to pick up only bits and pieces during the short time she was unwatched. Piecing it all together by herself resulted in lots of holes in her knowledge.

Cynthia closed her eyes, remembering the time she had seen Lohannes confront the Wyndelaces, and how she had whispered for him to fight. A little girl telling a demigod what to do. It was so silly.

Realizing frustration would get her nowhere, she prayed to Lohannes for strength and the ability to uncover how to reverse the Wyndelaces' takeover of the Marsians. Somehow, she had been immune, and she needed to understand why in order to help everyone else. As she prayed, her fingers began to tingle and then her nose. She thought little of it, figuring it was Jimmy trying to fight her, and kept praying while the tingling expanded into a ball of energy encompassing her head.

She opened her eyes, but was blinded by the bright blue light that now was covering her chest, arms, and legs. It didn't hurt at first, but then her muscles convulsed and she felt Jimmy writhing, trying to rip away from her. Her muscles fought to keep him attached, while the bluish energy expanded to fill the entire room. Shocking pressure pushed on her from all sides. Cynthia fell to her knees, gasping for air as she gripped her reddened neck. She fell to the ground, believing Jimmy had finally figured out how to kill her. Then the light softened, and the pain turned back to a tingling before disappearing completely. The room returned to its normal bleakness.

Cynthia didn't move for several minutes, looking around the room for any signs that something had changed. She closed her eyes and inhaled deeply to relax. However, in her mind she now saw the room perfectly laid out as if her eyes were open. She could identify every object, even down to a piece of tape stuck to the underside of the leftmost table. She exhaled and opened her eyes again. She walked over to her equipment, relooking at a page from the PCR manual. She closed her eyes again and could recall the entire page. Eidetic memory? No, something more. She not only remembered every word and each diagram, she understood it all. In fact, her mind now held a library full of biology and bioengineering information, beyond what any being should be able to possess. She was so amazed that she hadn't yet noticed the new athletic frame she possessed.

The small glass slide under a microscope caught her eye. It was the same slide that she had placed a drop of her blood on the night before. Curiosity prodded her to look at the slide through the microscope since it was now shifted sideways. When she did, the dried blood shifted and moved, creating four words on two lines.

Overthrow Aliens
Help Humankind

Cynthia stepped back, initially looking shocked before a wry smile spread across her face.

"Oh, Jimmy, you guys are sooo screwed!"

****

Withered and scarred fingers tapped slowly on the aqua-colored lines of a holographic keyboard for over an hour, only pausing to flex when they refused to work. With finality, Martha lifted her right hand, pointed her shaky index finger, and dropped it onto the period emblem. She closed her eyes and prayed to Lohannes, thanking him for the ability to write his life story so she could share it with all of his followers. Her task had started when he entered their village after escaping from the mine. She had shown him the rail he needed in order to get to the launch site, and then he rudely departed. Martha had gone back to her chores, expecting her life to continue as an elder member of the community. However, the next day she had received a message from the one called Bookworm. When she opened the message, she was surprised to find a summary of the duo's trip from the day before and a short note asking her to help him disseminate their journey to the demigod's followers. It was followed by several other messages, dating back to the first time Bookworm met with The President.

Every day after that, a new update appeared. What she wrote was not the same biography that Bookworm had written, as that one contained too much sensitive information and was heavily encrypted. Hers was the story of the fall and rise of the Darkened Demigod, crafted for the consumption of his devoted worshippers. And now that story was finished.

She rolled up the same black FlipFilm she had used during her encounter with Lohannes, nearly a decade and a half ago, and placed it within her desk before struggling to rise to her feet. It was a cold day, but the layers of brown clothing would keep her warm, along with the squirrel cap that had been her husband's favorite. Martha put on a brown jacket and tucked her gray hair carefully under the cap, having to redouble her efforts since her fingers didn't obey her commands like when she was younger. When she stepped outside, she looked at the bright winter sun and then at the frost that encrusted the ground. It would be slippery today, so she needed to be extra cautious in bare feet that had long ago lost feeling. As she walked, parents stopped to nod or bow, and the children did the same. She remembered when the parents were the children, and wondered how many children she had helped raise.

A path led out to the woods, and her feet eventually found their way onto it. No thoughts entered her mind as she continued to walk along the small dirt path, which she hadn't traversed since her only encounter with Lohannes. The memory of that day had been too painful. Martha listened to the chirping birds, many sitting atop a large, half-melted container. She paused briefly to look at it, recalling the written stories about it being one of the containers that had housed the alien invaders. Thanks to Lohannes, they had arrived as burning fireballs; the millions of enslaving aliens nothing more than black sludge upon their landing.

Martha continued, telling her feet and knees that it wasn't much further, then softly singing to her hips and back about their youthful days. She continued her singing, washing her body with the soothing music, until she entered an overgrown clearing. Small, broken domes were spread throughout the area, the weapons laying within having long since been destroyed. Shortly, they would be completely overrun by the raspberry bushes the local children had planted during a field trip several years earlier. She didn't stop to pick any of the ripe berries, instead walking to the center of the clearing where a thatch-work of rose bushes protected any stray children from falling into the mineshaft. With no hurry in her work, she spent hours unweaving the prickly vines with her aching fingers, until a wide gap lay before her. She stepped through and stopped directly in front of the hole. The memory of her unwavering husband, the one who carried so much guilt tied to an even greater burden, had never faded over the years. While she had been his caretaker after their daughter's death, he had been her undying love since she was a ponytailed schoolgirl. Vivid images reeled through her mind, replaying their life together through the romantic lens of Martha's heart.

When the story finished, Martha lowered her head and sent out a prayer of thanks to Lohannes. He had changed the destiny of humankind, moving from one of annihilation or slavery to one filled with incredible hope. He had sacrificed so much throughout his life, and in the end had received nothing in return. She also had sacrificed, pushing away the closure needed after her husband's death until her task was finished. Now it was.

"It's time for our bones to lie next to each other my love, so our souls can once again be intertwined."

With her final words vocalized, Martha closed her eyes again and took her first and last step over the hole.

Nothing happened, so she stepped again, and again. Only then did she open her eyes to see that she was indeed over the hole, floating by some unexplainable force. Too old to be truly shocked, Martha brushed away a strand of grayish-black hair from her face, noting how strong her fingers felt and how her joints were free of pain for the first time in decades. In fact, all her visible scars had been wiped away, replaced with a healthy new layer of skin. Her eyes easily focused on the tree line she hadn't been able to clearly see minutes earlier, and her heart pumped with a vigor she had left behind in her twenties.

"Sorry, my love. It appears that Loahannes isn't done with me yet," Martha stated. "Fear not, I'll return when I have written the story of how we defeated the aliens once and for all."

The rustling of branches caused her head to turn and her eyes to look at the vines she had moved aside. They had reshaped into powerful letters, forming two lines and three words.

Unite Earth
Lead

She returned to the path, a tear of pain held high on the creased smile that had spread across her face. An unwavering balance of pain and pleasure would continue to describe her life, but that constant was something she could handle.

As Martha restored order in her mind, she failed to notice that her bare feet floated inches of the ground as she walked.

ABOUT THE AUTHOR

Shawn Phillips wrote his first book, a young-adult fantasy novel titled *Dillon's Dream: Water in Earth*, in 2009 before following it up with his successful adult paranormal fiction novel, *The Doppler Affect*. *Darkened Demigod: Weapon of War* is post-apocalyptic novel that continues his creation of the fant2sci genre, where one uses science to merge fantasy and science fiction.

He spent his naïve, younger years embedded in southern Michigan farming communities before running to Holland, Michigan to pursue a chemistry degree at Hope College, which he completed in 1992. After migrating to the eye-opening California frontier, he continued his chemistry studies and obtained his doctorate degree in 1997. After a brief stint at DuPont, he signed on as a civil servant for the United States Air Force. As the director of The AFRL Rocket Lab, he has spent twenty years conducting and directing research for liquid, solid and in-space propulsion systems.

Shawn is happily (very happily…she might read this) married to his wife Yvonne of twenty years and barely survives the daily tortures from his sons Dakota and Colby.

Made in the USA
Columbia, SC
30 January 2018